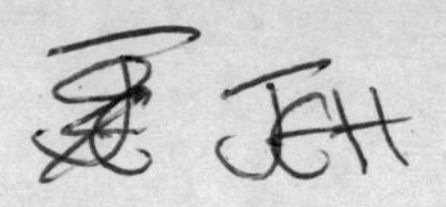

He couldn't, wouldn't, *ignore his own child…nor the baby's mother!*

Claiming His Secret Love-Child

Three exhilarating romances from three fabulous Mills & Boon authors!

Claiming His Secret Love-Child

MELANIE MILBURNE

CATHY WILLIAMS

MAGGIE COX

DID YOU PURCHASE THIS BOOK WITHOUT A COVER?

If you did, you should be aware it is **stolen property** as it was reported *unsold and destroyed* by a retailer. Neither the author nor the publisher has received any payment for this book.

All the characters in this book have no existence outside the imagination of the author, and have no relation whatsoever to anyone bearing the same name or names. They are not even distantly inspired by any individual known or unknown to the author, and all the incidents are pure invention.

First published in Great Britain 2011
Harlequin Mills & Boon Limited,
Eton House, 18-24 Paradise Road, Richmond, Surrey TW9 1SR

The Marciano Love-Child, The Italian Billionaire's Secret Love-Child and *The Rich Man's Love-Child* were first published in Great Britain by Harlequin Mills & Boon Limited in separate, single volumes.

ISBN: 978 0 263 88432 6

05-0311

Printed and bound in Spain
by Litografia Rosés S.A., Barcelona

THE MARCIANO LOVE-CHILD

BY
MELANIE MILBURNE

Melanie Milburne is married to a surgeon, Steve, and has two gorgeous sons, Paul and Phil. She lives in Hobart, Tasmania, where she enjoys an active life as a long-distance runner and a nationally ranked top ten Master's swimmer. She also has a master's degree in education, but her children totally turned her off the idea of teaching! When not running or swimming she writes, and when she's not doing all of the above she's reading. And if someone could invent a way for her to read during a four-kilometre swim she'd be even happier!

Don't miss Melanie's latest novel, *The Wedding Charade* and *The Man with the Locked Away Heart*, available from the Mills & Boon® Modern™ and Medical™ series in February and March 2011.

Dedicated to Jocey Anderson, Sue Mayne
and Katrina Henry, three wonderful members
of Talays Aussi Master's Swimming team,
who have bought each and every one of my books
so far. Thank you for being such faithful supporters
both in and out of the pool.
Happy reading and swimming!

CHAPTER ONE

IT HAD started just like any other Monday morning. Scarlett dropped three-year-old Matthew, at crèche after the usual tearful and heart-wrenching 'don't leave me, I miss you too much' routine, before fighting her way through heavy traffic to her small interior-design studio in Woollahra. And just like any other Monday morning her business partner and best friend, Roxanne Hartley, handed her a double-strength latte on her way in the door and asked her how her weekend had been.

'Don't ask,' Scarlett said wearily, and took a reviving sip of the creamy latte.

'So I take it the blind date your sister set up for you wasn't a success?' Roxanne said as she perched on the edge of Scarlett's desk.

Scarlett rolled her eyes expressively. 'Depends what you mean by a blind date. Clearly this guy's idea was to turn up blind *drunk*. He slurred his way through his sob story about his ex-wife for an hour and a half, until I finally managed to escape.'

'Poor you,' Roxanne said in empathy. 'But don't give up yet. There's got to be someone decent out there for you.'

'Decent would be good,' Scarlett said, booting up her

computer. 'A good father-figure for Matthew would be good, too, but as soon as men hear I have a three-year-old son they seem to lose interest.'

'Yes, well, men today can be so shallow,' Roxanne agreed. 'They won't commit, and they want sex on tap.'

'Tell me about it,' Scarlett said as she clicked on her computer mouse to activate the screen to check her list of appointments. She put her glasses on and blinked, once, twice, three times, her heart giving a quick, hard thud when she saw *that* name staring back at her.

'What's wrong?' Roxanne asked in a guileless tone.

Scarlett swivelled her chair to look up at her business partner, her face going pale with shock. 'You made an appointment for *me* to meet with Alessandro Marciano?' she choked.

Roxanne grinned at her excitedly. 'Yes. I wanted it to be a surprise, otherwise I would have called you over the weekend to tell you about it. He phoned on Friday afternoon just after you'd left. It's a huge contract, Scarlett. He's worth zillions, and if we get the deal think of what it will do for us. We'll be featured in every interior-design magazine across the globe. We won't have to pay rent any more, we'll be able to buy the building, no—' She clasped her hands together in glee and added, '—we'll be able to buy the whole street!'

Scarlett sprang to her feet, almost spilling her latte over her keyboard in the process. 'I'm not seeing him,' she said through tight lips. 'I don't want the contract. I want nothing to do with it.'

Roxanne slapped the side of her head as if she couldn't believe what she had just heard. 'Have you happened to look at our financial statements recently?' she asked as she slipped down off the desk. 'Come on, Scarlett, our business loan is stretched to the limit, you know it is. I know things are often a bit slow in January, while everyone is still on summer holidays, but this is a chance in a lifetime. This is just what we need right now. Alessandro Marciano has bought the old Arlington Hotel building in the city. He's going to turn it into a luxury hotel, with three floors of penthouse apartments for the super rich. And he wants us to do the interior design. *Us!* Can you believe it? It's like winning the lottery.'

'I can't see him, Roxanne,' Scarlett insisted. 'Please don't ask it of me.'

A light bulb seemed to come on in Roxanne's head as she peered at Scarlett. 'Hang on a minute, what… Have you dated him in the past or something?'

'More than dated,' Scarlett answered with a dark frown.

Roxanne gave her a probing look. 'What do you mean "more than dated?"'

Scarlett drew in an unsteady breath. 'He's Matthew's father.'

Roxanne's jaw dropped open, and her eyes went saucer-wide. *'He's what?'* she gasped.

Scarlett's expression became rigid with tension. 'I'm not going to see him, Roxanne. No way. I hate him for what he did to me, and I am not going to—'

The unmistakable throaty roar of a Maserati suddenly sounded on the street outside. Both girls looked out of the front window of the studio, and watched as the car's black, sleek body was expertly manoeuvred in between their tiny fuel-efficient vehicles parked outside.

Roxanne met her friend's startled grey-blue gaze. 'Looks like you're not going to have a choice,' she said, and added, with a little sheepish grimace as the front door opened with a cheery tinkle of the bell hanging on the back, 'Er…did I forget to mention the meeting was here, at nine-fifteen?'

Scarlett felt every pore of her skin and every hair on her body stand to attention as that imposing, darkly handsome figure stooped as he came in through the door. Her heart started going like a jackhammer, the pressure building in her chest so overwhelming she wondered if the heavy thumping would be visible through the lightweight white linen of her blouse.

His hazel eyes met hers, the brown-and-green flecks reminding her all over again of the myriad colours of a rainforest. But this time she felt as if there were mysterious shadows lurking in the depths of his gaze, as he stood looking at her in a watchful silence for what seemed like endless seconds.

'Hello, Scarlett,' he finally said in that stomach-tilting velvet drawl that had been her downfall close to four years ago.

Scarlett lifted her chin and turned to Roxanne, who was standing with her mouth opening and closing like a recently landed fish. 'Roxanne, would you please inform Mr…er…' She glanced down at her diary as if to remind herself of his name, before looking back up and continuing in the same haughty tone, '…Mr Marciano that I am not taking on any new clients as I am booked up until the end of the year.'

'But—' Roxanne spluttered, but was cut off by Alessandro who had stepped forward to smile at her with lethal charm.

'Miss Hartley, would you be so kind as to leave Miss Fitzpatrick and I to conduct out meeting in private?' he asked.

'No! Don't you dare leave,' Scarlett bit out hastily. *Please, oh please, don't leave me with him;* she silently begged the rest of the sentence with her eyes.

Roxanne pursed her mouth, and after a moment's hesitation scooped up her bag and half-finished latte. 'Sure, I can do that,' she said, smiling girlishly at Alessandro. 'I have to see a man about some tiles anyway. I'll be back at eleven.'

Scarlett sent her an 'I'm going to kill you for this' glare, before taking her place behind her desk in case her legs followed through on their current threat to fold beneath her.

The studio door opened and closed with another tinkle on Roxanne's exit, but to Scarlett it felt more like the sound of a vault locking down for good.

The silence thrummed in her ears, the air becoming so thick with it she felt as if a pair of hands was around the slim column of her throat, gradually increasing the pressure until she was sure she was going to choke.

'So you are not interested in doing business with me, Scarlett?' Alessandro asked with a coolly impersonal smile.

'No.' Her one-word response came out of her mouth like a hard pellet.

'Why ever not?' he asked with an ironic arch of one dark brow. 'I thought you would be jumping at this chance to get your hands on my money.'

She tightened her mouth even further, and forced her gaze to meet his. 'I am surprised you are interested in engaging the services of a filthy little slut—those were your words for me back then, were they not?'

There was no sign of anger in his expression, but Scarlett could sense it all the same. She had known and loved that face so well in the three months they had been together. Every nuance of it was imprinted indelibly on her brain. The smile that could melt stone, the gaze that could heat blood, the mouth that could kiss like a teasing feather, or with such hungry passion her lips had tingled and been swollen for hours afterwards. Even now, after all this time, she could still taste the salt and musk of his lips and tongue, and her lower body began to pulse with the memory of how if had felt with him plunging between her legs.

She crossed her legs under her desk, fighting the sensations brewing there. But it was almost impossible to control the hit-and-miss beat of her heart every time she encountered that brown-and-green flecked gaze.

'Your sexual proclivities, I would imagine, have no bearing on your talent at interior design,' he said with an enigmatic look. 'You have a good reputation professionally. That is why I am keen to have you wholly responsible for the project I am about to commence.'

Her chin went even higher. 'I told you, I'm not available.'

His mouth tilted slightly. 'Perhaps before you throw away this chance, Scarlett, you should at least look at what I am offering.'

'No amount of money you could dangle in front of me will induce me to conduct any sort of relationship with you again, business or otherwise,' she stated implacably.

A flicker of male interest darkened the brown in his eyes as they moved over her appraisingly. 'I was not going to suggest anything other than a business agreement between us, however…' He left the sentence suspended between them in the pulsing silence.

'Forget it, Alessandro,' she said. 'In any case, I'm already seeing someone.'

'Is it the same man you were involved with in Italy?' he asked, piercing her gaze with his. 'Dylan Kirby was his name, was it not?'

Scarlett felt her blood begin to simmer in her veins. 'I was travelling with him, not sleeping with him.'

Cynicism burned in his gaze. 'Ah, yes, that old story. I remember it well.'

'It's not a story, it's the truth,' she insisted. 'I met Dylan, Joe and Jessica on a bus tour. I told you all this four years ago. How many times do I have to repeat myself?'

'I am not interested in your lies, but I am interested in what you can do for me,' he said. 'Your business is in need of a contract as big as this, Scarlett. You would be a fool to throw it away as if it was worth nothing.'

She clenched her jaw. 'I hate to be the one to point out the irony in all this, but isn't that what you did to me?'

'I am prepared to be generous,' he said, ignoring her comment as if she meant nothing to him.

That was because she *did* mean nothing to him, she reminded herself. He had never spoken to her of love; he had simply enjoyed the delights of their affair while she had fallen in love with him, fallen hard.

Before she had met him she had been a little scathing at the notion of falling in love at first sight, or even of falling in love over a period of days. She had always thought the sort of love that was deep and abiding would build up over a period of time, as trust and respect grew between two people. But meeting Alessandro Marciano that hot summer morning in Milan had tipped her world upside down. Within three hours she had been kissed by him, within three days she had been sleeping with him, and within three months she had been pregnant by him.

Scarlett blinked herself back to the present when Alessandro handed her a document. She took it from him, her shaking fingers not quite able to avoid the fine-sandpaper brush of his against hers. Her whole body jolted in reaction and heat coursed through her, the thud of her pulse going at breakneck speed.

'If you are not happy with that amount, I will double it,' he said.

Scarlett looked down at the contract, her eyes almost popping out of her head at the amount printed there. It was an astonishing amount of money, although she would have to work very hard for it, she imagined. She knew enough about Alessandro Marciano to know he had exacting standards. His reputation as a hotelier was global. Guests staying at a Marciano hotel were treated to the utmost in luxury, and this one in Sydney would be no different, if the drawings his team of highly skilled architects had prepared were anything to go by.

But accepting this contract, as lucrative and career-enhancing as it was, would mean close contact with him, maybe even on a daily basis. There would be meetings with him to discuss her designs, fabrics to look over, light fittings, soft furnishings, plumbing fixtures—the list went on and on in her head. How could she get through it without damaging herself irreparably?

And more to the point how could she keep Matthew safe from knowing his father had refused to accept him as his? Although she couldn't help thinking one look at that child would remove all doubt, even in someone as cynical as Alessandro. They had the same hazel eyes, the same ink-black hair and olive skin, the same-shaped mouth—although Matthew's was still soft with the innocence of childhood.

'I will give you a day or two to think it over.' His deep voice invaded the private torture of her tangled thoughts.

She got to her feet in one abrupt movement. 'I don't need two—'

He held up one and then two long fingers against her mouth. 'Two days, Scarlett,' he said, holding her gaze. 'Think about it.'

Scarlett swallowed as her body remembered how intimately those fingers had known every pleasure spot she possessed. How she had felt that first frisson of passionate response when he had stroked the silken folds of her femininity for the first time—how she had quivered inside and out when he had explored her so thoroughly and so devastatingly with his fingers, his mouth, his tongue, and the hot, pulsing hard length of him.

He lifted his fingers, and she ran her tongue over where he had been, her stomach doing a sudden free-fall when she saw his eyes flick to her mouth.

And stay there.

The air tightened around them, as if an invisible clinging vine had silently insinuated itself into the room and was now pulling them closer and closer together.

Scarlett couldn't breathe; she wasn't game enough to draw in a breath in case he heard the betraying flutter of her pulse beneath her skin.

She stood very still as he reached out again, this time with just the index finger of his right hand, brushing it against the softness of her bottom lip, his eyes still locked on her mouth. The temptation to sweep her tongue over and around his finger was suddenly overwhelming. She had to clamp her teeth together to stop herself taking him in her mouth and sucking on him, as she had done so many times before.

And not just his finger…

His eyes came back to hers, a tiny frown pulling at the dark slashes of his eyebrows, the line of his mouth losing its inherent cynicism for just a brief moment.

'I had forgotten how very soft your mouth is,' he said in an even deeper, more gravelly tone than he'd used before.

Scarlett rolled her lips together, more to stop them buzzing with sensation than to draw his attention back to her mouth—but his eyes dipped again, and this time she felt the heat of his gaze like a brand on her lips.

'I-I think it might be time for you to leave,' she scratched out through her too-tight throat. 'I have nothing further to say to you. I don't want the work. You'll have to find someone else.'

He looked down at her for a long moment. 'I am not quite ready to leave, Scarlett. There are still some things I would like to discuss with you.'

Panic prickled at her insides as she stood stock-still in front of him. She couldn't step back because her desk was in the way, and stepping forward was out of the question, with the possibility of brushing against him to get past.

She was trapped.

'Four years ago you told me you were pregnant,' he said into the silence.

Scarlett felt her throat tighten even further, but somehow she managed to maintain eye contact with him. 'Yes…yes I did.'

'You also told me the child was mine.'

A glitter of anger lit her unblinking gaze. 'Yes, I did.'

'Did you go through with the pregnancy?' he asked after an infinitesimal pause.

She kept her gaze locked on his. 'At the risk of repeating myself—yes, I did.'

His expression remained as unreadable as a book with the pages glued together. 'Does your child have contact with its father?' he asked.

She frowned at him, angry at the way he was crossexamining her. 'What's with all these questions, Alessandro? You were the one who insisted the child couldn't possibly be yours. Why the sudden interest now? Have you suddenly changed your mind and decided I wasn't lying to you after all?'

He gave a little shrug of insouciance. 'No, of course I have not changed my mind. There is no way I could be the father of your child.'

Scarlett sent him a caustic glare. 'So you think.'

'I do not *think*, Scarlett,' he said with a granite-hard stare. 'I know it for a fact.'

She stood before him, silently fuming at his arrogance, her simmering hatred for him threatening to spill over.

His mouth tilted into a sardonic smile as his eyes roved over her lazily. 'Anyway, you do not look as if you have had a child. You are as slim and attractive as you were four years ago.'

She gave him a withering look. 'Thanks for insulting every mother out there who's put on a bit of weight after childbirth.'

'I did not mean to insult other mothers.'

'No, you're here to insult me,' she shot back. 'You can keep your contract, Alessandro Marciano. I don't want anything to do with a man who thinks I am a liar and a cheat and a whore.'

'So even after all this time you are still determined to have me nominated as the sire of your offspring, are you?' he asked with a curl of his lip. 'Why is that, Scarlett—because the other possible candidates would not pay up?'

She ground her teeth as she glared at him. 'There were no other candidates, and you damn well know it.'

The cynicism in the line of his mouth increased. 'You do not like admitting you got it wrong by singling me out, do you,

Scarlett? You thought you had landed yourself a meal ticket for the rest of your life when you met me. I wondered at the time why you had fallen into bed with me so quickly. It all made sense, of course, when you told me your news. You needed financial security, but you got it wrong in selecting me.'

She clenched her fists by her sides. 'I loved you, Alessandro. I *really* loved you. I would have given anything to have spent the rest of my life with you, but not for the reasons you're assuming.'

'Love?' He snorted. 'I wonder if you would still have claimed to love me if I'd told you at the beginning of our affair that I was not interested in having children—ever.'

'Why didn't you?'

Something moved in his gaze, like a shifting shadow. It was there one second, gone the next.

'We had only been seeing each other for three months,' he said. 'I was going to tell you within the next week or two, as I was concerned that you would have hopes for a future of marriage and babies with me. I realise it is a lot to ask of a woman, to relinquish her right to have a child with the man she loves.'

'So you *do* acknowledge that I loved you?'

The cynical slant to his mouth returned. 'I believe you loved the idea of marrying a multi-millionaire. Nothing awakens love so much as money, I have found.'

'Why are you so against having children?' she asked, still frowning. 'I thought all Italians loved children—having a loving family is everything to them, not to mention having an heir.'

'That has never been in my plans,' he said. 'I have other things I want to do with my life. Being tied down with a wife and children holds no appeal at all.'

Scarlett searched his face, wondering what had led him to such an intractable stance, but his expression was inscrutable.

'I will see you in two days' time, Scarlett, to discuss the terms of the contract.' He handed her a card with his business details on it. 'My private phone number is on the other side, if you should wish to contact me before then, otherwise I will see you at the Arlington Hotel on Thursday at ten a.m.'

Scarlett looked down at the gold-embossed card with its serrated edges, the pad of her index finger running over each and every letter of his name. But it wasn't until she heard the tinkle of the tiny bell hanging on the studio door that she realised he had left.

She looked up and watched as he went to his car parked outside, his tall, muscular body almost folding in half to get behind the wheel. He fired the engine and, just before he pulled out into the street, he glanced back and met her gaze, a small frown playing about his brow.

Scarlett turned from the window and drew in a scratchy breath, and held it inside her aching chest until the sound of his car had faded into the distance.

CHAPTER TWO

'I'M WARNING you, Scarlett, that if you don't take this Marciano contract on I'm out of here,' Roxanne threatened early on Thursday morning. 'This is what I've been hoping for ever since I graduated. It's what we've both been waiting for. You can't do this to me— damn it, you can't do it to *us*.'

Scarlett bit her lip, her eyes flicking to the clock again, which seemed to be gathering momentum every time she looked at it. She had less than twenty minutes to get into the city to meet Alessandro and give him her final answer. She had barely slept for the last forty-eight hours, agonising over what to do. Seeing him again had brought everything back, all the heartache and crushing despair of his disbelief and rejection.

'I know you're worried about some of the clauses in the contract,' Roxanne said. 'But we've handled complicated contracts before and sailed through without a hitch. This is an offer too good to pass up. Besides, you know how tight this industry is. If word gets out you turned aside a deal as big as this for personal reasons, how will we hold our heads up professionally?'

Scarlett sank her teeth into her lower lip. 'I know, but…'

'Don't blow this, Scarlett,' Roxanne said. 'If you haven't

signed on the dotted line when you get back to the studio later today, I want you to buy me out of the business.'

Scarlett felt her chest begin to thud with alarm. 'You know I can't afford to do that, Roxanne. It will ruin me. I have no savings, and getting a personal loan would be impossible right now.'

'You've lied to me for close to four years, Scarlett,' Roxanne said bitterly. 'You told me Matthew's father had died in a car accident in Italy. Do you realise how that makes me feel? Totally betrayed. I thought I was your best friend.'

Scarlett met her friend's wounded gaze. 'I know I should have told you, but I was so upset and confused when I came home. It seemed easier to tell everyone Matthew's father had been killed in an accident. I couldn't bear the questions from Mum and Sophie. They would have driven me mad. I wanted to tell you so many times, especially after all you've done for me, but I had to consider Matthew too. How is he going to feel in the future to hear his father wanted nothing to do with him?'

'I realise all that, but what's so hard about taking on several-hundred thousand dollars or more of business?' Roxanne returned. 'Get in the real world, Scarlett. So what if he doesn't believe Matthew's his kid? That's his loss. This is a business transaction. Put your private issues aside and get on with the job.'

'It's not that simple…'

Roxanne gave her a penetrating look. 'You're not still in love with the guy, are you?'

'No, of course not,' Scarlett said with an affronted huff. 'It's just that he's…he's…'

'Very attractive,' Roxanne offered helpfully. 'And super-rich.'

Scarlett glared at her. 'You know I'm not that sort of person, Roxanne.'

Roxanne blew out a breath. 'No, you're not, more's the pity. You're way too kind to people. You let them walk all over you.'

'If you're obliquely referring to the Underwood account, then don't,' Scarlett said with a little scowl. 'I felt sorry for Louise Underwood—her husband was a total brute. I couldn't leave her with all those bills to pay when he ran off with his mistress.'

'We're running a business not a charity, Scarlett,' Roxanne said. 'And, speaking of business, you'd better scoot or you'll never get there in time.'

'I'll get a cab rather than try and park,' Scarlett said as she grabbed her bag and sunglasses. 'God, I wish there was some way out of this.'

'There is,' Roxanne said. 'You sign the contract, you do the work, you say goodbye. Easy.'

Scarlett opened the studio door and grimaced. 'You think.'

When Scarlett arrived at the old Arlington in the city there were various workmen on site, as the building was in the first stages of being gutted. Scaffolding was wrapped around the outside, and the front doors were pinned back to keep them open, but even so the fine dust in the air made her nose start to twitch.

She walked across the threadbare carpet-runner to the reception desk, but she had to step aside as a worn sofa was carried past her to the service lifts. She carried on once the men had moved past, but the reception area was deserted, as the hotel had closed down several weeks ago.

She turned and looked up at the winding staircase and

locked gazes with Alessandro, who was standing on the next floor looking down at her. She felt her stomach fold over itself and her heart start to race as he came down the stairs, the sound of his footsteps echoing throughout the cavernous foyer.

'Hello, Scarlett.'

Scarlett felt the skin on her bare arms lift in goosebumps as he came to stand in front of her. His slightly wavy hair was glossy black with moisture, as if he had not long showered. She could smell the exotic spices of his aftershave, and the clean, male scent of his body, and her brain flooded with images of how he had looked wet and glistening in the shower.

'I was not sure you would come,' he said.

She blinked at him, her mind still back in the shower, her heart beating so quickly she could hear a roaring in her ears. 'Um…I need the money…' she said, but instantly regretted it when she saw the way his eyes hardened slightly. 'I mean, business has been slow over summer, and I don't want to get in too far over my head…or anything…' She bit her lip, hating that she sounded so unprofessional. She was usually so brisk and efficient with potential clients, but Alessandro was not just a client.

He was her little son's father.

Alessandro looked down at her for a lengthy moment. He had spent the last two days thinking about her, wondering what it would be like to have her in his bed again.

This reaction hadn't really surprised him; after all, he had felt the same way the first time he had met her. He could feel it now, the pulse of sexual attraction crackling in the air that separated them. Seeing her again had brought back a rush of memories of how responsive she had been in his arms. He had never experienced anything like it before or since. He felt his groin tightening even now, thinking about the pleasure her body had given him so uninhibitedly. Her slim, golden sun-kissed limbs had snaked around his, her body rocking and shuddering with the spasms of release, until he had exploded with mind-blowing pleasure time and time again.

He was glad now he hadn't told her he had fallen in love with her four years ago—certainly not after the way she had tried to deceive him. That would have been the ultimate in humiliation, to have had her know how deeply he had cared for her while she had been cleverly masterminding her plot to hoodwink him.

'So you have decided to work for me after all, Scarlett?' he said into the too-long silence.

Scarlett moistened her mouth with her tongue, her stomach feeling as if a large nest of bush ants had been disturbed inside it. 'Yes… Yes, I have…'

'Because you need the money.'

She swallowed twice before she could find her voice again. 'It's as you said—a big contract. It's also a very time-consuming one. I have some other clients that I—'

'Your business partner Roxanne Hartley can see to those while you work for me.'

'This is too big a job to do single-handedly,' she said. 'Roxanne will have to be in on it, as well as one or two other freelance designers.'

'I will leave you to make the necessary arrangements,' he said. 'I am sure you are more than capable of assembling a design team to manage this project.'

'It's not just that.' She took a breath to calm herself and continued. 'I'm concerned about how things are…between us.'

His eyes narrowed ever so slightly. 'What do you mean?'

She hoisted her handbag over her shoulder as she ran the palms of her hands down the sides of her skirt. 'We're not exactly friends, Alessandro.'

'We do not need to be friends in order to get down to business, Scarlett.'

'As long as this remains strictly a business arrangement,' she said with a pointed glance.

His expression contained a hint of mockery. 'Are you saying that for my benefit or your own?'

Her eyes flared. 'What do you mean by that?'

The brown flecks in his eyes darkened to the colour of espresso coffee. 'You can still feel it, can't you, Scarlett?' he said in a low, sexy drawl. 'You can feel that throbbing tension that fills the air as soon as we are in the same room together. I felt it the other day, and I know you did too.'

'That's complete and utter nonsense,' she said with a little toss of her head. 'Anyway, I told you, I'm seeing someone.'

'What is his name?'

Scarlett stared at him, her mind going completely blank. 'Umm…I'd rather not say.'

'How long have you been involved with him?' he asked, still pinning her with his gaze.

Scarlett pursed her mouth and glared at him irritably. 'I thought I was here to discuss the refurbishment of this building, not the details of my personal life. Now, can we get on with it, please? I have a full list of appointments, and I have to pick up my son at five-thirty.'

He held her gaze for a pulsing moment, but she couldn't decide what was going on behind the screen of his hazel eyes.

'Excuse me,' he said as his mobile started to ring.

Scarlett watched as he looked at the caller ID and frowned as he moved a few metres away. It gave her a chance to observe him while he wasn't watching, but she couldn't help wondering who he was talking to in such rapid-fire Italian, his voice sounding edgy and annoyed.

She drank in the sight of him—the long legs, the flat stomach, and the black silky hairs at his wrists where his shirt cuffs were casually rolled up. He looked every inch the successful and powerful man; the world was at his fingertips, and there was nothing he couldn't do if he put his mind to it.

Except acknowledge his son as his own.

Scarlett hated recalling the night she had told him about her pregnancy. She shrank back from the memories, but they marched right through her paltry blockade as they had done so many times before…

'Alessandro, I have something to tell you,' she had said as soon as he had come in from his office in Milan.

He'd placed his briefcase on the floor at his feet and leaned down to kiss her lingeringly on the mouth. 'Mmm,' he'd said, lifting his head momentarily. 'You have been eating chocolate again.'

She'd rolled her lips together and tried to smile, but her stomach had felt like it was unravelling. 'I know you're going to be terribly shocked,' she'd said, capturing her lip with her teeth before adding, 'I can't believe it happened myself… I should have been more careful. I know it sounds stupid and naïve but I just didn't realise how easy it was…'

He'd smiled and tipped up her chin with the pad of his fingertip. 'Let me guess. You have run out of credit on your mobile phone, no?'

'No, it's not that…' Her stomach had tilted again at his touch.

'I told you before, *cara,* money is not an issue with me,' he'd said, stroking her cheek with his thumb. 'I was the one who encouraged you to stay on in Milan for a few extra weeks, so it is only fair that I give you an allowance to tide you over.'

'No, I don't want to take money from you, Alessandro,' she'd said. 'I won't do it. I can get a job in a café or something if I run out.'

He frowned with disapproval. 'No, I do not want you working in a hot, crowded café. I like coming home to you fresh and happy to see me.'

'It's not about money,' she said. 'I have some savings from home I can transfer in any case.'

His thumb stopped moving as he held her gaze. 'You do not like the thought of being paid to be my lover?'

She frowned at him. 'Of course I don't like the thought of it. That's positively archaic, Alessandro. People don't do that, or at least not in the circles I move in.'

His expression was still unreadable as he looked into her eyes. 'I want you to be my lover, and I do not mind paying you to stay with me.'

Scarlett felt her breath stall in her chest. 'For…for how long?'

His thumb moved to her bottom lip and grazed it tantalisingly, his eyes holding hers like a magnet. 'How long would you like to stay in Milan?' he asked.

Her heart began thumping irregularly again. 'How long do you want me to stay?' she asked softly.

He kissed the corner of her mouth. 'The way I feel right now, I want you to stay for a long time—a very long time.'

Scarlett let out her breath in a long stream of relief. She had longed to hear him say he loved her, but it was almost as good knowing he wanted her to stay indefinitely.

'Alessandro…' She stepped up on tiptoe and kissed his mouth in a series of hot, passionate little touchdowns of her lips on his. 'I love you. I didn't think it was possible to love someone so much and so quickly, but I do,' she said, gazing up at him rapturously. 'I love being with you. I love it more than anything in the world.'

He smiled again and brought her closer, his hips pressing against hers. 'I know you do, and I enjoy being with you too. Now, *tesore mio*, tell me what you were so intent on telling me when I came in the door. I am all ears—is that how you say it in English, hmm?'

'Yes…yes, it is.' She took a little breath and announced baldly, 'Alessandro, I'm pregnant.'

He released her so abruptly she stumbled, only just managing to right herself because there was a priceless marble statue close by. She faced him, one hand still holding the statue, her stomach feeling like it was going to drop down between her suddenly trembling legs.

His expression was thunderous with anger, his eyes like chips of murky-coloured ice as they locked on hers.

'Vio slut ripugnante!' His words were laced with venom. *'Vio whore ripugnante.'*

Scarlett's eyes went wide with shock; she had been in Italy long enough to recognise a savage curse when she heard one. Although she had expected him to be surprised, and perhaps a little angry, to have him call her such horrible names was so unexpected she stood without speaking or defending herself for far too long.

'You tried to trick me into asking you to marry me,' he went on in the same cold, hard tone. 'You did not just want my money in exchange for a little affair—you wanted everything, did you not?'

'Alessandro—' She choked on a frightened sob. 'Why are you carrying on like this? I thought you cared for me. I—'

She flinched away as he stabbed a finger in the space between them. *'Siete una frode affamata dei soldi deceitful,'* he snarled.

She swallowed against the burning ache in her throat. 'I'm not sure what you're saying. Please, can you speak in English?'

He stepped closer, one of his hands coming down on her wrist like a manacle. 'You are a deceitful, money-hungry cheat,' he translated viciously, his eyes flashing with sparks of brown and green. 'You are a filthy slut, a filthy whore.'

Scarlett pulled against his iron hold. 'Stop it, Alessandro, please, you're hurting me.'

He flung her arm away and glared down at her. 'You are good at this, I will admit that, Scarlett. But then you are rather accurately named, are you not? You are a scarlet woman if ever there was one.'

She stood as frozen as the statue beside her. 'Don't say things like that, Alessandro,' she said, her heart squeezing in pain. 'You know I'm not like that.'

His bark of humourless laughter had an edge of cruelty to it. 'You opened your legs for me within three days of meeting me, but now of course I know why. You were looking for a father for your illegitimate child. You backpackers are all the same, screwing whatever comes along just for the hell of it. You got caught out and had to find a substitute father in a hurry. Who better than me, a knight dressed in Armani?'

Scarlett could scarcely believe what she was hearing. The malevolence in his tone was so foreign to her. She had never seen him lose his temper. He had never spoken to her so coarsely; she wasn't sure how to deal with it, or indeed how to defend herself. It seemed so out of character; it terrified her that the man she had given her heart and soul to had suddenly changed into someone else entirely.

'Get your things and get out of my house,' he bit out. 'I will give you ten minutes to do so.'

The hammer blows of panic inside her head made her vision start to blur. Her mouth was dry, her heart feeling as if it had been backed over by a truck. Her stomach churned with the nausea that had plagued her for days on end, but she fought against it valiantly as she tried to come to grips with what was happening.

She took a couple of deep, calming breaths. 'You don't mean that, Alessandro,' she said, keeping her voice soft and low. 'You know you don't. Darling, what's come over you?'

His eyes blazed as they looked down at her, his lips pulled tight by a rage so intense she instinctively moved back a step.

'You cannot possibly be carrying my child,' he said, with a flinty glare.

She nervously moistened her mouth. 'But of course it's yours, Alessandro. I've only been with you.'

His lips curled back in a sneer. *'Itete trovando!'*

Her chest tightened another painful notch. 'Please speak to me in English, Alessandro. I don't understand you.'

'You are lying!' He shouted the words so loudly they bounced off the walls, the echoes falling like slaps against her ears.

Scarlett was struggling not to cry. 'I'm not lying. I'd only had one lover before you, and that had been over a year before we met. How can you possibly doubt me?'

'You had been travelling for weeks with that Kirby man, but you tossed him aside as soon as you met me, no doubt because his wallet was running a little dry,' he said.

'That's not true! I have never slept with Dylan. I told him

and the others to leave without me, because I wanted to spend more time with you.'

His expression was cold with contempt. 'That was just a very clever act to worm your way into my affections, was it not?'

Her face fell. 'No…*no*. That's not true. How can you say that?'

'I can say it because it is true,' he said. 'You tried to set me up to pay for your bastard child, but there is one thing you miscalculated about me.'

She swallowed the thorny knot in her throat. 'Alessandro, you're not making sense. We've made love hundreds of times, a lot of times without protection. I went on the Pill too late. I thought it would be safe, but it obviously wasn't.'

His sneer turned to a snarl. 'I have heard of such ploys before. The unplanned pregnancy is a handy way of forcing a man into marriage, but these days it is all too easy to prove paternity.'

'I'll have a test done to prove it,' she said with rising despair. 'Then you'll have to believe me.'

His eyes raked over her from head to foot. 'I have all the proof I need. Now get out of my life.'

She looked up at him in stunned shock. 'You surely don't mean to throw me out on the streets at this time of night?'

His face was set in stone. 'It is where you belong, is it not?'

Scarlett opened her mouth to protest, but he had already turned to call one of the household staff, issuing a short, sharp command to have *Signorina* Fitzgerald's belongings packed immediately and brought to the front door.

Once the servant had scurried away, Alessandro turned back to Scarlett with another look of contempt. 'I must congratulate you on your ingenuity,' he said. 'I have been pursued by many women, but no one has ever got close enough for me to invite them to live with me, albeit temporarily.'

A bubble of anger inside Scarlett finally found its way to the surface. 'I was only ever a temporary diversion for you, wasn't I?' she said. 'You were only interested in a summer fling, and for your own convenience asked me to move in with you. You were never going to make things permanent between us.'

'Permanency is not something I have ever or will ever aim for in my relationships,' he said. 'I value my freedom too much.'

'You're going to end up a lonely old man with no one to love you,' she said, her heart sinking as the servant came down the huge staircase, carrying her backpack.

Alessandro gave a scornful sneer and opened the front door as wide as it would go. 'Goodbye, Scarlett.'

She picked up her backpack where the servant had placed it and slung it awkwardly over one shoulder, her eyes now streaming with tears. 'You're going to regret this one day,' she said, her voice breaking over the words. 'I know you will. You will hate yourself for not believing me.'

'The only thing I will regret is allowing you to fool me into thinking you were not like other social-climbing women,' he said. 'Now, get out before I have you thrown out.'

Scarlett stepped down the stairs with only her pride to keep her upright. She walked stiffly towards the wrought-iron gates, her heart splintering into thousands of pieces as she heard the front door of his house click shut with ominous finality behind her.

CHAPTER THREE

SCARLETT HAD to pull herself away from the past when Alessandro came back towards her with his phone clicked shut. 'I am sorry about that,' he said. 'One of my projects in Positano has been giving me some trouble. Now, let me show you around so you can get a feel for the place.'

She walked with him towards the staircase, her stomach feeling as if not only butterflies but bees and wasps were all vying for a landing space inside.

'I would like the foyer and reception area to make a statement,' he said as they climbed the stairs. 'Lots of marble—Italian, of course.'

'Of course,' Scarlett said, and tried not to react as his arm brushed against hers as she stood beside him on the first floor and looked down.

She was shocked that such a simple touch could affect her so much. She had thought she was immune to him by now, after what he had done to her. She had hated him for so long, the heat of it smouldering deep inside her, stoked every now and again by another milestone in her little son's life that Alessandro, out of arrogance, would never see. She had wanted to contact him so many times.

She had considered pursuing him legally, by insisting on

a paternity test to clear her name, but she had been frightened of the consequences. What if Alessandro turned out to be like her father, who had always made it so callously clear he had never wanted a second child? Her father's cruel words to her during her childhood had echoed well into her adulthood. She had lived with the stigma of being unwanted all of her life. She couldn't bear for her little son to suffer the same.

Sunlight came in from the dome above their heads and shafted down in golden rays on the floor below. Alessandro's arm brushed against hers again as he pointed to a shadowed area to the left of the reception desk. 'See that corner over there?' he said.

'Umm…yes,' she nodded, her nostrils flaring as the subtle but tantalising tones of his aftershave wafted past her face.

'What could you do to make that brighter and more open?' he asked, turning to look down at her.

Scarlett felt her heart come to a shuddering halt as his eyes met hers. She swallowed against the sudden thickness in her throat, her palms moistening where they were clutching at her handbag strap like a lifeline. 'I'd need to think about it,' she said. 'Lighting is one option, but there are others. For instance, if we choose a lighter colour for the marble it will throw more light everywhere, not just in that corner.'

His eyes were still locked on hers. 'You are good at this, no?'

She ran her tongue over the arid landscape of her lips, feeling self-conscious and terribly exposed. 'I enjoy it,' she said. 'I like the challenge of bringing new life to old interiors.'

He was standing so close Scarlett could hear the in-and-out of his breathing. She had only to take half a step for her body to come into contact with his, from chest to thighs. She sucked in a breath when he lifted his right hand and cupped her cheek, the touch so like a caress it made her whole body shiver in reaction.

'Don't,' she said in a hoarse whisper. 'Please…'

His thumb moved from her cheek to trace over her bottom lip, the movement slow but incredibly sensual. 'I have been thinking about how good we were together four years ago. Do you remember?' he asked softly.

How could she forget? Scarlett thought. Her body still rang with the echoes of the passion he had awakened. She could feel the pulse of it now as her blood charged through her veins. 'No,' she said. 'No, I don't.'

'No you do not remember, or no you do not want to be reminded?' he asked with a slanted smile.

'I'm here to work, Alessandro,' she said with as much assertiveness as she could muster. 'Nothing else.'

His eyes held hers for an interminable pause, before he stepped back from her and reached for a document lying on a table nearby. 'I trust you have had time to read through the contract I gave you?'

'Yes.'

She drew in a breath as he opened the folder and handed it to her. 'It is marked where you need to sign,' he said. 'Take your time.'

Scarlett bit down on her bottom lip as she looked through the folder page by page, her eyes skimming the words she had read, reread and agonised over for the last two days. She would be able to pay off all her debts and put enough money aside to pay for Matthew's education up to high school. There was even enough for her to employ a part-time nanny to take the strain off him being in child care for such long hours while she worked.

'I will give you carte blanche with the budget.' Alessandro's voice carved a deep hole in the silence. 'I want the best that money can buy.'

She looked up from the document to meet his hazel gaze. 'Why me?' she asked. 'Why are you choosing me for such a huge project?'

His expression gave nothing away. 'You are reputed to be one of the best,' he said. 'And I am in the habit of only settling for the best.'

She screwed up her mouth at him. 'That wasn't what you communicated to me four years ago. Back then, I was the lowest of the low.'

He held her pointed glare for several pulsing seconds. 'But you have since made something of yourself, have you not?' he said. 'No doubt I did you a favour by making you sit up and take responsibility for your actions.'

'A favour?' she spluttered. 'Do you have any idea what it's been like for me for the last four years?'

'That is neither my fault nor indeed any of my business,' he said, bending down to pick up the folder she had just dropped. He closed it, tucked it under his arm and met her gaze once more. 'I am prepared to pay you well to do this work for me, but if you are having second thoughts I can just as easily use one of your competitors. I have several from which to choose.'

Scarlett's eyes went back to the folder, her heart skipping a beat at the thought of some other design studio having the chance to work a miracle on this building. It was as Roxanne had said: a chance of a lifetime, and something they had both dreamed of since they had qualified as interior decorators.

'Do you want the job or not?' he asked after a lengthy moment.

She took an unsteady breath and put her hand out for the folder. 'I'll take it,' she said, dearly hoping she wasn't going to regret it.

He opened the folder without taking his eyes off hers, and handed his pen to her, clicking it as he did so.

Scarlett felt the warmth of his fingers on the pen as she took it from him and, to disguise her reaction, laid the folder on the table nearby, bent her head and signed all the relevant sections.

She straightened after she had finished and handed it back to him. 'There,' she said matter-of-factly. 'All signed.'

'Now all you have to do is deliver on your promise,' he said with another one of his enigmatic smiles.

'Umm…yes…' she said, shifting her gaze from the mysterious intensity of his.

He stepped back into her personal space and lifted her chin with two long, strong fingers. 'Four years is a long time, is it not, Scarlett?'

Scarlett felt the magnetic pull of his body, the heat of him so close to her reminding her of the intimacy they had shared in the past. 'Yes.' Her voice came out soft and whispery in spite of her attempt to sound emotionally detached. 'Yes, it is…'

'It is too long,' he said, placing his hands on her hips and bringing her body into closer contact with his. 'I have never felt like this with anyone but you. I have had numerous lovers, but not one of them can arouse me with the way you do. You are doing it now—the way you tug at your bottom lip drives me wild.'

Scarlett let go of her lip and swallowed nervously as she tried to ease out of his hold. 'Please let me go.'

He smiled crookedly as his hands subtly tightened on her

hips. 'You probably have no idea how much I want to kiss you right now, to feel your lips respond to mine as they used to do.'

She stood in the circle of his arms, her heart thumping in case he kissed her, and her stomach already twisting and turning with frustration in case he did not.

She held her breath as his head came down, the first touch of his mouth on hers making her body come to instant, throbbing life. Her breasts felt the press of his chest against them, and her thighs the full force of his arousal as it probed her with heart-stopping intimacy.

It was like coming home after a very long absence.

Everything felt so right.

The skating touch of his hands as they moved to her bottom and pulled her harder against him, the thrust of his tongue into the moist cave of her mouth, and the way he made a sound of pleasure at the back of his throat, made her feel as if the last four years hadn't passed.

The heat of his body warmed hers to boiling point, her mouth melting beneath the pressure of his, and her inner core turning to liquid.

His tongue tangled with hers, flicking then stroking until she was clinging to him without reserve. She kissed him back, her hands snaking around his neck to keep him close, her lower body grinding against the heated trajectory of his.

He angled her face with one hand as he deepened the kiss, his other hand going to her breast in a caress that was temptation and torture rolled into one.

Scarlett wanted more.

She wanted his mouth on her, sucking hard and then softly, as he used to do. She wanted to feel the graze of his teeth, to feel his skin on her skin, to taste his essence, to feel him move deep within her in the most intimate union of all.

She wanted to feel the length and strength of him in her hand, to shape him, to feel him tense with pleasure before he exploded with release.

He pulled back just as her hands brushed tentatively against the waistband of his trousers. 'Not here, Scarlett,' he said. 'We are in full view of the workmen. Why don't we go back to my house and finish this properly, hmm?'

The clinical detachment in his tone was all she needed to get her brain back into gear. 'I don't think so, Alessandro,' she said, stepping backwards, disgusted with herself at her lack of self-control. 'I've told you numerous times, I am not interested in revisiting the past with you.'

His mouth tilted sardonically. 'You did not give me that impression when you kissed me just then. What on earth would your current lover say if he saw you clawing at me so lasciviously?'

Scarlett felt as if her shame was emblazoned on every pore of her skin as she stood before him. She had no excuse for her behaviour. She didn't even understand why she had acted in such a disgraceful way when she hated him so vehemently. She hated him for denying the existence of his son. She hated him for coming back into her life just when she thought she had finally put his rejection behind her.

She drew in an uneven breath. 'I'm deeply ashamed of myself,' she said. 'I should have known this wouldn't work.'

His eyes pinned hers. 'You are reneging on the deal?'

She frowned at the steely glint in his gaze. 'I'm not sure what you are getting at. I told you this was to be strictly business between us. I can't do this any other way.'

'If you do not want to carry through on your commitment you will have to pay a severance fee,' he said. 'It is in the contract you just signed.'

Scarlett felt her insides drop alarmingly. Her eyes went to the folder he had placed back on the small table. She had momentarily forgotten about the severance clause. It had been one of two that had worried her, but she had assured herself the money would be worth it. Now she wasn't quite so sure.

He reached for the document and showed her a sentence just above the section where her final signature was written. 'Do you want me to read it out to you?' he asked.

'No,' she said through tight lips, trying not to look at the words printed there. She had practically signed her life and business away. She would have to pay, and pay dearly, to get out of the contract. She was starting to understand now why he had wanted her and only her. He would no doubt make it impossible to work with him so she would have no choice but to want out of the deal. He had used a thick wad of wordy pages to communicate one sure thing: he was going to ruin her.

She brought her eyes back to his and glared at him. 'I suppose you've done this deliberately, haven't you?'

His expression remained as inscrutable as ever. 'If you mean to imply that I have coerced you into working for me, then I think you need to examine the wording of the contract a little more closely,' he said. 'The terms and conditions are all there in plain English, and I gave you plenty of time to read them.'

She ground her teeth. 'I can see how this is going to be run. You want to pick up where you left off four years ago, and the only way you could do it was to lock me into a business deal that will ruin me if I pull the plug. Isn't that taking revenge a little too far?'

'It is not a matter of revenge, Scarlett,' he said evenly. 'About a year or so ago I came to Sydney on business and I visited a colleague who had recently had his penthouse redecorated. I was very impressed with the work and was intrigued, on asking, to find out it had been you who had done the design. I thought it would be interesting to meet you again, to see if what we had was still there.'

She flung herself away from him in disgust. 'I can't believe I'm hearing this,' she said. 'You tossed me out of your life as if I was a bit of rubbish, and never once checked up on me to see if I was all right. I could have been mugged or robbed or even murdered that night, for all you cared.'

Alessandro felt a familiar sharp needle of guilt stab at him. He had been so furious that night, he hadn't stopped to think of anything but getting her out of his life. But, after a young female British tourist had been brutally assaulted a year or so ago a few blocks from his house, he'd realised he should have had Scarlett escorted to the nearest bus shelter or train station at the very least. It had been late, and although he lived in a respectable part of the city she very easily could have met with danger, wandering alone at night.

'I hate you for what you did to me back then,' she continued. 'And I hate you for what you're doing to me now.'

'I am sorry,' he said in a gruff tone. 'I should have thought of your safety. It was wrong of me to treat you so appallingly.'

Scarlett turned around to look at him. 'I had your child, Alessandro, your *son*,' she said, her voice catching over the words. 'Haven't you ever wondered about him?'

His face became an unreadable mask. 'No, for I know he is not mine.'

She balled her hands into fists. 'If he was standing here right now you wouldn't be able to say that with the same arrogant certainty. He has your colouring, and the same eyes and hair.'

'I seem to recall your travelling companion had dark hair and eyes too—or have you conveniently forgotten that little detail?'

She eyeballed him determinedly. 'I did *not* sleep with anyone but you the whole time I was in Italy.'

He rolled his eyes and sighed with impatience. 'I am so tired of this conversation.'

'I am tired of you not believing me,' she threw back in frustration. 'Will you at least agree to meet him and see for yourself?'

'I do not need to see him.'

'Which means you don't *want* to see him,' she said with an embittered look.

'Yes, that is right,' he said with a cutting edge to his voice. 'I do not want to be reminded of your duplicity. Even after all this time it sickens me to think of you lying to me like that.'

Scarlett felt like screaming, and stalked over to the balustrade on the landing to get control. She drew in some deep breaths, her chest feeling so constricted she felt as if hundreds of tiny sharp knives were embedded between her shoulder blades, nicking at her every time she tried to breathe.

'I will leave you to look over the rest of the building,' he said into the taut silence. 'You have my contact details if there is anything you need to check with me.'

Scarlett turned to look at him. 'Why do you want me to work for you when you refuse to believe me about your—'

'Do *not* say it again,' he cut her off abruptly. 'I am not the father of your child, and no amount of times you insist to the contrary is going to change that fact.'

'I just want you to meet him to see it for yourself.'

His brows came together over his eyes in a furious frown. 'I am warning you now, if you bring him to this work site at any time I will sever the contract myself. You will be responsible for whatever debt is incurred as a result.'

'You can't do that,' she said, but there was terror wobbling in her voice at the fear that he could.

He gave her a gelid look. 'Go read the fine print, Scarlett,' he said. 'Then tell me what I can and cannot do.'

Scarlett didn't need to, she already knew.

CHAPTER FOUR

'SO HOW did it go?' Roxanne asked as soon as Scarlett came into the studio at lunchtime.

Scarlett dropped her handbag to the floor with a little thud. 'I signed the contract,' she said, her tone heavy with resignation.

'Yippee!' Roxanne jumped up and down, sending her riotous bright-red curls bouncing. 'We're going to be famous!'

'Yes, but there are terms.'

'Terms?' Roxanne stilled and frowned at her. 'What terms?'

Scarlett flopped down in her office chair. 'I can't get out of the contract until I complete the job.'

Roxanne blinked at her. 'So?'

'So I am in over my head,' Scarlett said. 'Both of our heads, actually. If for any reason I don't finish the project, I am liable. We both are.'

'But you're going to finish the job, right?'

Scarlett bit her lip. 'What if he makes it impossible for me to do so?'

Roxanne's throat began to move up and down. 'You mean you think he put that clause in there on purpose?'

Scarlett's brow was still heavily furrowed. 'I'm not sure. I can't help thinking he's very cleverly luring me into his orbit. He told me he'd seen some work of mine and really liked it. I think it must have been Tomasso Venetti's in Bellevue Hill. That's the only penthouse I did last year.'

'You did a fabulous job on that place,' Roxanne said. 'No wonder he liked it. You really have a way with old buildings, Scarlett. I'm sure that's why he's asked you to oversee the Arlington.'

'I can't do it without you,' Scarlett said. 'It's a huge project, and I'm starting to suspect the devil will be in the details.'

'We can handle it, Scarlett,' Roxanne reassured her. 'You just have to keep your head when you're around him.'

'That's the whole trouble,' Scarlett confessed, and dropped her head into her hands. 'I can't think straight when I'm anywhere near him.'

'Look, why don't you get your mum or Sophie to babysit Matthew, and we can go out and have a drink to celebrate landing this contract? We need to think positively about this, instead of dwelling on the negatives. We could go to Dylan's in The Rocks. Everyone is raving about the place since we did the makeover for him. It's one of the most popular restaurants down there now. Besides, we haven't seen him since he broke up with Olivia.'

Scarlett dragged her head up out of her hands. 'You're right,' she said. 'I do need to take my mind off the negatives, and seeing Dylan would be nice. I'm probably being paranoid about Alessandro anyway.'

'Did you tell Alessandro about Matthew?' Roxanne asked.

'Yes, but I got the same response. He still refuses to accept the possibility he could be his child.'

Roxanne rolled her lips together, her brow creasing into a frown as she looked at Scarlett.

'You're giving me that look again,' Scarlett said with an irritated scowl.

Roxanne sat bolt upright. 'I'm not doing any such thing.'

'Yes, you are,' Scarlett said. 'I can see it in your eyes. You don't believe me any more than he does.'

'That's not true.'

Scarlett angled her head pointedly.

Roxanne blew out a breath. 'All right,' she said. 'I confess—I did harbour the thought that you might have somehow got it wrong. For a while there I thought you and Dylan might have had a bit of a holiday fling back then, as even now he always seems to prefer your company to mine. But Matthew is a dead ringer for Alessandro, don't you think?'

'I don't think—I know.'

'Have you told your mum yet?'

'No.'

'Don't you think it's time you did?'

Scarlett released a long-winded sigh and reached for the phone. 'I just know what she's going to say.'

'But, darling, how could you have *lied* to me for all these years?' her mother cried. 'I can't believe you didn't trust me enough with the truth.'

'I wanted to avoid this sort of reaction, that's why,' Scarlett said. 'He's not interested in being a father to Matthew.'

'Not interested?' Her mother's voice was sharp with disapproval. 'Why on earth not?'

'Because he doesn't believe Matthew is his.'

There was a short but telling pause.

'Mum?'

'Darling, you can be straight with me, you know,' her mother said. 'I am your mother after all.'

'Of course I'm being straight with you. There's no possibility of Matthew being anyone but Alessandro's son.'

'None at all?'

Scarlett could hear the doubt in her mother's voice, but this time chose to ignore it. 'No, Mum, there's no doubt at all.'

'Well, then.'

'I know what you're thinking.'

'I'm not thinking anything.'

'Yes, you are,' Scarlett said, mentally rolling her eyes. 'You're thinking what you thought when you said goodbye to me at the airport four years ago—that I would fall in love like you did with a totally unsuitable man and ruin my life.' *Which is pretty much what I did do*, she thought ruefully.

Lenore let out a sigh. 'It's just I can't help worrying about you,' she said. 'You're not streetwise like Sophie.'

'You make me sound like a naïve infant.'

'In many ways you are, Scarlett,' Lenore said, her tone softening with maternal concern. 'You are so trusting of people. I think that's why you ended up with a child out of wedlock. You and I are alike in that sense. We think the best of people when they're not worthy of it. You have to toughen up, love. I've had to—I wouldn't have survived if I hadn't.'

Scarlett let out a sigh as she pinched the bridge of her nose. 'I know.'

'Have you told Sophie about this…this horrible man?'

'Alessandro's not a horrible man,' Scarlett said in his defence. 'He's Matthew's father.'

'He doesn't want the role, Scarlett, so there's no point in thrusting it upon him. Some men are like that, your father being a case in point. You'd be better to move on without him, for Matthew's sake.'

Scarlett knew her mother was right, but a part of her—the part where her pride was stored—wanted Alessandro to accept his son as his own. She felt as if she couldn't move forward until he did. It was like a wrinkle in a carpet—it was going to be a tripping point until it was smoothed out.

'I know how hard it's been for you,' Lenore said. 'You were in a terrible state when you came home from Italy.' Her voice broke as she continued. 'I sometimes think if it wasn't for Roxanne's support in getting your business up and running you would have given up all hope and…done something drastic…'

'Mum…'

Her mother sniffed. 'It's true, darling. You were so thin and run down. But we all assumed you were grieving.'

'I was.' *And I still am,* she added silently. 'It felt like a death at the time.'

'Break ups are like that,' Lenore said. 'The only difference in this case is there's still a body to deal with.'

And what a body, Scarlett thought, recalling how Alessandro had felt under the touch of her hands.

'Will you be all right dealing with this man on a day to day basis?'

Scarlett felt her stomach tremble again at the thought. 'I think so.'

'I'm worried about you.'

'I appreciate your concern,' Scarlett said with heartfelt sincerity. 'But I can handle Alessandro Marciano. He's a part of my past—he has nothing to do with my future.'

'He might have more to do with your future if he suddenly

realises he has a son,' Lenore pointed out. 'What if he meets Matthew some time in the future?'

Scarlett pressed her lips together. 'He doesn't want to meet him, and to tell you the truth I'm starting to think he doesn't deserve to, for what he's put me through.'

'It's understandable that you're angry with him,' Lenore said. 'But think how dreadful it would be if you still felt something for him.'

There was another short but loaded silence.

'You don't still care for him, do you, Scarlett?' her mother asked with an anxious edge to her tone.

'No, Mum. I feel nothing but hatred towards Alessandro Marciano,' she said, trying not to think of how his mouth had felt on hers earlier that day. 'I will never forgive him—ever.'

'Why did you agree to take on this project if you loathe him so much?' Lenore asked.

'I've worked for difficult clients before.'

'You will be careful, won't you, love?'

'Mum, stop worrying about me. I know what I'm doing.'

'How much is he paying you?'

'A lot.'

'How much?'

'Enough,' Scarlett answered. 'I'll be able to get into the black with my business loan.'

Lenore sighed. 'I wish I'd been able to help you a bit more, but my welfare payment is hardly enough to live on and—'

'Mum, stop it. We've been through this a hundred times before. I'm twenty-six years old, far too grown up and independent to be taking money off my mother.'

'I know, sweetheart, but Sophie's done so well, I just wish—'

'Mum, this is me you're talking to, not Sophie. I want different things for my life. I would go crazy living like Sophie does. I hate coffee mornings and bridge parties. I don't want or need a rich husband and designer clothes to feel good about myself.'

'I know that, darling, but sometimes I wish you were a bit more established financially,' Lenore said. 'Wouldn't it be nice if you could find a nice man to settle down with, perhaps have another child, a little half-brother or sister for Matthew?'

Scarlett closed her eyes as she fought against the ambivalence of her feelings. She had one child, a perfect little son who was the image of his father. She wasn't ready to think of having another child by another man. The few dates she had been more or less coerced into by her sister had confirmed she wasn't quite ready to move on.

'Scarlett?'

'I'm OK, Mum, really,' Scarlett reassured her. 'It's just been a heck of a day, that's all.'

'Yes, love, of course it has,' Lenore responded. 'It must have been so hard seeing him again.'

'Yes… Yes, it was…'

There was a small silence.

'Scarlett?'

'It's all right, Mum. I'm not in any danger of making the same mistake twice.'

'I know, but history has a habit of repeating itself, as you know from my experience. I took your father back, and while I'm glad I did, because it meant you were born as a result of our brief reconciliation, I wouldn't want to see you get hurt all over again.'

'I'm not going to allow myself to get hurt,' Scarlett said with a confidence she didn't really feel. 'I've grown up in the last four years, Mum. I'm not going to get my heart broken again.'

* * *

A courier arrived mid-morning with the floor plans of the hotel, but there was no accompanying note inside. Scarlett knew it was inconsistent of her to feel so out of sorts, for she was the one who had insisted it was a business deal and nothing else.

She spent the rest of the day worrying that Alessandro would walk in the door of her studio, and yet as she shut her computer down at five p.m. she felt strangely disappointed and aggrieved that he hadn't.

Matthew was tired, but excited when she picked him up from crèche when she told him his granny was going to babysit him that evening.

'I drewed you a picture,' he announced proudly, unrolling the piece of art paper he had in his hands.

Scarlett smiled as she looked at the bright smudges of paint. 'Wow, that's beautiful, darling. What is it?'

'It's a cat like Tinkles, only not dead.'

Scarlett frowned as she thought about how she had handled the recent death of their neighbour's cat. She had couched it in euphemistic terms, but it seemed Matthew had understood it in his own way.

'It's lovely,' she said. 'Can you do one for Mrs West as well? I'm sure she'd love to have a reminder of Tinkles.'

'Can we get a cat?' he asked as they came to the car. 'Or what about a puppy? I'd *love* a puppy.'

'Darling, we live in a flat,' she said. 'It would be cruel to have a kitten or puppy locked up inside all day.'

His little face fell in disappointment. 'But Mrs West had a cat.'

'I know, but Tinkles was very old and used to living inside, and Mrs West was home with him all day so he never got lonely.'

'What about a daddy?' he asked after a moment. 'Can we have one of those?'

Scarlett disguised her shock by concentrating on unlocking the car and settling him into his car seat. 'I'm not sure about that, sweetie.'

'I wish my real one wasn't dead,' he said as he wriggled into the seat and automatically lifted up his arms so she could snap the restraining belt in place. 'What if we prayed to God and asked him to make him come alive again?'

She had to look away from those big hazel eyes. 'I've prayed and prayed, darling, but it's not going to happen.'

'I'm still going to pray,' his little voice piped up from the back seat as she got behind the wheel a few moments later.

Scarlett met his beautiful green-brown gaze in the rear-view mirror and smiled, even though it hurt. 'Let's hope God is listening,' she said, and took the turn towards home.

Dylan saw Scarlett as soon as she came in the door of his restaurant and, smiling broadly, embraced her in a solid hug. 'It's so good to see you, Scarlett. I was thrilled when I looked at the bookings and saw you and Roxanne had booked in for tonight. It's been a few months since I saw you both. My fault more than yours, so don't start apologising. I've been a bit antisocial since Olivia left.'

'I understand,' Scarlett said, returning his hug.

'So how's the business and Roxanne?'

'I'm expecting her any minute,' Scarlett said. 'She's probably having trouble parking. I had to shoehorn my way into the tiniest spot.'

Dylan smiled. 'Let's have a quick drink together while you wait for her,' he suggested, and signalled for the drinks waiter. 'The apprentice chef I have is brilliant, so I can trust him to hold the fort for a few minutes. The dinner crowd hasn't trickled in yet.'

After two glasses of champagne were set down in front of them, he asked, 'How's Matthew?'

'He's good,' she said with a smile. 'Growing up all the time.'

'He's a cute kid,' Dylan said. 'I loved those photos you emailed me a while ago.'

Scarlett wondered if she should say something about Alessandro, when out of the corner of her eye she saw a tall figure stoop slightly as he came into the bar area with an attractive, willowy blonde on his arm.

'What's wrong?' Dylan asked, leaning forward in concern.

Scarlett swallowed the bitter taste of bile in her throat. 'Er…nothing. I just thought I saw someone I knew, that's all.'

Dylan glanced towards the entrance. 'That's Velika Vanovic, the model everyone is talking about. See how popular you've made me?' he said, turning back to smile at Scarlett. 'Everyone famous or high profile wants to come here and enjoy the ambiance.'

'I think I've seen her on a billboard, she's very beautiful…' Scarlett answered feebly, staring at the bubbles in her glass, hoping the knives of jealousy currently attacking her insides would soon disappear.

'The man with her seems vaguely familiar,' Dylan commented, frowning slightly. 'I wonder where I've seen him before…. Hey, isn't he that guy you were seeing in Milan?' He swung his gaze back to her in confusion. 'Scarlett, didn't you tell us he was dead?'

She shifted position in the hope that Alessandro wouldn't see her. 'I can explain…'

'Oh look, they're coming this way.'

Scarlett felt her stomach clench as Alessandro and the glamourous model approached.

'Good evening, Scarlett,' Alessandro said, running his gaze over her appraisingly. 'What a coincidence, seeing you here like this.'

Scarlett rose with Dylan from the sofa. 'Yes,' she said. 'It is.'

Dylan offered a hand to Alessandro with a pleasant smile. 'Hello, Alessandro. It's been a long time. What, nearly four years?'

For a moment Scarlett wondered if Alessandro was going to ignore Dylan's outstretched hand, but after what was probably only a nano-second of hesitation he took it and shook it cursorily. 'Yes, something like that,' he said, his eyes flicking towards Scarlett with an inscrutable look. 'Velika, this is Scarlett Fitzpatrick, the interior designer I was telling you about. Scarlett, this is Velika Vanovic.'

'Pleased to meet you,' Scarlett said, and took the other woman's cold, thin hand briefly.

'Likewise,' Velika said in a husky tone, although the chill of her light-brown eyes belied her comment.

'So,' Dylan smiled pleasantly. 'You're here for dinner as well?'

'Yes,' Alessandro said, his gaze shifting to take in the twin glasses of champagne on the coffee table.

Scarlett felt the scorch of Alessandro's gaze as it met hers; she felt as if every layer of her skin was being lasered off by the heat of it. She knew what he was thinking; she could see it in the rigidness of his jaw. In spite of her assurances to the contrary, Alessandro had always been convinced Dylan had designs on her. He had only met him once or twice, as Dylan, Jessica and Joe had been keen to get on with their tour. But

Scarlett knew that finding her here sharing a drink with Dylan was hardly going to convince Alessandro that nothing but platonic friendship bound them to each other.

'I hope you enjoy your evening with us,' Dylan said. 'I'll organise the head waiter to see you to your table, unless you would like a drink in the lounge first?'

'Thank you, but I think we will go straight to our table,' Alessandro said. 'Velika and I have somewhere else to go after dinner.'

To bed, most likely, Scarlett thought with another sickening wave of jealousy.

Alessandro looked down at her as if he could read her thoughts. 'Enjoy your evening, Scarlett.'

'We will,' she answered with a little hitch of her chin.

Dylan waited until Alessandro and his partner were led to their table before he spoke in a low undertone. 'OK, so you have some explaining to do, young lady,' he said in mock reproach. 'That's Matthew's father, isn't it?'

Scarlett gave him a 'please forgive me' look. 'Yes.'

'I can see the likeness, it's absolutely unmistakable,' he said. 'To tell you the truth, I never really did buy that story about Matthew's father dying in a car accident, but I figured you had your reasons so I kept quiet.'

'I'm sorry…I should have told you. Roxanne is still furious with me about it. You and the others had gone to the States by then. By the time you came back home, I couldn't really tell you one thing and everyone else another.'

He took one of her hands in his and gave it a little squeeze. 'So what gives?'

Scarlett could feel her hand shaking beneath the gentle pressure of his. 'He doesn't believe Matthew is his.'

'Hasn't anyone told him about DNA tests?' he remarked

wryly. 'A friend of mine bought one off the internet. All it takes is a quick swab and the results are back in a couple of days. It puts an end to the argument over paternity right then and there.'

'I begged him to have one at the time, but he point-blank refused. By the time I thought about pursuing it legally, I realised he might not be such a good person to have in Matthew's life.'

'Why's that?'

She picked up her glass and watched as the miniature necklaces of bubbles rose to the surface. 'My father made it a point to remind me whenever he could of how I was unplanned and unwanted. I didn't want to risk Matthew being exposed to the same.'

Dylan gave her a look of concern. 'You still hold a bit of a candle for him, don't you?'

Scarlett met his clear grey eyes. 'No,' she said with steely emphasis. 'I don't think I will ever be able to forgive him for what he's done. Every day I think about how Matthew has missed out on so much. I can't forgive Alessandro for robbing our child of what he should have had.'

'It's upset you, seeing him with that woman, hasn't it?' Dylan said gently.

'Yes,' she said. 'Of course it upset me. He's living the life of the rich playboy while I've been bringing up his son without support.'

'Money isn't everything,' Dylan put in. 'You've given Matthew a much greater gift in loving him.'

'It's not about the money,' Scarlett said on a sigh. 'It's about the emotional support. It means everything to me.'

Roxanne came in at that point, looking flustered. 'I'm *so*

sorry I'm late, but my car broke down, and I—' She pulled up short when she saw Dylan. 'Oh…hi.'

'Hello Roxanne.' Dylan rose and gave her a brief kiss on the cheek. 'How nice to see you again.'

Roxanne's cheeks became pink, and she looked even more flustered. 'Thanks. You too.'

'Well, I'd better leave you girls to get on with your evening,' Dylan said. 'I can see one of my kitchen staff waving at me.'

He gave Scarlett a close hug and kissed her lightly on the mouth before releasing her. 'Take care, Scarlett.'

Scarlett's smile died on her lips when she caught sight of the slow burn of Alessandro's gaze from across the restaurant. A faint shiver scuttled up her spine as she thought of the power she had given him in agreeing to work for him. Any length of time in his presence was going to be dangerous—and not just professionally…

CHAPTER FIVE

'WOULD YOU mind if we do this some other time?' Scarlett asked Roxanne briefly, describing what had occurred earlier.

'Sure,' Roxanne said, slinging her bag over her shoulder. 'The last thing you need is to see that woman draped all over your son's father.'

Scarlett knew Alessandro had had numerous lovers since her, but even so seeing him with the glamorous model had hurt her more than she had expected it to. She hadn't thought it was possible to be affected in such a way, but her stomach was twisting and turning with anguish even now at the thought of him rushing through dinner so he could take that woman back to his hotel with him.

She tugged herself away from where her thoughts were leading. Why should she care what he did? It wasn't as if she still felt anything for him. She hated him with a vengeance, and nothing but nothing was ever going to change that.

'So, what's going on with Dylan and you?' Roxanne asked as they made their way out to where Scarlett's car was parked.

Scarlett glanced at her friend as she pressed the remote-control device. 'What makes you ask that? You know we've always been friends. There's nothing going on.'

Roxanne rolled her eyes. 'Sometimes you can be so naïve,'

she said. 'Dylan was all over you. No wonder Alessandro was giving you the evil eye.'

Scarlett frowned as she strapped on her seatbelt. 'Dylan's still getting over Olivia. He's lonely, that's all.'

'Lonely baloney,' Roxanne said with a cynical look.

'Are you jealous or something?' Scarlett asked.

'Of course not!' Roxanne insisted. 'He's a restaurateur. He works the most ungodly hours. I pity the woman he eventually marries, she'll never see him.'

Scarlett secretly wondered if her friend was being rather too emphatic in her dislike of Dylan. They had never quite hit it off, skirting around each other on the few occasions they had met, like two wary dogs.

'You know, I've been doing some thinking,' Roxanne said a few minutes later as Scarlett wove her way through the city traffic. 'What if Alessandro changes his mind some time in the future?'

Scarlett glanced at her. 'You mean about Matthew?'

'One look at that child is going to make him have some serious doubts about his convictions,' Roxanne pointed out.

Scarlett's hands tightened on the steering wheel, her teeth nibbling at her bottom lip. 'I know.'

'He could make things very difficult for you,' Roxanne said. 'I have a friend whose sister went through a very acrimonious divorce a couple of years back. As a result, their only child has to travel back and forth on access visits to Melbourne every second weekend. If Alessandro Marciano decides he wants his son to spend time with him in Italy, it's going to be tough on you, not to mention little Matthew.'

Scarlett felt her stomach start to clench again in dread. She had been down this road many times as a young child—forced into access visits that had never turned out the way she had hoped.

Roxanne was right.

Alessandro lived in Milan; he was only here to redevelop the old Arlington Hotel. He hadn't indicated any permanent plans to reside here in Sydney. If he did somehow come to the realisation that he had fathered a child, he might insist on regular access, not stopping to think of how it would affect Matthew to be transported like a parcel through the post.

Matthew was in many ways still a baby. He had not long come out of nappies at night, and still had the occasional accident. He was certainly bright and advanced for his age, but a long-haul flight would be out of the question. Unless of course Alessandro insisted she accompany him, which would throw up a whole lot of other problems—the main one being her ongoing attraction to him. She fought against it assiduously, but each time he was in the same room as her she felt every cell in her body swell in awareness, every fibre of her being tingle in remembrance of the passion they had so briefly shared.

'I feel so torn,' she confessed. 'For years I've wanted Alessandro to face the truth about Matthew, but now I'm worried about what might happen if he does.'

'You're still in love with him.'

'How many times do I have to tell you I'm not?' Scarlett asked in frustration. 'I hate the man.'

'Look, Scarlett, I sometimes think I know you better than I know myself,' Roxanne said. 'You still feel something for him, I can tell every time you mention his name. You get a certain look in your eyes.'

Scarlett gave her a withering glance. 'You're imagining it.'

'Am I?'

Scarlett let out another sigh. 'Look, I admit when I saw him at the restaurant tonight with his latest lover I felt physically ill, but that's because he's hurt me more than anyone else I know. Even my father's crappy behaviour is nothing to what Alessandro's done.'

'Listen, Scarlett, you were in love with him four years ago,' Roxanne said. 'It makes sense that you could fall in love with him again. Believe me, it happens.'

'Yes, I know,' Scarlett said. 'I swore I'd never end up like my mother, falling in love with a man who consistently let her down.'

'I hardly think Alessandro Marciano is in the same category of scum as your father,' Roxanne commented wryly. 'You've only seen your father once since you were a young child, and that was when he came to ask you for money. What a creep.'

'Don't remind me,' Scarlett said with a little grimace of distaste.

Roxanne gave her a reassuring smile. 'You'll get through this, Scarlett. I know you will. We're a team, remember?'

'I know…thanks.'

'We'll knock this project over together and then you can get on with your life. Alessandro will be back in Italy before you know it, and you'll never have to think of him again.'

'Yes.' Scarlet began to gnaw at her bottom lip, a frown almost bringing her brows together over her eyes.

'But you will, won't you?' Roxanne said. 'Think of him, I mean.'

Scarlett released her lip and sighed as she looked at her friend. 'I'm trying not to, but it's hard when I have his son as a constant reminder.'

* * *

As soon as Scarlett arrived at the studio the next morning Roxanne handed her the telephone, cupping her hand over the mouthpiece to whisper, 'It's Alessandro. He wants to speak to you.'

Scarlett took the receiver with an unsteady hand and held it to her ear. 'Scarlett Fitzpatrick speaking.'

'That was a very clever trick, Scarlett,' Alessandro drawled. 'Dangling the opposition in front of my nose to make me want you all the more.'

She felt her face growing hot, and was glad he couldn't see it. 'I don't know what you're talking about. Now, did you want me for something or is this simply a nuisance call?'

'I want to see you.'

'So make an appointment like everyone else does,' she clipped back.

'That is exactly what I am doing,' he said. 'I want to see you this evening at my house.'

Scarlett's heart felt as if it had just slammed into a brick wall and bounced off again. 'Your house? You've got a house?'

'Most people do, do they not?' he said, his tone sounding faintly mocking.

'But…but I thought you'd be staying at a hotel, or a serviced apartment or something.'

'I prefer to have my own space,' he said. 'I bought a house before I arrived.'

Scarlett had to peel her dry tongue off the roof of her mouth so she could moisten her lips. 'So…so how long are you expecting to stay in Sydney?' she asked.

'As long as it takes to see to the business I have here.'

'The Arlington Hotel, you mean?'

'That and some other loose ends,' he responded.

Jealousy rose like a bubbling, hot tide of lava inside her. 'I suppose Velika Vanovic is one of those loose ends?' she put in churlishly. 'You'd better be careful, Alessandro, she's been around the block a few times, or so I've heard.'

'I like a woman who is up front about what she wants,' he returned.

'I hate to imply you have little else going for you, but women like Velika Vanovic are after one thing, and one thing only.'

'Yes, I know,' he said. 'Sex, and plenty of it.'

Scarlett clenched her teeth. 'I meant money.'

'Velika is at least open about it, unlike you, who went about it by more devious means.'

She gritted her teeth. 'I did no such thing.'

'I will expect you here at eight p.m. We will have dinner together to discuss your ideas on the project so far,' he said as if she hadn't spoken.

'I'm not having dinner with you,' she said with stiff force. 'I have another commitment.'

'Cancel it.'

Three beats of silence passed.

'I don't usually see clients out of office hours,' she put in guardedly.

'I am sure you will not mind making an exception for me, since we are old acquaintances, hmm?'

'So what we had together has been downgraded to mere acquaintances, has it?' she asked with bitterness sharpening her tone.

'Old friends, then.'

'We were *lovers*, Alessandro Marciano, and as a result you are the father of my child,' she said through tight lips. 'Don't you dare insult me by referring to me as a mere acquaintance.'

'Are you suggesting you wish to be elevated to the role of my mistress?' he asked.

'Of course not!' she spluttered in indignation.

'It can easily be arranged,' he put in smoothly. 'In fact, I have been thinking about it since I ran into you last night with your boyfriend. He seems pleasant enough, but I bet he has not been able to make you writhe and scream the way I did.'

'It's none of your business what I do or who I do it with.'

'And yet you responded to me so delightfully when I kissed you. I had only to touch you and you went up in flames.'

Scarlett knew she had no way to defend herself, but it didn't stop her trying. 'Lots of ex-lovers temporarily revisit the context of their past relationship. It doesn't mean anything.'

'It means you are still attracted to me, in spite of your involvement with another man,' he said.

'You're a fine one to talk,' she shot back. 'If you're so heavily involved with Velika Vanovic what business did you have kissing me?'

'Ah, but that is what I wish to discuss with you this evening,' he said. 'I will send a car for you, so do not think of trying to wriggle your way out of it.'

'Can I bring my son?'

The silence stretched and stretched, until Scarlett seriously wondered if he had hung up on her.

'I do not think a small child should be up at that hour, do you?' he asked. 'If money is an issue I will pay for a babysitter.'

Scarlett let another little silence slip past.

'Don't send a car,' she said, on a sigh of resignation. 'I'll make my own way there.'

'I am sending you a car and I expect you to use it,' he said in a tone that brooked no resistance.

She felt her top lip go up in a sneer. 'Is this a late show of concern for my welfare on the streets alone at night?'

There was a tiny almost immeasurable pause.

'Yes, it is, actually,' he said gravely. 'I deeply regret the way I treated you four years ago. It was ungallant and unfeeling of me.'

'It was also totally unjustified.'

There was another small, tense silence before he broke it by saying, 'I will see you this evening. *Ciao*.'

Scarlett let out her breath in a whoosh, and replaced the receiver on its cradle with a little clatter. 'Ooh I hate that man!' she growled.

'Do you need me to babysit?' Roxanne asked.

Scarlett folded her arms and began to pace the studio. 'I'm not going. I swear to God, I'm *not* going.'

'I'll be there at seven-thirty,' Roxanne said. 'That'll give me time to go to my Pilates class first.'

'I can't believe I signed that contract with that stupid clause in it.' Scarlet was still pacing, her expression thunderous. 'I should have known he would want to tighten the screws, so I had no choice but to get involved with him again.'

'Whoa! Back up a bit,' Roxanne said. 'I think I missed something somewhere. What's this about getting involved with him again? Do you mean involved as *involved*?'

Scarlett scowled. 'He implied something along those lines, but I'm not going to stand for it.'

'Are you sure you can resist him?' Roxanne asked with a concerned look. 'He's one hell of a package, Scarlett. If I wasn't so off men at the moment, I'd be tempted myself.'

'I've changed my mind,' Scarlet said, putting up her chin.

'I'll go around to his house tonight and prove to him that I'm not interested. I'll take some sketches and layouts, and keep things formal and businesslike at all times.'

'Yeah…right.'

'What do you mean, "yeah…right"?'

Roxanne didn't answer, but her expression was communication enough.

'You don't think I can do it, do you?' Scarlett said.

'I think you're in very great danger of getting hurt all over again,' Roxanne said. 'History has a habit of re-marking its territory.'

'Repeating itself,' Scarlett corrected. Roxanne was always mixing her metaphors. 'History has a habit of repeating itself, not re-marking its territory.'

'It's kind of the same thing, though, isn't it?' Roxanne said.

Scarlett was glad the front door of the studio was opened by a client at that point, so she didn't have to answer.

CHAPTER SIX

MATTHEW WAS already sound asleep by the time Roxanne arrived, so Scarlett offered her a drink and sat down to chat to her while she waited for the car Alessandro was sending for her to arrive.

At ten minutes to the hour the doorbell rang, but instead of seeing a chauffeur standing there Scarlett came face to face with the tall, commanding figure of Alessandro himself.

'Oh…It's you.'

He cocked one dark brow at her. 'You were expecting someone else?'

'No, but you said you'd send a car for me. I thought it would be a limo driver or…or something.'

'I was not prepared to take the risk that you would refuse to be transported to my house by my driver, or indeed not turn up at all.'

She glowered at him. 'I'm not that much of a coward.'

Alessandro cast his gaze around the small flat, and encountered Roxanne sitting on the sofa with a bemused expression on her face. 'Good evening, Miss Hartley,' he said. 'Are you babysitting for Scarlett?'

'Yes, but don't hurry back,' she said. 'I've brought a good

book, and there's a late-night movie on the TV I've been dying to see.'

Scarlett sent her a 'what do you think you're doing?' glare, but Roxanne deflected it by sending a beaming smile in Alessandro's direction.

'That is indeed very kind of you, but I will not keep Scarlett out too long,' he said. 'I have an early flight to catch in the morning.'

'Milan?' Scarlett couldn't quite remove the trace of hopefulness from her voice.

His eyes collided with hers. 'Melbourne, actually.'

'Another hotel makeover?'

'Yes,' he said. 'But I will make some time for pleasure as well.'

Scarlett wished she hadn't asked. She followed him out to his car with her stomach churning with jealousy all over again, imagining him with yet another glamorous starlet hanging off his arm. She sat stiffly and silently in the passenger seat as he drove the short distance to the exclusive suburb of Double Bay, but her eyes couldn't help but widen when he turned the powerful car into a driveway she was all too familiar with.

She swung her gaze to look at him. 'You knew I redecorated this property, didn't you?' she asked.

'Yes. I like what you have done to the place. That was one of the reasons I thought I would use you for the Arlington makeover.'

Scarlett didn't give him time to come around to her door, but leapt out clutching her portfolio to her chest like a shield. Her brow was furrowed as she followed him into the house, her thoughts going off in all directions like a box of out-of-control fireworks.

'What would you like to drink?' he asked as he led her into

the huge living area she had designed with meticulous attention. 'I have white wine, champagne, and all the usual aperitifs.'

'White wine, thank you…' she said, still trying to get her head around things.

She had spent a lot of time on this house; the makeover had been total, and she had felt so thrilled with the results. It had gone from being a large but tired 1930's house to a luxury mansion with every modern fixture and appliance. The kitchen and walk-in pantry were huge, the living area twice the size of her flat. Each of the six bedrooms had an *en suite* done in Italian marble, and the main bathroom was second to none in terms of opulence. It had been one of the biggest projects she had ever done, and the payment she had received had helped her and Roxanne move out of the cramped office they had rented in the outer suburbs to their current studio in trendy, upmarket Woollahra.

Alessandro walked to where she was standing, and handed her a glass of white wine as he raised his glass in a toast. 'To a successful completion of our contract,' he said.

A little hammer of suspicion was tapping away inside her head as she held his inscrutable look. 'What's going on, Alessandro?' she asked.

'We are having a drink, are we not?'

'I mean about you happening to be the owner of this house,' she said. 'It wasn't just a coincidence, was it?'

He gave her one of his enigmatic smiles. 'I had one of my employees oversee the work. He spoke very highly of your professionalism and meticulous attention to detail.'

'That would be Mr Rossi, wouldn't it?' she asked, her mouth pulled tight. 'So, he was acting for you.'

'I trusted him to see that the house was brought to a satisfactory standard.'

Her fingers tightened around the stem of her glass. 'I hope you're happy with what I've done.'

His eyes glinted. 'Very. The master bedroom in particular is pure sensual indulgence. I can see your touch everywhere.'

Scarlett could feel a blush rising from the soles of her feet to pool in her cheeks. 'I only did what I was asked to do,' she said, with a white-tipped set to her mouth.

'Yes, but you did it with your own personal flair,' he said. 'It is like making love, no? You have moves and touches no one else can even imitate.'

She gripped her glass even tighter, trying not to be pulled into his force field. She could feel the magnetism of his presence: the way his eyes held hers, the way his too-close body radiated its warmth and very male scent, so that her nostrils flared of their own volition to take more of him in.

He put his wine glass down and stepped closer, tipping up her chin with a lazy finger. 'Just like the properties you have designed, you have left your indelible mark on me, Scarlett,' he said softly. 'No one has ever been able to erase it.'

Scarlett could feel herself drowning in the deep green and brown of his eyes, her whole body on high alert. The blood rushed through her veins, her skin prickled, her breasts felt tight, and her stomach began kicking with excitement as he took the glass from her nerveless fingers and set it down right next to his, all without once releasing her gaze.

Her tongue sneaked out to moisten her lips. 'Alessandro… I can't do this.'

His thumb stroked the side of her mouth, close but not quite touching her pulsing lips. 'But you want to, don't you, *cara*? You want to as much as I do.'

She couldn't stop staring at his mouth, her heart going like an out-of-control jackhammer in her chest. 'It…it doesn't make it right,' she said. 'You already have a mistress, and I have—'

His hands came down on her shoulders and held her fast. 'Do not play games with me, Scarlett. I will have what I want, no matter what hurdles or obstacles you put in the way. We have unfinished business between us.'

'Yes, the birth of your son being one of them,' she threw back.

His jaw was set in taut lines. 'Why do you persist with this? I told you, he cannot possibly be mine.'

'There are ways of finding out for sure.'

His fingers tightened momentarily before he released her, using one of his hands to bring back the hair that had fallen forward over his frowning forehead. 'I do not need to find out anything. I know everything I need to know. I saw you with Kirby; there is an easy familiarity between you. Anyone can see you are intimately involved. I am not surprised he is still on the scene. He never really went away, did he? In fact, it would not surprise me if you cooked the whole scheme up between you.'

She looked at him with contempt. *'What?'*

'Money was your motive,' he said, holding her glare with consummate ease. 'Your job was to land yourself a billionaire so you could get your hands on half of the assets and split them with your lover. It has been done before, and no doubt will be done again.'

'Will you agree to have a paternity test done?' she asked, ignoring his insulting summation of her character.

He looked at her in silence for what seemed a very long time, his expression as closed as a clenched fist. 'If that is the only thing that will stop you going on with this nonsense, then yes, I will agree to it.'

Scarlett suddenly felt suspended between relief and worry. What if on finding out the truth he decided he wanted full custody of his son? What if he insisted on Matthew spending up to half a year in Milan? Matthew was generally a secure little boy, but he was still a toddler, and the slightest change in routine would be enough to make him have nightmares or set him back developmentally. She might very well have started a chain of events that, once in motion, would not be easily halted.

Alessandro was a determined and no-nonsense man. Once he found out the truth, he would want control, and she had virtually handed it to him by pressing the issue so persistently.

'We don't have to rush into things…' she said, knowing it sounded as if she was backtracking.

His lip curled. 'Having second thoughts, Scarlett?'

She forced herself to hold his gaze. 'No, but I'm concerned about the effect on my son. I've always told him his father is dead.'

'He is very young to understand the concept of death,' he commented. 'He must be a very intelligent child.'

'He is,' she said, lifting her chin. 'But then, so is his father.'

He picked up their glasses, handing her the one she hadn't yet tasted. 'Dinner is ready,' he said. 'I had my housekeeper prepare it earlier.'

Scarlett followed him to the dining area she had designed for a happy family gathering, never once at the time imagining that a few months later she would be sitting in it in a stony silence, opposite the man who had so ruthlessly broken her heart.

She sat, staring at the food on her plate, wondering how on earth she was going to get it past the aching lump in her throat.

'You are not eating,' Alessandro said after a few moments. 'Is the food not to your liking?'

She picked up her knife and fork. 'It's fine…lovely, in fact. You must have a very good housekeeper.'

'Yes, I have,' he said. 'She only comes in twice a week, however.'

Scarlett looked up in surprise from rearranging the food on her plate. 'Is that all? I thought you'd have a daily, if not full-time help.'

He picked up his wine glass and met her gaze. 'I do not like sharing my living space with people who are virtually strangers. I thought you would have remembered that about me.'

Scarlett did, but she thought with his billionaire status it might have changed. Alessandro had always been very particular about his privacy. She hadn't met any member of his extended family in the whole time she had lived with him. When she had asked about his parents, whether they were coming to visit or if they could visit them, he had told her they were on an extended cruise and wouldn't be back for months. All he had told her was that he was an only child, but now she wondered if there was more to his background than he was prepared to reveal.

'How are your parents?' she asked after a slight pause.

'Fine.'

'Where are they based now?' she asked. 'Do they live in Milan close to you?'

'No, in Sorrento,' he answered. 'They have a nice place overlooking the sea.'

'So you see them often?'

'No.'

'They must miss you,' she offered into the ensuing lengthy silence.

His eyes fell away from hers. 'Yes…' he said, with a slight frown pleating his brow. 'I imagine they do.'

Scarlett picked up her glass and took a tiny sip. 'Will they come out to visit you while you're here in Australia?' she asked.

'They have talked about it once or twice, but nothing has been confirmed.'

'Do you have a photograph of them?' she asked.

His eyes were shadowed as they met hers. 'No, I do not.'

'Are you close to them?'

'Yes and no.'

'What does that mean?' she asked.

He let out a frustrated sigh. 'Look, my parents do not have a particularly happy marriage. I do not spend much time with them for the simple reason I do not like hearing them bicker with each other all the time. It grates on me.'

'Why don't they get divorced?'

'They do not believe in divorce.'

'How ironic,' she said with an ironic twist to her mouth, 'That you—their only son—doesn't believe in marriage.'

'It is not that I have anything against marriage, Scarlett. I know of several very happy marriages where both parties love and respect each other.'

'But you don't want that for yourself.'

'No.'

Scarlett let her gaze fall away from the determined depths of his. 'I told you four years ago you'll end up a lonely old man.'

'I am prepared to risk a bit of late-life loneliness to have my freedom now.'

She brought her eyes back to his. 'So you go from one relationship to the other, a month with one woman, a week or two with another? That's such a shallow way to live.'

'You are entitled to your opinion, but it is not the way I see things.'

She threw him a disgusted look and said, 'Go on, tell me—what's the longest relationship you've ever had?'

His gaze meshed with hers for several heart-chugging seconds. The silence was so intense, Scarlett could hear the sound of her own breathing.

'It was the one I had with you, *cara,*' he said with a little smile. 'Three months, two days and nine-and-a-half hours.'

Scarlett's mouth went completely dry. 'You…you counted the days and hours?'

She wasn't completely sure, but she thought his crooked smile contained a hint of sadness. 'I missed you after you had gone,' he said. 'I was angry at first. Angry for days, weeks even, but then I kept finding things you had left behind—an earring or a little souvenir you had bought, and forgotten to put away with the rest of your things.'

She ran her tongue over her lips. 'What did you do with them?'

'I kept them.'

She frowned at him as he rose from the table. 'But…but why?'

He came around to help her to her feet, his fingers warm and vibrant on the bare skin of her arms. 'Do you know, that to this day I am still not sure,' he said, turning her to face him, his hands going to her waist, his fathomless gaze holding hers. 'Perhaps I always hoped we would see each other again.'

Scarlett felt her breath catch like a tiny fish-hook at the

back of her throat. 'Did-did you feel anything for me back then, Alessandro, anything at all other than desire?'

He lifted one hand from her waist and brushed the back of his bent knuckles over the curve of her cheek, his eyes now more brown than green. 'Why do you ask? You do not still have feelings for me, do you, *cara*?'

She didn't answer for the simple reason she couldn't get her voice to work. She had locked away her feelings for him four years ago, but her chest felt like it was going to explode with the effort of keeping them back.

His thumb stroked over the teeth marks on her lip in a tender caress. 'You are wavering, are you not?'

Her startled gaze flicked back to his. 'No…'

He smiled a sexy blood-heating-to-boiling-point smile. 'That did not sound very convincing, *tesore mio*.'

'No,' she said more stridently this time, although she shivered all over when he brought her hips up against his.

'Can you feel the effect you have on me?' he asked in a husky tone. 'How we still affect each other?'

Scarlett could, but she didn't want to admit it. She tried to put some space between their bodies, but his hold was both gentle and determined. She was breathing too hard and too shallowly to get her brain to work. Her body was taking over, just like it had all those years ago. One touch from him and she was going weak at the knees, her heart racing with excitement, her blood surging to all her pleasure points in preparation for the exquisite torture of his touch.

His head came down, and she did nothing to stop his lips making contact with hers. Instead she closed her eyes, a soft sigh escaping from her mouth into the warm, dark cavern of his as he held her captive under the searing pressure of his kiss.

His tongue searched for hers in a single commanding thrust that sent an earthquake-like reaction right through her. Aftershocks of pleasure reverberated throughout her body, each of her limbs beginning to tremble with the sheer force of being in his arms again.

His hands shaped her with the confidence of a lover who knew her body well and desired it greatly. She revelled in the possessive clamp of his teeth against her breast as he roughly freed it from the barrier of her clothes, the almost primitive action sending hot sparks of desire to every part of her body. His mouth suckled on her hotly, his tongue laving her nipple, his teeth grazing her again.

Somewhere at the blurry back of her conscience she knew she should be pushing him away, not clutching at him in passionate desperation, but there was nothing she could do to hold back her response. It was as if it was hard-wired into her system; every time he touched her he set her alight with burning need, just as he had done four years ago. One kiss had started something that was way beyond her capability to withstand.

When he lifted her skirt to her waist and searched for her hot, melting core she did nothing to resist him. Instead she gasped with mind-blowing pleasure as his fingers pushed aside the lace of her knickers to find their honeyed target, the movement so sensual, so devastatingly sexy, she arched upwards to have more of him.

'Please…*oh, please*…' she begged as he teased her mercilessly.

'You want me, *cara*?'

'Y-yes…' she panted as he brushed against the swollen pearl of her need.

He smiled a victor's smile as he cupped her face with his

hand. 'I knew you would not be able to resist,' he said. 'You are the same as you were four years ago—wanton and shameless in your quest for fulfilment.'

His words were enough to bring Scarlett back to earth with a jarring thud. She stepped out of his hold and smoothed down her skirt with what precious little dignity she had left. 'As far as I recall, this wasn't part of the contract,' she said with a cutting edge to her voice.

'I am prepared to pay double time for out-of-hours work,' he put in with suave smoothness.

She glared at him, affronted. 'You think you can afford *me*, Alessandro?'

His cynical smile cut through her like a scalpel. 'You can name your price, Scarlett. I will pay it to have you in my arms again. And, yes, I can afford you.' The dark gaze raked her mercilessly. 'Easily.'

She folded her arms across her body, more to stop one of them slapping that arrogant look off his face. She couldn't believe his audacity, to think he could buy her like the whore he thought she was. 'I want to go home,' she said with a petulant toss of her head. *'Now.'*

'You will go home when I say you can go home.'

She sent him a glowering look. 'You can't hold me here against my will.'

He stepped towards her, backing her against the wall as he stroked his hands down the length of her bare arms, his touch like silk sliding over a warm, smooth surface. 'But it will not be against your will, will it, *cara*?' he asked. 'I can see the longing in your eyes. You would be on that floor flat on your back by now, if your pride had not got in the way.'

Scarlett wanted to deny it, but knew he would never believe

her, not when she had allowed him to touch her so intimately just moments earlier.

She mentally cringed in shame. How could she have allowed herself to succumb to his lethal charm in such a degrading way? It confirmed all his misguided opinions of her as a shallow, money-hungry tart who would open her legs for the highest bidder.

'At least I have *some* measure of pride,' she tossed back after a tense pause.

His hazel gaze pinned hers. 'How much do you want to be my lover again?'

She flattened her spine against the wall. 'I told you, Alessandro, you can't afford me.'

His eyes hardened with chips of cold-green purpose. 'How much, Scarlett? How much to have you in my bed again for the time I am in Sydney?'

CHAPTER SEVEN

SCARLETT eyeballed him with gritty determination. 'It may have escaped your notice, but I don't have a "for sale" sign stamped on my forehead.'

His mouth tipped up at one corner. 'Like a lot of women I know, Scarlett, you have a price. But what you are doing by these delaying tactics is trying to drive up the price a little further, is it not?'

She sent him a caustic glare. 'I am *not* going to be used by you, not for any price.'

'It is a very clever manoeuvre,' he said as if she hadn't spoken. 'And well known in the circles I move in.'

'Yes, well, I don't care for the circles you move in,' she said primly. 'Your model friend is a case in point. She's looking for prestige and notoriety by hanging off your arm. I would have thought by now you would have been able to pick it up a mile off. She's after money and nothing else.'

'Velika has nothing to do with the arrangement we have made between ourselves,' he said.

Scarlett felt like stamping her foot. 'There *is* no arrangement between us!' she insisted.

He lifted one dark brow meaningfully. 'Aren't you forgetting something, Scarlett?'

She swallowed convulsively as she saw the flecks of brown in his eyes darken, her stomach turning over itself as he tilted her chin up with the point of one finger. 'You signed a contract, Scarlett, remember?' he said, his eyes locking on hers. 'Your business will fall over if you have to pay your way out of your contract with me.'

She ran the tip of her tongue over the dryness of her lips, her heart beginning to pick up its pace alarmingly. 'Are you…?' She cleared her throat when her voice dried up and began again. 'B-blackmailing me into your bed?'

His smile was slanted at a devastatingly sexy angle. 'Blackmail is rather a distasteful term, is it not? I was hoping you would agree to resume our affair without having to resort to using such underhand tactics,' he said. 'After all, you have made it very clear you are still attracted to me.'

'That's totally irrelevant!' she argued. 'Physical attraction to someone doesn't give automatic licence to have an affair with them. There's such a thing as self-control, you know.'

He ran his hands down her arms to encircle her wrists again, his long, strong fingers like twin bracelets of velvet-covered steel. 'I do not feel any self-control when I am around you, *cara*,' he said as his eyes held hers in the magnetic force-field of his gaze. 'I never did, and I sometimes wonder if I ever will.'

Scarlett could feel the slow melt of her bones under his touch, her belly doing tiny, jerky somersaults as each of his thumbs began stroking the sensitive undersides of her wrists. Desire pulsed hot and thickly through her bloodstream, her skin tingling in response to his drugging caresses. Her legs were weakening beneath her, and she felt the involuntary loosening of her spine as one of his hands went to the lower curve of her back and brought her up against his hardness.

'Kiss me, Scarlett,' he commanded softly. 'Kiss me the way you used to do, with your whole body and soul.'

Scarlett's gaze dropped to his mouth and her belly did another sudden flip-turn. 'I-I don't think—'

His hand at her back pressed her even closer. 'What are you frightened of, *tesore mio*?' he asked.

She moistened her lips with a tentative movement of her tongue, in case it accidentally brushed his mouth hovering so close to hers. 'I-I'm not frightened,' she said, even though fear had already thickened her throat so she could barely swallow.

His lips nibbled at the side of her mouth, so close to the tingling fullness of her bottom lip she felt her legs begin to tremble, his warm breath dancing over her face and mouth tantalisingly. She felt the brush of his tongue against her cheek, and then along the seam of her mouth, the sensual movement making all hope of resisting him impossible.

She gave a little whimper and opened her mouth under the next sweep of his tongue, taking him inside to her moist warmth, mating with him in a dancing duel that mimicked what their bodies had done so well together in the past. Passion flared like a bush fire, the hot, licking flames sending Scarlett's heart-rate soaring as his pelvis ground against hers, his hardness against her velvet softness making every scrap of sense she possessed move even further out of reach of reason and rationality. She clung to him, her mouth on fire beneath the passionate onslaught of his, her teeth nipping at him as he nipped at her, her tongue flicking as his thrust, her body turning to liquid as his grew rock-hard and insistent.

His hands went back to her breasts, pushing aside her scooped neckline to gain access, his mouth a hot brand as he sucked on each engorged nipple in turn. Scarlett was vaguely aware of crying out in pleasure, partially aware too of digging her fingers into the thick hair of his scalp as she arched her spine to have more of his heat against her.

'You are just as passionate as you were before,' Alessandro said against her neck, his tone husky with desire. 'Perhaps even more so.'

Scarlett pulled away from him with an effort, her conscience an unbearable burden. She couldn't do this. Not while he thought she was only coming to him in exchange for money. It sullied everything they had shared in the past. It tainted everything she had given of herself. She had adored him; she had worshipped him in every way imaginable. To be reduced to a mere plaything was anathema to her.

'What is wrong, *cara*?' Alessandro asked.

She moistened her dry lips. 'Please take me home,' she said, tears shining in her eyes. *'Please…'*

Alessandro frowned as he considered talking her into staying a little longer. He knew it would not take much to persuade her—she was clearly as aroused as he was—but something about those tears in her grey-blue eyes warned him he had pushed her a little too far too soon. He had plenty of time; after all, the Arlington project would take several months to complete. He would no doubt have numerous opportunities to convince her to be his mistress again. He would have to be patient, that was all. He had waited this long; he could wait a little longer.

He reached for his keys and gave her a twisted smile. 'Come, *tesore mio*,' he said. 'I have found out what I needed to know in any case.'

Scarlett wanted to ask him what he meant, but she had a feeling she already knew. She followed him out to his car and sat in a miserable, guilt-stricken silence as he drove her back to her tiny flat.

He walked her to the door and waited until she had unlocked it, before he bent down to press a barely-there kiss to both of her cheeks. 'Sweet dreams,' he said. 'I will see you soon, no?'

Scarlett's throat was almost too tight to reply. 'Y-yes…'

Once Roxanne had left a few minutes later Scarlett went into her son's bedroom. One of his little arms was flung over the edge of the bed, the other clutching a matchbox car close to his face. She gently unpeeled his little fingers, her heart contracting painfully when she found a shiny-black Maserati lying there…

'Phone for you,' Roxanne said when Scarlett came inside the studio the next morning. 'It's Alessandro. By the way, I told him you're not involved with Dylan. And you can stop looking at me like that. He asked and I answered.'

Scarlett was still scowling as she picked up her extension. 'Hello, Scarlett Fitzpatrick speaking.'

'So you have decided to concentrate your efforts on the biggest return, eh, *cara*?'

'That is a despicable thing to say,' she said, turning her back on Roxanne.

'Are you missing me, *cara*?'

Scarlett felt her heart miss a beat at that low, velvet drawl, her stomach crawling all over again with desire.

He suddenly laughed, the deep rumble sending tiny shivers of reaction to the core of her being. 'You cannot help yourself, eh, Scarlett? You want me even though you do not want to do so. It is the same for me. I did not think I would feel this way about you, but I do.'

Scarlett held her breath. 'What are you saying?'

'I am saying I want to see you tomorrow night when I get back from Melbourne.'

She flattened her lips together, stalling as she tried to withstand the temptation.

'I will come to your house, if you like,' he offered. 'My flight back to Sydney is not a late one.'

Her hand tightened on the receiver. She wanted more time to prepare Matthew for a visit from his father. She wanted Alessandro to know for certain he *was* Matthew's father when they met for the first time. She had been lucky before, as Matthew had been fast asleep in bed and Alessandro hadn't seemed to notice the photos on the wall unit, but if he came around for any length of time…

'Umm…I don't think that's such a great idea,' she said, knowing it sounded pathetically lame. 'I'd rather meet on neutral ground.'

'I will book a hotel room and then no one will disturb us.'

'No! That's sound so…so terribly tacky,' she said and releasing a breath of resignation, added, 'I'll come to your house…after I've put my son to bed. But I insist on making my own way there.'

'All right,' he said. 'If you insist.'

'What about Velika Vanovic?' she asked after a tiny but tense pause.

'What about her?' His tone was impersonal and cool.

'She's your current mistress, isn't she?'

'She is not relevant to us, Scarlett.'

'Are you still seeing her and sleeping with her?'

'Why are you so interested?' he asked.

'I don't like sharing.'

He laughed again. 'You are so delightfully transparent. I like that about you. I like it a lot.'

'And yet you think I lied to you about our son.'

The silence this time was taut as a wire strained to its limits.

'I will see you tomorrow evening, Scarlett,' he said in a curt tone.

'I might not be here,' she said with reckless abandon. 'I might change my mind at the last minute.'

'You will be there,' he said, and ended the call before she could contradict him.

Roxanne came over to Scarlett's desk. 'Let me guess, you want me to babysit again, right?'

Scarlett bit her lip and nodded.

Roxanne gave her shoulder a tiny squeeze. 'You're doing the right thing, honey,' she said. 'You have to sort this out one way or the other, and now's the time to do it.'

The following evening Scarlett stood on the doorstep of Alessandro's house with legs that trembled as she heard his footsteps approach the front door to answer her summons.

She clutched her folder to her chest and forced her eyes to meet his as he opened the door. 'I have some preliminary mock-ups for you to look over,' she said, nervously moistening her mouth.

'Come and show me what you have been up to,' he said with an unfathomable smile.

Scarlett followed him to where he had drinks and nibbles set out and, pushing her reservations to one side, took a glass of white wine and sat next to him on one of the sumptuous leather sofas. She took a tiny sip, trying not to notice how close his thigh was to hers. She could see the bunching of his muscles as he leaned forward for the bowl of crisps, her stomach beginning to prickle with desire at the thought of those long, strong legs entrapping hers, the way they had done in the past.

'Do you want some?'

Scarlett blinked at him vacuously.

He smiled as he held the bowl under her nose. 'You have gone all glassy-eyed on me, *cara*,' he said. 'What is going on in that beautiful blonde head of yours, mmm?'

Scarlett wondered he couldn't see what was going on for himself. She felt as if her need for him was written all over her skin, every fine pore ached to feel the glide of his hands on her flesh. Her cheeks felt hot, indeed her whole body felt as if it was smouldering, and she knew one touch from him would send her into flames.

She put her glass on the coffee table and began to get to her feet. 'Maybe I shouldn't have come here tonight…'

One of his hands came down over hers and held her fast. 'No, Scarlett,' he insisted. 'Do not leave.'

Scarlett looked at their joined hands and felt a feathery sensation run up her spine. Her breasts began to tighten beneath the soft lace of her bra as his thumb began to stroke her wrist, her pulse going like a threshing machine as he pulled her closer to bring his mouth into contact with hers.

She tasted wine and salt and sex, a devastating combination that left her with no hope of resisting. It was as if her body was specifically programmed to respond to him and him alone. She kissed him back without reserve, her tongue tangling with his in a sensual dance of dangerous desires finally unleashed. She felt the increasing urgency in him as he pushed her back to the cushioned comfort of the sofa, his weight coming over her, his erection nudging at her intimately as his hands went to her breasts.

She drew in a sharp little breath as he shaped her through

the thin fabric of her dress—but her breathing stalled altogether when he deftly unzipped her and unclipped her bra, so he could have his mouth on her bare skin. His lips closed over one tight nipple, making her back arch, and her toes curl so much her shoes fell to the carpeted floor with two soft little thuds.

He took her other nipple and suckled hard, the drawing of his mouth on her flesh making her whole body writhe in response.

'I want you, Scarlett,' he said as he removed the rest of her clothes before starting on his own. 'I want you so badly I cannot think of anything else.'

She looked down and touched him, almost reverently. He was so hard, so fully aroused. She wanted to reach down and taste him, to feel him move within the moistness of her mouth, to feel his control straining at the leash as she subjected him to one of the most intimate acts of all between lovers.

'If you want me to stop then you had better tell me now,' he said, even as he separated her tender folds in preparation for his entry.

She answered by kissing him on the mouth, her tongue meeting his in a dance of mutual desire that left words totally unnecessary. She felt him surge fully into her warmth, the thickness of him after so long making her wince slightly as her slim body accommodated him.

He pulled back and looked down at her in concern. 'Am I hurting you?'

'No…'

'Am I going too fast for you?'

She shook her head, unable to speak for the emotion clogging her throat. It felt so good to have him so deep and warm and hard inside her. Her body had missed him so much;

for nearly four years she had lain awake at night, aching for exactly this, feeling his flesh on her flesh, his skin on hers.

He brushed her mouth with his in a kiss that was as light as air but as hot as fire. 'I have been going mad with the need to do this,' he groaned, easing himself inside her gently. 'You feel so perfect.'

Scarlett let out a breathless gasp of pleasure as he filled her completely, his slow, gently rocking motion making her want him harder and faster. She clutched at his buttocks with her fingers, and he responded by upping his pace until she was writhing against him uninhibitedly, her legs like jelly as she felt each hard thrust bring her closer and closer to the release she craved with all her being.

Suddenly she was there, her body exploding with an orgasm so intense she felt as if she had momentarily lost consciousness. Wave after wave of pleasure swamped her being, her nerves twitching and jumping with the aftershocks of such a cataclysmic response to his love-making.

She felt him prepare for his final plunge into oblivion, the tension in his muscles building and building, before he thrust forward with a groan of pure ecstasy.

The silence pulsed for a moment or two as Scarlett tried to get her breathing back under control.

'Scarlett…' Alessandro said, lifting her chin with the pad of his index finger, his hazel eyes taking in the creeping colour staining her cheeks. 'Do not be ashamed of what just happened between us.'

Her teeth began to savage her lip. 'It shouldn't have happened. I can't believe I let things go that far…'

His hands came down on the tops of her shoulders. 'Listen to me, *cara*,' he said. 'I wanted that to happen. We both did.

We are both consenting adults who have a fierce attraction for each other. Why not enjoy it while it lasts?'

She slipped from beneath his hold and, scooping up her dress, fumbled her way back into it. 'I-I can't do this, Alessandro…' she said, her voice catching over the words. 'It's not what I want for my life.'

'What do you want for your life?' he asked after a beat or two of heavy silence.

She turned to look at him again, her expression so sad it pained him to see it. 'I want to get married to a man who loves and adores me,' she said. 'I want a normal life. I don't want a short-term affair with someone I no longer…' she hesitated for a fraction of a second '…love.'

'You might not love me, but you certainly desire me,' he said. 'Or are you going to deny that after what we just shared?'

'No…of course I'm not going to deny it,' she said, shifting her eyes from the determined probe of his. 'I am still attracted to you…' She bit her lip again before adding, 'Much more than I realized.'

He stepped towards her again and captured her waist with his hands. 'I want you back in my life, Scarlett,' he said with an implacable edge to his voice. 'I want you like I've wanted no other woman.'

She lifted her gaze to meet his. 'But for how long? You're well known for your fly-by-night relationships, Alessandro. I can't do that, living holding my breath as if each day could be the last we have together.'

'I cannot answer precisely,' he said, dropping his hands from her waist. 'It depends on how things go with the Arlington redevelopment…and other things.'

'I suppose by other things you mean your current mistress,

Velika Vanovic?' Scarlett asked with a scathing set to her mouth.

He gave her a level look. 'I am no longer involved with Velika Vanovic. You are the person I am now involved with, and after what just happened here I am not going to give you up without a fight.'

'But you said you weren't going to blackmail me any more,' she said as the pit of her stomach began to quake in alarm in case he changed his mind. 'Surely it is up to me whether this goes any further?'

His expression communicated nothing but iron-clad determination as he reached for her again. 'I do not need to blackmail you. I can see how much you want me. You have already proven it.'

'No,' she said, making a vain effort to push him away—but somehow her hands wouldn't cooperate, instead clutching at him with clawing need. 'I don't want to be involved with you again.'

'Yes you do, Scarlett,' he said, beginning to nibble on her earlobe in the way that made her spine instantly turn to liquid. 'You want me again. Once is never enough for you, or for me. I am already hard again.' He captured one of her hands and placed it on the hard ridge between his legs. 'Do not leave me in this state, *tesore mio*,' he groaned. 'I want you right now.'

Scarlett's fingers began stroking him almost of their own volition, the temptation of his body too much to withstand. How could she possibly deny herself the magic of his lovemaking? It was all she had ever wanted from the moment she had met him—to be in his arms, spinning out of control with the passion that constantly smouldered between them.

He groaned again. His teeth gritted as he fought for control, his head thrown back as she sank to her knees in front of him, her soft breath wafting over him tantalizingly, before she began stroking him with the tip of her tongue. His hands went to her head, his fingers delving into her hair as she slowly tortured him, each moist glide of her tongue taking him that much closer to the point of no return. She felt the power she had over him and it excited her, just as much if not more than it had done in the past.

His fingers dug deeper into her scalp. 'No, *cara*, I cannot take any more,' he said, breathing heavily.

Scarlett kept on caressing him, stroking then sucking in turn, until he exploded with a muttered curse, his body sagging against her once it was over.

She straightened, and was about to step backwards when he stalled her by encircling one of her wrists with his hand. 'No,' he said. 'This is a two-way street, Scarlett, remember? Just like in the past, you do not get to do that to me unless I am allowed to return the favour.'

Scarlett pulled ineffectually at his hold but her heart wasn't in it, and she could tell he knew it. She drew in a gasping little breath as he picked her up in his arms and carried her to the bedroom she had designed only months ago, her excitement building as his eyes burned into hers with sensual promise.

'You are so very sensual, Scarlett,' he said as he joined her on the bed, his weight pressing her into the mattress. 'I cannot get enough of you. I have craved this for so long—to see you again, to feel you again, to make love to you again as we used to do. I have missed what we had so much.'

'I've missed it too,' she said in a soft whisper as she stroked the lean line of his jaw. 'You have no idea how much.'

He traced the point of his index finger from her belly button to the tiny landing-strip of dark-blonde hair that shielded her femininity. 'I have never forgotten the taste of you,' he said in a low growl. 'God, the nights I have lain awake thinking of the taste of you.'

Scarlett drew in a ragged breath as he bent his head to her moist warmth, his tongue moving against her swollen point of pleasure with exquisite expertise. She had no control over her response; it shook her from the inside out, each movement of his tongue sending her into a vortex of feeling that reverberated throughout every part of her body.

He moved back over her, his thighs entangled with hers in an erotic embrace as he entered her silken warmth in a strong, gliding thrust that sent sparks of pleasure from her head to her curling toes.

His mouth came down on hers, the sexy saltiness of her body mingled with his warm breath as he played with her lips, tugging at them with his teeth, teasing her tongue into a passionate duel. She nibbled at his bottom lip, sucking on it, pulling at it with her teeth and then sweeping over it with the tip of her tongue, the deep groans of pleasure he was emitting from the back of his throat thrilling her, and inciting her to do it all over again and again.

He responded by increasing his pace, his body driving into hers with tender force, the thick, hard length of him caressing her in all the right places. She only had to tilt her hips upwards to feel the first flicker of release, the second and third quickly following, until she lost count as she shuddered her way through another mind-blowing orgasm.

Her body was still pulsing with the aftershocks when she felt his whole body tensing above hers in that final second or two before he finally lost control. His face contorted with pleasure as he sucked in a harsh breath before releasing it in a rush as he spilled himself with explosive power.

In the silence that followed Scarlett felt her conscience

begin to prod at her. She wasn't a sleep-around sort of woman, she never had been. She had only had one lover apart from Alessandro and now, with the responsibilities of a small child, she could never treat any relationship with a man as just physical. And certainly not this man—the father of her son.

Alessandro propped himself up on his elbows to look down at her. 'This feels so right,' he said with a wistful look coming and going in his dark, intense gaze. 'This part always felt so right between us.'

She compressed her lips, trying not to show how emotionally affected she was. 'But I want much more than you are prepared to give…'

He got off the bed, reached for a bathrobe, and tied it around his waist. 'I have told you the rules,' he said with a curt edge to his voice. 'This is all I can offer you, Scarlett. Believe me—you should be content with that.'

Scarlett reached for her wrinkled clothes and struggled back into them, hoping she wouldn't betray herself by crying uncontrollably. 'I need to go home. It's getting late.'

He came from behind and held her against his solid, hard male warmth. Her breath whooshed out of her lungs as she felt his growing arousal behind her, the thin barrier of her clothes not enough to stop her from responding with a soft whimper of pleasure as his mouth began to nuzzle against her neck, and his hands cupped her already tingling, peaking breasts.

'You do not really want to go home right at this very minute, do you, Scarlett?'

'No…' she whispered huskily as he turned her to face him, his mouth coming down to hers. 'God help me but, no, I don't…'

CHAPTER EIGHT

ROXANNE WAS out on a call at a client's house when Alessandro arrived at the studio the next morning. Scarlett heard his car first, and a ticklish feeling ran up her spine as she swivelled on her office chair to look out the window.

She watched as he unfolded himself from the vehicle. His hair looked like black satin in the morning sunshine, his lean face cleanly shaven, his dark pin-striped trousers emphasising the length of his legs and trimness of his waist, and his light-blue business shirt highlighting the olive tone of his skin.

Her stomach flipped and then flopped as he stepped onto the pavement, his eyes meeting hers through the window. She pushed herself away from the desk and stood up as he came in the door, her hands going to her thighs to smooth down her skirt.

He moved across the small space of the studio and, cupping her cheeks with both hands, kissed her thoroughly. Scarlett breathed in the heady fragrance of musky male, sharp citrus and tortuous temptation. All her carefully rehearsed reasons for not agreeing to a resumption of their relationship were suddenly deleted from her brain as his tongue flicked erotically against hers.

Still cupping her face in his hands, he lifted his mouth off hers and smiled down at her. 'I knew you would be here waiting for me,' he said.

She screwed up her mouth at him. 'It *is* my studio after all,' she pointed out. 'Where else would I be?'

He tucked a strand of silver-blonde hair behind her ear, the brush of his fingers against her face making her tremble deep inside. 'You are still fighting it, yes?'

She lowered her gaze. 'I don't want to get hurt…'

He brought her chin up. 'I am only involved with you, Scarlett. You have my word.'

Scarlett wondered if she was being fobbed off. How could she tell? He was a notorious playboy; women flocked to him wherever he went. He had said it himself: he wasn't the settling-down type.

'If you do not believe me, read this morning's paper,' he added.

Scarlett's gaze went to the folded newspaper lying on Roxanne's desk. They usually had a quick flick through it during their coffee and lunch breaks, but with Roxanne still out at a client's house, and with the number of calls Scarlett had had to make in her partner's absence, there hadn't been time to even put on the kettle.

'There is a short article about us on page three,' he informed her.

'About us?' she asked, her eyes going wide. 'What do you mean "about us"?'

He walked over to Roxanne's desk, picked up the paper and opened it to the page where a small paragraph was headed: *Billionaire Hotelier involved with Local Interior Designer.*

Scarlett read the accompanying paragraph with her heart kicking like a wild brumby in her chest. It was only a few words about her and the studio, and thankfully no photograph accompanied it. It simply stated she was the new love interest of Alessandro Marciano.

She closed the paper and handed it back to him. 'Well, that just goes to show you can't believe everything you read in the press,' she said with an embittered look. 'I am not your love interest, am I, Alessandro? I am just someone to sleep with, someone to slake your lust with. You just want a fill-in affair while you are here—let's not go calling it anything else.'

His hazel eyes caught and held hers. 'Love is a favourite word of yours, is it not?'

'It's not just a word,' she said. 'It's a feeling, and in some ways almost a way of life. You've always shunned it, but you don't know what living is all about until you allow yourself to love someone more than life itself.'

She swallowed as he stepped towards her again, his hand tilting her face so she couldn't avoid his penetrating gaze.

'Love is a very cruel mistress,' he said with a rueful twist to his mouth. 'She takes hold of you, and then dumps you when you least expect it.' He released her chin to brush the curve of her cheek with the pad of his thumb, the touch so light she wondered if she had imagined it. 'I learned not to love a number of years ago, long before I met you,' he continued. 'I decided it was not worth the suffering once that person is no longer with you.'

'That seems a very selfish way of viewing things. What if the person you loved didn't leave?'

He dropped his hand from her face and moved back from her. 'Sometimes there is no way to control such things, Scarlett.'

'Alessandro…' She took a step towards him, but his eyes had already shifted from hers and before she could stop him he moved past her to look at the screen-saver that had come up on her computer. She watched with baited breath as he looked at the montage of images of Matthew she had constructed, his body becoming as still as a lifeless statue as his eyes roved each and every photo.

Every milestone was there—the first ultrasound picture, the first few minutes after birth, Matthew's first tooth, his first birthday, his first wobbly steps, even his recent third birthday with the racing-car cake she had made for him.

The silence stretched to the point of pain.

Alessandro was not aware of his hands gripping the edge of the desk until he finally registered his fingers were numb. His heart was beating, but too fast and too hard. His stomach contents were liquefying, his vision was blurring. He couldn't swallow, he couldn't breathe, he couldn't even think.

'His name is Matthew.' Scarlett's soft voice carved through his swirling thoughts. 'He turned three a couple of months ago.'

Alessandro counted back the months and gripped the desk even tighter. It couldn't be true. It was a lie. He had seen the test results. He was infertile, as planned.

But the child *looked* like him.

God, he even looks like Marco, Alessandro thought with a gut-wrenching pang of grief that he'd deluded himself into thinking he had locked down long ago.

Somehow he found the wherewithal to turn away from the computer screen and face Scarlett. His heart was still doing leap-frogs in his chest but, seeing her there, standing so still and silently before him, was like a stake being driven right through his body.

'He's yours, Alessandro, even if you don't want to ever acknowledge it,' she said, holding his gaze determinedly.

He scraped a hand through his hair and drew in a breath that scalded his throat. 'I need proof. I am sorry if it offends you, but I need to have proof. It is…' He swallowed deeply. 'It is important.'

She gave him one of her scathing looks as she folded her arms across her body. 'I believe you can buy a DNA kit off the internet. I am quite willing to allow you to use it.'

She wasn't supposed to say that, Alessandro thought with another wave of dread. Not if she had lied to him. The way she had suggested a test the other day and then instantly backed down had made him think she was still lying. But there was no way she would give him the go-ahead for a test that would prove without a doubt who was the child's father. Besides, she'd had three years to try and force a paternity test on him and yet she hadn't done so. The legal system was full of such cases these days—men who had been paying out large sums of money for children had begun to fight back, insisting on proof the children they were supporting were actually biologically theirs.

'I don't know what to say…' He hated admitting it, but it was true. He was lost for words. He had never been in a situation like this before. He had always prided himself on being in control, which was why he had insisted on having a vasectomy in the first place. He didn't want a repeat of what had happened to Marco. He couldn't bear to put a child of his through it, not knowing what he knew about himself and his family.

'"Sorry for not believing you" would be a very good start,' she said with crispness in her tone.

He swallowed again to clear his throat. 'I will have to save that for when I know for sure.'

She rolled her eyes in disdain. 'You can't do it, can you?

You can't even for a moment harbour the possibility that you got it wrong.'

His jaw felt so tight he thought his teeth were going to crack. 'Do you have any idea of what this is like for me? *Do you?*' he asked.

She glared at him with chips of grey-blue fire in her gaze. 'You're not going to get the sympathy vote from me, Alessandro. I was the one who carried your child for nine miserable months, and delivered him after an eighteen-hour labour without his father there to support me.

'Don't talk to me about how this is for you. You don't even know half of what it's been like for me. I have struggled to provide for my child. I've had to put him in crèche when I would much rather be at home with him, but what other choice did I have? I can't even afford to send him to the school of my choice when the time comes, because his arrogant, always-right untrusting bastard of a father wouldn't accept that he might have somehow got it wrong.'

Alessandro felt as if an avalanche had hit him. The first glimmer of tears in her eyes was like the blunt end of a telegraph pole hitting him in the mid-section. He moved towards her, but she swung away and snapped up a tissue from a pretty little box with primroses on it. *Funny, the little inconsequential things you noticed when everything else was spinning out of control,* he thought as he watched her wipe at her eyes and discreetly blow her nose.

'I'll arrange to see a doctor tomorrow,' he said. 'It might take a day or two to get the sperm-test results back from Pathology.'

Scarlett turned and looked at him with a puzzled frown. 'Sperm tests?'

His eyes were full of pain as they met hers. 'I had a vasectomy performed when I was twenty-eight years old. I was declared infertile three months later.'

Scarlett stared at him in a stunned silence. No wonder he had denied fathering a child so vehemently. What man wouldn't have reacted in exactly the same way? He had believed himself to be incapable of fathering a child; he had taken the necessary steps to ensure it would never happen. Looking at it from his angle, he had every right to be suspicious—although a part of her still felt he should have trusted her regardless.

'Scarlett…' he said, dragging a hand through his hair, his expression still tortured with anguish. 'I never thought something like this could happen. It never once occurred to me that it could. The chances of it must be a million to one at least.'

Her slim shoulders began to shake, and he moved across the room. His hands came down on her shoulders and turned her to face him. Emotion clogged his throat at the grey-blue of her tear-washed eyes. He realised then that, if he had ever had a choice in the matter, she would have been the mother of his children. She would make the perfect mother. She was gentle and nurturing, and yet strong and determined—so like his own mother used to be until life dealt her such a cruel hand. His mother was not the same mother he had adored, even though Marco had been buried long ago.

He hardly realised he was doing it as he lifted Scarlett's chin with the point of his finger. 'If you do not want to continue with the project I will cancel the contract. You will not incur any expense as a result.'

She bit her lip so hard he was sure bright-red blood was going to spring from it. He brushed his thumb against her teeth and her lips trembled in response.

'It's all right,' she said on an expelled breath. 'I will do it.

But I want you to know I'm not doing it for you or for me, but for Roxanne.'

He lifted one brow quizzically.

'She's worked so hard for what we've built up,' Scarlett explained. 'We both have, but I've been a bit hamstrung with my commitments to Matthew. She's been so good, and I don't want to let her down.'

Alessandro placed his hands on the top of her shoulders and gently squeezed. 'We will sort it out, Scarlett, do not worry.'

She lowered her gaze. 'He's so like you…' she whispered.

He closed his eyes against the sudden and unexpected sting of tears; his chest felt like a clamp had been placed on his heart and lungs.

'I wanted to send you photos,' she went on, her voice still barely audible. 'So many times I wanted to prove to you how like you he is. He even does that little thing you do when you sleep.'

'What thing?' His voice sounded like a croak, but at least he had been able to get it to work.

'He sprawls all over the bed,' she said. 'With his arms and legs everywhere. It's so cute.'

Alessandro stood in silence as he breathed in the scent of her silver-blonde hair; it had always reminded him of the fragrance of sun-warmed jasmine.

Something inside his chest began to loosen, like a too-tight knot that had resisted all attempts to be untied for years.

What if the thing he suspected had indeed happened? Would she agree to resume their relationship on a more permanent basis for the child's sake, or would she always resent him for not believing her in the first place?

He had shut off his feelings for her four years ago, but he

knew it wouldn't take much to switch them back on again. Hadn't last night proved how close to the wind he was sailing? He could feel the tug of desire even now as she stood silently in his embrace. His body was stirring against her; she surely could feel it, although so far she hadn't made a move to step backwards from him.

His mind started to run with the possibilities—but then he was brought back to earth with a jarring thud as he remembered there was the other issue of the child's health. He was only three now, but Marco had shown signs not much earlier than that…

She eased herself out of his hold and, without looking at him, tucked a strand of hair behind her left ear. 'I'm sorry…this must be so hard for you,' she said. 'I mean, learning about the existence of a child you never wanted.'

It was on the tip of his tongue to say how much he would have loved children of his own, perfectly healthy, robust children—a boy, a girl, what did it matter? He had never understood parents who claimed to have a preference for one or the other sex. As long as it was healthy was all that mattered, but that was one thing he could not guarantee.

It had been taken out of his hands on the day he'd been born.

'Yes,' he said, feeling his chest go down in a sigh. 'It is hard, but we will know for sure in a day or so.'

It was totally the wrong thing to say; he knew it as soon as he said it. She stiffened like someone who had been sprayed with quick-setting glue, her mouth went tight, her eyes turned to blue chips of ice, and her bitterness cut through the air like a sharpened blade.

'How typical,' she said, 'how absolutely typical.'

'What I meant to say was—'

She stalked across to the door and held it open, the tiny bell tinkling in startled protest. 'What you meant to say was you still don't believe me,' she bit out. 'There's still a small part of you that won't accept Matthew as your son. Now please leave, before I change my mind about the DNA test or the contract.'

It was not in Alessandro's nature to back down. He had fought long and hard for many things in his life, and certainly being dismissed by a tiny silver-blonde virago was not something he was used to accepting. But the set to her mouth told him it was probably a good time to leave.

He brought two of his fingers up to his mouth and pressed his lips against them in a mimic of a kiss, before placing them on the stiff but somehow still-soft bow of her mouth. 'I will be back in a couple of days with the results,' he said.

'I can tell you the results right now,' she replied, swiping at her mouth as if he had tainted her with his touch.

He held her embittered gaze with determination. 'I have to be sure, Scarlett. I know it's hard for you, but you have to understand my position on this. You have no doubt at all he is your child. You physically gave birth to him, you needed no other evidence—but I am afraid that I do.'

She spun away with a frustrated sound that was somewhere between a scornful snort and a sigh. 'Please leave,' she said. 'There's no point in continuing this conversation until you have what you want.'

But I can never have what I want, Alessandro thought as he drove away a short time later, his eyes fixed on the road ahead in case he was tempted to look back.

I can never have what I want.

CHAPTER NINE

'ARE YOU sure?' Alessandro asked Dr Underwood two days later. 'There is absolutely *no* doubt?'

Dr Underwood shook his head. 'No doubt at all, Mr Marciano. Your sperm count is positive. I don't know who did your vasectomy, but from the test results we've received it clearly wasn't entirely successful. That doesn't mean the surgeon was incompetent, by any means, it's just that—as I am sure he or she would have explained at the time—there is about a one percent failure-rate for the procedure. That's why we insist on the three negative sperm-counts after three months post-surgery.'

Alessandro frowned. 'But I had three counts done in Italy and they were all negative. What are the chances of a rejoin after three negative readings?'

Dr Underwood scratched at his closely cropped greying beard for a moment. 'It's less likely,' he said. 'At least half the failures occur in the first three months after the operation, but the rest can occur up to five years later.'

Alessandro stared at him, his heart chugging, his skin breaking out in a sweat in spite of the air-conditioned comfort of the consulting room.

He was a father.

Something he had never intended to happen had happened.

He was the father of a three-year-old boy.

Oh, dear God, what had he done?

Dr Underwood leaned forward on his desk. 'You can always have the procedure redone. I can organise a referral to a surgeon for you.'

'Yes,' Alessandro said without hesitation. 'Yes, I would like you to do that. I want it done as soon as possible.'

The doctor's brows moved closer together. 'You were quite young when you had it originally performed. You are what age now…?' He looked down at his notes. 'Only just thirty-three. You seem very determined about this. Do you want to discuss it with a professional, such as a counsellor or psychologist, first?'

'No, I made up my mind a long time ago that I do not want to have children.'

The doctor scribbled on his notepad and, tearing the page off, placed it in an envelope and handed it to Alessandro. 'Let's hope this time it works,' he said with a crooked smile.

'Yes,' Alessandro said, rising to his feet. 'Thank you for your time.'

Dr Underwood pushed back his chair and got to his feet as well. 'If you change your mind at any time about seeing a counsellor, just let me know. You know…' He gave a somewhat philosophical smile this time. 'Sometimes these things are just meant to happen.'

Alessandro didn't respond. He couldn't. His voice was trapped somewhere deep in the middle of his chest, where he could feel a sensation like a hand squeezing his heart with cruelly tight fingers.

* * *

'You've been staring at that phone for the last two hours,' Roxanne said. 'He will ring or contact you when he feels ready to do so.'

Scarlett chomped on her bottom lip for the hundredth time that afternoon. 'I'm so confused,' she confessed. 'I've been so angry towards him for all this time, but then when I stop and think about what he's going through I feel terrible. If only he had *told* me at the time. I would have insisted on a test. I feel partially to blame now for all he's missed out on. I shouldn't have let it go. I shouldn't have let my experiences with my father interfere with Alessandro's rights as a father.'

Roxanne came over and perched on her desk, as was her custom. 'Why did he have the cut done in the first place?' she asked. 'Does he generally hate kids, or is there some other reason?'

Scarlett leaned back in her chair and blew out a breath. 'I don't know,' she said. 'I feel a bit ashamed to admit it, but we never really got around to talking about those sorts of issues. Besides, I always knew I was more in love with him than he was with me. He never said the three magic words. I think he was more interested in a short-term affair. He never once mentioned the future—it was as if he didn't expect to have one, certainly not with me.'

'He's absolutely gorgeous looking,' Roxanne said, and, glancing at the screen saver on Scarlett's computer, added, 'Matthew's the spitting image of him.'

Scarlett put her head in her hands and let out another sigh. 'What am I going to tell Matthew?' she asked. 'He thinks his father is dead.'

'I think the truth always works best with kids,' Roxanne said. 'I hated finding out I was adopted at the age of ten. I should have been told when I was much younger. I know

Matthew's only three, but he's one smart kid. He understands far more than you give him credit for.'

Scarlett dragged her head up to meet her friend's gaze. 'You're right,' she said. 'I need to tell him, at least to prepare him in some way, for once Alessandro finds out the truth I'm sure he will want to take control.'

'What sort of control are you talking about?' Roxanne asked with a little frown of concern.

Scarlett's bottom lip suffered another indentation with her teeth. 'I'm not sure…but knowing him as I do I think he will want to have things his way. He's been so confident for so long that Matthew's not his child. It will be a blow to his ego to find out he is wrong.'

'Do you think this is just about ego?' Roxanne asked with another frown. 'Most men are proud of the fact they can cut the mustard, or whatever the saying is.'

Scarlett couldn't help smiling, but it faded as she answered, 'I don't really know. I've met plenty of men who were adamant they didn't want children. I've met women just as strident about avoiding motherhood. As I said earlier, Alessandro and I never really got around to discussing the marriage-and-babies thing. I wanted to, many times, but you know how it is with a new relationship—you tread so carefully in case you scare them off.'

'But weren't you on the Pill?' Roxanne asked.

Scarlett shifted her gaze from the probe of her friend's. 'Yes and no.'

'What does that mean?'

'It basically means no.'

Roxanne rolled her eyes. 'Yeah, that's what I figured.'

'I was young and naïve,' Scarlett said in her own defence.

'I didn't for a moment expect to become involved in a full-on relationship while I was overseas.'

'Yes, well, someone should have warned you about men like Alessandro,' Roxanne said with a wry look.

Scarlett turned to look at the screen saver and sighed again. 'He's missed out on so much… Maybe I should have sent him some photos right from the start. I wanted to many times, but then I thought of the way he threw me out on the street that night and I changed my mind.'

Roxanne placed a hand on her shoulder. 'It's not your fault, Scarlett. You did your best and he refused to listen. Maybe it had to happen this way.'

Scarlett gave another deep sigh. 'How am I going to tell Matthew his father is alive?'

Roxanne gave her shoulder a little squeeze. 'You'll think of a way.'

'How was crèche today, darling?' Scarlett asked as she lifted Matthew into his evening bath.

Matthew's bottom lip came forward slightly as he settled amongst the bubbles. 'Robert taked my car off me, one of my favourite ones.'

'Robert *took* your car off you,' she corrected automatically. 'That's terrible, darling. Did Mrs Bennett or Miss Fielding get it back for you?'

He shook his head and his little shoulders went down. 'No.'

'I'll have a word to them about it tomorrow,' she promised. 'Maybe Robert doesn't have many toys and really enjoyed playing with yours.'

'I don't want to go there any more,' he said, big tears

forming in his hazel eyes as he looked up at her. 'I want to come to work wif you.'

'Darling, you know that's impossible. We've talked about this before, lots of times.'

Another little sigh puffed out of his mouth. 'I know…'

She took a break to prepare herself. 'Matthew, remember I told you that you didn't have a daddy, like your cousins Angie and Sam and Michaela have?'

He nodded solemnly.

'Well…' She moistened her mouth and picked up a handful of bubbles, watching as they lay suspended there in the palm of her hand. 'Well, the thing is…'

The sound of the doorbell ringing stalled the rest of her sentence. She tossed the bubbles aside and quickly pulled the plug out of the bath and, scooping Matthew up in his towel, called out, 'Just a second.'

'Who is it, Mummy?' Matthew asked as Scarlett did her best to dry him as she walked to the front door of her flat. 'Are we having pizza again?'

'No, darling,' she said. 'It's not the pizza-delivery man. It's…it's…'

'A surprise?' he asked, with excitement building in his eyes. 'What sort of surprise?'

'Er…I'm not sure…it could be Mrs West. She might have run out of milk again.'

Scarlett opened the door, already knowing who it was, for she had felt it in every single cell of her body at the first sound of that bell.

Alessandro stood there, his eyes going immediately to the child wriggling in her arms. Such a rush of pain, panic and guilt passed through his body he felt as if he was not going to be able to keep upright. He tried to speak, but for some reason his throat refused to work. He swallowed half a dozen times but still nothing came out.

'Who is it, Mummy?' Matthew asked in a small-toddler sibilant whisper.

Scarlett looked at Alessandro with a direct and somewhat challenging look. 'This is your father, Matthew.'

Matthew wrinkled his brow and looked at her again. 'He's not dead, like Mrs West's cat Tinkles?'

'No, darling, he's not dead. He's very much alive.'

A silence measured the erratic pace of Alessandro's heartbeat before the little boy whispered up against his mother's ear, 'Can he speak?'

Scarlett smiled in spite of the tension of the moment, and when she looked at Alessandro his mouth, too, had tilted a fraction.

'Hello, Matthew,' Alessandro said, not knowing whether to offer his hand or bend down and kiss the child.

What did one do these days with small children?

He didn't know.

Over the years he'd actively avoided children of any age, knowing how much worse it made him feel about the decision he'd been forced to make.

'Hello…' the child said with a shy but totally engaging smile. 'Do you like cars?'

Alessandro felt a sharp pain begin in his abdomen and travel right through to his backbone, like a savage drill. 'Yes…yes, I love cars. I have several.'

The boy's eyes lit up, and Alessandro couldn't help noticing they were exactly the same colour as his, fringed with thick, sooty lashes.

'I've got twenteen,' Matthew announced proudly.

'Twenteen?' Alessandro glanced at Scarlett with a quizzical look on his face.

'Twenty, darling,' she said, addressing the child. 'Remember how it goes after ten? Eleven, twelve, thirteen, fourteen—'

'Fifteen, sixteen, seventeen, eighteen, nineteen, twenty!' Matthew crowed.

'That is indeed a lot of cars,' Alessandro said, still struggling to hold himself together.

'Umm…perhaps you should come inside,' Scarlett said when she noticed a neighbour she didn't particularly like hovering in the stairwell.

'Thank you,' Alessandro said, stepped inside and closed the door.

Scarlett brushed a strand of her hair back with her one free hand. 'Umm…would you excuse us while I get Matthew into his pyjamas? He was in the bath when you rang the bell.'

'Sorry,' he said, looking uncharacteristically uncomfortable. 'Perhaps I should have phoned first.'

Scarlett wondered why he hadn't. But then, looking at him now, she realised he had probably needed time to gather himself. The news would no doubt have shocked him. He had clearly not expected to be proved wrong.

She felt for him, even as she felt angry that she had suffered alone for so long. It was a bewildering mix of emotions: resentment, regret, hate, love…

No she didn't love him any more, she decided. How could she? She had suffered too much as a result of his lack of trust. She wasn't going to allow herself to get caught out a second time.

'Can I wear my racing-car jammies?' Matthew asked as she carried him out of the small living-room.

'Sure you can,' she said. 'I washed them yesterday.'

'You won't tell Daddy I still sometimes wet the bed, will you Mummy?' he asked in another whisper, but his little voice carried regardless.

'No,' she said. 'Not if you don't want me to.'

Alessandro turned to look around the room, knowing it was pointless feeling shut out and angry. It was his fault for being so arrogantly confident. He should have at least given her the benefit of the doubt. He could have repeated the tests. He could even have checked the statistics on the internet like any other layman, for God's sake. He'd done it after he'd left the doctor's surgery, ashamed that he hadn't thought of it earlier.

It was all there. He'd even read of two pregnancies occurring five years after surgery.

He wondered how those two men had treated their partners. Had they cut them from their lives, accusing them of being unfaithful. Or had they stayed close, supporting them, and guiding them through what to all intents and purposes was an unplanned pregnancy.

It shocked him to the core that he hadn't once considered Scarlett's feelings about being pregnant at twenty-three. That was considered young these days, when most women got their career established before they thought about settling down. She had not only been young, but only just qualified as an interior designer. And he had thrown her out on the street, late at night in a foreign country, pregnant and alone.

No wonder she still hated him.

His eyes went to a photograph sitting on a side table and he picked it up and looked at it, emotion beginning to tighten his chest. It had obviously been taken the day she left hospital after the birth of Matthew. He could see the run-down outer-suburbs hospital building in the background.

Scarlett was holding him, a tiny bundle of blue in her arms, her still-swollen stomach visible, her breasts fuller than normal, and her gaze full of love as she looked down at the infant. But there was sadness in her smile. He could sense it.

You should have been there, the voice of accusation thundered in his brain. *You missed the birth of your child out of arrogance, ignorance and prejudice.*

Three whole years had passed.

He had not been there for a moment of his son's life. Not a single moment. He hadn't felt the first fluttery kicks in Scarlett's womb with his hand pressed against her abdomen. He hadn't been there for the first ultrasonic image of his son. He hadn't witnessed the moment of birth, heard that first mewing cry, had never been woken in the night by the howls of hunger that only an infant could perform with such fervour. He had missed everything, but he had no one to blame but himself.

Scarlett had faced it all alone, and how in the world he was going to make it up to her, or even to Matthew, was anyone's guess.

But he wanted to.

Oh, dear God, he wanted to—but there were several hurdles in the way.

The first one was to find out if Matthew was healthy. He certainly looked it; his limbs were strong and rounded with the plumpness of early childhood, his hair was glossy black, and his eyes clear and bright.

But Marco's had been too, until their world had been turned upside down…

CHAPTER TEN

SCARLETT tucked her son's night nappy out of sight under the elastic waist of his pyjamas and led him by the hand back out to the small living-room.

Alessandro was standing with his back to them, a photograph in his hands, and as he heard their footsteps he placed it back on the side table and faced them.

'Matthew would like to say goodnight,' Scarlett said, with a look he couldn't quite decipher.

He looked down at the child, the ache in his chest so unbearable he felt like he was going to cry, like he had done so uncontrollably at Marco's funeral.

'Can I call you Daddy?' Matthew asked, blinking up at him.

'Of course,' Alessandro said, squatting before him. 'But in Italy where I come from children call their father *Papa.* Can you say that?'

'Papa,' Matthew said with a dimpled grin. 'Is that right?'

Alessandro reached out and touched his child for the first time. He laid a hand on the boy's shoulder, but then, wanting more skin-on-skin contact, he placed his hand on the curve of his tiny cheek. 'That is perfect, my son,' he said, his voice breaking slightly over the words.

'Will you tuck me into bed and read me a story?' the little boy asked—and then, glancing briefly at his mother as if to ask her permission, added as he turned back, 'Mummy won't mind. She's always tired after work and she even skips a few pages. She thinks I don't notice, but I do.'

Alessandro smiled even though it hurt. Marco had been the same. He'd only had to hear a story once to have it memorised word for word. 'Sure, I would like to do that, very much,' he said. 'That is, if your mother does not mind.'

Scarlett met his gaze. 'No,' she said, trying but not quite managing to smile. 'I don't mind at all.'

A few minutes later Alessandro read a story about a wombat and an echidna, and how they managed to have a workable friendship in spite of their many differences.

He looked down after he had finished the second-last page, and saw the fan-like lashes of his son's eyes flutter a couple of times then close over his eyes, a soft sigh of total relaxation deflating his tiny chest, covered by a thin cotton sheet. In his hand was a tiny matchbox car, a black Maserati, the sight of which had affected Alessandro almost more than anything else so far.

He looked at that tiny chest moving up and down, and wondered if Scarlett had any idea of what could be lurking inside there, waiting like a time bomb to leap out in the future and cast a dark shadow over all of their lives.

When he came back out Scarlett was sitting with a magazine in her hands, her reading glasses perched on her nose, giving her that studious, intellectual look he had always found so incredibly sexy.

She looked up and removed her glasses. 'Is he asleep?'

'Yes,' he said, taking the sofa-chair opposite, a particularly uncomfortable one, he noticed. A spring of some sort was protruding into his left buttock, and he had to move a few times to avoid its insistent prong.

A silence threatened to halt all communication, but Alessandro had things to say and didn't want to let any more time pass. 'Is he well?' he asked somewhat abruptly.

She blinked a couple of times. 'Yes…mostly.'

He found himself leaning forward on the sofa, which activated the prodding spring once more. It made him realise how hard she had struggled to provide for their son. The irony of it was particularly heart-wrenching—she decorated penthouses worth millions, and yet she lived in a tiny cramped flat with furniture that looked like it had come out of a charity shop.

He cleared his throat, as if by doing so he could clear away his guilt, but it was pointless. It rose like a debris-ridden tide inside him, making his voice sound husky. 'What do you mean by "mostly"?' he asked.

'Alessandro, he's three years old.' Her tone was matter-of-fact. 'He's had numerous colds and stomach bugs. He's a little kid—they get sick all the time.'

'How sick?'

She frowned at the intensity of his gaze. 'Not enough to be hospitalised, although he came close once.'

He leaned forward even further. 'What happened on that occasion?'

Scarlett found his penetrating stare almost too much to cope with; she had to really fight to hold his gaze. 'He had a serious chest infection,' she said. 'He became wheezy, and it took a while for the antibiotics to kick in. The first lot the doctor prescribed gave Matthew an allergic reaction.'

'But he was not hospitalised?'

'No. I took a few days off work and treated him at home with an alternative antibiotic. He was fine in a week or so. It was a bad winter. Everyone went down with the same bug.'

'Is he particularly susceptible to chest infections?'

She chewed her lip as she thought about the other mothers she knew at crèche and what she knew of their children. 'No,' she answered at last. 'No more than the average child. Why are you asking such questions?'

He gave a little shrug, his expression giving nothing away. 'I have missed out on three years of his life. I am just trying to fill in the gaps.'

Her grey-blue gaze hardened as it met his. 'You could have been there from the first moment, but you chose to disbelieve me. I take it the doctor you saw confirmed my version of events?'

He let out a sigh that snagged at his throat like a mouthful of barbed wire. 'Yes. It has now been confirmed. It is rare, but it does occasionally happen. I have had a spontaneous rejoin of my *vas deferens*.'

'Do you need a DNA test to confirm Matthew as your son and not someone else's?'

Alessandro was ashamed to admit he had thought of it—but as soon as he had seen that child he had known he was his. A DNA test would only confirm what he already knew—Matthew was his son, the living breathing image of himself and his younger brother Marco, with all its harrowing burdens and consequences.

'No,' he said, not meeting her gaze. 'That will not be necessary. I have all the information I need.' *For now,* he added silently. A DNA test would have to be performed at some stage, but not the one she was thinking of.

Scarlett sat opposite him, trying to push her righteous anger to one side, but she couldn't quite manage it. She was secretly terrified he might take it upon himself to insist on regular access to Matthew.

Matthew had only known her as his chief care-giver. He hated being at crèche, in spite of the loving and well-trained staff, and on the few occasions Scarlett had been out at night the only people he liked babysitting him were Roxanne or her mother.

'Scarlett…' He pushed a hand through the black silk of his hair and met her gaze. 'I would like to discuss the role I want to play in Matthew's life now that I know he is mine.'

Here it comes, she thought, her stomach twisting and turning with dread. 'He's only three years old,' she said, sending him a flinty look. 'I hope you're not expecting him to fly back and forth like a parcel between Sydney and Milan several times a year? Because I won't allow it.'

A frown drew his brows together. 'I was not thinking of any such thing, not yet in any case. He is too young to be without his mother for one thing, and the other…'

Scarlett waited for him to continue, but instead he let out a sigh and got to his feet. She watched, her breath feeling as if she was drawing it into her lungs through a crushed drinking-straw, as he reached down and picked up the hospital photograph again. He stood looking down at it for endless seconds. His face side-on was like an expressionless mask, and yet she was almost certain she could see a film of moisture in his eyes as he put the frame back down and faced her fully.

'Tell me about him,' he said in a voice that didn't sound like his at all. 'Tell me everything.'

Scarlett wasn't sure where to begin. She didn't want to overload him with guilt, but neither did she want him to think it had been a breeze having his child without emotional and financial support. 'He's a lovely child,' she said. 'He was born at eleven in the morning and weighed seven pounds and three ounces. He's very advanced for his age; he walked at ten months, and spoke in full sentences at eighteen, which is unusual for boys; they are often slower with language. He loves cars, as you can see, and he loves animals. I wish I could have given him more than I have, but… Well, I gave him what I could when I could.'

'You did your best,' he said. 'I am amazed that you have achieved what you have while trying to raise a small child.'

'It wasn't always easy,' she admitted. 'But my mother has been down this road before, so I more or less knew what I was in for.'

Scarlett looked at his tortured expression. Seeing him finally accept Matthew as his son had been so incredibly poignant, it had moved her to tears. It would take him a few days, maybe even weeks, to realise the full extent of what he had missed out on in his son's life so far. He was so obviously affected by the realisation that he had made the biggest mistake of his life. He was doing his best to find a way to make amends, but how that was going to impact on her and Matthew remained to be seen.

'I want an active role in his life,' Alessandro said. 'I know it will be hard for you to accept, but I want to be a real father to him now.'

She didn't answer, just stood there before him with uncertainty and fear in her gaze. And no wonder, Alessandro thought. He still found it hard to believe just a thin wall of plasterboard separated him from the sleeping form of his son. The son he had betrayed by being so adamant Scarlett had lied to him.

Three years of Matthew's life had gone past, each and

every day containing a thousand memories that he would never have access to. It was gone for ever; the babyhood of the only child he would ever have was gone.

His eyes went to the photograph again. It was like a magnet. Every time he tried to avert his gaze, it tracked back to that small rectangle of truth as if pulled by powerful strings.

He should have been standing there beside her with a smile as wide as any proud father's. Instead he had been several-thousand kilometres away, seething with hatred.

But now he was here, and he had to do something about preparing Scarlett for the burden of knowledge that had deadened his soul for so long. She would surely be devastated to find out Matthew could have a life-threatening condition. What parent wouldn't be?

He let another silence pass for a moment or two.

'I was thinking we could get married as soon as possible,' he finally said.

Her eyes bulged with shock, or was it anger? He couldn't quite tell. *'Excuse me?'* she said, her mouth so tight it looked like it had been stitched into place. 'What did you say?'

He cleared his throat. 'I said I thought we could get married.'

'For what reason?'

He didn't like the sound of her tone, or the contentious look she was firing his way, but he soldiered on regardless. 'We have a son,' he said. 'He has a mother, but he has not had a father for the first three years of his life. I am prepared to step into that role and do what I can to make it up to him.'

'You can *never* make it up to him,' she said, her eyes flashing with venom as they hit his. 'You have your evidence now, but where were you when he and I really needed you? How dare you think you can waltz back into our lives on the basis of a pathology test and suddenly become father of the year?'

'I have some rights, surely?' he argued, even though he understood her position. 'I know I did not plan for this to happen, but it has, and I am prepared to face the consequences.'

She threw him a blistering look. 'I don't want to marry you. You're only asking me because of Matthew. How do you think that makes me feel?'

'Your feelings or even mine do not come into it,' he said. 'I am trying to do what is best for our child.'

'You seem to have forgotten something,' she said with a glittering glare. 'I hate you for what you did to me, Alessandro.'

'I hope to God you have not communicated that to my son,' he inserted into the taut silence.

Scarlett wasn't entirely sure what she had been expecting him to say in response, but it certainly hadn't been that. He seemed to be genuinely concerned about Matthew. It made her feel ashamed that she hadn't factored in her little boy's feelings and needs in this most complicated of situations.

'No…' she said on an expelled breath. 'Of course not.'

'But you told him I was dead.'

Her head came up, her eyes reluctantly meeting his. 'Yes. I thought it was the best thing all round. My mother was deserted by my father before I was born. She struggled so hard to provide for my sister and me. I knew I couldn't come home and announce I was pregnant to a man who refused to acknowledge my baby's existence. I was so distraught, I found myself telling Mum and Sophie the father had been killed in a road accident. It seemed believable.'

'Did you tell *anyone* the truth?'

She shook her head and looked down at her hands. 'Not until the other day when you came into the studio. Before that I was tempted to many times, to Roxanne mostly, but I didn't see the point. You had denied all responsibility. I didn't see that changing any time soon.'

He sent a hand on a rough pathway through his hair again, making it stick up at odd angles. 'If only you had sent me a photo or two,' he said heavily. 'I would have had no choice but to sit up and take notice.'

She lifted her gaze back to his. 'So now it's my fault for not pressing the issue a bit harder, is it?'

Alessandro jerked back as if she had struck him. 'No, I am not saying that. I just wish…' He didn't finish the sentence. He couldn't think of the words to say. He wished he could rewrite the past. He wished he could have told Scarlett four years ago of his love for her, but the burden that was attached to that love had prevented him. He wished he could tell her now of how worried he was that her world, her relatively secure world, could come crashing down at any moment.

And it was *his* fault.

Scarlett swung away in despair. 'I can't believe you have the audacity to come here and expect me to fall into your plans as if the last four years haven't happened.'

'I understand your reluctance, but I am thinking about our son. He deserves better than this.'

She spun back to glare at him. 'What do you mean, "he deserves better than this"? Are you somehow suggesting I'm not doing a proper job of raising him?'

He gave the room a sweeping glance before returning his gaze to her combative one. 'This is a small flat. It is up three flights of stairs, and as far as I can tell has no air-conditioning. It is not the place for a young child.'

'The air-conditioning broke down a couple of weeks ago,' she said. 'The landlord hasn't got around to fixing it yet. And, besides, I can't afford to rent a house with a garden as much as I'd like to. I have bills enough as it is, trying to run a business.'

'I will take care of all of your expenses, Scarlett,' he said. 'I will pay off any of your loans and credit cards. I will also arrange for Matthew's name to be put down at the school you would like him to attend when he is of age.'

She gave him a narrowed-eyed look, her tone deliberately sarcastic. 'Forgive me if I'm wrong, but I can sense a list of conditions attached to that very generous offer?'

His eyes glinted with determination. 'Just the one, actually,' he said. 'Marriage to me.'

'No.' She clamped her lips tight over the word.

'Do not make me resort to more forceful means, Scarlett,' he said, with rising frustration. 'I am trying my best to be patient and understanding with you. We once had a good relationship. We could work towards having one again for Matthew's sake.'

Scarlett threw him a scornful look. 'You think by just walking in here and offering marriage everything is going to magically turn out right? What planet have you been living on? We hate each other, Alessandro. I don't see that changing just by shoving a wedding band on our hands and smiling for the cameras.'

'I realise you have every reason to hate me,' he said. 'But for Matthew's sake I must ask you to please try and control those feelings. I do not want him to grow up in a hostile environment.'

'I'm *not* marrying you.'

'You are only saying that because you want to punish me.'

She rolled her eyes at him. 'No, I'm saying it because it's actually true. I apologise if your ego finds it a little hard to accept—but, thanks but no thanks, as the saying goes.'

He stepped towards her and took her by the upper arms in a hold that was on the surface gentle, but Scarlett could feel the steely strength of his fingers the moment she tried to pull away.

'Listen to me, Scarlett,' he ground out, his eyes locking on hers. 'You will marry me or I will close your business down. You will be begging on the streets for your next meal, I guarantee it.'

Her eyes flashed with hatred. 'If you ruin me you'll be ruining your own son. What sort of man are you?'

'I have the sort of legal connections that will ensure I gain full custody of Matthew,' he said, his voice hard and determined. 'You will see him only if and when I say you can.'

Scarlett felt the cold, hard stone of despair land in her stomach, the weight of it threatening to send her insides to the floor at her feet.

She had underestimated him.

He had the sort of money to do anything he wanted. If he took it upon himself to ruin her, he could do it. If he wanted full custody of Matthew, he would and could get it. The only way she could stop him would be to do what he wanted her to do.

But marrying a man she had once loved with all her heart, only to have been rejected so cruelly and unfairly, was more than she could bear. Her anger towards him had festered for close to four years. It was like a hard nut deep inside her that wouldn't dissolve. If she allowed herself to be coerced into a loveless marriage, what damage would it do to her? Not to mention Matthew, who would surely sense the enmity between his parents. He was a deeply sensitive and highly intelligent child; it would gradually erode his self-esteem to find his parents were only together for the sake of appearances.

She slowly dragged her tortured gaze back to his. 'Don't make me do this, Alessandro. Do you really want me to hate you more than I already do?'

His eyes were more brown than green as they held hers. 'It is a strange sort of hate, don't you think? Your eyes burn with it, and yet your body burns with something else.'

Scarlett became increasingly aware of the heat of his body against hers and the warmth of his breath as it caressed her face. She nervously moistened her lips, tasting wine and temptation as his mouth slowly but inexorably lowered towards hers.

The first touch of his lips against hers was like an explosion of flammable materials. The blood thrummed in her ears as she felt the sensual glide of his tongue against the seam of her mouth, not asking but demanding entry.

She gave it without hesitation, her lips opening on a deep sigh of pleasure as his tongue invaded her mouth, sweeping and stroking and thrusting against hers with earth-shattering expertise. She felt as if she was on fire. Her whole body was leaping to life; her breasts became heavy and tingly, her legs loosened, her spine melted, and her arms moved to his chest, her fingers splayed at first, then clutching at him as his kiss became even more intensely sexual.

He nipped at her bottom lip in a teasing manner and she responded by doing the same, but a little harder. He groaned deep at the back of his throat and nipped again, his tongue sweeping over the indentation of where his teeth had been. She bit him again, but softer this time, sucking on him, tugging on him until he took control again, his tongue playing with hers in a teasing come-and-get-me manner.

Scarlett knew she had to put a stop to this before she melted into a pool at his feet. She could already feel the dew of desire between her legs, the throbbing pulse building to fever pitch until she could barely stand.

She pulled out of his embrace—obviously catching him off-guard, for otherwise she knew he would not have released her until he was ready to do so.

She stood, desperately trying to get her breathing back under control, her lips tingling as if a thousand electrodes were attached while her heart thudded haphazardly. 'You sh-shouldn't have done that,' she said, annoyed that her voice sounded so breathless and uneven.

His eyes still burned with desire as they held hers. 'Why not?' he asked.

She glared at him. 'You know why.'

'As of three days ago we were already involved, so I do not see the problem.'

'I was only involved with you as I had no choice. You practically blackmailed me into your bed.'

'It did not take too much pressure to get you there,' he said. 'It makes me wonder just how many other men have been in your life since we broke up.'

Scarlett felt like slapping him, but then she realised she was just as angry at herself. As he had pointed out, she hadn't really put up much resistance, which didn't give her much moral high-ground to stand on. 'I know you'll find this hard to believe, but there's been no one since you,' she said.

'What about Kirby?'

'I have never been involved with Dylan,' she said. 'He's always been like a brother to me.'

His brow was creased in a frown. 'So there has been no one?'

'No. Being a single mother makes dating difficult. You have to be so careful these days with whom you allow your child to have contact. I decided it was too much effort.' She sent him brittle glance and added, 'It's probably hard for a man like you to understand, but I never once considered getting rid of him.'

Alessandro met her flashing eyes and inwardly sighed. One of the reasons he'd had a vasectomy was to prevent any lover of his having to face such an agonising decision.

'Was it a difficult pregnancy?' he asked after a little pause.

She took her time answering, her bottom lip suffering a little nibble by her teeth before she released it in order to speak. 'It was hard being alone. I wanted to share the whole experience with…with someone, but that wasn't possible.'

'If only I had known back then what I know now,' he mused.

Her expression instantly hardened. 'You no doubt would have insisted I have a termination, wouldn't you? The last thing you wanted to be was tied down with a wife and a child. You've said it several times since. You lived the life of a playboy when I met you, and still do; I always suspected I was nothing more than a temporary diversion, for if I had been anything else you would never have doubted me.'

'I cannot change the past any more than you can, Scarlett,' he said. 'We have a son who needs both his parents. Marriage is our only option. I will not settle for anything less.'

Scarlett didn't bother hiding her contempt. 'You weren't so keen on marriage and babies a few days ago.'

His hazel eyes darkened as they clashed with hers. 'There will be no other babies. I want you to be clear on that right from the start.'

There was a taut silence.

'What if I am already pregnant?' she asked.

A tiny jackhammer seemed to be at work beneath his skin at the side of his mouth, which was pulled tight. 'Are you saying you are not on the Pill?'

'Why would I be?' she asked. 'As I told you—I haven't slept with anyone since you.'

He swung away from her, his expression clouding with something she couldn't quite identify. She watched as he paced the room back and forth, his long strides having to shorten considerably to fit between the sofa and the shabby wall-unit.

When he finally turned back to look at her his face was ashen. 'If it has happened…' he swallowed deeply '…then we will deal with it. How soon will you know?'

She chewed at the inside of her mouth, trying to recall where she was in her cycle. 'I'm due in a few days,' she said, not able to meet his eyes.

'I have organised to have the procedure redone,' he said. 'I'm going to hospital as a day case.'

Scarlett felt as if she had been struck by something heavy and blunt deep and low in her abdomen. 'You're asking too much, Alessandro,' she said, lifting her gaze back to his. 'I want another child. I don't want Matthew to grow up without a brother or sister.'

His jaw was set in intractable lines. 'Well, I do not want another child. I did not want the one I have, but there is nothing I can do about it now.'

She glared at him in outrage. 'How can you *say* that? Matthew is a living, breathing child. He's the most precious little person. He's your flesh and blood, for God's sake. He's already halfway to loving you.'

He raked a hand through his hair and turned away on a

rough sigh. 'Yes…yes, I know, but I did not intend to pass on my flesh and blood…to anyone. I thought I had done everything possible to prevent it, but somehow…'

'Why, Alessandro?' Her voice came out as a hoarse whisper. 'Why are you so determined about this?'

'I do not want to inflict suffering on anyone, and least of all a child.'

'But how will you do that?' she asked, her brow wrinkled in bewilderment. 'You have so much to offer a child.'

'I have nothing but money,' he said, turning to face her again. 'Believe me, it is not nearly enough.'

Scarlett frowned as she looked at the flicker of pain come and go in his eyes. 'Money isn't important, it's love that counts.'

His mouth slanted mockingly. 'There you go using that four-letter word again.'

'I don't want to marry a man who isn't capable of love,' she said. 'What sort of father will you be if you can't even express love to your wife and child? It's not normal.'

'When we marry you will be my wife in every sense of the word, Scarlett, so that will make it very normal—very normal indeed.'

'What if I don't agree?' she said, lifting her chin a fraction.

His jaw became even more rigid. 'You know I have the power to do what I threatened to do.'

'Yes, and the lack of morality to do it,' she threw back. 'I can't bear the thought of being tied to you indefinitely. I can't think of anything worse.'

There was a heartbeat or two of silence.

'I do not recall saying we will remain married indefinitely,' he said.

Scarlett felt the wind drop right out of her self-righteous

sails. She stood for a moment, trying not to show how his statement had affected her. But even so she felt her teeth sink into her bottom lip again before she could stop them, and this time she tasted blood.

'I want Matthew to legally bear my name,' he said. 'The best way he can do that is for you to marry me. The marriage will continue for as long as I feel it is necessary.'

'Necessary for what?' she asked, her heart skipping all over the place.

His eyes were unreadable as they held hers. 'I will meet you tomorrow at the old Arlington Hotel building at ten a.m. to discuss the arrangements. In the meantime, I will deposit funds in your bank account which should see to your business loan and any other outstanding debts you might have.'

Scarlett watched as he opened the door to leave, the words of protest stuck—along with her tongue—to the roof of her mouth.

He turned back from the door to look at her. 'Do not think of rejecting my offer of marriage, Scarlett,' he added. 'It would not be in Matthew's interests if you did.'

'And what about *my* interests?' she asked. 'Have those been factored in somewhere in your scheme of playing temporary happy-families?'

A shutter seemed to come down over his brown-green gaze. 'I am doing my level best to make up for what you have suffered,' he said in a deep, gravelly tone. 'I made a mistake that I will probably regret for the rest of my life.'

'You're about to make another one,' she said. 'Marrying me is not going to solve anything—if anything it's going to make things worse.'

'You will be well rewarded for your efforts.'

She glared at him. 'Don't insult me by offering me disgusting amounts of money—or is that how you usually buy female affection these days?'

His expression barely changed, but Scarlett saw the way his knuckles turned to white beneath his tan as he gripped the door knob. 'I will see you tomorrow,' he said in a deceptively even tone. 'If you do not turn up, then I will have no choice but to assume you are not only putting your business on the line but your son as well.'

Scarlett wanted the last word but he closed the door before she could even think of it, much less get it past the knot of tension in her throat. She whooshed out a breath and sagged against the nearest flat surface, and closed her eyes as she heard the rumble and roar of his car as it left.

CHAPTER ELEVEN

'I CAN'T believe you lied to us for all these years,' Scarlett's sister Sophie said over the phone later that evening. 'I don't know what I'm going to say to Hugh when he gets home. I saw that article in the paper and immediately called Mum. What on earth were you thinking?'

Scarlett sent her eyes heavenwards. 'This is not about you, Sophie.'

'Of course it's about me!' her sister railed. 'Hugh and I are high-profile people. I have told everyone for years that you are a grief-stricken single mother, and now I find out you've been lying about your child's father. I feel *so* betrayed.'

Scarlett felt like grinding her teeth, but only stopped because her sister had acute hearing for that sort of thing, being married to a cosmetic dentist. 'I didn't mean to hurt you, but I was trying to do what I thought was the best—'

'When can we meet him?' Sophie cut her off. 'What about tomorrow night? I can get our housekeeper to make a special meal.'

'Alessandro's a very busy man,' Scarlett said. 'He won't have time to traipse around meeting all my relatives.'

'They will be *his* relatives once you are married,' Sophie pointed out.

'Ahem.' Scarlett pointedly cleared her throat. 'I haven't exactly said I was going to marry him.'

'For God's sake, Scarlett, he's your son's father!' Sophie cried. 'You have to marry him. Or hasn't he asked you?'

'Yes, he has, but I don't like the conditions.'

'Listen, Scarlett, when you're marrying a billionaire you don't think about the conditions,' Sophie said with typical older-sister pragmatism. 'Even if the marriage only lasts a year or two you'll be set for life.'

'I don't want to be set for life, I want to be happy.'

'Do you feel anything for him?' Sophie asked.

Scarlett rolled her lips together as she thought about it. 'Yes, but I don't think it's the best way to start a marriage.'

'What is that supposed to mean?'

'It means I'm not sure what I feel about him,' Scarlett answered. 'He's Matthew's father, so I can't exactly hate him, but I don't want to feel what I felt for him before.'

'You don't have to love him to marry him,' Sophie said. 'Plenty of marriages survive on much less.'

Scarlett couldn't help feeling her sister was talking from experience. Sophie had always been very determined about her life plan. She'd had a checklist from the age of fifteen, and any man who hadn't got a tick in all the boxes had been summarily dismissed as potential husband-material.

Hugh Gallagher was the first one who'd come along who had met all her demands, but Scarlett often wondered if her sister had sold herself short. At the time of night when most secure couples would be cuddling up in bed, Sophie rang to chat about nothing and everything. And every time Scarlett asked where Hugh was, her sister would answer somewhat dismissively that he was operating on a private patient.

Scarlett felt like asking just how many wisdom teeth there were in Sydney to be taken out at close to ten p.m.

'What does Matthew think of him?' Sophie asked.

'I'm not sure he's old enough to really understand what's going on,' Scarlett said. 'But he seemed to really enjoy having him here this evening.'

'When are you going to see Alessandro again?'

'Tomorrow,' Scarlett answered with another flutter of unease in her belly. 'We're meeting to go over the designs I've been working on.'

'Wow, that's going to be quite a feather in your cap,' Sophie said. 'I read about it in the weekend supplement. The new Marciano Palazzo hotel is going to be one of the most luxurious Sydney has ever seen.'

'Yes, I know.'

'Don't blow this chance, Scarlett,' Sophie said. 'This is an opportunity of a lifetime. Think of what he could give Matthew.'

Scarlett tightened her mouth. 'I just want him to love him, that's all.'

'What about you?' Sophie asked. 'Do you want him to love you too?'

Scarlett released a long sigh. 'That's every girl's dream, isn't it?'

'Yes, but sometimes love is not enough.'

'You're starting to sound like Alessandro,' Scarlett said. 'He's as cynical as they come, but I still don't really know why.'

'He'll tell you when he's ready,' her sister said. 'It's a guy thing. They hate revealing their vulnerability.'

'I have never seen Alessandro as someone who would

allow himself to be vulnerable. He likes to be in control at all times and in all places.'

'Then you'll have to stick by him until he feels safe enough to do so,' Sophie said. 'This would have knocked him for six, I imagine, finding out he'd fathered a child he had no intention of ever fathering.'

'I know,' Scarlett said, looking at the photograph that had transfixed Alessandro so much while he had been there. 'I realise how hard it is for him, but I have had close to four years of dealing with this alone. I'm not quite ready to forgive him.'

'You don't have to forgive him, just marry him, and let the rest take care of itself,' Sophie advised. 'It's really the only thing you can do.'

'He doesn't want another child.'

'Oh… Well, then, I guess you'll have to accept that. Remember how hard it was for Mum? I swore I'd never let it happen to me, and I haven't. You need to grab this chance while you've got it. If you keep him dangling too long he might withdraw the offer.'

'Alessandro doesn't *offer*,' Scarlett said with a little scowl. 'He demands.'

'Marry him, Scarlett,' Sophie said. 'He deserves a chance to put things right. You never know, he might even fall in love with you this time around.'

'Yeah, right, as if that's going to happen,' Scarlett said as she hung up the phone a minute or two later.

Scarlett caught sight of Alessandro's striking figure as soon as the Arlington came into view. He was wearing a hard hat, standing beside a much shorter man who was similarly attired, and who she assumed was one of the engineers he had employed. They had their heads together over some plans, but

Alessandro looked up as if he had felt her presence, his eyes locking with hers.

'Good morning, *cara*,' he said, removing his hat to bend down to brush a brief, hard kiss to her mouth before she could counteract it. 'Barry, this is my fiancée, Scarlett Fitzpatrick. Scarlett, this is Barry Alder, my chief engineer.'

For the sake of politeness Scarlett had no choice but to shake the other man's hand, although the glare she sent Alessandro's way threatened to save the painters the job of stripping the old paint off the walls. 'Pleased to meet you,' she said, stretching her mouth into a stiff little smile.

Barry Alder took off his hard hat and smiled back. 'I saw the announcement in the paper this morning. Alessandro is a lucky man. Congratulations on your engagement.'

Scarlett felt her stomach drop. 'Umm…thank you.'

Alessandro handed the engineer his hat as he put an arm around Scarlett's waist and drew her into his side. 'We will leave you to it, Barry. I am taking Scarlett out to choose an engagement ring. Call me if there is anything you need.'

'It all looks pretty straightforward,' Barry said. 'The foundations are fine. I'll get back to you on those quotes about the footbridge. It shouldn't take more than a day or so.'

'No hurry,' Alessandro said. 'I have other things on my mind right now.'

Scarlett waited until the engineer had moved on before spinning out of Alessandro's hold. 'What the hell is going on?' she asked with a glittering glare. 'I don't recall saying I was going to marry you.'

He captured one of her hands with his and tugged her closer. 'You do not have any choice, *cara.* I thought you understood that.'

'I have no intention of marrying you. I don't care how

many press releases you make to the contrary, I am *not* going to bow to your commands as if I have no mind of my own.'

'You have a choice,' he said smoothly. 'You either marry me or you lose your business and your son.'

'You can't do that,' she said, but she knew he could and would if pressed to do so.

His eyes hardened as they clashed with hers. 'You think you can take me on in a legal battle, Scarlett? You do not have a chance. You are foolish to even consider taking me on in a battle of wills. I will always win.'

'You have lost three years of your son's life because of your arrogant confidence,' she threw back. 'How much else are you prepared to lose?'

He held her defiant look for a lengthy moment. 'We will be working and living together in a matter of a week,' he said. 'It would be advisable to get any ill feeling out of the way now.'

'It's going to take me decades, much less weeks, to forgive you.'

'I am not asking you to forgive me,' he said. 'In fact, I am not asking you to do anything. I am *telling* you what is going to happen and when it will happen. We will be married in a week's time. I have organised a special licence. You and Matthew will move into my house in Double Bay tomorrow, and from that moment we will live as man and wife.'

'I am *not* going to sleep with you.'

A hint of a smile lurked at the edges of his mouth. 'It took me three days to get you into bed four years ago, and less than that the second time around,' he said. 'Do not lock yourself into any tight corners, *cara*. You know you will have to back down eventually. It is the way things are between us.'

Scarlett felt her face heating with shame at how she had

responded to him so unrestrainedly. There wasn't a part of her that hadn't been affected by him. Even now she could feel her pulse racing, and her breathing becoming shallow and uneven in his disturbing presence.

'Where is Matthew?' he asked.

'He's at crèche. I pick him up at five-thirty.'

He frowned. 'Isn't that rather a long day for a small child to be in care?'

'I don't have any other choice,' she said with a stinging glare. 'I can't afford a nanny.'

'I can arrange a nanny for you. Even a few hours a week would surely help? The rest of the time I would like to spend with him. I need to establish my relationship with him.'

'You can't rush things with a small child,' she said. 'He needs time to understand you are his father. It's a big thing for him.'

'It is a very big thing for me,' he said and, raking a hand through his hair, added, 'God knows I am still trying to come to terms with it.'

'Well, bully for you,' she said with a curl of her lip. 'You're the one who wouldn't believe me when I told you I was expecting him.'

Alessandro looked down at her grey-blue gaze that was burning with resentment, wondering if he should tell her why he had so desperately avoided becoming a father. But then he recalled the devastation on his mother's face the day Marco had been diagnosed. It wouldn't be fair to dump that burden on Scarlett in the middle of a busy city-street with the noise of jackhammers and traffic going on in the background. He would have to prepare her carefully for the shock of her life. He wasn't sure how he was going to do it, but it would have to be done, and sooner rather than later.

'I cannot change how I reacted back then, Scarlett. If I could turn back the clock, I would, but we have to move on now for Matthew's sake. I want to be a father to him, a real father in every sense of the word, and the only way I can do that is to be your husband.'

'Even though you don't love me?' she asked with a sudden film of moisture shining in her eyes.

He reached out with the pad of his thumb, stalled the progress of the first tear that escaped and blotted it gently against her cheekbone. 'I am willing to learn how to be a good father, *cara*, so who knows?'

Scarlett drew in a scratchy breath as he led her away from the dust and debris of the building site, the hard edges of her anger softening so much she felt as if she was melting from the inside out.

She *wanted* to be angry with him.

She *needed* to be angry with him to stop herself from…

She gave herself a brisk mental shake and strode along the uneven pavement alongside him, her head down in fierce concentration. She wasn't even going to think about loving him again. He didn't deserve it for not trusting her.

But even so, when his arm came out like a barrier to prevent her stepping in front of a turning car, Scarlett felt a tremor of awareness rumble through her being as his gaze briefly engaged hers. She looked up into the depths of his eyes and felt another layer of anger peel away until all she had left was her unprotected heart, aching for what might never come to pass….

Although it had not been her intention to simply go along with his plans, Scarlett found herself just minutes later sitting in an exclusive jeweller's shop with an exquisite diamond on her finger.

'Do you like it?' Alessandro asked, his hand gentle and protective on her shoulder.

'Yes, but—'

'We will take it,' he said to the jeweller. 'And the wedding rings as well.'

Scarlett watched as he signed the credit-card slip with a quick, dark slash of his signature, her stomach caving in when she turned to see the media already gathered outside to have the first photograph and interview. TV cameras were being angled at her, big fluffy microphones poised for when she and Alessandro walked into the hot summer sunshine.

'Do not worry, *tesore mio,*' Alessandro said as he drew her to her feet, his arm going about her waist. 'I will handle the press. Just smile and look happy.'

'Mr Marciano.' One of the three television interviewers got in first. 'Congratulations on your engagement to Scarlett Fitzpatrick. Does this mean you will be staying longer in Sydney than you had originally planned?'

'But of course,' Alessandro said, smiling politely.

Scarlett listened as a volley of questions and short, impersonal answers flew back and forth until an older rather, forceful-looking female journalist jostled forward with her microphone.

'Is it true, Mr Marciano, that Scarlett Fitzpatrick is the mother of your three-year-old son?' she asked. 'A son you had not even known existed until a week ago?'

Scarlett felt the tension in Alessandro's body as he stood beside her with his arm encircling her waist. 'Yes, she is,' he said in a clipped tone. 'Now, if you will excuse us, we have to—'

'Do you have any comment to make on the current medical condition of your son, Mr Marciano?' the journalist persisted.

Scarlett glanced up at Alessandro in confusion but his expression was inscrutably tight. 'No, I do not have any comment to make, other than he is a very healthy little boy,' he said. 'Now, if you will please make way—'

'Miss Fitzpatrick.' The journalist shifted targets with consummate ease. 'You must be very relieved to have your little son declared healthy. Were you worried he might also be a carrier?'

Scarlett felt the colour drain out of her face, and her chest suddenly felt as if someone very heavy had just sat upon it, crushing her lungs so she couldn't draw in a breath. 'Umm…a c-carrier?' she stammered, glancing up at Alessandro for help but his features were stonier than a statue.

She turned back to the journalist, her heart beginning to hit and miss a few beats. 'A carrier of…of what?'

CHAPTER TWELVE

'I WAS going to tell you,' Alessandro said as he bundled her into his car a few tense minutes later, his expression still looking as if it had been carved from granite.

Scarlett was opening and closing her mouth, as she had been doing ever since he had dragged her away from the press, her chest still so tight she could barely breathe, let alone get a word out.

The journalist hadn't minced any words. It seemed the older woman had found out a whole lot more about Alessandro Marciano's background than the young woman who had loved him and given birth to his son.

Still loved him, Scarlett corrected herself. She had been fooling herself into believing otherwise, but there was no point denying it now.

'I just did not want to dump it on you like that bitch of a journalist just did,' he said through gritted teeth as he started the car with a roar. 'I wanted to prepare you for the possibility that Matthew might have cystic fibrosis like my brother Marco, or if not he could—like me—be a carrier.'

Scarlett looked down at her still-shaking hands. The news had totally stunned her. She had not expected anything like this. She had believed Alessandro to be a playboy by choice, a man who actively sought no strings in his relationships for selfish reasons. She had never once thought there could be some other explanation. She couldn't begin to imagine how he had suffered and agonised over his decision to become sterilised, especially at so young an age.

The loss of his younger brother had clearly devastated him. In the whole time she had known him he had not once uttered a word about having a sibling, let alone having lost him to the debilitating and all-too-often ultimately fatal respiratory illness.

'My brother was three and a half years old when he was diagnosed,' Alessandro said into the silence. 'He had been more or less healthy until that point. He had the occasional chest infection, but things went downhill from there. He spent most of his childhood in hospital, and when he was not in hospital he was being pummelled by physiotherapists at home trying to clear his lungs.'

'I'm so sorry…' Her voice came out as a broken whisper. 'I am *so* sorry…'

'You have nothing to be sorry for,' he said. 'I should have told you earlier. I have not spoken of Marco's death for many years to anyone, not even my parents. It still upsets them both so much. Marco lost his childhood due to his illness and his future due to his death. He spent every day suffering while I looked on helplessly.'

Scarlett wanted to reach out to him and hold him close but he was concentrating on negotiating his way through the thick city traffic.

'I would have gladly changed places with him,' he continued in the same ragged tone. 'I felt so damned guilty for being the healthy one. When the doctors suggested genetic testing, I felt marginally better to find out that I had not exactly escaped. I was a carrier.'

'Is that why you…?'

He didn't wait for her to even frame the rest of her question. 'Yes. I decided I was not going to take any chances. Although both parents need to be a carrier to produce a child with cystic fibrosis, I was not prepared to risk it. I had seen enough. Neither of my parents knew they were carriers until Marco was diagnosed. Their marriage which had been steady enough to that point fell apart. They each wanted to blame the other. They *still* blame each other.'

'But it's no one's fault,' she said. 'How can it be anyone's fault? It's just the way the dice fall.'

He let out a long, uneven sigh. 'I know, but I can also understand how each of them feels. It is hard when you carry the genetic blueprint for a disease. You just want to get rid of it from your life, to pretend it is not there.'

'And the only way you could do that was to remove any chance of becoming a father,' she said, beginning to chew at her lip.

'Yes,' he said, flicking a quick, shadowed glance her way. 'But now I *am* a father.'

Scarlett prayed fervently that her gut feeling was right on this, even though the hammer of doubt began to pound inside her brain with deafening force. 'I don't think Matthew has it, Alessandro. He's fine. He's a healthy little boy.'

His hands tightened on the steering wheel. 'How can you be sure?' he asked. 'He will have to be tested. Even if he does not develop the disease, he could be a carrier. Either way we have to have the test done so we will know what we are dealing with.'

'Is that why you are insisting on marrying me?' she asked after a short pause.

He didn't answer immediately, but Scarlett couldn't tell if that was because the car in front had just done an illegal manoeuvre which Alessandro had to quickly counteract, or whether he was still thinking about how to respond. 'Marriage is our only option,' he finally said. 'It will give Matthew my name, which is important to me for legal reasons. He is and will remain my only heir.'

Scarlett surreptitiously pressed her hands against her flat stomach. They had made love without protection. He had assumed as he had four years ago that he wouldn't need it—however she…

'I am sorry you had to hear it the way you did,' he said. 'I would have given anything to spare you that.'

She reached out a hand, laid it on his thigh and gently squeezed. 'It's all right, Alessandro,' she said softly. 'I understand your reluctance to tell me sooner, I really do.'

He picked up her hand, brought it up to his mouth and held it tightly against his lips so she felt the movement of each agonised word against her skin as he spoke. 'I do not want to lose him, Scarlett. I have only just realised he is mine. I have already missed three years of his life. I could not bear to lose him again now.'

She fought back tears as he released her hand. 'I won't let that happen,' she said, gripping both hands tightly in her lap. 'Nothing and no one is going to take my son off me. *Nothing.*'

He gave her a bleak look as he turned into his driveway. 'You sound exactly like my mother,' he said as he activated the remote control on the gates. 'But, when she should have been celebrating Marco's coming of age, she was preparing for his funeral instead. He died the day before his eighteenth birthday. She has never quite recovered from it, nor has my father.'

'I'm sorry,' she said again.

'We will have lunch together, and then I want to collect Matthew and spend the afternoon and evening with him. I have organised for the doctor to come to your flat to take some blood for testing. I thought it would be less stressful for Matthew than taking him to the surgery. Is that all right with you?'

'Of course,' she said, moistening her dry lips, her heart beginning to thud again with dread. 'Yes, of course it is.'

He came around to open her door and as she got out he kept her hand in his and brought her up close. 'We will marry at the end of the week. I know it is short notice, but I do not want to waste any more time.'

She tried to get her hand back but he held it firm. 'Surely we don't have to rush things?'

'I know how you feel, but I do not want the press to go on and on with this. Believe me, they will hound us relentlessly. It is a matter of personal privacy. Also, I do not want to miss another moment of my son's life. I want him under my roof and under my protection. My parents will want to fly out to meet Matthew, but I will not have them come here until the media attention dies down. It will be best if we marry quickly and get on with our lives so that we are left alone.'

Scarlett could understand his position, but she felt as if things had escalated out of her control. Just a couple of hours ago she had been adamant that she was not going to be railroaded into marriage with him, but now…

She looked at him covertly as he led the way into his house, his face now devoid of the heart-wrenching emotion she knew was lying just under the surface. He was a deep and complex man, nothing like the arrogant self-serving playboy she had made him out to be. He was responsible and caring, and deeply hurt by the cruel hand of fate.

He turned to look at her as he pushed open the door for her to precede him. 'He looks like him,' he said, his voice sounding rough and uneven.

She felt her stomach clench. 'Matthew looks like Marco?'

'Yes.' His broad shoulders went down in a sigh as he closed the door and leaned back against it. 'If I hadn't seen your computer screen-saver the other day I would still be insisting he could not possibly be my son.'

She went to him then, hugging him around the waist, her head buried against his chest. 'At least you know now,' she said huskily. 'That's all that matters.'

Alessandro bent his chin to the top of her head and breathed in the summer-jasmine fragrance of her hair. 'Yes,' he said, his heart feeling like a lead weight in his chest. 'I know now.'

'Mummy!' Matthew said gleefully, and then when he saw the tall figure two steps behind added with even more excitement, *'Papa!'*

Alessandro scooped up his son and held him close. The tiny but strong limbs clutching at him reassured him just as much as they tortured him with guilt. 'How was your day?' he asked.

'Good. I made a special thing for you.'

'Oh really?' Alessandro asked, looking a little bewildered.

'Box work,' Scarlett said in an undertone, pointing to the cardboard boxes and other craft materials on the small tables scattered about the room. 'He made a jewellery box for me the other day. It's bright green, with pipe cleaners for handles.'

'Oh.'

Matthew came over with a proud smile and handed his

father a teetering assortment of small cardboard-cartons and yogurt containers pasted together rather haphazardly.

'Wow,' Alessandro said, holding it a little gingerly. 'What is it?'

'It's a hotel,' Matthew announced. 'Like the one you and Mummy are building together.'

Scarlett looked at her son in surprise. 'How did you know about that?' she asked.

'Roxanne told me,' he said. 'She said it was the biggest con…con-something you had ever done.'

'Contract,' she said. 'It's like an agreement or a promise, but it's written on paper and both people sign it.'

'When I grow up I want to have lots of hotels too,' Matthew said. 'And lots of cars, just like *Papa* does.'

Alessandro felt a knife-like pain rise in his chest. What if his son didn't get the chance to grow up? Like Marco, he might not even get to see the day he came of age. He couldn't believe how much it hurt him to even think about the possibility of losing his little son. He had only known him a few days, and yet the love he felt for him was as strong as any devoted father's, he was sure. It filled him, it consumed every waking moment—the need to protect his flesh and blood in every way possible.

He forced a smile to his face and bent down to be on a level with Matthew. 'We have come early because we have something special to tell you.'

Matthew's eyes became bug-like with excitement. 'Am I getting a puppy?' He started to jump up and down. 'Am I? *Am I?*'

'No, darling,' Scarlett said. 'It's not a puppy.'

Alessandro watched as his son's little shoulders slumped, Matthew's bottom lip trying not to pout in disappointment but failing. 'We will think about a puppy,' he found himself saying as he laid a hand on Matthew's little bony shoulder.

'Really?' Matthew asked, eyes wide with anticipation.

Alessandro gave the little shoulder under his large hand a gentle squeeze. 'Of course we will. You can even choose its name.'

Scarlett sent Alessandro a cautionary glance but he ignored it as he continued, 'Matthew, your mother and I are getting married in a few days. That means basically that you will not be living in the flat alone with your mother but with me at my house.'

Matthew's little face fell, his hazel eyes wide with worry. 'Is…is Mummy going to be there too?' he asked.

Alessandro frowned. 'Of course she is. That is what being married means. Two people living together.'

Matthew worked at his bottom lip for a moment before releasing it. 'But Ben's parents are married, but his mummy lives with someone else now.'

Alessandro looked at Scarlett for help. 'Can you explain this? I do not seem to be doing such a great job of it,' he said with a rueful grimace.

Scarlett ruffled her son's hair and smiled at him tenderly. 'Ben's mum and dad are going through a divorce, which means they don't want to live together any more. Your father and I, er, do want to live together so we can both be with you all the time.'

'So I will always have a live daddy now?' Matthew asked.

'Yes,' Alessandro said, his throat feeling tight. 'I will always be there for you. Now, run along and get your things as we are going out tonight to celebrate becoming a family.'

Scarlett had to wait until Matthew was out of earshot. 'I

don't think you should have said you were going to be with him indefinitely.'

He looked down at her. 'Why not?'

She hoisted the strap of her bag back over her shoulder and checked to see where Matthew was before she answered. 'You intimated to me that our marriage was going to be temporary.'

'It will last as long as it needs to last to provide for my son. I want him to visit my country. I want him to learn my language.'

She threw him another reproachful look. 'Promising him a puppy was totally out of line. Dogs need a lot of care and attention, and unless they spend inordinately long periods of time in quarantine they cannot travel overseas.'

'I want to give him what he wants—surely that is my privilege as his father?'

'You're trying too hard,' she said, conscious of Matthew scampering over towards them with his little backpack slung over one shoulder.

'Do not tell me how to be a father to him,' Alessandro said in a harsh undertone. 'You are his mother, you know nothing of what being a father involves.'

Scarlett gave him a stringent look. 'I have been both mother and father to him for the last three years, so don't tell me what I do and do not know.'

Grey-blue eyes warred with hazel, but in the end it was Matthew who broke the gridlock. 'Where are we going to celebrate being a family?' he asked.

Alessandro took his son's little hand in his. 'Where would *you* like to go?' he asked.

'I just want to be where you and Mummy are,' he said with an engaging smile. 'But somewhere where there is chips would be good. I love them, but Mummy won't always let me have them.'

'That's because I want you to be as healthy as you can possibly be, darling,' Scarlett said. 'I want you to grow up big and strong.'

'Just like *Papa*?' Matthew asked, doing a little skip as he held tightly to his father's hand.

Scarlett saw the up-and-down movement of Alessandro's throat and the shadow of grief come and go in his eyes as they briefly met hers. 'Yes,' she said softly. 'Just like *Papa.*'

'Is he asleep?' Scarlett asked, peering around Matthew's bedroom door later that evening after she had seen the doctor out.

Alessandro stood up, his sudden increase in height making the room seem even smaller than it was. 'Yes,' he said, closing the book he had been reading. 'He fell asleep on the first page, but I kept reading.'

Scarlett looked at the title and inwardly frowned. 'That's probably a bit advanced for him,' she said, indicating the copy of C. S. Lewis's *The Lion, the Witch and the Wardrobe* in his hand.

He turned away from her to place it back on the small shelf amongst the picture books and children's Bible. 'I know, but my brother really loved it when he was a child. I used to read it to him when he was in hospital for long periods. I just thought…'

She took a step towards him even before she realised she'd moved. 'Alessandro…'

He turned back to face her, his expression frighteningly grave. 'We need to talk.'

'Yes—yes, I know.'

He led her out of the room, reaching for the light switch at the same time she did, his hand coming over hers.

Scarlett met his gaze in the semi-darkness, her heart feeling as if it was going to burst from her chest as his long warm fingers curled around hers.

She didn't pull away when he took her hand in his and led her through to the small sitting-room, where he took the sofa opposite once she was seated.

'The DNA test will tell us if he is a carrier or likely to develop the disease,' he said into the silence. 'We need to prepare ourselves for the results.'

Scarlett could feel the hammer of dread she had been trying to ignore begin to pound again deep inside her, the shock-waves reverberating with terrifying, sickening clamour inside her head.

She couldn't bear the thought of her precious little boy becoming ill in any shape or form, much less with a disease with no known cure at this point in time. The thought of Matthew being a carrier was perhaps a little less distressing, although she imagined it would be a heavy burden for him to carry when he became an adult and started thinking about having children of his own.

Alessandro sent his hand through the thickness of his glossy black hair and met her gaze once more. 'I have so many regrets about how I have handled this situation,' he said. 'I realise there is very little possibility of you ever forgiving me for letting you down the way I did, but I beg that you will try and find in it in yourself to do so.'

There was a beat or two of silence.

'I do forgive you, Alessandro,' she said, surprised that she actually meant it.

His eyes contained a hint of moisture, and his throat looked as if he was having trouble swallowing. 'I do not deserve such ready forgiveness, Scarlett,' he said. 'You should be making me suffer much more for my sins.'

She gave him a twisted smile. 'I think there has been suffering enough on both sides without any more being added to the pile. Matthew is the important one now. We have to concentrate on what his needs are now and in the future.'

'Yes,' he said, sighing as he looked down at his hands for a moment before raising his gaze again. 'Whatever happens…' he paused as he fought for control. 'I want to thank you for having him. It is an experience I had so very determinedly decided I would never have—and yet seeing him living and breathing, laughing and smiling, has made me realise my life would have missed something very precious if fate had not stepped in the way it did.'

'You believe it was fate?' she asked.

He gave her a glimmer of a smile. 'Meeting you that day in Milan was fate, was it not?' he asked. 'Remember?'

Scarlett remembered it all too well—the way she had tripped over something on the pavement and had pitched headlong into Alessandro's tall body coming the other way, her face practically buried in his groin until she had righted herself with the help of his strong hands on her upper arms.

The instant jolt of attraction had taken her completely by surprise. Her heart had felt as if it had been short-circuited by the electricity charging from his body to hers where he'd been still holding her. She had smiled up at him in embarrassment, her stomach doing somersaults and backflips when he'd smiled back.

'Yes…' she said, moistening her mouth. 'I remember.'

'The ceremony will be a simple one at five in the afternoon,' he said after a short pause.

'I see,' she said, not sure there was anything else she could say to stop the fast-moving train of Alessandro's determination.

Things were rapidly moving out of her control, and yet she could barely get her voice to frame a protest. It seemed Alessandro was intent on getting things done, and done quickly, and nothing and no one was going to stand in his way. It worried her that she was so willingly going along with everything, but she couldn't find it in herself to try and stop the process of her life being totally subsumed into his. He was trying to make up for lost time, and yet he had not once mentioned his feelings for her. He cared for Matthew, that much was clear, why else would he have insisted on giving him the protection of his name?

As to what he felt for her, that remained a mystery. He desired her, but then physical attraction was always so much less complicated for men than for women. It had been that way in their relationship four years ago. She had fallen in love with him but he had not once voiced the reciprocation of those feelings.

'I have also organised an appointment with a dress designer, as well as a hair and make-up session. I will take care of Matthew while you are otherwise occupied.'

'You seem to have thought of everything…' she said with a little frown. 'But what about my flat and all my things? I still have six months on my lease.'

'The lease I will take care of,' he said and, rising to his feet, gave the sitting room a cursory glance before he added, 'But there does not seem to be very much to move. My staff will see to it during the ceremony so as not to disturb you or Matthew.'

'What about guests?' she asked. 'Am I allowed to invite anyone?'

'If you would like to do so, then of course, but I would like to keep things fairly low-key and simple. We will not have a full reception, just some champagne and hors d'oeuvres before we settle in as a family at my house.'

She gave him a look that contained a hint of petulance. 'There doesn't seem much for me to do except turn up at the church on time.'

'I have tried to make things easier for you by taking care of every detail, Scarlett,' he said with an element of frustration in his tone. 'It would be unfair to expect you to organise a wedding at short notice on top of your work commitments.'

'You are controlling everything as if I'm a puppet that has to dance when you say so,' she said as she rose from the sofa in one jerky movement. 'What about what I want? Have you thought about that?'

He drew in a breath and came to stand in front of her. 'I know that you want what is best for Matthew,' he said. 'That has been your number-one priority thus far, has it not?'

She pressed her lips together and lowering her eyes, she nodded. 'Yes. Yes, of course it has.'

He tipped up her chin and locked gazes with her. 'Then on that we are united, *cara*,' he said. 'Is that not a good place on which to start a marriage?'

'I just wish…' She gnawed at her bottom lip momentarily. 'I just wish things were different…you know…between us.'

Scarlett felt him tug her towards him. It was such a gentle movement, but she could feel the steely purpose underpinning it. She went all too willingly, her body coming into contact with his from chest to thigh. She moistened her mouth again, her eyes going to the sensual curve of his, her body set alight by the embers smouldering in his hazel gaze as it secured hers.

'I want you like I have wanted no other woman,' he said, skimming his hands down to her cup her breasts, and shaping her intimately until she began to whimper in response. 'I want you now. I told myself I would wait until we are officially married, but I cannot stop this urge to have you in my arms again. I have been fighting it all day.'

'I've been fighting it too,' she confessed. 'I thought I hated you but.....but I.....but I don't....'

His hands stilled on her. 'I do not want your pity,' he said, frowning. 'You do not have to sleep with me because you feel sorry for me.'

'It's not about that,' she said in earnest. 'I want you just as much as you seem to want me, maybe even more so.'

His hands gently cupped her face. 'I cannot give you what you want, Scarlett. I cannot give you what you deserve. You spoke of your longing for another child.You must realise I cannot agree to that.'

'But I'm not a carrier,' she said. 'Matthew is fine. I just know he is.' *I am praying he is,* she inserted silently. 'We could have another baby, another two babies, and they could be just as healthy as he is.'

His hands fell away from her face. 'No. I will not allow a child of mine to suffer the way Marco did.'

'I'll have a test! Then you'll see it's OK.'

'You are forgetting something, Scarlett,' he said heavily. 'It is not a matter of playing Russian roulette. I am a carrier, Matthew could be too, and so too could any other child I father. I had genetic counselling years ago. There is a fifty-percent chance of me fathering a child who is a carrier. I do not want that on my conscience.'

She looked at him in despair. 'But…but I could already be pregnant.'

He brought her chin up so she had to meet his gaze. 'We will deal with it,' he said. 'We will deal with it if it turns out you are pregnant.'

She swallowed back the painful restriction in her throat. 'You're not asking me to…to…'

He shook his head. 'No, of course not. That is your decision and one I will support either way.'

'I can't do it, Alessandro,' she inserted passionately. 'My father asked it of my mother, and she wouldn't do it. I wouldn't be here today if she had done what he had insisted.'

He cupped her face once more, his eyes warm as they held hers. 'I would not ask that of you. You were very brave to have gone ahead with the pregnancy with Matthew. You had no one to support you, but if you are pregnant this time I will stand by you. But in the meantime all I am asking of you is to give me a chance to be a father to my son.'

'I w-won't stand in your way,' she said, emotion contorting her voice. 'I want you to be there for him. I really do.'

'So you will agree to marry me next Friday?'

'I can't believe I'm saying this, but yes, I will marry you.'

'I hope you will not regret doing so, Scarlett,' he said. 'I will make sure you are well provided for if things do not work out.'

'You mean…if…I mean when we get divorced?'

'If anything should happen to Matthew…' He swallowed tightly and continued. 'I would not want you to be tied to me, as my mother has been to my father, in a loveless, pointless marriage.'

She looked up into Alessandro's tortured face and felt the last, hard nut of her anger dissolve completely. 'You love him, don't you? You love Matthew even though you've only known him such a short time.'

He put his hand to the nape of her neck and pulled her back against his chest. 'Yes,' he said on the tail end of a deep sigh. 'I did not think it was possible, as I have not allowed myself to feel anything more than mild affection for anyone for many years.'

She lifted her head and met his hazel gaze. 'Is that what you felt for me four years ago—mild affection?'

A small frown began to pull at Alessandro's brows as he looked down at her. 'No,' he said. 'What I felt for you was different.'

She ran her tongue over her lips in an apprehensive gesture, her gaze still locked on his. 'Are you going to tell me?' she asked.

He lifted her off her feet and carried her to her bedroom next door. 'I would much rather show you,' he said, and kicked the door shut with his foot.

CHAPTER THIRTEEN

SCARLETT WOKE during the early hours of the morning to find one of Alessandro's hair-roughened thighs lying heavily over one of her smoother ones, and her breasts pressed against the possessive band of his arm. Her bottom was wedged against his pelvis, the hard ridge of his erection nudging her provocatively from behind.

She wriggled experimentally, and his mouth began to nuzzle against her neck. 'You are not tired of me yet, *cara*?' he asked in smouldering tones.

Scarlett knew she would never be tired of him. He made her whole body pulse and hum with erotic delight, and even though they had made love twice earlier she felt her need for him building all over again. 'I thought you were asleep,' she said, too shy to admit how much she wanted him.

He turned her over, his body pressing its delicious temptation against hers. 'I was, but I was dreaming of you,' he said. 'I have done that a lot just lately.'

Hope lifted like a balloon in her chest. 'Have you?'

He smiled and pressed a teasing kiss to the side of her mouth, so close to, but not quite touching, her lips that tingled for his touch. 'Not just lately,' he confessed. 'For years, actually. I have never forgotten how you felt in my arms.'

Scarlett felt her love for him rising to the surface of her skin like champagne bubbles spilling over the rim of a glass. She was overflowing with love for him. Every pore of her body was soaked with it. She touched his face, her soft fingers catching on the stubble that had grown along his jawline in the hours they had been in bed, her stomach doing a little fluttery movement as he reached past her for where his wallet was lying on the bedside table.

'I have only one condom left,' he said as he tore open the packet with his teeth. 'That is, unless you have a supply handy.'

A tiny frown pulled at her forehead. 'I told you, Alessandro, I haven't slept with anyone since you. Don't you believe me?'

It seemed a long time before he answered. 'Yes, I believe you.'

She looked at him, her stomach tripping over itself at the look of respect she could see in his eyes as they held hers.

'You have been a wonderful mother to my son,' he said in a husky tone. 'I know I have said it before, but I do not know how to thank you for protecting him the way you have done. You have sacrificed your own life to provide for him.'

'I love him, Alessandro,' she said softly. 'As soon as I knew I was carrying him I loved him.' *And I love you too*, she desperately wanted to add, but she realised he wasn't quite ready to hear it.

So much had happened in such a short time. He was struggling with a host of complex emotions—regret, guilt and grief at what he had lost so far in his little son's life. She could see the pain in his eyes; it was etched too in every chiselled feature on his face. She would only be adding to his burden of guilt to tell him she had never stopped loving him.

Besides, he might not believe her. He might think she was only saying it out of pity, as he had hinted at earlier. He was a private man, but a very proud one for all that. There would hopefully be time after they were married and Matthew's health status was established.

She reached up and stroked his face again, his gaze burning with sensual promise as it held hers.

'I cannot wait much longer,' he said, his now-sheathed body searching for the silken warmth of hers. 'I do not want to make you sore, but I cannot quench my desire for you.'

'I'll be fine,' she said, opening her legs to accommodate him, sighing in bliss when he surged into her heated core. 'It feels as if you have never been away.'

He kissed her deeply, his tongue setting fire to hers as his body rocked against her in the passionate climb to the summit of sensual release. Scarlett was with him every step of the way, her body tensing exquisitely, inexorably, as he brought her breathlessly to that final moment of suspension between agony and ecstasy.

She finally tipped over with a high cry of pleasure that came from deep within her body, the waves rolling her over and over until she was lying totally spent in his arms. Her breathing was still choppy and uneven as she felt him pump himself to paradise, his harsh groan of release making her skin lift in a shiver of delight that she had brought him to this moment.

She stroked his back with her fingers, up and down in slow, sweeping, caressing movements that brought another sigh of deep pleasure from his throat. 'You have such a sensual touch,' he said against her neck, the movement of his lips tickling her sensitive skin.

'I'm a little out of practice,' she said, becoming bolder as she stroked the taut curve of his buttocks.

He propped himself up on his elbows to look down at her. 'I am sure we will get you back up to scratch in no time at all.'

She toyed with a strand of his hair that persisted in falling forward. 'How long do you think our marriage will last?' she asked, not quite able to meet his eyes.

He frowned, and captured her hand to still its movements. 'I cannot really answer that,' he said. 'No one can answer that these days. It is up to so many variables.'

'It's a big commitment,' she said, bringing her eyes back to his. 'And a legally binding one.'

A glint of cynicism entered his gaze. 'I have already told you that you will be well provided for if or when we decide to bring the marriage to an end.'

'I wasn't suggesting—'

'Before we marry there are legal papers to sign,' he said. 'I have to protect my business interests and my shareholders. I do not mean any offence, but that is the way it has to be. Prenuptial agreements are more or less commonplace these days.'

'Not between couples who trust each other,' she said. 'You seem to be suggesting that I will take the first opportunity I can to grab half of your assets.'

'You have every motivation to do so, Scarlett,' he reminded her. 'What better revenge than to have me lulled into a false sense of security? I have let you down—not intentionally, of course, but no less despicably, and dare I say unforgivably. Even though you say you have forgiven me, you could very well be quietly plotting and planning your revenge—but I am not going to allow it to come to fruition for one reason and one reason only.'

'Let me guess,' she said with a scornful glare as she tried ineffectually to get out from under the erotic weight of his body entrapping hers. 'Your pride is the issue at stake here. That's all you really care about it, isn't it? Your damned pride.'

'No,' he said, capturing her flailing hands and holding them above her head. 'This is not about my pride. It is about our son. He does not deserve to be exposed to whatever bitterness we feel towards each other.'

Scarlett felt tipped off course emotionally as she struggled against his hold. *She* was the one who was supposed to be feeling bitter, not him. What did he have to feel bitter about? It wasn't as if she had kept their child a secret from him. She had been upfront and honest from the word go, but *he* had chosen not to believe her. 'Let me go,' she bit out, arching and bucking beneath him.

His green-brown eyes glinted as her body came into intimate contact with his. 'You do not really mean that, Scarlett, now do you?'

She arched her spine again, but it only intensified the intimacy. She couldn't resist him now. She gasped in submission as he slid inside her needy warmth, her body wrapping around him tightly, almost greedily.

'No, you don't,' he said, sweeping his tongue over the trembling bow of her lips. 'You want me even though you hate me, but I do not care. I would rather have you hating me than not have you at all.'

I don't hate you, Scarlett mentally chanted as his mouth came down like a burst of flame upon hers.

* * *

'You're getting *married* to him?' Roxanne asked incredulously. 'Wow, that man sure can sure charm the birds from the bees.'

'Trees,' Scarlett said, mentally rolling her eyes.

'Have you told your mum?' Roxanne asked.

'I called her this morning after Alessandro left.'

'And?'

'And she's happy for me.'

'Are you happy for you?' Roxanne asked with a penetrating look.

Scarlett let out a little sigh. 'I'm so frightened for Matthew. We both are. We have to wait a few days for the test results. I feel like an axe is hanging over our heads. It could drop at any moment.'

'But he might not have it,' Roxanne said, echoing what Scarlett's mother had said earlier. 'You might be worrying for nothing.'

Scarlett looked at the screen saver and wondered how many years of photographs she would have of her son if it turned out he was a sufferer. 'I just can't imagine what life would be like without him,' she said, biting her lip.

Roxanne bent down and gave her a big hug. 'You're not going to lose him, Scarlett,' she said. 'Don't even think about it.'

Scarlett was working on some of the layouts for the Marciano Palazzo Hotel when Alessandro arrived with his lawyer. She forced a smile to her lips as she greeted the older man, who after exchanging a few cursory words placed the papers in front of her to sign.

She picked up a pen and, sending Alessandro a brittle little glare, bent her head to the documents, reading through each one with studious deliberation. She was conscious of the minutes ticking by as she turned each page, but finally she came to the end and signed the highlighted spaces.

Once the lawyer had left Alessandro turned to Scarlett. 'Do you have time for a coffee, *cara*?' he asked.

Scarlett considered refusing, but Roxanne was within earshot. 'All right,' she said, removing her glasses. 'But I haven't got long.'

'You are not working too hard, are you?' he asked as he held the door open for her.

'It's what I'm being paid to do, isn't it?' she returned.

He took her elbow as he led her across to where his car was parked. 'The hotel refurbishment is not high on my list of priorities right now,' he said heavily. 'All I can think about is Matthew.'

Scarlett felt her defenses take a tumble. 'Me too,' she said, glancing up at him, her expression full of fear.

He gave her elbow a gentle squeeze, his eyes softening as they met hers. 'We will not know anything for at least a week. I know it is hard, but at least we have the wedding to distract us.'

They sat in a café a short time later with steaming coffees in front of them. Scarlett poked at the foam on hers with a teaspoon, her brow still wrinkled with worry.

'Here is the number of the dress designer.' He handed her a card across the table. 'She will fit you with whatever you need for the day at my expense.'

Scarlett looked down at the bridal designer's name on the card before returning her surprised gaze to his. 'You want me to be a real bride?' she asked.

'But of course,' he said. 'Is that not every young woman's dream?'

She pressed her lips together as she tucked the card into

her purse. 'I was expecting a quick civil service,' she said. 'I'm surprised you want to go to so much trouble, especially given the limited time.'

'I am trying to right the wrongs of the past,' he said. 'You said you wanted marriage and babies. I cannot agree to another child, but the least I can do is give you a wedding day to remember.'

Scarlett concentrated on pushing at the foam on her coffee again rather than meet his eyes.

'I am going to have the surgery redone tomorrow,' he said after a protracted silence.

She looked up at him again. 'Would you like me to come with you?'

'That will not be necessary,' he said. 'It is a simple procedure.'

'But it still requires a general anaesthetic, right?'

He gave her a lopsided smile. 'Do not concern yourself with my welfare, Scarlett. I know you would prefer it if I met with a dastardly end, but as you see I am in excellent health.'

She frowned at his tone. 'I don't wish any such thing on you or anyone,' she said. 'I just thought you might like some support. It's scary going into hospital on your own.'

'Are you offering to accompany me just to make me feel even guiltier about the support I refused to give you four years ago?' he asked with a flinty look.

'No, of course not,' she said, still frowning.

He shifted his gaze and pushed his barely touched coffee away. 'I am suffering enough as it is without you heaping burning coals upon my head.'

Scarlett felt tears burning at the back of her throat. 'I know,' she said. 'I'm sorry.'

He reached for her hand and brought it up to his mouth,

kissing it softly as his eyes met hers. 'I am being a brute, *tesore mio*,' he said in a gruff tone. 'It must be pre-wedding jitters, no?'

She tried to smile but couldn't quite pull it off. 'We're both on edge,' she said, suppressing a tiny shiver as his lips pressed against her fingertips once more. 'We both stand to lose the one person we love more than any other.'

His fingers tightened momentarily around hers. 'We are not going to lose him, *cara*,' he said. 'Not if I can help it.'

CHAPTER FOURTEEN

'ARE YOU sure about this?' Scarlett asked Roxanne the following evening. 'I mean, Alessandro's not really expecting me to drop in, so if you want to cancel…'

'Stop fussing, Scarlett,' Roxanne said. 'Besides, I think it would be a nice gesture to turn up with some flowers. Alessandro would be feeling pretty sore and sorry for himself, I would imagine.'

Not that he would ever let on, Scarlett thought as she drove to Alessandro's house a few minutes later. The lights were on downstairs, which signalled he was still up, but it seemed an age before he answered the doorbell.

'Hi,' she said, thrusting the flowers forwards. 'Umm…I thought you might like these.'

He took the flowers from her after a small hesitation and, raking his fingers through his tousled hair, stepped back from the doorway. 'I wasn't expecting visitors.'

'I know, but I just thought…' She shuffled from foot to foot. 'You know…that you might not want to be alone right now.'

She heard him pull in a breath as he put the flowers to one side, the sound of the cellophane wrapping as it crinkled under his fingers sounding like gunshots in the silence.

'How are you feeling?' she asked.

He turned to face her. 'I am fine. A bit sleepy, but that is to be expected.'

There was another short silence.

'Have you eaten?' she asked.

'I am not hungry.'

'I could make you something,' she offered. 'An omelette or a boiled egg, or—'

'Why are you here?'

Scarlett flinched at his sharp tone. 'I'm here because you shouldn't be alone right now.'

'What if I want to be alone right now?'

She waited for two or three seconds to ask, 'Do you want me to leave?'

He held her gaze for a moment before turning away to stare at the flowers she had brought. 'That was my mistake four years ago,' he said. 'I should never have sent you away. I should have checked and double checked before I did that.'

'You weren't to know,' she said in a creaky voice. 'You didn't do it on purpose, it was just the way things turned out.'

He swung around to look at her. 'How can you stand there and be so damned charitable about this?'

She moistened her paper-dry lips. 'Because you are my son's father.'

He sucked in a harsh breath and swung away again. 'But what sort of father am I?' he rasped. 'I have given him a legacy that is going to be with him and his offspring for God knows how many generations.'

'I don't see it that way,' she said. 'You can give him so much. And I don't mean in terms of money. You have so much that is good in you, Alessandro. You are a wonderful person. You could have turned your back on him, but you didn't once you knew for sure he was yours. He loves you. He told me so this evening when I tucked him into bed before Roxanne came around to babysit. He *loves* you.'

She saw his knuckles whiten where he was gripping the small marble table where he had laid the flowers down. 'I should not have doubted you, Scarlett,' he said. 'I have robbed myself of the first three years of my son's life. How can I ever repair that damage?'

'Children are not like adults,' she said, fighting back tears. 'They don't hold grudges and they don't judge. I am sure by the time Matthew is of school age he will not even remember that you weren't there for the first three years of his life. You are his father now—that is all that matters.'

He turned back to face her, his expression so tortured she felt an answering pain deep inside her chest. 'I want to be a father to him,' he said in a tone raw and deep with emotion. 'I want to do the things with him that my father could not do because of Marco's illness.'

'You will do that, and more,' she said softly. 'I know you will.'

He let out a sigh and took the three steps that separated them, his arms enfolding her into his rock-hard embrace. 'I do not understand how you can be so gracious. I would not be the same in your place. I would never have been able to forgive what you have forgiven. You are a much better person than me.'

'That is not true,' she said. 'I haven't had to face the issues you've had to face.'

'But you have to face them now.'

'I know, but I still don't think Matthew's—'

He put her from him abruptly. 'Wishing and hoping does not cut it I am afraid, Scarlett,' he said. 'Do you not think my parents did not do the very same? They prayed and wished and hoped and begged, but it did nothing to change what happened in the end.'

'I know. It's just I want to keep positive for as long as I can for Matthew's sake.'

He let out a sigh and sent his hand through his hair again. 'Go home, Scarlett,' he said. 'You do not have to be a devoted wife until Friday. These are your last days of freedom—do not waste them on me.'

Scarlett reached up on tiptoe and pressed a kiss to his cheek. 'I hope you're feeling better soon,' she said softly.

He brushed the side of her face with the back of his knuckles in a caress so gentle she felt tears start to well in her eyes. 'I will see you in church,' he said. 'I have to go back to Melbourne for a couple of days. If there is anything you need in the meantime, do not hesitate to call me.'

She moistened her lips and stepped back to leave, but he caught her arm and brought her up close, his mouth pressing down on hers in a brief but possessive kiss that sent flames of need to every sensual spot in her body.

It was over as quickly as it began.

She stood blinking up at him when he released her, her heart going like a misfiring engine, and her stomach coiling with need.

'Go home, Scarlett,' he repeated.

Scarlett let out a shaky sigh and left.

The day of the wedding arrived with brilliant sunshine and humid heat, but Scarlett barely noticed as she and Matthew arrived at the cathedral in the car Alessandro had sent for them.

Clutching the bouquet of fragrant gardenias he'd had delivered to her flat that morning, Scarlett gave her little son a smile as they walked past the flashing cameras of the press to where Alessandro was waiting at the end of the aisle for them both.

The vows were exchanged before the public kiss that seemed to Scarlett to contain such a private promise of passion.

She looked into Alessandro's eyes as he lifted his mouth from hers and felt her belly quiver with anticipation. She could see the desire shining in his eyes, and her heart began to clip-clop erratically at the thought of being his wife in every sense of the word.

'Mummy?'

Scarlett was jerked out of her eye-lock with Alessandro to the little figure standing between them. 'Yes, darling?'

'Are we a family now?' Matthew asked, his stage whisper echoing throughout the cavernous cathedral.

She felt her heart contract when Alessandro bent down and lifted him into his arms. 'Yes, Matthew,' he said, the mist of emotion unmistakable in the hazel depths of his eyes as they met hers. 'We are a proper family now.'

After Scarlett had introduced Alessandro to her mother and sister there was barely time for photographs before he said it was time to leave. She could sense his impatience to get away from the persistent press, but she realised it was because he was trying to protect Matthew more than anything else.

Matthew chattered non-stop in the car on the journey back to Alessandro's house, which relieved Scarlett of the task of thinking of something to say. She still found it hard to believe she was now legally married to him. Four years ago she would have given anything to have his ring on her finger and yet, looking down at the simple white-gold band now, she couldn't help wondering how long it was going to stay there.

'You are savaging that lip of yours again, *cara*,' Alessandro said as he carried a now fast-asleep Matthew into the house a short time later. 'Do I make you so nervous?'

She let her lip go, feeling a blush steal into her cheeks. 'No… It's just that it's a big change, you know, being married instead of single.'

'I enjoyed meeting your mother,' he said as he handed her the keys to unlock the front door. 'She reminds me of you.'

Scarlett concentrated on fitting the key into the lock. 'Yes, we're very alike,' she said, thinking of how hurt her mother had been by her father. She only hoped history wasn't going to repeat itself in her life with Alessandro.

Matthew opened his eyes and blinked a couple of times. '*Papa?* Is this your house?' he asked looking around the huge foyer with wonder.

'Yes, my son, it is,' Alessandro answered. 'But now it is also yours and your mother's home too.'

Scarlett turned away from his glinting look to address her son. 'Matthew, it's time you were in bed. It's been a long day.'

'But I'm not tired,' Matthew protested. 'And I want to look around my new house.'

'You can do that tomorrow, but for now—'

'I will show you around for a few minutes before I tuck you in,' Alessandro said to Matthew. 'You should at least know where everything is the first night in a new place.'

Scarlett glared at him silently.

'Your things have been placed in my room,' he said to her with an inscrutable expression on his face. 'Matthew will be in the room closest to ours. My housekeeper has already unpacked everything, so you will be able to get changed.'

She turned away without responding, her arms going across her body in an attempt to control her emotions. She felt like she was already losing her son. Alessandro was taking command of everything, leaving her with no authority where Matthew was concerned. She could see how within weeks she would have no place in her son's life. She would be shunted to one side while Alessandro took control, indulging Matthew, giving him the things she had never been able to afford to provide.

'Mummy, are you going to come up and kiss me good-night?' Matthew asked a few minutes later as he and Alessandro returned from a tour of the lower floor and garden.

Scarlett met Alessandro's gaze with an arch look. 'Am I allowed to?' she asked.

His brows moved together slightly. 'He is your son as well as mine, Scarlett,' he said. 'You do not have to change your routines with him on account of me.'

'Don't I?'

His frown deepened. 'We will talk about this later. Come, Matthew, we will do your teeth and get you into your pyjamas so that Mummy can tuck you in.'

'But I want *you* to tuck me in,' Matthew said with a little pout. 'Mummy's done it heaps of times, but I want you to do it now.'

Scarlett gave Alessandro a 'see what you've done now?' glare.

He held her look for a tense moment before addressing Matthew with quiet authority. 'We will both tuck you in on the nights we are here together.'

Matthew's little brow wrinkled. 'But aren't you going to be here every night from now on?' he asked.

'I sometimes have to travel,' Alessandro said after a small

pause. 'I also sometimes have to work long hours, but I will try to be here as much as possible.'

'I don't want you to go away without me,' Matthew said, and with a beseeching look added, 'Can't Mummy and I come with you everywhere you go?'

'That might not always be possible, Matthew,' he said, briefly meeting Scarlett's gaze. 'I have a business to run in Italy, and your mother has her business to see to here.'

'I know! Mummy can sell her business to Roxanne, and then we can be with you all the time,' Matthew said, clearly proud of his solution.

'We will see about that,' Alessandro said with another inscrutable look at Scarlett, and led the way upstairs.

Scarlett had barely closed the door on her son's sleeping figure a few minutes later when she rounded on Alessandro. 'How dare you override my authority like that?'

He fixed her with a level stare. 'Keep your voice down,' he commanded quietly.

She glared at him, her hands in fists at her sides. 'Don't tell me what to do. If I want to shout at you, I will shout.'

His eyes became hard as they clashed with hers. 'You will not raise your voice to me, and certainly not within the hearing distance of Matthew,' he said, still in the same quiet but steely tone.

Scarlett brushed past him to stomp into the master bedroom where she proceeded to remove her things from the walk-in wardrobe in a haphazard fashion.

'What do you think you are doing?' he asked.

She spun around to face him, her arms full of clothes. 'I'm not going to share a room with you,' she said. 'I'm not going to share anything with you. I wish I'd never married you.'

'Put the clothes down, Scarlett,' he commanded.

Tears shone in her eyes. 'You're going to take him away from me, aren't you?' she asked, holding the clothes like a shield against her. 'That's your plan, isn't it?'

'You are talking rubbish, Scarlett. I have no such plan.'

'I don't believe you,' she said, struggling not to cry. 'As soon as you realised he is yours, you've been systematically eroding my place in his life so when we divorce he'll want to live with you instead of me.'

'That is not true.'

'I won't let you do it, Alessandro,' she said. 'I won't let you turn him against me.'

He let out a breath and came towards her. '*Cara*, the last thing I want to do is take him away from you. You are his mother.'

'But you said our marriage was temporary.'

'I have said a lot of things I am deeply ashamed of saying,' he said. 'But how else was I to get you to do what I wanted you to do?'

She swallowed as some of the clothes in her grasp slipped to the floor. 'I'm not sure what you're saying…'

'I am saying that the only way I could see to get you to agree to marry me was to leave you no choice in the matter,' he said. 'I let you down four years ago. I turned my back on you and our son out of sheer ignorance and arrogance. I will never forgive myself for that. Every time I see that photograph of you standing outside that hospital with him in your arms, I feel like a saw is tearing at my insides.'

'You…you do?'

He nodded as he removed the rest of the clothes from her arms and laid them to one side. 'I should have been there for you, *cara*. I cannot get that time back no matter how much I want to. If it had not been for my medical history, I would have asked you to marry me four years ago.'

Her eyes went wide. 'You…you would?'

He touched her bottom lip with his thumb. 'I had only realised a couple of days before you told me you were pregnant that I was in love with you. I was fighting it for weeks, as I knew it would bring up the difficult issue of children. You were so young to give up that dream. I did not think I could ask it of you.'

'I would have given it up for you,' she said softly. 'I would have done anything to have stayed with you.'

His thumbs blotted the steady pathway of tears making their way down her cheeks. 'But it was already too late,' he said. 'You were carrying my son.'

She choked back a little sob. 'Yes.'

'I love you, Scarlett,' he said. 'I think perhaps I always did, even when I thought you had lied to me. That is why I reacted the way I did. If I had not cared for you, I would not have felt so betrayed.'

She looked at him in amazement. 'You still *love* me?'

'Yes, *cara*, I do. But it has taken me a long time to realise it.'

'Alessandro, I am so happy, but so frightened at the same time,' she confessed. 'I thought I'd lost you for ever, and now I have you, but Matthew could be…' She bit her lip and blinked back fresh tears.

His eyes were shadowed with pain as they held hers. 'We will have the results of the test in a day or two,' he said. 'I do not know how to prepare Matthew if it turns out he is affected or is a carrier. Either way, I feel as if I have let him down all over again.'

Scarlett grasped at his hands and squeezed them tightly.

'You mustn't think like that,' she said. 'I love you, Alessandro. Matthew does too. Whatever the test shows is not going to change that.'

His eyes misted slightly. 'I do not deserve your love,' he said. 'I think I found it easier when you said you hated me. That at least I deserved.'

'I can't hate you any more,' she said, wrapping her arms around him. 'I've tried to, but I can't. I loved you from the moment I tripped and fell into your arms.'

He brought her closer, his chin going to the top of her head. 'I wish I could protect you from whatever the future holds,' he said. 'I loved my brother *so* much. Losing him was like losing a part of myself. I have felt empty ever since.

'It was not until I met Matthew that I realised how locked down I was emotionally. But when I was reading to Matthew the other night I recalled a conversation I had with Marco not long before he died. I think he knew he did not have long. He told me how much he had enjoyed the life he had had. At the time, I could not understand why or how he would say such a thing. From my perspective he had endured nothing but constant suffering, but he did not seem to see it that way. He said he had learned so much about the value of relationships, how the love and care he had received had made him a stronger person even though he was weak physically.'

'He must have been a very brave and special person,' Scarlett said softly.

Alessandro nodded sadly. 'Indeed he was, and he would have been delighted to have been Matthew's uncle. I *want* Matthew to be well, *cara,* I want it with all my being, but I do not even know at this point if our little boy has a future. That is the worst agony for me—knowing that if he doesn't it is my fault.'

Scarlett hugged him tighter. 'We will have whatever has been allotted for us, you, me and Matthew,' she said. 'There is nothing else we can do but live in love and hope.' But even as she said the words fear leaked like a thick, choking tide into her bloodstream, making her feel weighed down with the terror of the unknown.

CHAPTER FIFTEEN

SCARLETT SAT with Alessandro in the waiting room of the doctor's surgery, her fingers encased in the warmth of his. She looked down at their joined hands and felt a fluttery feeling go through her as she recalled the intimacy they had shared over the last few days as man and wife. Passion had flared as fiery as ever between them, heightened by the love they had both confessed.

She still couldn't quite believe he still loved her, and yet every time she caught him looking at her she saw it in his eyes. They were soft and warm, in spite of the shadows he did his best to hide from her.

'Not long now,' Alessandro said, giving her hand a little squeeze.

'No…' She released a jagged sigh as she returned the pressure of his fingers.

Just then the doctor came out to the waiting room. 'Mr and Mrs Marciano? Come this way please.'

Scarlett exchanged a quick, worried glance with Alessandro as he helped her to her feet before following Dr Shaftsbury to his room.

'I have some very good news for you both,' Dr Shaftsbury

announced with a smile. 'Your son does not have cystic fibrosis.'

'Is he…?' Alessandro cleared his throat and began again, 'Is he a carrier?'

The doctor smiled. 'No, he is not.'

Scarlett burst into tears as she saw her relief reflected on Alessandro's face. He clutched at her hand and held it so tightly she felt her wedding and engagement rings cut into her flesh, but she didn't even wince.

'I can't believe it,' Alessandro was saying, shaking his head. 'All this time I have dreaded passing it on…'

'Matthew is one of the lucky ones,' Allan Shaftsbury said. 'As we discussed last week, there is a fifty-percent chance of your offspring becoming a carrier. That is an issue you will have to consider if you plan to have any more children.'

'We are not planning on any more,' Alessandro said.

Scarlett shifted restlessly in her chair.

Alessandro looked at her. 'Scarlett?'

She couldn't hold his gaze.

'Is there something you should have told me before now?' he asked.

She ran her tongue over her dry lips. 'It's too early to tell, I might be late for a whole lot of reasons.'

Alessandro reached for her hand. 'How late are you?' he asked.

She lifted her eyes to his. 'A week—eight days, actually…'

Dr Shaftsbury leaned his arms on his desk. 'If it turns out you are pregnant, you can have the foetus screened and make a decision as to whether or not to continue,' he said.

'No,' Scarlett said. 'That's not an option for me. I will love the baby no matter what.'

Alessandro's thumb began stroking Scarlett's palm as he

faced the specialist. 'I agree with Scarlett, Dr Shaftsbury,' he said. 'Sometimes these things are meant to happen.'

He got to his feet and shook the doctor's hand. 'Thank you again for your help.'

'It has been a very great pleasure,' the doctor answered with another smile.

Scarlett waited until they were outside the surgery before she spoke. 'Did you mean what you said in there?' she asked. 'About the baby?'

He stood looking down at her for a long moment, his eyes so warm with love she felt her heart contract. 'I meant it, *cara*,' he said. 'If we are indeed expecting a baby then it is what is meant to be. We will love it no matter what. You have taught me that lesson, if nothing else.'

She smiled at him with love shining in her blue gaze. 'I love you, Alessandro Marciano.'

He pressed a tender kiss to her forehead. 'I love you too, *tesore mio*. No matter what the future holds.'

Eight months later

Scarlett stood silently at the door of the lounge, watching as Alessandro looked down at his tiny daughter cradled in his arms, his expression so full of wonder and joy it brought tears to her eyes.

The news that their little girl was a carrier had been accepted with great sadness, but also a sense of relief in that she was not going to suffer in the way Alessandro's brother had done. Yes, there would be issues to face in the future, but for now they would enjoy the miracle of her infancy and childhood.

Alessandro's parents Sergio and Lucia had grown a little

closer to each other as they had got to know Matthew when Scarlett and Alessandro had visited them in the summer. And the news of Scarlett's pregnancy had clearly brought them much joy, as they had seen the happiness and fulfilment on Alessandro's face each time he looked at his little family.

They were flying over for the christening in a couple of weeks, and Roxanne and Dylan had agreed to be godparents; their recent engagement was something Scarlett had seen coming for several months.

'Is she finally asleep?' Scarlett asked Alessandro as she came into the room.

Alessandro smiled as he met her gaze. 'Yes, she is, but I am not ready to put her down. It will not hurt to hold her while she sleeps, will it?'

She came to perch beside him on the sofa where he was seated, and gently caressed the black silk of his hair. 'No, of course it won't hurt her,' she said softly. 'You are her father, and she needs to get to know your touch.'

'I am her father,' Alessandro said, still looking down at the perfect features of little Mia—the name he had chosen not just because it was Italian but because it meant 'mine'. 'I never thought I would ever say those words to anyone, but now I have two beautiful children, thanks to you tripping into my arms that day in Milan and capturing my heart.'

Scarlett pressed a soft-as-air kiss to the top of his head. 'It was meant to happen, darling,' she said. 'And I for one am very glad it did.'

'Me too,' Alessandro said, reaching for her hand and giving it a loving squeeze, his hazel eyes full of adoration as he cradled his daughter protectively against the steady beat of his heart. 'Me too…'

THE ITALIAN BILLIONAIRE'S SECRET LOVE-CHILD

BY
CATHY WILLIAMS

Cathy Williams is originally from Trinidad, but has lived in England for a number of years. She currently has a house in Warwickshire, which she shares with her husband Richard, her three daughters, Charlotte, Olivia and Emma, and their pet cat, Salem. She adores writing romantic fiction and would love one of her girls to become a writer—although at the moment she is happy enough if they do their homework and agree not to bicker with one another!

CHAPTER ONE

JUST at this precise moment in time, life seemed very good to Riccardo di Napoli indeed. He knew, of course, that the feeling wouldn't last. Even at the young age of twenty-six, he was already keenly aware that disappointment was the shadow forever lurking round the corner, but just right now…

He had a feeling of perfect satisfaction as he briefly considered where he was. Metaphorically. The golden and only child of a couple whose name in Italy was a byword for wealth. From the moment of his birth—and probably, he thought with wry amusement, from the instant of conception—he had been lavished with everything vast sums of money could offer. He had been a child doted upon by his parents and reared to inherit the mantle of his father's massive business concerns. It was a legacy which had sat easily on his shoulders. He was bright, and to the deep and lasting approval of his father had refused to accept his birthright without earning it.

He had spent the past eight years adding credentials to his title, first from Oxford University, then Harvard, and then had come his working stint in London which had been fulfilling and hugely successful.

He had felt his first real taste of power, had noted and rather enjoyed the reluctantly won admiration from men far older than him. He had witnessed the sharpening of knives behind backs, had tasted the heady rush that comes with the making of money, and had thrilled to it.

And now here he was, poised and ready for the invigorating and cut-throat career that lay ahead of him. This little break in the Tuscan hills, as he dipped his toes into the one area of his family businesses which he had so far ignored, was proving to be as educational as it was enjoyable.

He had always been happy to drink the wine but it was interesting to get a taste for its production.

Nothing too involved, of course. His area of expertise would always be primarily in the financial arena. Still, he never suspected that the brief interruption to his pre-destined and rapid upward climb would prove as fruitful as it now was.

His eyes slid to the woman lying next to him, who was basking in the night-time warmth where the air was alive with the sounds of tiny creatures, and the sultry stirring of the trees and undergrowth in the gentle breeze.

It was too dark to make out her features, but he didn't have to. He had spent the past seven weeks almost exclusively in her company and her face and body were imprinted in his head. He would have been able to trace every small contour of her fabulous body with his eyes shut.

Oh yes. Life felt very good indeed.

As if on cue, Charlie turned onto her side and propped herself up on one elbow. She couldn't help herself. She reached out and splayed her fingers through his hair. Dark, dark hair that was worn longer than the boys she knew in England, with their silly, prissy haircuts and their infantile behaviour.

'I wish you weren't going tomorrow,' she repeated for the millionth time. 'I know you probably think that I'm being clingy, but it's just going to be so *lonely* here without you.'

Riccardo caught her hand and planted a kiss on the soft underside of her wrist. It made her squirm. It always did. Every time he touched her. They had just made love. Right here. With the night around them and only a blanket separating them from the prickly grass. Still she could feel her nipples hardening and every muscle in her body tensing in exquisite anticipation.

'You are insatiable,' Riccardo said huskily. He dropped his hand to her waist, running it up and under her tee-shirt, and felt the now familiar perfection of her rounded breast. He massaged it slowly, rubbing the hard nipple with his thumb.

She whimpered with gratifying eagerness, and with a smile of pleasure he pushed up the tee-shirt. The faint light from the moon showed her breasts in all their glory. True, she might be slightly built with almost no hips to speak of, but she had the breasts of a real woman. Full and rounded with big, pink nipples that were designed to be licked and teased.

As he proceeded to do now.

Charlie moaned and curled her fingers into his hair.

'No,' she gasped, not wanting the conversation to slip past, because she was so desperate to find out whether he would miss her as much as she knew she was going to miss *him.*

Riccardo ignored the protest. Actually, he was only vaguely aware that she had spoken at all. The rush of blood to his head and the fierce stirrings of his body cocooned him in a glorious bubble of pure sensation. The feel of her nipple against his tongue…the touch of her thighs as he impatiently shoved up her thin cotton skirt and pulled down her underwear…the dampness between her legs then as they obligingly parted for his questing hand…the throbbing nub of her clitoris as he roused it with his fingers. He continued to bombard her breasts with his mouth, sucking hard on first one nipple, then the next, while his own body surged to heights he couldn't remember attaining.

'Riccardo…stop…' she pleaded, making no effort to pull away from him. In fact, just the opposite. 'If you don't, I won't be able to stop myself…' She tugged his hand, and before he could return to his devastating caresses Charlie pushed him onto his back. Her near-climax was sending waves of sensation racing through her body, making her movements frantic as she did away with the clothes separating their feverish bodies. Then she slid onto him and flung her head back, eyes shut, her breasts bouncing as she controlled the rhythm of their lovemaking, until he shuddered under her just as she reached her body's nirvana.

She sagged forward, spent, and enjoyed the gentle touch of his hands on her breasts as he came down with her from his own personal peak of satisfaction.

'Have I told you that you have beautiful breasts?'

Riccardo asked, and Charlie subsided onto him with a smile.

'I believe you have. But please don't let that get in the way of repeating yourself.' She grinned and nuzzled him on his chin, loving the way the faint abrasive feel of his bristle felt against her smooth skin. She didn't think that any of the boys in her circle of university friends had *bristle*. Ever since she had become involved with Riccardo, she had blithely lumped all her male acquaintances into some indistinct category with the heading 'young and therefore immature'.

Of course, they would be, she thought guiltily. They were, after all, only eighteen. The same age as her. Not that Riccardo was aware of that little fact. She quickly shoved the thought to the back of her head and concentrated on the matter in hand—namely trying to find out how he *felt* about her. And not just the lust bit.

She clasped her fingers together under her chin and surveyed him seriously.

'Will you miss me?' she asked.

With her breasts squashed against his chest, and in the languorous aftermath of unbridled passion, Riccardo didn't find it too hard to tell her that he would.

'Not that I would call three days a lifetime,' he teased, brushing back her hair.

'I know it's not a *lifetime*, but it's a *long* time. I mean, we've been in each other's company for *weeks*. It's just going to be a little…odd, working here at the vineyard and not seeing you around and about.'

In *my* vineyard, Riccardo thought proudly, although she wasn't aware of that. As far as she was concerned, he was just bumming around, doing a bit of this and a bit of that on the production side. Since he had never in his life done any bumming around, he was quite charmed to be thought of in that light.

More realistically, there was no way he was going to give her any inkling as to what he was really all about. Gold-diggers swarmed around wealthy men like flies to a honey pot, and it was refreshing to spend his time with a woman without crazy suspicions proliferating in his head.

'It'll give you time to catch up with those friends of yours.'

'I guess it *is* only a few days,' Charlie sighed. She slid off him. 'There, you can breathe now that I'm off you.' She reached for her tee-shirt and he stopped her.

'Not yet. I like looking at you naked.'

'Just a shame most of it has to take place outdoors,' she said wistfully. 'Honestly, the amount of times I've tried to hint to Jayne and Simone that they should go spend a night somewhere so that we could have the place to ourselves…'

'A night where?'

'Oh, I don't know.' She giggled. 'Wherever it is people go to when they want to give other people space in a cramped flat.'

'Ah, *that* mystery place. I suppose if they knew of its existence they might have been more obliging.' He linked his hands behind his head, comfortable in his own nudity, and appreciated the lines of her body. The sun had turned her skin a healthy golden colour, which suited her long, streaky blonde hair and wide blue eyes. He thought, not for the first time, how much younger she looked than her twenty-four years, but then that was probably because she wore next to no make-up, which was always ageing on a woman.

'And also,' Charlie ventured tentatively, 'I'm not going to be around for much longer. I have to get back to England.'

'Yes. And that will be exciting for you. Taking up a new job, meeting new people.'

'Um, yes,' she said indistinctly, thinking of the university life looming in front of her. Two months ago, she couldn't wait to get there. Now she was dreading it after her heady summer in the sun. 'And then you'll be off as well… Do you realise you've never actually told me exactly where your next port of call is going to be?' Although, she now thought, she had told him practically everything about herself. About her dad dying when she was six, and being brought up by her mother who had worked her fingers to the bone so that her two daughters didn't have to do without. About her mother being the victim of a hit-and-run accident which had put Charlie off cars for a long time. About her sister now living in Australia, happily married and with a brand-new baby whom Charlie had never seen except on her computer.

Okay, so she had told a couple of white lies about her age, but instinct had told her that he would not have come near her if he had known that she was only a teenager. In the great scheme of things, a few white lies were easily justified.

Mostly they had been happy to be in each other's company, and that was fine.

'Who knows?' Riccardo gave a little shrug. 'The life of a wanderer…'

'And what are you going to do when you're finished wandering?'

'Settle down, get married, have six children.'

Charlie laughed, but she felt a little frisson at the thought of his kids, all with his dark hair, dark eyes and olive skin.

'You don't mean that.'

'You're right.' Riccardo thought of the life that lay ahead of him. 'I don't. At least, not yet. I have too much living to do to even go near the thought of settling down with a woman and having a family. Now, are we going to go for that drink in Lucca or not?'

'I don't know if I can be bothered.' Charlie stretched. 'Besides, I don't feel too good about using Fabio's pool. I know he and Anna are out for the evening, but I shouldn't think they'd like the thought of one of the workers flapping around on their property.'

Fabio and Anna ran part of the vast vineyards and had their own little villa and pool. Charlie, Jayne and Simone shared a flat in the nearby village and biked in every day to do their work. The arrangement worked, and Charlie didn't want to ruin it by taking advantage of her employer's absence. But Riccardo was having none of it. Youth, arrogance and a certain desire to impress the delicious woman staring up at him raced through his blood like fire. The boy who was mature beyond his years in the world of finance was right now just a young man willing to indulge an under-used wild streak.

'It's either the pool or else break into his house and use their shower…'

'Don't even say that!' But she was laughing, caught up in the energy of the moment.

'And we're here now, aren't we? In their grounds?' *Or should I say* my *grounds,* he thought realistically. 'In their grounds…in their pool…where's the difference?' Before she could say anything, he stood up and swiftly gathered up all their clothes, holding them high up and out of her reach as she scrambled to her feet, laughing.

'You're right, of course. We could always walk back to your place, but we'll have to do it wearing nothing.'

'You wouldn't dare!'

'Never challenge a man like me.' Riccardo grinned, dangling the bundle of clothes away from her frantic attempts to grab, until she subsided with a little 'humph' of mock disgruntlement.

The pool was really only a few minutes' walk through the vineyards which layered the hill in neat, orderly rows. And, once in the water, she had to admit that it was absolute bliss, beautifully cold and refreshing. And fun, touching him in the water, having him touch her. It was wicked, but how could she resist when he hoisted her to the side of the pool, lay her down with her legs dangling in the water and spread them wide apart so that he could lean at the side of the pool and taste her? A leisurely feasting with his tongue which flicked and darted, probed and squirmed. How could she resist something that felt so good?

This was what he had done to her—turned her from an ordinary, pretty teenager with ordinary, controllable relationships into a woman who was willing and eager to try anything with him. A whole new world of experiences had opened up and she had soaked them up like a sponge, loving the way he made her feel, loving *him.*

She climaxed with a long shudder of mindless ecstasy, amazed that her body could respond yet again with such involuntary urgency. Then she was content to lie there for a while before drawing her legs up and watching him as he swam like a fish up and down the lengths of the pool, before heaving himself out and then shaking off the water like a jungle animal surfacing from a river. He had utter confidence in his nakedness. He didn't seem to give a jot that she was staring at him. She was like that now with him, but at the start just the knowledge that his eyes were on her had made her want to cover her nudity with her hands. No man had seen her before without clothes, and she had shied away from his rampant masculinity, fascinated and scared at the same time.

Watching him now as he walked towards her, she wondered how he would have reacted if she had told him that she had come to him a virgin.

With horror, perhaps. Because he certainly hadn't come to her inexperienced. Anything but. Experienced men liked experienced women, was her reckoning, and besides she was supposed to be twenty-four. How many twenty-four-year-old women were totally inexperienced? He would have seen through her little white lie in an instant and that would have been the end of that.

'Ready?' Riccardo asked, running his fingers through his hair and liking the way she was eating him up with her eyes. Her amazing, big blue eyes. 'If we don't go now then we might as well head back to our respective places because I have an early start tomorrow.'

That had her on her feet in minutes. They walked hand in hand back through the vineyard to where they had left their bikes, stopping to get into their clothes when they were more or less dry.

Riccardo, thankfully, had a car. A battered old thing which he told her he had bought on his travels through the country. He was going to be using it to visit his mother the next day. She had no idea what he would do with it when he decided to push on with his travels, but he was a free spirit. She looked at him and smiled at what she saw. A man with one hand on the steering wheel, the other resting half out of the car, breeze whipping back his black hair, his classically perfect profile in frowning concentration. He drove like an Italian, as though he owned the roads.

In between their companionable silence, they made sporadic conversation until they reached Lucca, with its dramatic walls that framed the city, and which never failed to make her draw breath in appreciation.

Once parked, they went to their favourite bar which was buzzing. Riccardo slung his arm over her shoulder and drew her into him, surprised to find that he really *would* miss her over the next few days, and not just her body. She made him laugh with her amusing chatter. She was a holiday from the type of woman he usually dated.

'We should eat first,' he told her.

'Okay. Shall we go to the usual place?' Charlie, ever conscious of a bank balance that seldom reached heights that could be called truly healthy, favoured the cheap and cheerful venue.

'No, somewhere a little more upmarket, I think.'

'I can't afford anywhere expensive, Riccardo. You know that.'

'Yes, yes,' he said impatiently. 'I know. You're saving for a down payment on a house when you start your job.'

Since the only accurate part of his statement was the 'saving' bit, Charlie saw fit to change the course of the conversation just a little. 'What about you?' she protested. 'You'll need to put money aside too, if you're going to travel and see the world.' They had arrived at an expensive-looking restaurant with tables set outside. The starched white linen and bowls of flowers on the tables were a clear giveaway that her fragile bank balance would be feeling a little queasy were she to dine there. She stopped abruptly and looked up at him.

'No way.'

'You're being stubborn.'

'I'm not dressed for a place like that.' She yanked him aside so that a middle-aged couple of understated elegance could get past. 'And neither are you, for that matter!'

A lifetime of fabulous privilege had given Riccardo a keen disregard for what other people thought of him, and he shrugged.

'Honestly, Riccardo. You can be so *infuriating* at times!'

'Hmm. Does that mean you won't miss me when I'm gone?'

'Stop trying to change the subject!'

'I've never seen you hot and bothered before. Cute. Anyway, it doesn't matter what we're wearing. Who cares? Certainly not the proprietor. Competition is stiff.

He'll be very grateful for our contribution to his kitty, whatever our attire happens to be.'

Charlie gazed at him, half impressed by his easy self-confidence, half determined not to be swept out of her reality zone.

'Come on.' Riccardo cupped her elbow and guided her to the front. 'And, before you start telling me about your financial situation, this is on me.' He didn't give her time to reply. He spoke rapidly in Italian to the head waiter, so rapidly that she couldn't keep up with the translation in her head, and whatever he said must have been funny because the stiff, proper Italian actually cracked a smile.

It was the first proper restaurant Charlie had been into since she had come to Italy. The clientele was mostly over fifty, and she could feel their eyes on her, which made her self-consciously twiddle her fingers under the table until Riccardo raised his eyebrows.

To further disconcert her, he ordered wine, shooting her a quelling look just in case she interrupted.

This, he had discovered, was one of the more boring aspects of being a so-called wanderer. He was supposed to be penniless. Or at least conserving all his money for some mysterious sensible future that lurked around the fictitious corner. Despite his relief that he didn't have to be on his guard with her, there was still a part of him that would have liked to spend money on her. After all, it wasn't as though he didn't have an endless reserve of the stuff. He supposed it all came down to a pretty human desire to quite simply show off. Strange.

'You'll regret this,' Charlie said, stifling her awkwardness by very quickly downing a glass of cold, white Italian wine. 'When you're backpacking your way through some bit of Europe and you haven't got enough cash to get the train…'

'That will never be the case,' Riccardo said truthfully. Persuaded by him, she had stopped wearing a bra, and his eyes drifted to her ample breasts pushing against her tee-shirt.

He prided himself on his sophistication, but there was nothing sophisticated about what his body was doing right now. He hurriedly focused his attention on her face. Safer.

'Because?'

'Because I will…make sure I always have sufficient to get by.'

'That's fine to say, but you don't know what's around the corner.' Her friend Pete's dad had, quite suddenly, been made redundant at the age of sixty-two. They had been forced to sell the family home and move into a tiny terraced house. Life never quite worked out the way you thought it was going to.

'No, but you can hazard a pretty good guess. God, as they say, helps those who help themselves.' He lazed back in his chair and looked at her with hooded eyes. Without turning, he snapped his fingers and a waiter came charging over. Charlie marvelled at his air of command. Where on earth did he get *that* from?

'And where would you like God to help you get?' she asked, smiling, relaxed, blossoming under his languorous gaze.

'Oh, all the usual places. To a sprawling house with the sprawling lawns and the fleet of fast cars…'

'You don't really mean that, do you?'

'Why not?' Riccardo shrugged. 'When you strip away all the nuts and bolts, isn't that what everyone wants, whether they care to admit it or not?'

'I don't think so.'

'You're telling me that you wouldn't want all the things that money can buy?'

'You don't need money to enjoy life.' Charlie thought that she had never been happier than she had been over the past few weeks and money hadn't been involved. Since when had money been able to buy the beauty of the Tuscan hills with a man you loved right there by your side?

'But it enables one to eat…like this.' On cue, their starters were brought for them, a bowl of massive tiger prawns smothered in butter and garlic.

'You talk like someone who has oodles of it, Riccardo,' Charlie laughed.

'And you, *cara,* talk like an idealistic young kid who's never sampled the reality of life.'

Which abruptly reminded her that he was probably right. She needed to edit her opinions just a fraction, because really, as a woman in her mid-twenties about to strike out in a brand-new career, she would be looking towards a future that involved making money, as much as she could, so that she could enjoy all the things money could buy. Nice house with a cosy mortgage, a small house but with a bigger one on the horizon just as soon as she had settled into her imaginary job and started climbing the imaginary ladder. She nearly grimaced at the dreary prospect of it all.

'I'm trying to hang on to my inner child,' she teased.

'And so should you. I mean, you're not exactly the old man of the sea as yet. You have plenty of time to start thinking about making money.'

If only you knew. He felt a twinge of discomfort at his deception.

'I mean…' she licked her fingers before dipping them into the bowl of water with the lemon bobbing in it '…you're a free spirit. Somehow it's hard to picture you behind a desk with a mound of paperwork in front of you, and the telephone ringing and the boss yapping at you to bring him that report you should have done three days ago.'

Riccardo couldn't help it. He laughed at the comical picture she presented.

'Maybe,' he said smoothly, lowering his eyes. '*I* will be the boss yapping orders.'

'Oh no, please don't be one of those boring office people. Promise me!'

'Okay. I promise. Now, shall we enjoy this meal? The last before I head off to visit my dear mother.'

Charlie wondered about his mother. He had let slip precious little about his personal life. Oh yes, she knew what turned him on, she knew his thoughts on politics and politicians and what his favourite foods were, and all the places he had been to, but his family background was a dark area.

'Tell me about her.' Their second course was brought and, as Charlie watched the waiter deposit large white plates laden with their heavenly dishes, she missed the sudden shutter that snapped down over Riccardo's eyes. When she next looked across at him, he was back to his normal, teasing self.

'She is a typical Italian *mama*, very protective of her little boy.' That much was true. Riccardo dug into his piece of rare steak, a pleasant change from his recent diet of pasta and pizzas, and told her just enough to sate her curiosity without having to indulge in any out-and-out lying. Only when she asked where exactly his mother lived did he grow more circumspect.

Charlie knew why. There was no shame in having to admit to a parent living in reduced circumstances, but sometimes it could hit hard. Hadn't she once felt that very same thing herself? She had won an assisted scholarship to a private girls' school when she was eleven, and between the ages of eleven and sixteen, before she had left for a sixth form college, she too had sometimes found herself ashamed about her own comparative lack of money, loath to draw attention to the fact that she wasn't a member of the 'two-car, three-times-a-year-holiday-abroad' club. She tactfully and sympathetically changed the subject but it gnawed away at her, that little window into a wealth of information that would make their relationship so much deeper, that would set it on a course she was so desperate for it to follow.

Much later she was to think that love and desperation were a fatal combination.

For now, though, bitterness was an emotion with which she had never had contact. For now, she just appreciated the exquisite food and drank the exquisite wine, and wondered how she could manoeuvre the conversation back to the more fertile ground about *him*.

But he was an adept conversationalist. He didn't want to talk about himself, and so he didn't. He only had a couple more hours in her delectable company, he thought, and he wasn't going to waste it trying to dodge questions about himself. In fact, he could think of something far more profitable they could be doing…

Riccardo liked that thought. Less acceptable to him was the suspicion that he would miss more than just her willing body. Involvement with a woman, *any* woman, was not at this point in time part of his game plan.

They couldn't go back to her place. Her two friends would be there. They were 'entertaining' tonight. Riccardo had assumed that that meant having boyfriends around, but no, just an English couple they knew who were stopping by for the night. And his place was out. Which, unfortunately, just left the car. But when it came to sexual experiences, he was game for pretty much anything.

And so, he discovered, was Charlie.

Not the most comfortable place on the planet, Charlie admitted wryly to herself, but beggars couldn't be choosers, and she just wanted to touch him yet again, have him touch her once more, before he left to see his mother. She didn't even lodge a faint protest when he pulled down one of the twisting side roads and killed the engine. By now it was very late and here, away from the lights of the town, very, very dark. She was also slightly tipsy, she realised, after the better part of a bottle of some very expensive wine.

'You have some making up to do,' Riccardo murmured, wishing to hell he was driving something decent instead of this clapped-out heap of rust which he had bought because it suited the image he had wanted her to have.

'Meaning…?'

'Meaning that I satisfied you at the pool…'

'Oh, yes, so you did.' She remembered his dark head buried between her thighs and the rhythm of his tongue snaking along her most intimate places until she had bucked and moaned and reached orgasm.

They made love with the inventiveness of two people who knew each other's bodies intimately and were comfortable with the knowledge. And this time neither was left unsatisfied. In fact, Charlie thought with a sigh of contentment as they reluctantly drew apart, she seriously doubted satisfaction could get any higher.

She could have fallen asleep. In fact, she was beginning to drowse when he flipped open the car door and shifted his weight from under her.

'Nature calls,' he told her, placing a kiss on her nose. 'And then I'm going to drop you off, my little witch.'

He left the car door slightly ajar, and that was when she saw it—there, nestled in a little wad of papers which must have slipped out of his pocket in their love making. The envelope was folded in two and there, in bold type, was his mother's name and address.

Charlie picked up the envelope, suddenly very wide awake, and committed the name and address to memory. If she had had a pen and piece of paper handy she would have scribbled it down, but then that would have taken time and he wasn't going to be away for ever. She glanced nervously out of the car, made a mess of the papers and then slumped back onto the car seat where he found her a couple of minutes later.

'What's all this?' he asked.

'All what?' She yawned and sat up. 'Oh, not mine. I try and confine my bits of paper to my handbag. Must be yours. Gosh, I hope you haven't lost any more…' She began searching on the ground while he stuffed the papers back into his trouser pocket.

'Forget it. Come on. Time to go, little one.'

Charlie smiled. She believed in fate, and fate had been working overtime when it had shown her that envelope with that all-important address on it.

Because how else would she have known where he was going? And how else would she have been able to think of the one way she knew to show him that, whatever his background, he had nothing of which to be ashamed?

What better way to get to know him than by paying him a surprise visit…?

CHAPTER TWO

'BUT, Mum, I don't *like* that kind of ham! Why can't I just have some chocolate instead? *Everybody* in my class gets to bring a bar of chocolate for lunch! I'm the *only* one who brings in yucky sandwiches with yucky ham and yucky brown bread!'

'Brown bread's good for you.' Charlotte Chandler barely heard the familiar lament from her eight-year-old daughter. She was running late for work and was not open to a lengthy debate on the quality of sandwich fillings or, for that matter, the nutritional value of chocolates for lunch. 'Where's your homework, Gina?'

'In my room.'

'Well, honey, run and get it! Oh, for goodness' sake!'

She waited, tapping her heels by the front door, looking at her watch and waiting for her daughter.

Sometimes, at moments like this, she was assaulted by one of those 'what if' moments that always left her shaken.

What if, eight years ago, things had turned out differently? *What if* she hadn't decided on a stupid whim to trek in Riccardo's wake so that she could pay him a surprise visit? *What if* she had just stayed put with the two friends with whom she now had zero contact and just waited for him to return? *What if* he had loved her the way she had loved him? *What if, what if, what if?*

She had devised a method of dealing with the past, though. In her head she visualised a box, and into that box she put all those nasty, sad memories, and then she visualised herself shutting the lid of the box and sealing it down with masking tape. Most of the time, though, life was just too hectic for her to indulge her quiet regrets. And certainly, when Gina had still been a vociferous, demanding toddler, she had spent her days working flat out to meet the cost of the rent and the child minder and then flopping, exhausted, into bed at night, too tired from coping to have had much room in her head for anything.

Only now, Gina was older, and her quiet moments were no longer few and far between. It didn't seem fair that the memories that should have naturally died a death as time passed by should now start clamouring for attention.

Gina reappeared, homework in hand, already looking slightly disheveled, although it was the start of the day and she had been perfectly neat an hour before when she had got dressed for school.

Charlotte automatically reached down and smoothed some of the dark curls back into position. 'Okay. Now, you're *sure* you've got everything?'

'Sure!'

'How sure?'

'Two thousand sure.' They grinned at each other, enjoying this little game they had been playing before school since time immemorial, and then they were off.

Yet another busy Monday. A short drive to drop Gina off to school and then a far longer one for Charlotte, heading north, giving her ample time for all those unwelcome thoughts and memories to begin jostling in their box until, as she cleared the Hammersmith flyover and eased her little car onto the M4, she just sighed and allowed her mind to drift.

She knew why this was happening, of course. It was because of Ben. Because she was finally trying to get her life back on track, so to speak, by jumping back into the whole dating game instead of standing on the sidelines watching the world go by, and making excuses whenever her friends tried to encourage her to go out and meet some guys.

It was inevitable that she would be reminded of *him.* She was emerging from eight years of cold storage, for heaven's sake! *Any* guy she now saw would generate comparisons in her head.

And she was pretty sure that the comparisons were unfair, because after such a long time there was no way that she could actually remember Riccardo in any detail to speak of. She had taken no photos of him, something for which she was eternally grateful. In her head, she could still catch his smile, though, that lazy, sexy smile when he'd turned to her and reached out, and she could still remember the way her foolish heart had fluttered at the slightest contact.

She was aware of passing the Heathrow turn-off as she headed out towards the M25. She knew this route to their Midlands branch and could drive it with her eyes shut. It gave her plenty of time to think, and while she tried to make an effort to think of Ben—lovely, upwardly mobile, fantastic-catch Ben—she found herself thinking of Riccardo instead. Riccardo, who had been so shocked when she had turned up on his doorstep like an unwanted parcel that should have been delivered to another address.

She hadn't been Charlotte then. She had been Charlie. Charlie the teenager without a care in the world, madly in love, and crazy enough to have thought that the man she loved might just love her back. After all, he had *wanted* her, hadn't he? He'd told her so a million times! And how could you make love with someone with such tenderness and passion without there being just a tiny bit of love somewhere?

Finding his mother's house had been a nightmare. It had been a steaming hot day, one of those days when too much walking about made you feel slightly sick, and she had stupidly worn trousers and a tee-shirt that had clung to her like glue. Even eight years on, she could still recreate in her head all those nauseous feelings that had assaulted her as she'd tiredly travelled the distance that must have taken Riccardo, in his car and knowing the roads, no time at all.

Of course, in retrospect, she knew where the sickness had sprung from, but at the time she could remember thinking that if she didn't get to the house pretty soon then she would have to blow some of her money on a meal in one of those expensive air-conditioned restaurants as soon as she got to Florence.

Because Florence had been her destination, or rather the outskirts of Florence.

Where, exactly, she couldn't quite remember. Having committed the address to memory, she'd realised that her memory wasn't quite as obliging as she had hoped.

She had ended up spending far too much money on a mediocre meal simply because she'd been too tired to carry on trekking, and her broken Italian combined with her white-blonde hair had made her feel strangely vulnerable. Lingering over coffee, she'd realised just how much Riccardo had protected her from the open stares of Italian men. She had felt their eyes boring into her, on top of her sickness, and she had been halfway regretting the impulse to follow him.

But there had been no turning back, and besides she'd *wanted* to meet his mother, had *wanted* to prove to him that she loved him whatever his background. She hadn't cared if he didn't have any fixed plans or career path!

In the end, it was sheer luck that she landed up in the right place. After several hours, she could only remember bits of the wretched address, and she had forlornly managed to find a taxi driver with only the despairing hope that he could piece together what she recalled and somehow work out where she was supposed to go.

But, of course, she had Riccardo's name—di Napoli. And that was the key that eventually unlocked the door.

He knew the family name. In fact, knew exactly where to find the house, looked at her curiously, although she was too relieved to notice that fleeting glance.

She arrived late in the evening, and even in the fading light could see that this was not the house of a destitute woman.

'Are you sure you have the right place?' she asked the taxi driver anxiously. 'Are you sure you have the right di Napoli? I mean, there must be hundreds of them!'

A mansion faced her. It was of that distinct washed terracotta colour, but this was no simple dwelling. Portico after portico stretched along its clean main façade, and above them rows of windows and yet more doors sitting squarely behind a long balcony that extended the width of the building. And the pattern was repeated yet again. Surrounding the villa were extensive manicured lawns and trees that looked as old as time. Behind her, the taxi driver was talking rapidly in Italian, way too fast for her to understand a word he was saying, but she recognised the name Elena di Napoli, and if nothing else that was enough to make her realise that she had reached the right place. And no insignificant little place with dodgy electricity and erratic plumbing.

Charlotte felt her stomach constrict now as she remorselessly replayed the remembered scene—the old lady who'd answered the door, the old lady who had not been Riccardo's mother but one of the maids. Then his mother had arrived, then Riccardo, and from thence on her hopeful dream had turned into a nightmare.

She switched on the radio, but the distraction failed to work. Riccardo had been literally horrified, and while she had stood there, clutching her bag with all her worldly goods, stammering out that she had decided to surprise him with a visit, he had looked at her as a stranger would, with cold, black eyes, talking between her and his mother—English with her, Italian with his mother, who had the autocratic bearing of someone whom the daily inconveniences of life as most people would know it had not touched for decades. She had been tall, erect, with a long aquiline nose down which she'd stared at Charlie as though she was something the dog had chewed up and decided to spit out. Right onto her gleaming marble floor.

The minute Charlotte had managed to get Riccardo on his own, she had demanded to know how he could have lied to her, told her that he was penniless, led her to assume that he was just someone on a mission to see the world.

'I didn't *lie* to you. I allowed you to go along with your own fabrication, because things would have been rather more complicated had I not.'

Now, Charlotte switched up the volume of the music, because this particular snippet of memory was one of the most destructive. The way she had clung to him, her eyes welling up, begging him to try and explain why he was being so cold. She had been so *young*! She hadn't once, not once, clocked that he was just too accomplished to have been any ordinary person. He had been born into fabulous wealth and had the self-assurance to show for it. And even when the scales had been ripped from her eyes she had still clung to the hope that maybe, just maybe, his background wouldn't come between them. Okay, so he had lied to her about that, but she could have seen her way to forgiving him.

What a chump, she muttered to herself, driving along and frowning hard. The fog was only now beginning to lift. It was going to be one of those dank, dark days, the sort that reminded you that sunshine in late January was a rare sighting. And it was as cold to match. Her coat was flung in the back seat, and even with the heater going top whack she could still feel the iciness trying to penetrate her layers of shirt and V-necked jumper.

The trip up to the office took a little over an hour and a half, and by the time she made it there she was her usual brisk self with no outward hint that she had spent the past hour rehashing the unpleasant details of her past.

Aubrey, who owned the agency and its five branches, was as usual fulsome in his flattery and apologetic about dragging her out of the London office.

'But you're the expert on big, old houses,' he gushed.

'There's no need to lay it on with a trowel, Aubrey. It was no bother.' It was a huge bother. She had paperwork piling up on her desk, and a couple of touch-and-go sales that would require her intervention, but Aubrey had kick started her career and she owed him a great deal. Not many people would have taken her on, four months pregnant, with a stillborn university career and absolutely no experience in selling houses, never mind big ones. He had.

'How's that gorgeous daughter of yours? Any boyfriends yet? Ha, ha. Little joke.'

Charlotte grinned, nodding pleasantly at the people in the office, all of whom she knew, following Aubrey through to his separate room, fired up to get on with the viewing so that she could drive back and hopefully arrive home as early as possible. Elaine, her babysitter, was going to be there but she still enjoyed her night-time routine with Gina.

'I've told her, no boyfriends until she's through university.' Charlotte settled into the leather chair opposite him and reached forward for the particulars of the house.

'My dear girl, you mustn't let your own experiences influence you now…'

'I try not to, Aubrey, but it's difficult. Now, this house. Wow.'

'Wow indeed. We've just this minute got the particulars printed up. In fact…' he leaned back and folded his hands on his not inconsiderable stomach '…it's not even on the open market as yet.'

'And you have someone interested?'

'Several, in point of fact.'

'So it's a myth that big country houses aren't selling.' She flicked through the glossy brochure, which was presented over several pages, each with eye-wateringly tempting colour shots of various rooms and the extensive gardens. Charlotte was accustomed to these big, old properties. She asked all the relevant questions, and whether there were any sinister things wrong that would put a prospective buyer off. Many a promising sale was lost to rising damp or dry rot.

She shouldn't have made that passing remark about steering Gina away from boyfriends. She didn't want to come across as bitter, and most of the time she succeeded, but Aubrey was one of the few people who knew about her ordeal with Riccardo. He was also Gina's godfather, and so qualified to observe, not that he did that very often. Still. She stuck the brochure in her briefcase, keenly aware that he was looking at her with genuine concern and not really wanting to get into an in-depth conversation about her emotional life.

'Still seeing that young man of yours?'

Charlotte stood up and raised her eyebrows wryly.

'I'm twice your age. I'm qualified to give you little lectures about your life. Call it senior citizen advantages.' He stood up and moved round the desk and briefly put his arm around her shoulder. He was a big man. Tall and, as he enjoyed saying, a fully paid-up member of 'the fat brigade'. He dwarfed her.

'I'm taking it slowly with Ben,' Charlotte told him. 'He's a nice guy, but I'm not going to rush anything.'

'Wise girl. Right, then. I'll probably be gone by the time you finish this viewing. You have all the details in the folder. It's a woman. Phone and let me know how it goes, and let's put a date in the diary for you to come up with the little one for the weekend. Diana says it's too long since she saw you!'

'You've got a deal.'

'And feel free to bring the young man…'

'I'll have to think about that one. Maybe.' Introducing him to Aubrey and Di would be like introducing him to family, a big psychological step towards cementing their relationship onto another level. By now, they had enjoyed dinners out, the occasional theatre outing and one Sunday lunch, and she was content to keep it to that level until something kicked in and told her that the time was right to accelerate things. She had only been seeing him for three months. Why rush things along?

'Is our viewer a local person?' she asked, walking with Aubrey to the door. 'Will they be familiar with the property, or do I have to play up the location?'

'Definitely not from around here, so yes, let's hear it for the great transport links and rural setting.'

Rural being the operative word, Charlotte thought, as she left behind all vestiges of bustling provincial life and drove out into the country. It was stunning scenery. A profusion of trees raising naked branches upwards, and wintry fields stretching on either side of the winding road. In summer she imagined it would be awash with greenery.

She found herself slowing down so that she could absorb her surroundings. It really didn't matter how many big houses she walked around in London, none could compare to something in a setting like this because there was no such thing as perfect privacy in the city. You could part with millions and still have neighbours around within shouting distance. Whereas here your millions would buy you all the solitude you could ever need.

She wouldn't have minded having a look around the gardens before her viewer but that would have been an indulgence, and she was slightly relieved to find that the option was denied her because, lo and behold, there was her car randomly parked at an angle in the courtyard—a long, very expensive silver Bentley Continental, the sort that cost roughly the same price as some people's houses. Unfortunately for Charlotte, no one was in it. Nor was the woman anywhere to be seen at the front of the house. Well, there was no way she would be *inside*, not unless she had decided to embark on a little breaking and entering.

With a sigh of frustration, Charlotte walked back up to the front door and glanced around her, then she set off. She had to look at the brochure to see where the boundaries of the house lay. Frankly none were within sight, and the prospect of trekking through acres of land in search of one errant old lady with more money than sense filled her with dismay.

She was circling the back of the house, vaguely admiring the lawns and the extensive copse behind, which was all part of the package, when she heard his voice from behind her and for the first few seconds she really didn't recognise it. But only for a few seconds. Then her body froze in utter shock. Just an ordinary, polite apology that he had missed her.

Charlotte turned around and there he was: the man who still visited her in every sweet dream and every nightmare she had had over eight years. God, she had been thinking of him only this morning! Had that been some sort of dreadful, sick premonition? She blinked to dispel the reality of him standing not more than five metres away from her, and then she closed her eyes and, for the first time in her life, she blacked out.

She surfaced to find herself flat on her back with her head resting on something soft, like a cushion. There was also someone peering down at her. *Oh God.* She struggled to sit up and wriggle away from him at the same time, all the while keenly aware of the image she would be presenting—neat bob all over the place, snappy grey suit creased and soiled beyond redemption, hands covered in dirt and little chips of gravel from where she had tried to hoist herself away from him.

'Well, well, well…' Riccardo said softly. 'It's *you*, isn't it?'

'What are *you* doing here?' She sat up, gritting her teeth to ward off the sudden giddiness, and shakily got to her feet.

He hadn't changed. At least, not much. When she had occasionally imagined herself bumping into him again, she had always helpfully reconstructed him as overweight, balding and prematurely aged from the stress of all those little Italian *bambinos* his mother told her he would one day have, *with an Italian girl from his own class and not a foreigner without a penny to her name.*

But eight years had sharpened his killer looks. The black hair was short now and there were a few lines on his face but he was still devastatingly good looking. He had been kneeling next to her and he bent to brush the knees of his trousers, his expensive, hand-tailored trousers which were probably as ruined as her skirt would be but had cost ten times as much. *Tough.*

A ball of resentment welled up inside her like acid. 'I was told to expect a Mrs Dean.'

'You've changed.' He circled her like a tiger that had somehow managed to corner some interesting prey and didn't want to devour it just quite yet.

His eyes on her felt like a physical assault and she found herself cringing back. It would have to stop, she told herself. She was no longer a vulnerable eighteen-year-old girl! She was a woman with a child...*Gina.*

Fear rammed into her but she managed to keep her expression steady. She would have to get rid of him, and fast, because there was no way that she was going to allow him to find out that she had had a child by him.

No way! She had left Italy eight years ago with her life in ruins and she wasn't going to let it happen again.

'I realise you might think me unprofessional, but I'm afraid I'm going to have to let someone else show you around this house.'

'Why?'

'Isn't it obvious? We had a disastrous relationship eight years ago and that's bound to be reflected in my attitude towards you.'

'If I want this house then I'll buy it, whatever your attitude happens to be.'

'That's as may be,' Charlotte said coldly. 'But I'm not prepared to be in your company.' She reached into her bag for her mobile phone, but before she could flick it open his hand was around her wrist and he was *there*, invading every atom of her precious personal space.

'Well, that's just too bad. I've driven quite a way to get here, and I'm not about to get back into my car until I've seen this house, so you're going to get the key out of that briefcase of yours and you're going to show me around, room by tortuous room, until I'm satisfied. Got it?'

'Or else what?'

'Or else I lodge a formal complaint to your boss and make sure he understands that he's lost a potential sale, a very *big* potential sale, because of you.' Riccardo looked at her, hands stuffed into the pockets of his camel coat. His jacket, she realised, was still on the ground from where he had folded it to put under her head.

'I apologise for your jacket.' She stooped to pick it up and then stretched it out to him, making sure not to close the safe distance between them. Inside, every bit of her was shaking like a leaf.

Cornered, she stuffed the phone back into her bag and pulled out the keys to the house.

'Good girl,' Riccardo said approvingly. He had been shocked to see her, and even more shocked by his reaction which was a certain curious satisfaction, as if the wheel had come full circle, as if he had been waiting for just this moment.

Which, of course, he hadn't been. That episode in his life had been consigned to history a long time ago. She had been the casual fling who had turned, suddenly, into someone hell-bent on pinning him down. Still, it was amusing to see how much she had changed. Gone was the long, streaky hair, the fresh face, the open smile. In its place was a tailored bob and a guarded, wary expression. She was still as slender as she had been then, though, he thought as his eyes appraised the lines of her body under the business suit. As though it had been yesterday, he remembered the feel of her body under his, and was disconcerted by the impact that fleeting memory had on him.

Abruptly, he turned away, knowing that she was following him.

'I suppose you ought to know that the land extends to…there…' Charlotte pointed to various landmarks and made sure she didn't look at him. 'There's the option to buy the adjacent field, but that wouldn't be necessary as this is all a green-belt area. There's no chance that planning permission would be given for any domestic housing.'

'Estate agent. Not what I would have expected of you. But, then again, I really didn't know you very well, did I, Charlie?'

'The name is *Charlotte*.' She opened the front door, which had a series of locks, and switched off the alarm. All this was done without looking at him, although she could feel him right there next to her, sending her nervous system into panicked overdrive.

Riccardo ignored the interruption. 'No. There I was, thinking that I was dealing with a woman, and instead I was dealing with an adolescent.'

Charlotte stuck her chin up and refused to rise to the taunt. Not that she could. She hadn't *felt* like an adolescent, not when she had been around him. She had felt all woman then. But she had just been a teenager after all, as his mother had triumphantly pointed out, having rummaged in her backpack the minute Charlie had been in the shower, crying and trying to figure out what to do next. His mother had rummaged and found her passport which Charlie had brought with her rather than leave behind *just in case*.

'I point that out just in case you raise any more arguments about being the poor, deceived victim.'

'I wasn't about to raise any more arguments,' Charlotte informed him coolly. 'I was, in fact, about to point out features to the house which you might be interested in. The flooring is all original oak, as is the balustrade and banister leading up to the first floor. If you would like to follow me, there's a cellar just there…'

'Not that I intend to have a vast collection of wines stored here.'

She wanted to tell him that she really didn't give a damn what he intended to store or not store in the house, should he choose to buy it, because *he* and whatever *he* chose to do was none of her business and she could not care less.

'Oh, and that would be because…?'

'Why don't you look at me when I speak to you?'

'You were a huge mistake in my life.' She looked at him squarely in the face and thanked the Lord that he couldn't hear the wild beating of her heart. 'And why would I want to look at my past mistake?'

Riccardo forgot that over the years she had crystallised in his head as a *narrow* escape. The bottom line was that no one had ever referred to *him* as a mistake. No one. He was, frankly, outraged by her remark. Success and power accumulated rapidly over the years had built a circle of devotees around him, insulating him from the effects of personal criticism. But she was already moving on, vanishing through the door ahead of him, and he followed her with an angry scowl.

'The breakfast room.' Charlotte swept a glance round a room that was the size of most people's living areas. A huge circular table dominated the centre. To one side were two sofas, and opposite a fireplace which had retained its original Victorian tile surround. She dutifully pointed this out, aware of him behind her, releasing a force field of invisible energy that she found draining and disturbing.

'And did you manage to rectify the mistake?' Riccardo moved smoothly to stand in front of her. He wondered how he could have forgotten the blueness of her eyes and the fringing of dark eyelashes that was so dramatic against the colour of her hair.

'*This* is why I didn't think it a good idea to show you around this house,' Charlotte told him bluntly. 'Because I didn't want to be bombarded with personal stuff. There's no point to rehashing the past. It's long forgotten.' *Ha.* But to make her point, to show him that she was now a fully fledged adult, she smiled. It wasn't a warm smile but she hoped that it would prove to him that, whatever she had said, he no longer affected her.

The smile infuriated Riccardo almost as much as the 'mistake' remark. It was patronising. Yet another novel and deeply unpleasant insult to his personal pride. Thank God their relationship had ended when it had, he told himself. The woman had turned out to have the makings of a shrew in her.

'Of course it is,' Riccardo agreed, touching the Victorian tiles and giving Charlotte the distinct impression that he was only half listening to what she had said. 'If I came across as bombarding you with personal stuff then…' He glanced over his shoulder at her. 'Please accept my heartfelt apologies.'

Charlotte looked at him suspiciously. She wouldn't have put him down as the apologising sort of man, but who was to say what kind of man he was now? One thing was certain—she didn't want to antagonise him. Some instinct inside her told her that that would be a very unwise thing to do indeed. She would get through this viewing, and the best way to do it would be with a smile on her face, then she could get back to her life. Besides, maybe *she* had been at fault, bristling for no good reason and reading innuendo when there had just been curiosity.

'Sure.' She shrugged and then grinned at him reluctantly. 'I guess we're both a bit shocked to find ourselves here, facing each other after all this time.'

'So let's start again, shall we?' Dangerous curiosity began to uncurl inside him. Was she married? There was no ring, but nowadays that didn't say a hell of a lot. Maybe she was divorced. 'You look well. Life must agree with you... Are you married?'

Just at that precise moment in time, her mobile phone rang. Ben. Charlotte mouthed a 'sorry' and half turned so that she could conduct a whispered conversation, then, as she snapped shut the phone, she turned to Riccardo and said brightly, 'Not married, no. Not yet, anyway...'

There! If that didn't establish some well-defined boundaries between them, then what would?

CHAPTER THREE

RICCARDO let that ride. So the teenager had matured into a woman involved in a relationship and on the brink of marriage. It had always been her dream. Thinking back, he could remember snippets of conversation when she had confided in him that there was a little bit of her that was jealous of her sister, jealous of all that domestic stability. He could remember laughing and denigrating an institution that was based around cementing two people together, usually when they were way too young to recognise the compromises it involved, but conversations like that had only ever lasted for a short while because there had always been better things to do.

Then she had shown up on his doorstep, clutching dreams of commitment and marriage, and he had been forced to recognise that perhaps he should have paid a bit more attention to those tenuous threads of conversations that he had allowed to waft by.

He made a big mental effort to be magnanimous on her behalf, but his head was playing weird tricks on him, forcing him to remember the tantalising feel of her body writhing under him, and the way he had not been able to get enough of her. From that springboard, that slow curl of curiosity began to swell. He wondered what the man was like and felt an unwelcome jolt of jealousy.

'So…what happened to the university plans? When I found out how old you were—or should I say how *young* you were—you told me that you were on your way to university to study…what was it?'

'Land management.' Now they were entering perilous waters, and Charlotte could feel little pinpricks of perspiration breaking out all over her body.

'So what happened to the land management dreams?'

'Oh, you know…' she said vaguely. 'Dreams come and go. Look, have you seen enough of this room? Because I have a bit of a drive back home.'

'Oh yes? And home would be…?'

'Not around here!' Charlotte laughed and briskly took the lead, sweeping out of the breakfast room and heading towards the kitchen which she intended to describe in such depth that he would probably keel over in boredom. Anything to avoid him questioning her. Yes, his questions were harmless, and pretty predictable given the history they had briefly shared, but they still had her on tenterhooks.

'Now, the kitchen! As you can see, this is the perfect kitchen for entertaining!' She could hear herself teetering on the brink of a Stepford-wife impersonation. 'Double Aga, great for preparing meals for large numbers of people, and big enough to house a table for eight. The conservatory is a recent addition to the house, one of the few, but I think you'll agree that they've done an excellent job in maintaining the Victorian aspect of the house!'

'You certainly seem to be involved in what you do,' Riccardo commented dryly, bemused by her sudden departure into manic-salesperson pitch. 'Yes. This is a very...charming kitchen, although I don't intend to be doing much cooking in it.'

'No wines for the wine cellar, no food in the kitchen... what *exactly* is the purpose of the house, if you don't mind my asking?'

'Investment. I think the time is right to add a country house to my portfolio. I guarantee that in five years' time this place will have quadrupled in price.'

'In that case, is there any point in showing you around? You could get everything you need from the particulars you have in your hand.'

'Oh, I think I need to have a close up view of whether any work needs doing. It's boring, and I can't afford the time, but my assistant inconveniently caught some kind of bug over the weekend and couldn't make it.'

Charlotte looked at Riccardo's dark, sexy face and shivered at the man he had become. The winning confidence of youth had been honed into cold self-assurance. Years ago, in the aftermath of their showdown, he had coolly informed her that his future was mapped out for him, waiting for him to seize. He had obviously seized it, but it didn't appear to have made him happy because happiness wasn't etched into his features.

'Why, can't you afford the time?' she heard herself asking, and he must have detected the sarcastic edge to her voice because he directed all his frowning attention onto her.

'I'm a very busy man.'

'Oh yes. Forgot. All those big plans you had for that brilliant, golden future that had been planned for you since birth. I guess taking time out *would* be a little tricky.' Charlotte could have kicked herself for launching into a provocative personal attack, but he was just so damned *arrogant*, standing there, black eyes sweeping condescendingly over a house that was achingly beautiful and deserved to be more than just bricks and mortar bought to make money for a man who obviously didn't need it!

'Do I detect a certain amount of sarcasm in your voice? Is that part of your selling routine?'

'I apologise,' Charlotte muttered under her breath. 'Look, shall we get this over with?'

'Do I make you feel uncomfortable? Or is it just being confronted with your past mistake that's putting you on edge?'

'I'm not on edge.' She brushed past him, heading through to the main body of the house. This was not going to be a quick once-over. The place was so big that she could be doing her sales patter for much longer than she wanted, especially if he kept butting in with questions and observations.

It just showed the ugly bones of their relationship—she confused and sickeningly affected by him, and he cool as a cucumber and happy to stampede straight through her 'keep off' signs.

She virtually ran through the ground floor. She forgot about laboriously pointing out interesting features. That just took up valuable time, and she wanted to be far away from him so that she could breathe properly.

Upstairs came the bedrooms. She actually wanted to just leave him to get on with it, but she couldn't afford to have him running back to Aubrey with complaints about her performance. She loved her job and she needed it. So on they went. Guest rooms one, two, three and four, and then yet another sitting room and a study, and then the main bedroom.

Riccardo walked in and looked around the stunning oak-panelled walls. Large bay windows dominated two of the walls and through both lay extensive views of fields and woodland. He noticed that she hadn't followed him in but that she had remained hovering by the door, clutching her brochure.

Impatience mingled with irritation. So, yes, she had admitted that she had made a mistake with him, but did she have to take her aversion to such obvious lengths? She clearly couldn't wait until they were outside and she could speed off in the opposite direction. He supposed it said something that she could still be affected by his presence after all this time, but he wasn't idiot enough to think that that something was remotely flattering. Anyone bitten by a snake would probably shy away from too many future personal encounters with the species.

Accustomed to the adulation of women, Riccardo gritted his teeth and did what he had come to do. He peered at the woodwork, looked at the window frames, tried to work out what fundamental work would be needed if he bought the place. Behind him, he could sense her waiting, keen to leave, probably looking at her watch.

'There's another floor,' Charlotte said, as soon as he turned around. 'It's been used as a suite of guest rooms, but it could be turned into pretty much anything. Would you like to have a look?'

'No. I'd like to give that a miss, because I really don't object to tossing a couple of million at a property having only seen a fraction of it. I'm really getting a little impatient with your wounded-party act, Charlie.'

'*Charlotte,*' she said quickly. 'I'm not that girl you knew any more!'

Riccardo took a couple of steps towards her, and Charlotte swallowed hard but stood her ground until he was towering over her, face grim, ebony brows winged into a dark frown. Everything about him terrified her. Life for the past eight years seemed to have been a pleasant, trouble-free walk in the park compared to just this one single moment in time.

'No, you're not. You're a woman about to be married who clearly can't stand the sight of me and isn't mature enough to conceal it.'

'Can you blame me?' Charlotte said in a high, accusing voice. Logic and common sense flew through the window, and in its place was a red mist of remembered hurt, misery and resentment. 'You led me on…'

'I promised *nothing*!'

'You slept with me.'

'I wasn't the first!'

'Yes, you damned well were!' She had never told him. Now it was out, and he stared at her in shocked silence.

'You couldn't have been. I would have known.'

'How?' Charlotte demanded, her cheeks burning. 'How would you have *known*?'

'There was no…there were no signs…'

'Oh, please! I was eighteen and you swept me off my silly feet.'

Would he have slept with her if he had known that she was a virgin? Riccardo asked himself. No. No, he wouldn't have, because his keen antennae would have alerted him to the inherent problems. He also would have started asking a few more questions about her age because twenty-four-year-old virgins, in his experience, were pretty thin on the ground. He surfaced to find that she was still attacking him, fuelled by eight years of blistering resentment.

'No, you don't!' he cut in harshly. 'If I had known that you were a virgin, whether you were eighteen, twenty-four or fifty-six, I wouldn't have slept with you!'

'Because?' She heard herself ask the question with dismay and knew that she should have listened to her head and not allowed her emotions to run wild.

'Because you would have been vulnerable!'

'And all you wanted was sex,' she whispered bitterly.

Riccardo swept his fingers through his hair and flushed. 'That is *not* what it was all about!'

'No? And that would be why you stood up for me when your mother started ranting about my unsuitability?'

Riccardo released a long, audible hiss of frustration. Those big, accusing blue eyes were making him feel like a cad and, damn it, he didn't deserve that!

'My mother wanted…'

'Oh, yes! I know what your mother wanted—a good Italian girl for you! Someone with all the right connections! She made herself perfectly clear on the subject. In fact, she mentioned a certain *Isabella*. Perfect credentials! Did she make it to the altar after all?'

'No one made it to the altar,' Riccardo muttered, glowering at her. Her face was suffused with angry colour. She might have changed the haircut, and swapped her tee-shirts and short skirts for a business suit, but look past that and there was still the same girl underneath.

'You're right,' he said heavily. 'I should have stuck up for you a bit more.'

'*A bit more?* You didn't stick up for me at *all*! In fact, if my memory serves me, you were horrified that I'd landed on your doorstep!'

'It was unexpected.'

'An unexpected and unpleasant surprise,' Charlotte amended, recalling it as if it had all happened the day before. 'Especially to a young, vulnerable kid who thought that the first man she slept with might just turn out to be somebody who cared.'

'And I was twenty-six who thought he had been having a pleasant fling with a twenty-four-year-old woman. A twenty-six-year-old with his career stretching in front of him and no thoughts of marriage on his mind!'

'I never said that I wanted to *marry* you!' But she had wanted a relationship, not just a meeting of bodies until they went their separate ways. And where else had that been heading but down an aisle somewhere along the way? Why kid herself? She shifted uneasily on her feet and tried not to see his point of view, but like it or not it still crawled under her skin and she reluctantly had to admit that he had just run scared, confronted by someone he thought wanted to tie him down. The age thing had probably been the final straw.

And now there was Gina.

'And you have to understand that my mother is a traditionalist. A young, blonde English girl appearing on her doorstep would have been her worst nightmare.'

Charlotte was finding it somewhat harder to picture his mother as a kindly old lady who just happened to have been caught in a time warp.

'Well, now that we have got that out of the way, maybe we could finish this tour of the house,' she said tightly. They said that confession was good for the soul but, having spilt her guts, she just felt confused.

By the time they were back in the hallway, Charlotte was wrung out, even though nothing further had been said between them. She had said all the right things about the house and he had asked all the expected questions.

It was already dark And gloomy outside, even though it was still just mid-afternoon, and it was cold.

'So…' She looked at him when they finally made it outside, already feeling safer with her little car next to her. 'If you're interested, then you can get in touch with Aubrey James at our Henley office and he can take it from there.' His face was all dark angles, and she shivered and wrapped her coat tighter around her.

'Why not you?'

'I beg your pardon?'

'Wouldn't it be more logical to get in touch with you, considering you were the one to show me around the house?'

'No!' She clicked her remote and yanked open the door of her car. 'I mean, no, it wouldn't, because I don't actually work at Aubrey's branch.'

'Well, where *do* you work?'

'In London,' Charlotte admitted reluctantly. 'But I have a good track record with selling grand old houses, and Aubrey likes to think that that makes me some kind of expert.'

'Handy when the boss gives his employee special favours.' Riccardo wondered whether this was the fiancé, to whom she was as good as married, bar the details. 'Is this the soon-to-be bridegroom?'

'The…? Oh.' She remembered her passing remark about Ben, that distance-creating manoeuvre that hadn't worked. Poor Ben. What would he think if he knew that he had featured as a likely fiancé? She grinned, her first genuine smile of real amusement. 'No. No, Aubrey isn't any bridegroom in the making. In fact, he's very happily married and twice my age, height and girth. Father figure sooner than bridegroom, I would say.'

Riccardo watched that smile, just the shadow of it, in the swiftly descending gloom and drew in his breath sharply. He'd remembered that, kept the image of it somewhere in his head, even when time had moved on. Curious. And unsettling.

'So, who *is* the lucky man?' he asked lightly, and Charlotte couldn't find a reason not to name a name. It would have been odd if she had tried to withhold the information, she reasoned, because women on the verge of marriage were supposed to be happy and proud of the fact.

'Ben.'

'And Ben is…?'

'Oh, the usual. A man. Couple of arms, couple of legs, head.'

Riccardo gave a rich, throaty chuckle of amusement, and in the darkness Charlotte blushed and remembered that she needed to be on her way, far from the man standing in front of her, who it seemed still had the ability to get her hot and bothered. She had to get back to her daughter.

Their daughter, her mind flung back at her.

'And what does the arms, legs and head do?'

'Nothing! I really must be off now. I don't want to end up driving in the dark. Especially as it's such a long drive back to London.'

'Surely if your boss has such a high opinion of you he would get you somewhere to stay for the night, save you the drive down?'

'Oh, no, I can't stay here!' No sooner were the words out than she wanted to swallow them back down. 'I mean… I mean…'

'I know what you mean,' Riccardo interrupted her brusquely. 'Young love. I guess the man whose job is *nothing* is waiting for you somewhere in London with a spread in the oven and candles on the table. You have to be careful, you know.'

'Careful? Careful of what?' It was difficult keeping up with him, especially when his conclusions were so far off-target—a fact for which she was extremely grateful.

'Men who kick off a relationship by making sure you're chained to them. It might be flattering to start with, but no one enjoys being a captive.'

'I don't know what you're talking about,' Charlotte said waspishly. It particularly made no sense, considering she and Ben were still in a 'maybe, maybe not' situation. Nevertheless, in view of the fact that she had been creative with the truth, Charlotte felt morally obliged to defend his good name. 'I'm not a captive, for goodness' sake.'

'Then why the panic?'

'I really have to go.'

'I'm heading down to London myself. I could always follow you, make sure you get to your house safely, for old times' sake. These roads can be treacherous in winter.'

'No!'

Riccardo put up both his hands in mock surrender. His curiosity was now seriously piqued.

'I'm fine to drive back unescorted, thank you very much. I've done longer trips.'

'And travelled back to London on the same day? When it's getting dark? In that tiny little sewing-machine of yours?'

'It's very reliable!'

'But not exactly equipped for long-distance driving.'

'I don't believe in great, big gas-guzzlers.' She looked meaningfully at the great, big gas-guzzler parked behind him.

'Yet in the event of an accident, on a dark road in the middle of winter, you might find yourself regretting that you cared more about the planet than your own safety. Is that a company car? If it is, then I think I shall have a word with that boss of yours, find out what he thinks he's playing at, sending you all over the country in something that's only fit for city driving…'

'Don't you dare!'

'You know, you should never mention my name and the word "dare" in the same breath…'

Charlotte wondered whether he was joking. It was hard to tell, because the light was so poor and she couldn't read the expression on his face, but still a little whisper of danger fluttered along her spine.

'Why are you so jittery?' he asked curiously. Riccardo knew that this was a conversation that was going nowhere. She would drive off and so would he, and later he would just think of their meeting as one of life's strange coincidences. But for the moment he had the strangest need to carry on talking to her. 'I mean, it's soon going to be dark.' He shrugged, a casual, elegant movement that she remembered well. 'So where's the rush? Why don't I take you out to dinner? You can continue ranting at me, and then when you're through we can do some civilised catching up.' Riccardo liked his use of the word 'civilised'. It made him sound ferociously controlled, and papered over the alarming suspicion that for the first time in years he was not responding to a situation with his head. His head was definitely not telling him to ask out a woman who was treating him like an infectious disease.

'Sorry, can't.' She opened her car door and flung her bag and briefcase in the passenger seat, then she clambered in. But before she could slam the door behind her he was there, propping it open with one lean, brown hand, and bending down to stare at her. And unfortunately for her, with the car light on, there was no way she could conceal the agitation on her face. She knew how she looked: red faced and as guilty as hell. Naturally he wouldn't know *why* she looked guilty, but he would be curious, and even after all these long years she knew him well enough to realise that there was one trait he possessed which would surely not have changed—tenacity. He had always found pursuit in the face of a challenge very invigorating.

'My boyfriend. Well, fiancé…' She sat on her hands and crossed her fingers.

'Ben with the nothing job.'

'Actually, he's a chartered surveyor. And—and you were right. He's actually waiting for me. He's cooked me a meal. He always does that whenever I happen to be on one of these jobs…you know…when I won't be getting back until late. He's a great cook. Loves it.'

Riccardo frowned heavily, and Charlotte, feeling a lot more comfortable now that she had established an alibi for her red face, laughed lightly and started her engine. 'Yes, I know you'd probably disapprove. I guess, coming from that traditional Italian family of yours, you probably think men who cook are wimps, but there you go! Ben is a fantastic cook, and there's nothing he enjoys more than looking after me!'

'He must have a very flexible working environment,' Riccardo drawled. 'If he can find the time to hurry home and indulge his love of cooking whenever you happen to be on the road after five thirty.'

How had she known that he would manage to shape his remark into a veiled insult? That great, big fat ego of his probably couldn't stand the thought that she had bagged herself the perfect man.

She sighed a sigh of resounding pity for him. 'You know, all that paper chasing…'

'Paper chasing?'

'*Money*, Riccardo. Selling your soul for pots of gold…sacrificing everything for a big bank balance… Well, that's the domain of the dinosaur! It's the twenty-first century, and these days people are finally waking up to the fact that there are more important things in life than foreign holidays and big cars! And Ben is a twenty-first-century man. He arranges his time so that he can really fit in the things he enjoys doing!'

'Cooking…and what else? Cleaning, ironing and needlework?'

Charlotte chose to ignore his predictable sarcasm. 'Ha ha, Riccardo. You might think you enjoy working twenty hours a day so that you can rake in more and more money, and buy beautiful old houses like that one as *investments*, but as far as I'm concerned Ben has discovered the *real* secret of happiness. He's said good-bye to *greed* and hello to a more spiritual and *fulfilling* life.'

'And you're content with all this tree-hugging stuff?' Riccardo laughed shortly. 'I don't believe it!' He worked damned hard, he told himself, and he enjoyed it. Not because of the money. Hell, it wasn't as though he *needed* to make any more of the stuff! He enjoyed it because it fired his blood, made him feel alive.

'Well, I don't actually care *what* you believe. Now, if you don't mind, I want to go. To that delicious hot meal waiting for me. And a man who knows that there's more to life than a fat bank balance!'

Driving away, Charlotte had the feeling that she had won the battle, and the war as well. She had established herself as a thoroughly modern woman who had moved on with her life and now had her priorities firmly in place.

She even found herself humming along to the radio station until that kick of triumph started wearing off, at which point she realised that she had won nothing at all.

Sure, in *his* eyes, she had succeeded in fabricating the image of a woman in control, the complete opposite, in fact, of the dithering kid he had demolished eight years previously.

But, in reality, there was no fabulous fiancé rustling up mouth-watering dishes for her every evening. She didn't even know if Ben could boil an egg! They had eaten out whenever they had met. And, yes, she really *did* disapprove of a man whose *raison d'être* was money. But she worked her socks off to maintain a decent lifestyle for herself and Gina, so where was that twenty-first-century road she had proudly declared herself going down? Somewhere on a very distant horizon!

And should she have told him about Gina? The thought filled her with horror. Who knew what he would do? The worst case scenario filled her head like suffocating poisonous fumes—he would go ballistic and then his Italian side would kick in and he would take his daughter. He would use all that fabulous wealth at his disposal to guarantee Gina at his side, whatever the cost. She shuddered.

In the morning, she would telephone Aubrey to let him know how the viewing had gone, and in passing she would mention the identity of the prospective buyer and swear him to silence on the subject of his goddaughter. Just in case Riccardo decided to ask any questions about her. She very much doubted that he would, but just in case…

It was always better to be safe rather than sorry.

CHAPTER FOUR

CHARLOTTE propped her chin in her hand and looked intently at Ben, whose niceness over the past two weeks had been teetering precariously on the brink of boring. She was determined, however, not to find him boring, and in fact at moments like this, when her mind was beginning to glaze over as he enthused over some particularly tedious event at work, Robinson, Hathaway & Sons, she reminded herself that niceness was the stuff of all good, successful relationships. All that 'frisson' business was much overrated, as she had discovered to her cost. And she and Ben were beginning to have a relationship. They hadn't slept together but they had shared a few lingering kisses, which he had attempted to progress. But she had firmly told him it was simply too soon and he had gallantly respected her decision.

She had breathed more than one sigh of relief that Riccardo, having appeared from thin air to throw her into panicked disarray, had also disappeared similarly quickly. He had spoken to Aubrey, who had been fully briefed on fending off any questions about her, had told him that he would go away to think things over in connection with the house, and that had been the last the agency had seen of him.

The fact that his appearance had reignited a maelstrom of memories was just something she knew she would have to deal with. And she was, by really focusing on Ben and harnessing her stubborn mind with frequent, stern lectures.

She snapped out of her daydream to find that Ben was waiting for her to say something. *What? What? What on earth had he been talking about?*

'Yes,' she said automatically, which produced a smile of pleasure.

'Great. I know some women don't like being the first on the dance floor, but you're a game gal. My lady…this dance!'

Charlotte watched in horror as she realised what she had agreed to. They were in a jazz club, one which was currently sporting an empty dance floor, despite the fact that the music was good and the tables arranged around the circumference were brimming with people. And she was about to make a complete fool of herself by strutting her stuff with Ben.

'Sorry!' She smiled brightly and ignored the outstretched hand. 'Misheard. Thought you asked if I'd ever been to France!'

Ben had started doing a little wiggle in front of the table, hand still beckoning. Lord, why? Even though he was not in full flow, Charlotte could see that he would be one of life's enthusiastic dancers as opposed to one with rhythm.

Now he was threatening to move round the table and

hoist her to her feet and she stood up, glancing with deep embarrassment around her, and took to the dance floor.

'You should have warned me about this!' she yelled into his ear. 'I would have prepared myself!'

'How?'

'By drinking twelve bottles of wine beforehand!'

'You're doing fine!'

She swore that the wretched live band stretched the short number out for as long as possible just for the cabaret spectacle, and even more mortifying was the round of applause that greeted them at the end of the number. And she had been right about Ben. He flung himself around the dance floor like someone hopping on red-hot bricks and, having broken the ice, didn't seem inclined to do the decent thing and scuttle back to the table.

But at least the dance floor was filling out the way it did when two people had broken the ice by making perfect fools of themselves. And it was a slow number, so no more kangaroo hops, at least for the moment. When he wrapped her in his arms, Charlotte forced her body to relax against his and was just beginning to believe that really, yes, she was feeling some kind of physical link between them, when she felt a tap on her shoulder. She raised her head and there he was, staring at her with something close to amusement, and she felt her stomach clench into a knot of pure horror.

What on earth was Riccardo doing in a jazz club in the centre of London? Didn't he have empires to run and universes to conquer? And how was it that, having been absent from her life for the past eight years, he had now been seen twice in the space of a fortnight?

'May I?' He was looking at Ben with a pleasant smile and, poor innocent that he was, Ben was responding with a warm smile back. Couldn't he see that the man was a viper? 'I'm an old friend.'

Charlotte felt Riccardo's hand on her elbow and opened her mouth to stage a protest, only belatedly remembering that she and Ben were supposed to be engaged. What if Riccardo decided to offer his heartfelt congratulations to the happy couple? She plastered a smile on her face and stood between both men, her back to Riccardo, physically keeping them as far apart as she could to prevent any unfortunate conversations taking place.

'You sit!' she shouted to Ben over the music. 'You can get me something to drink—one of those cocktails!'

'Obedient little puppy, isn't he?' Riccardo said, swooping her into a twirl and then pulling her back into him so that their bodies met with way too much force for her liking. Like sleight of hand, he had managed to manoeuvre them into the corner, where the music didn't seem quite as loud so Charlotte didn't have to yell to reply.

'What are you doing here?'

'Do I read disapproval in that question? As far as I am aware, I don't need a special pass from you to get into a jazz club in London. If you remember, I happen to like jazz very much.'

Charlotte was remembering lots of things, and his love of jazz music was the least disconcerting of her memories. She remembered dancing with him out in the open to some tinny music from the speakers on her radio, she remembered the feel of his body pressing against her and the way she had laughed, throwing her head back, looking forward to where all that sexy dancing was going to go later.

'I saw you on the dance floor with the fiancé,' he murmured into her ear. 'Very brave of you.'

'Yes, well, Ben is adventurous like that,' Charlotte said coolly. Every time she tried to inch away from him, he pulled her gently back, his hand placed firmly in the small of her back.

'The man is a paragon.'

'Who are you here with?' Charlotte asked in an attempt to steer the conversation away from her paragon non-fiancé. He would be there with *someone*, or more probably several people, all of them high profile and ultra-glamorous. Riccardo was not a man to indulge his love of jazz by coming to a club on his own.

'A very attractive blonde, as a matter of fact.'

Charlotte felt a jab of pain. 'And you've left the poor woman on her own, to dance with someone who doesn't want to dance with you?'

She felt his hand tighten fractionally, and that felt good because she knew that her remark had got to him. The great Riccardo di Napoli wouldn't like being told that a woman didn't want his company. The great Riccardo di Napoli, with his attractive blonde who was probably sulking in the corner at being left on her own. Well, Charlotte only hoped that it would point the poor thing in the right direction, namely the nearest door through which she could exit as fast as she could if she knew what was good for her.

'He's exactly as I imagined from what you said,' Riccardo drawled. Out of the corner of his eye, he could see Lucinda focus on them, and even in the subdued mood lighting he could detect her frown of displeasure. She was getting demanding and that, didn't sit well with him. He would have to deal with that, but later. Right now, all he could think of was the woman he was holding, the one who wanted to get away. He moved them expertly around, so that his back was to Lucinda's pouting face. 'Looks like a sensitive guy.'

'I'm not going to have this conversation with you.'

'You used to believe in fate. Do you remember?'

'That was then and this is now, Riccardo.' So *that* was his date! Hard to miss, Charlotte thought sourly, considering her height. Six feet at least, with those lethal-weapon stilettos, and hair down to her waist. The sort of woman accustomed to turning heads, several of which were obeying the primitive laws of attraction and swivelling predictably in her direction. Charlotte wished she had worn heels now, if only because they were brilliant at bolstering confidence. But she wore heels every day to work, sensible pumps, and on weekends she liked reverting to flats.

Unfortunately she felt at a depressing disadvantage as she looked up at Riccardo's lean, dark face and met black eyes staring right back at her.

'I gave up believing in fate roughly eight years ago, as a matter of fact. I thought that fate had prompted me on that journey to your house and I couldn't have been more wrong. These days I prefer to make decisions a little more rationally.'

'So you don't think fate had a hand in bringing us together at this point in time?'

Was he flirting with her? Voicing some kind of academic question? Playing with her like a cat plays with a mouse, just to see what it will do? She stiffened.

'Only if fate has a sick sense of humour.'

The music came to an abrupt halt and she quickly pulled away as the leggy blonde Lucinda weaved a dramatic path through the little crowd on the dance floor.

'I think your date's calling, Riccardo!' Charlotte sniggered. 'And she doesn't look too impressed. I should watch out if I were you. Looks like she can pull a mean punch.'

There was nothing more satisfying than getting the last word, she decided as she headed back to Ben, who had obediently got her the cocktail which she no longer wanted.

Before he could say a word, she sat down and leaned closely towards him.

'Small problem,' she said as casually as she could. 'It's really about that man.'

'The man who twirled you across the dance floor? He's very good on his feet, isn't he? I always think that's the problem with Englishmen. They can be a bit stiff when it comes to dancing. Bit like me.'

'You're great, Ben.' She had visions of Riccardo swooping over with the blonde draped on his arm, asking the ridiculous but obvious question 'so when is the big day?' She gulped down a generous mouthful of her Up Against The Wall cocktail. 'But that man is Gina's father…'

Ben's mouth dropped open, and into the surprised silence Charlotte quickly gave him the bare bones of her little white lie.

'I'm truly sorry, Ben. I know I shouldn't have involved you in this, but I honestly didn't know what to do. He doesn't know about Gina and I can't risk him finding out, and…and…'

Ben looked at her shrewdly. 'So we're engaged. Well. Hasn't he noticed that you're not wearing a ring?'

Charlotte shrugged and looked at her slim, smooth ringless fingers. 'And there's something else,' she admitted sheepishly. 'He's… Well, one of these arrogant types, and I sort of implied that you were completely the opposite… You know, loves cooking and listening to music, you know what I mean…'

Ben made a face. 'I can't cook to save my life.' He grinned. 'So we're not engaged,' he said, reading the situation. 'But we're good friends, and if pretending is what you want then we might as well make a good job of it.'

'We probably won't have to!' Charlotte said but when she saw Ben raise his eyebrows and glance over her shoulder she knew that pretending was precisely what they were going to have to do. She looked around to find Riccardo and his Amazon model girlfriend approaching their table. Together they made a striking couple, and as Charlotte had predicted Lucinda was hanging onto his arm, making sure that any greedy female knew that this was her man. Poor, misguided woman, Charlotte thought.

'Riccardo!' She was aware of Ben playing his little game of ownership by placing his hand possessively over hers. 'You're still here! And you must be Lucinda?' She smiled broadly and then, wide-eyed and the picture of innocence said, 'Riccardo couldn't stop talking about you when we were dancing!' Oh yes, that met with the predictable response. Delight in her, tight-lipped disapproval in him. 'I gather you two are in a very serious relationship. Tell me, Riccardo, are congratulations in order?' It was all she could do not to burst out laughing as he tried to back out of the corner into which he had been pushed. He deserved it. Any man who made it his business to string women along deserved to occasionally face the consequences of his actions.

If looks could kill, Charlotte thought that she would have been six feet under by now. She was playing with fire but, with her so-called fiancé at her side, was safe in the knowledge that there was no way she could be burnt.

'Because they are for us!' Ben piped up while Riccardo continued to seethe. 'I've found the perfect woman!' He leant towards Charlotte and playfully rumpled her hair, which didn't strike her as the most romantic of gestures but it worked, judging from the brooding frown on Riccardo's face.

'And Charlie has spoken a lot about *you*,' Riccardo said smoothly, detaching Lucinda from his arm so that they could sit. He had used her nickname deliberately, knowing that it would resurrect memories she wanted to exorcise. If she wanted to play games with him, then who was he not to oblige?

'Yes, I have!' Charlotte gritted her teeth at the familiar use of 'Charlie' and gave Ben a wide, Tinseltown smile. 'I've told him what a gem you are! Always there, making sure I eat well and look after myself.' She looked at Lucinda. Lord, but the woman was a beauty. Right now a vaguely bored looking beauty, but she even managed to pull off bored without losing her glamour. Something about the way she tossed that mane of hair and let her lips fall into a natural pout. 'Guess you find that yourself…?' She flashed a woman-to-woman smile at her and felt Riccardo's glare.

Lucinda gave her a blank look. 'Well, Ric doesn't cook much, if you know what I mean…'

'No?'

'No,' Riccardo said flatly. 'Why cook when someone else can do it so much better?'

'I guess it depends on how much money you have to toss around in restaurants.'

'Oh, I also have my own personal chef.'

'And so do I,' Charlotte returned snidely.

'Bossy lady, isn't she?' Riccardo said to Ben, who had been following their back and forth conversation with interest. 'Like being called someone's "personal chef", do you?'

Charlotte felt a flare of anger and swallowed it back. *Bossy lady!* Coming from the king of arrogance, that was rich! She stood up, not giving Ben time to try and think of something clever to say. He was no match for Riccardo and she wasn't going to sit back and watch him demolished.

'Aubrey says you haven't been in touch about the house,' she said, changing the subject. 'Have you found a better investment somewhere else?'

'It's still under consideration.' Riccardo looked her straight in the eyes. Still as sexy as hell, he thought. Lucinda might be beautiful, but Charlotte was sharp and he liked that. In fact, he had forgotten just how much of a turn-on it was. His dark eyes slid across to where Ben was hurriedly downing the remains of his drink and standing up. The man was either firmly under her thumb, a complete bore with no mind of his own, or the perfect soulmate in a passionless love match, because he wasn't reading anything in their body language.

He shifted so that he could look at them both, and was invigorated by the thought that *he* seemed to rouse her passion a hell of a lot more than her fiancé. Her fiancé who was obviously tight with money, judging from her lack of ring. Of course, her passion might not be of the hop-into-bed variety, but there was a fine line between the passion of anger and the passion of lust. Two sides of the same coin, he thought. He felt the sudden pull of forbidden attraction, and for a few seconds, staring at her, there was no club around them, no fiancé, no Lucinda. He was back in Italy, his body on fire, his head filled with thoughts of when, how and where he was going to bed her.

'And I'll be in touch.'

'What?' Charlotte said sharply.

'About the house. I'll be in touch.'

'Well, you have Aubrey's number.' She turned away, leaving a goggle-eyed Lucinda suddenly very much interested in conversations about houses.

'He'll hate that,' she confided triumphantly to Ben as soon as they were outside, settling themselves into the back of a black cab. 'Some woman with stars in her eyes at the thought of houses and domesticity.' She was so involved in savouring her small bittersweet victory that she missed Ben's thoughtful expression as he watched her, as she leaned forward slightly, her eyes fixed on a distant horizon.

'Least of all a woman who doesn't conform to the well-connected Italian *signorina* he's signed up for. Poor Lucinda. All the looks in the world couldn't buy her an entry into that rarefied Italian world of his.'

It was half an hour before she found that the taxi had stopped outside her house, and only then did she realise that she had been boring the pants off Ben for the entire journey. But the babysitter was waiting inside and there was just no time for lengthy apologies. Just for a grateful peck on the cheek that he had rescued her from a hole that might just have caved in around her.

She hadn't expected him to get in touch with Aubrey. There was no reason for him to buy his big investment house in any particular place, and he would take his time, making sure that he didn't throw good money behind something that wasn't going to reap him the maximum profit.

Anyway, he would be too busy trying to disentangle himself from the lovely Lucinda, just as he had disentangled himself from *her* eight years ago when she had foolishly believed that they'd been more than just a passing fling.

So on the Saturday morning, half an hour after she had returned from dropping Gina to play with one of her friends from school who lived a couple of streets away, Charlotte thought nothing when the doorbell went. She lived in a semi on a pretty, busy side street which looked deceptively peaceful because someone, years ago, had thought to plant trees here and there along the pavements. She was accustomed to people knocking on the door trying to sell her anything, from window cleaning to one-to-one power-yoga tuition.

Dressed in faded dungarees, hair scraped back with an Alice band and with her furniture polish in one hand—because she'd been going to utilise her Gina-free time by getting down and dirty with her cleaning stuff—she pulled open the front door, and froze.

'You're going to ask me what I'm doing here. I know.' Riccardo glanced behind her to the white, white walls, the glimpse of abstract paintings, the bare pine floorboards, then he returned his attention to her shocked face. All her colour had drained away and her eyes looked enormous. He could see her think about closing the door on him, but she must have realised that the gesture would have been a futile one because he knew where she lived and he would come back. Also, he had managed to inveigle a position in the doorway which would have made any door slamming pretty difficult.

'Go away,' Charlotte said shakily. 'You can't just…just *show up* on my doorstep like this! If you want to discuss the house, you have to talk to Aubrey. How did you get my address anyway? How do you know where I live? Did Aubrey tell you?'

'No. Are you going to invite me in?'

Charlotte considered her options quickly. She either forced him to go, somehow managed to slam the door in his face, which would certainly involve a struggle, and he would return. She knew he would. Or she stayed on her doorstep holding forth and thereby risking Gina appearing unexpectedly. Or she politely invited him in, listened to what he had to say, and then dispatched him without fuss. No contest—option three. She pulled open the door and stepped back so that he could brush past her.

'How did you find out where I lived?'

'I have my ways. Nice place.' He started heading towards the kitchen and she quickly forestalled him. The fridge was a riot of childish drawings and bits of paper announcing various school happenings. A danger zone, in other words.

'If you want to go into the sitting room, Riccardo, but I can't be long. I'm...I'm on my way out.'

'Clutching a can of furniture polish?'

Charlotte had forgotten about that. 'After I do a bit of dusting, naturally. And change. I do all my housework on a Saturday.'

'I'm surprised your fiancé doesn't help out there. Seems the kind of guy to enjoy a spot of dusting. Where is he anyway?'

'What do you want, Riccardo? Why have you come here?'

'Because you've been on my mind.' Their eyes met, and Charlotte felt a sickening lurch somewhere in her stomach. God, his voice could still do things to her! And looking at him now... He was casually dressed. On most other men, the dark grey trousers and grey jumper would frankly have looked insipid. Riccardo looked devastating. He had a body that was fashioned for those immaculately tailored Italian clothes he wore. Tall, broad shouldered, lean hipped. Charlotte swallowed and told herself to focus.

'Oh yes?'

'Oh yes,' he mimicked her gravely as he sat on one of the sofas and crossed his legs.

Around him the little room, which she had taken so much time and effort to decorate with honey, cream and oatmeal colours, looked average and uninspired. She didn't sit down, preferring to remain hovering by the doorway significantly, even though she felt a mess in her dungarees and thick, padded socks. She had to do something with the hair, though. She needed the comfort of feeling it around her face, providing cover, so she yanked off the Alice band and continued to look at him blandly.

'That was a pretty annoying stunt you pulled the other night,' Riccardo said. 'Letting Lucinda believe that there was more to our liaison than there was.'

'I don't happen to think it's fair the way you treat women. I could tell that she wants more from you than a hop in the sack, and if you can't provide that "more" then you should be upfront.'

'And, just in case I wasn't, you were prepared to jump in and be upfront on my behalf. Or at least land me in as much bother as you could. Payback for bumping into you accidentally after eight years.'

'Okay. If you've come here looking for an apology, then I apologise. Satisfied?'

'No.' Riccardo stretched out his long legs and settled back into the sofa. 'I told you. You've been on my mind.'

Charlotte went across to the chair facing him and flopped bonelessly into it. Standing by the door, trying to be a woman in control, was difficult when your legs felt like jelly. 'I'm not interested, Riccardo.'

'Aren't you? Is that why you're shaking like a leaf? Because you're so *indifferent* to me?' Riccardo watched her nervously sweep her fingers through her hair. He could almost hear the cranking of the gears in her head as she tried to formulate a verbal deterrent. Really and truly, he hadn't known what he was going to say to her once he arrived on her doorstep. Yes, he'd been annoyed at her interference with Lucinda, but that had not been anything he hadn't been able to deal with.

More complex was his reaction to Charlotte. Ever since he had bumped into her, he had been behaving out of character, and for the life of him he couldn't understand why. He just knew that he had resurrected an old relationship with Lucinda to prove to himself that the blonde who had surfaced after eight years meant nothing to him. It hadn't worked, and he couldn't figure out how a man like him, a man who could have any woman he wanted, would find himself going crazy with thoughts of a woman who wanted nothing to do with him.

Bumping into them, seeing her with her fiancé, had clarified at least one piece of the puzzle.

He wanted her. Whether he liked the fact or not. Hence sitting here now, on her sofa, watching her seethe in impotent frustration at his presence in her house.

'Why don't you just tell me what you want, Riccardo? I've apologised over the Lucinda thing, and I meant it. What you do is no business of mine.' But watching him squirm had been worth its weight in gold!

'And what *you* do shouldn't be any business of *mine*, but I find that it is.'

Charlotte felt faint. Out of the corner of her eye she could see the hands of her watch ticking. Time was creeping by and Riccardo was showing no signs of leaving.

In one split instant, she realised that she had made a

fatal error. She had hoped to quench Riccardo's curiosity by producing a fiancé and she had also, she'd thought, killed two birds with one stone because she'd figured that a fiancé would show him just how much her life had moved on.

She should have known that his curiosity over Ben would not have politely stopped the minute she'd hopped in her little car and driven away. Riccardo was not a polite person. If he hadn't bumped into her at that club, then sooner or later he would have tracked her down, because he would have wanted to meet the man he thought she was intimately involved with.

He was staring at her, waiting for her to respond, and knowing that with each passing second of silence her discomfort was increasing.

Casually he let his eyes drift through the room. Pale colours. Not what he would have expected from a woman with a deeply passionate nature, but then maybe she was trying to stifle that passion. A small flat-screen television was perched on top of an antique pine bookcase. And in front of that row of books…

Riccardo stood up and strolled towards the bookcase, then he squatted down and looked at the framed pictures. They were all of the same person. He picked one up and stood up.

'Who is she? That niece of yours in Australia?'

Charlotte literally couldn't answer because her vocal cords seemed to have seized up. Nor could she get to her feet and do something useful like snatch the photo from him. Not when her legs had turned to lead.

Nor did she have to, because as his question hung in

the silence the sound of the doorbell was already answering his question.

'Are you going to get that?' He replaced the photo on the shelf, but remained standing where he was. 'Might be someone important.'

Charlotte stood up shakily and looked at him.

'Yes. Yes, I'm sure it will be…'

CHAPTER FIVE

GINA had been to the corner shop with Amy and her mum and had returned the proud owner of a very large bag of teeth-destroying sweets. Despite a daily diet of healthy foods, and stern chats about the horrors of eating sweets, she still saved her pocket money for her weekly sugar fix. For once, Charlotte didn't frown, shake her head and tell her that there was no way she would be allowed to eat the lot in one go. In fact, she opened the door and stood there, looking at her beautiful daughter who bore such a stunning resemblance to the man sitting in her lounge.

'Are you feeling sick, Mum?' Gina frowned anxiously. 'You could have one of my sweets, if you like,' she said kindly. 'But not any of the orange ones.'

'Come in, baby.'

Gina looked at her mother in alarm. This was not the normal Saturday sweet-buying routine. She popped a Fruit Pastille nervously into her mouth and was even more alarmed when nothing was said. 'I promise I'll tidy my room *right now*,' she declared.

'There's someone I think you need to meet, Gina.'

'Is it Mr Forbes?' Her eyes began to well up. 'Because it wasn't my fault that I forgot to do my homework!'

'You forgot to do your homework?' Charlotte was momentarily distracted, then she remembered Riccardo in the lounge and gave Gina a reassuring smile. 'No, it's not Mr Forbes.' Very gently she helped her daughter out of her puffy black coat, then the black boots, until she was left just in her pair of jeans and long-sleeved black jumper. Charlotte had given up trying to coax her daughter into pink a long time ago.

'Okay?' Charlotte asked, and Gina nodded and slipped another sweet into her mouth which, pleasantly surprised, she got away with.

Charlotte was holding Gina's hand as they walked into the lounge to find Riccardo standing by the window, arms folded. They both stopped by the door and, on a roll, Gina dipped her hand into the bag of sweets, only for Charlotte to relieve her of it and place it on a side table.

'Riccardo, I'd like you to meet Gina.'

Gina stood stock still by her mother's side and stared unblinkingly at the man looking at her.

'That's a pretty name,' Riccardo said, for want of anything better. He had next to no experience of children. As an only child, there had been no nephews or nieces. 'How old you are?' he asked, discomfited by the silence that greeted his trite remark.

'Gina's eight,' Charlotte said quickly, waiting to see if the penny would drop. But of course it didn't. There was no reason for him to think that Gina was *her* daughter, and in the absence of that crucial piece of information she would just be a random kid to him.

She could feel tension clawing its way in her stomach, and she licked her lips and tightened her grip on Gina's hand. Riccardo was beginning to look faintly bored. Didn't he wonder at all what an eight-year-old child was doing in her house?

'I'm in Year Four at St Bart's Primary school,' Gina piped up. 'I'm top of my class in maths *and* english,' she said proudly. 'Last week I got a *star* award!' She looked at Charlotte. 'Didn't I, Mum?'

Charlotte watched as Riccardo's brain shifted into gear, heading towards the inexorable conclusion. He went very, very still and his eyes sharpened on Gina's face, taking in the dark, tumbling curls, the big brown eyes, the slightly olive skin—putting two and two together.

Having broken the ice, Gina, self-assured like her father, began to chat about her star award, offering to fetch it for a viewing, while Riccardo looked at her in frozen silence.

'Eight years old,' he said finally, in an oddly unsteady voice. 'And when exactly is your birthday, Gina?'

'Gina, you need to go and clean that room of yours now… And as a special treat…' Charlotte snatched the bag of sweets from the table and thrust it into her daughter's astounded hand with a strained smile. 'But only this once! Because I need to have a private little chat with Riccardo. So, after you clean your room, you can… you can…' She could feel Riccardo's eyes boring into her, and she didn't need to read the expression in them because her imagination was well equipped to provide it for her. 'You can play on your games console!' Whilst not quite as bad as the sweets issue, Gina's computer games were a limited treat. She grinned happily and didn't wait for her mother to change her mind which, she had discovered, adults had a way of doing. She dashed up the stairs, and Charlotte closed the door gently behind her. She had to lean against the closed door to support herself.

'Oh, dear God, tell me that you weren't… Dios! Tell me that you weren't pregnant…' Riccardo said in a flat, stunned voice. For the first time in his life he felt as though life had turned around and kicked him in the stomach, and then, having done so, had returned to repeat the exercise. He sat down heavily on the sofa and rested his elbows on his knees. The thoughts in his head were moving so quickly that he felt physically sick. He dropped his head in his hands and stared down at the floor.

'Look,' Charlotte said awkwardly. 'I didn't mean for you to find out this way.' She took a couple of tentative steps towards the chair, and Riccardo turned his head to look at her with savage contempt.

'What you're saying is that you didn't mean for me to find out at *all*!' That small dark-haired child whom he had viewed with just mild curiosity was his own *flesh and blood*! Riccardo felt a surge of rage wash through him with the force of a tidal wave, and he had to breathe deeply or else succumb to a violence he had never felt before. Which wouldn't do. Already his mind was working quickly, trying to figure out how best to handle the unbelievable.

Charlotte didn't say anything. He was beginning to scare her, not because she felt he might become physically threatening, but because there was a coldness in his eyes that was even more menacing. 'You don't understand!' she said defensively.

'Then why don't you enlighten me?'

Charlotte could see that the last thing he wanted was enlightenment. He was not going to be prepared to listen to what she had to say, but there was no way that she was going to remain silent.

Riccardo watched as she walked tentatively towards the chair. She looked as though one false move on his part and she would run a mile, and she would be right, he thought, because right now his precious self-control was wearing very thin at the edges. His head was cluttered with images of the child who had told him about her star award, to whom he had shown only passing, polite interest.

'When I left Italy I had no idea that I was pregnant,' Charlotte said tightly. 'We were so careful. Just a couple of times. Well, that was all it took. '

'And so, when you discovered that you were, you just decided that you would eliminate me from the picture,' Ricardo said, his voice cold and steady.

'You made it perfectly clear that I had been a passing fling. You didn't need your life cluttered up with a clingy girlfriend. The last thing you would want would be your life cluttered up with a responsibility that would last a lifetime.'

'My own child.' Riccardo tried to get his head around that and found that he couldn't. 'How *dare* you sit there and calmly tell me what I would or would not have wanted when it came to my own flesh and blood!'

'And how dare you sit there and imply that what I did was a deliberate act of cruelty!' Charlotte returned hotly.

She glanced at the closed door and lowered her voice, because children had a knack of appearing just when you didn't want them to. 'I was in pieces when I left Italy. How do you imagine *I* felt when I found out that I was pregnant, alone here, with no means of income and a university career that was over before it had had a chance to begin? Don't you think that I wished I could turn to you for support?' Charlotte took a bitter trip down memory lane. 'Yes, I admit it briefly crossed my mind to get in touch with you, although that would have been difficult enough. Every time the thought crossed my mind, I imagined what your reaction would be. To not want someone to be part of your life and then find out that you're lumbered with their offspring…'

'That's no excuse! What kind of monster do you think I am, that I would deny my own child?'

'Actually there are quite a few men who turn tail and run the minute they know their girlfriend's pregnant. Believe me, it's not exactly a unique reaction!'

'I am not "quite a few men"!'

Charlotte took a deep breath and looked at him. 'I was scared, Riccardo. I had walked out of a lion's den. I wasn't about to head straight back into it. You didn't want me…' God, it still hurt even now to say that. 'You didn't want me, and the way I saw it was that, even if I went straight back to Italy and broke the happy news to you, you would either send me on my way again or else take my baby away from me!'

'*Our* baby!'

'There's no point getting into a great big argument about it now, Riccardo. What's done is done.'

'It never occurred to tell me at *any point* along the way that I was a father?'

'I built my life without you. It's not like I chose the easy option.'

Riccardo stood up abruptly, so abruptly that it took a few seconds for Charlotte to register that he was going. But going where?

'You're not taking my daughter away from me!' She sprang to her feet, ready to do anything it took to avert that eventuality. 'Don't imagine that you can use your money and influence to have Gina!'

'I cannot stay under this roof a minute longer,' Riccardo said savagely. 'I need to go away and think.'

'Think about what?' She reached for his arm, and he shrugged her away.

'I'll be back, and when I return, believe me, I will come with a solution!'

'A solution?' What kind of solution? Did he imagine that this was an intriguing little conundrum that could be sorted out, the way he sorted out his problems at work?

But she was relieved that he wasn't storming up the stairs, two at a time, so that he could shake Gina's world to its foundations. Although, she knew that the time had come to tell her daughter about her dad. Of course she had asked questions in the past, but really not that many. They had been content to live in their happy little bubble, and Charlotte had shoved the future and all its attendant problems, when Gina got older and grew more curious, to the back of her mind.

But she would wait a while, and over the next four days the waiting nearly killed her. She lived on her nerves, expecting the doorbell to go at any moment, with Riccardo and his lawyer standing on her doorstep demanding custody, even though she knew, thinking rationally, that there was no way he could pull that off. But, then again, Riccardo could pull off anything or at least that was the impression he gave.

In the end, she telephoned Aubrey and bared her soul. She wanted to hear him soothe all those irrational fears away, which he did, but it wasn't enough. She had to find out what Riccardo was up to; she had to steal his march.

'Aubrey, I just have to know where he is. I have to get in touch with him.'

'Leave it with me.'

And less than two hours later she knew. All those years, and she could have bumped into him at any time. She had lived her life in blissful ignorance of the danger lurking virtually on her doorstep. Because his offices were in London, not a million miles away from where she worked, and shockingly close to a couple of penthouse suites she had sold to overseas investors. They probably would have bumped into each other at that jazz club much earlier if she had had any kind of active social life. She knew the area well, as he no doubt did too, and they both loved jazz.

Of course, she knew that he would probably not have spent all of his time in London, but still.

It took all her courage to take the bull by its horns and confront Riccardo on his own turf. It had been bad enough dealing with him in the safe confines of her own house, but, as she dressed carefully for the meeting she had never really anticipated, she could feel her stomach work itself into a series of knots.

Her normal morning routine had a nightmarish feel to it, and she had even sent Gina off to school with a chocolate bar nestled next to her sandwich and yoghurt. Then she had looked at herself in the mirror, a long, hard look. Not that it would make a scrap of difference, she wanted to present herself as a model human being. Fat chance of him falling in line with *that* plan, she thought, heading out and hailing the first taxi she could find so that she didn't have to battle with the underground.

She didn't know whether he would be in or not, and, as the taxi dropped her off in front of one of those paeans to modern architecture that left her cold, she half hoped that he would be out—somewhere safely abroad, tucked away on a continent far from her and Gina.

However, if he did happen to be around, then she was pretty certain that she would be ushered up to his office the minute she gave her name. A bit like a rabbit being shown straight to the lion's den.

It was an analogy she wished she hadn't thought of, as the girl at Reception put through a call and was told that Mr di Napoli was indeed in and, yes, having been given Charlotte's name, he would see her.

Better than that, his secretary would fetch her from Reception! The girl at the desk looked at Charlotte with new-found respect. Maybe the neatly turned out blonde with the frankly unadventurous outfit had a bit more going for her than she'd originally thought.

Charlotte's unadventurous outfit had been planned for a purpose. The purpose was to show Riccardo that when it came to Gina she meant business, that she was not going to be steamrollered by him, but neither was her intention to wage war or go on the immediate attack. Hence she had decided on a suit in a sensible colour. Grey. But it was a trouser suit, and she was wearing a cheerful burgundy jumper with the trousers.

Now if she could only get her mind to be as relaxed and confident as her outfit, she thought as the elevator purred its way up to the top floor, she might be getting somewhere.

But her mind refused to be reined in. Riccardo *affected* her. She wished it was simply a case of hate, which was what she had been at pains to imply, combined with a healthy dose of apprehension and resentment at the situation in which she now found herself, but there was something else. It was like a dangerous snake rustling in the undergrowth, and Charlotte knew that there was still an attraction there for her. Worse, she suspected that it had always been there, just lying in wait, and now that he had shown up on the scene it had surfaced and was gathering force.

Poor Ben. She had seen him the evening before and had apologetically told him that he should think of finding someone else.

'I don't deserve you, Ben,' Charlotte had said truthfully, reaching across the table and linking her fingers through his. 'You're a nice guy, and you need a woman who doesn't come with an armful of complications.'

'You mean a woman who doesn't come with a rival.'

'No!' She'd made a dismissive, snorting noise. 'Riccardo? A rival? Not in a million years! But I'm in a messy situation just at the moment, and it's not fair that you get caught up in the undertow.'

'Maybe it's a good thing that he knows about Gina.'

'You wouldn't say that if you knew the man.' She had been pleased and relieved that Ben had taken it so well. In fact, they had parted on the best possible terms, agreeing to remain friends. Later she wondered whether he could ever have been right for her, or she right for him, if breaking up had been such a painless affair.

The elevator shuddered to a stop. She was aware that Riccardo's secretary had been making polite conversation with her, and she wondered whether she could get away with murmuring something vague because the last thing she needed was a chat with someone she didn't know. Not when she was fighting to control her desire to run away. She wondered what the pleasant, middle-aged, grey-haired woman would say if she blurted out the truth: that she had come to discuss her boss's parental visiting rights to his eight-year-old daughter. How much greyer could grey hair turn?

Riccardo's office was at the very end of a long corridor, on either side of which thick doors alerted the uninitiated that the people sitting behind them were *very* important. The double-fronted wooden doors at the end of the corridor thereby sent the clear message that the person behind them was *beyond* very important.

And of course, Charlotte thought as his secretary pushed open the door, a beyond-very-important man wouldn't do something as crazily simple as come to the door to greet them. He would be staring out of his virtually floor-to-ceiling glass windows at all those small, lesser folk tramping the city streets below, as Riccardo was now doing.

She heard the door shut gently behind her and took a deep breath as Riccardo slowly turned around. For him, the past few days had seen him suffer the agonies of confusion that everyone endures at various points in their lives, but which for him were novel and unwelcome emotions. He could count on the fingers of one hand the number of hours' sleep he had had, and he was functioning at work on automatic level.

He had given himself nearly a week to absorb the situation, because he really hadn't trusted himself to return to her house and deal with it in a controlled and adult manner. Now he was glad that she had appeared on his doorstep, so to speak, because she was in his territory. He recalled that feeling of trying to walk in quicksand when he had been at her house, as he had watched the foundations of his orderly world disappear out of reach, and his mouth tightened.

'I realise you said that you would be in touch,' Charlotte said without bothering with any phoney pleasantries. 'But I can't just sit around and wait until you decide the time is right to come knocking on my door with your so-called "solution".'

'Sit.' It was a command rather than an invitation, and Charlotte momentarily hesitated, not liking the fact that he was issuing orders. He had never been like this years ago, had he? Then she told herself that it was not in her interests to keep remembering the man who he had once been. It distracted her from the man who he now was, and this was the man she had to keep at a distance, whatever physical connection existed between them in the form of their daughter.

She sat and was relieved when he followed suit, although in his case it was behind his grand desk, which was a feat of modern carpentry, multi-grained wood with lines so smooth that it looked untouched by human hand.

'So?' Riccardo pushed himself away from the desk so that he could cross his legs at an angle, then he looked at her, in no rush to break the silence. Of course, he was mildly interested in what she had to say and would certainly give her her chance to speak, but already he knew his solution. As he had watched her hovering there by the door, it had come to him as an almost inevitable conclusion.

'I don't want to talk about the past. I know how you feel, I know you think that I should somehow have appeared heavily pregnant on your mother's doorstep, even if I was terrified that you would have taken my baby away from me. I guess, in your mind, I should have been prepared to do that as well. I was just a scared, disillusioned kid, but I should have mustered up the courage and taken whatever was doled out to me by you and your mother.'

Riccardo scowled. Put like that, he could feel a reluctant sympathy. In fact, put like that, he didn't much care for the person he had been eight years ago. He was guiltily aware of how terrifying it must have been for her to have shown up unannounced, only to find her arrival greeted with rejection. Of course, that was no excuse to have denied him his rights as a father, but he could reluctantly see her point of view.

'But I didn't, and, yes, don't imagine that I didn't think about letting you know when Gina was born, when she was growing up.'

'But you successfully managed to squash the temptation.'

'Temptation isn't exactly the word I would have used,' Charlotte admitted truthfully. 'It felt more like a duty that I just…well, could put off. I imagined how you would react, and it was easier to walk away from dealing with the situation.'

'Would you *ever* have mustered the courage or would you have been happy to let sleeping dogs lie—maybe tell Gina that her father had died, make up some story when she started asking too many questions?'

Charlotte looked at him with genuine horror. 'What kind of person do you think I am?'

'The kind who takes the easy way out!'

'Not to the point of lying to Gina about you! I always knew that sooner or later she would demand to know who you were, and I was prepared for that!'

Riccardo didn't point out that by that indeterminate point in the future he would have been a complete stranger to his daughter, and the possibility of any bonding would have been close to zero. She was right. It would be easy to become locked in perpetual arguing over who had been right and who had been wrong, but in the end there was fault on both sides.

Although, he told himself piously, *he* had obviously been the loser.

'So you came here to tell me…?' Riccardo dragged the matter out of the boxing ring and back into civilised territory.

Charlotte took a deep breath. She had given the matter a great deal of thought. 'I think I should be the one to tell

Gina about you.' She held up her hand to stave off an interruption that hadn't been voiced. 'And then you can meet her. Of course, you'll want to get to know her…'

Charlotte had visions of Riccardo becoming a semi-permanent figure in her life, a man who didn't want her but was tied to her because of an accident that had happened in the past. Would he resent her more and more as time went on? How would she feel when he got married, had children of his own? 'And I'm not going to stand in your way. We can work out the nuts and bolts of where and when, but basically I'm willing to be generous with access. Also—' she had nearly forgotten this point '—I don't want any money from you. Eight years ago your mother accused me of being a gold-digger, even though I told her that I hadn't known your financial background, and—'

'When?' Riccardo asked sharply.

'When she showed me up to that room.'

'I didn't know.'

Charlotte shrugged. 'It doesn't matter now, but you need to understand that I don't want anything from you. Nothing. Not a penny.'

His mother had done more damage than he had thought. What else had she said? She was frail now after a fall, but would still be too proud to admit to having made errors in the way she had handled the situation way back then. Another unwilling tug of sympathy.

He stood up and strolled across to the window, which had splendid views over London. For a few seconds he idly followed the progress of people scurrying across pavements as he marshalled his thoughts, then he turned around to look at her.

'So I see my daughter, say, once a week? Twice a week? When I happen to be in London? Because I travel a hell of a lot. And how long do I see her for?—maybe an hour or two after school? Because she would have homework to do, I suppose.'

'There *are* weekends,' Charlotte pointed out, not liking the direction of his comments, or his tone of voice. 'You could see her every other weekend…'

'Except when she's going out, I guess.'

'Why are you making this difficult, Riccardo? It works for loads of other people.'

Riccardo shrugged and walked towards her. For a tall, muscular man his movements had always been graceful and economic, but she still felt to cringe back in the chair, especially when he leant over her and placed his hands on either side of her, palms gripping the arms of her chair.

Up close like this he literally did take her breath away. It was as if she had to create a force field to ward off his dynamism, and she could just about have succeeded, but the minute he closed the physical gap between them she had no protection against the stark power of his presence.

'But not for me. It doesn't work for me, Charlie.'

Charlotte didn't have the strength to remind him that she no longer used that abbreviated nickname. She felt trapped by those amazing eyes with their idiotically long lashes. She used to tease him about that!

'No?' she managed to croak.

'No. I don't intend to be one of those part-time dads, trying to forge a bond for four hours a week. Nor do I intend to watch another man raise my own flesh and blood.'

It took a few seconds for Charlotte to realise that he was talking about Ben. She opened her mouth to protest, but he wasn't about to let her interrupt. She had had her say. Now it was time for his.

'Gina is my daughter, and she will take my name and have all the privileges that are her due!'

'What are you saying?' Charlotte whispered.

'We will be married. Of course. That way I will see my child and be responsible for her on a full-time basis.' He thrust himself away from her and Charlotte remained in a little pool of stupefied silence.

Eventually she said, 'You're kidding, aren't you?'

'Why would you think that?' He perched on his desk and stared down at her.

'Because it's a ridiculous suggestion?'

'To you, maybe. To me, it makes perfect sense. I can give Gina everything she could possibly need or want, and in addition I would have her there, would be able to fulfil my fatherly duties full time, have a say in the decisions that will affect her as the years go by. We get married, and you won't have to work. You can be a full-time mother. There are no drawbacks to this plan. So you can wipe that expression off your face.'

'And my role would be…?'

'You're her mother, of course. Your role in her life would remain unchanged.'

'But aside from that every other aspect of my life would be turned on its head, but that would be okay just so long as you get your own way.'

'There's no point arguing about it, Charlie. We will be married.'

'When did you become like this, Riccardo?'

'Like what?'

'Arrogant. Intransigent. Thinking that you can have whatever you want with the click of a finger.'

Riccardo flushed darkly and glared at her. 'Because I'm not soft? Because I don't subscribe to the theory that men should not be ashamed to cry? That doesn't make me arrogant.' But he *was* arrogant, and the admission made him wince inwardly. 'My solution would be for the best.'

'You solution is insane!' She stood up and controlled the shaking of her hands by dusting off some non-existent specks of fluff from her trousers. 'I know you feel that I've deprived you of time you should have spent with Gina, but I won't allow you to steal my life because you want to create a false family unit.'

'Steal your life?'

'That's right.' She looked at him squarely in the face without flinching. 'Marriage at all costs for the sake of a child might be the Italian way, Riccardo. But it's not mine.'

CHAPTER SIX

AND they hadn't even got around to his fulminating diatribe about the fiancé!

Riccardo glared at the bottle of wine staring reproachfully at him from his gleaming black, granite kitchen counter. One glass for Dutch courage, something he had never needed in his life before, but which he seemed to need now because he was about to see his daughter for the first time.

After her incredulous rejection of his marriage proposal—something he fancied very few women would have turned down without even bothering to give it a second thought—Charlotte had stalked out of his office and he had stayed put, imprisoned by his own pride which had absolutely forbidden him to follow her, beg her to reconsider and listen to the advantages. The obvious advantages.

Four hours later he had phoned and coldly told her that he would respect her ridiculous refusal to listen to common sense, but he'd demanded that she tell Gina about him.

'Of course I will,' Charlotte had said, for all the world

as though anything else would have been incomprehensible. 'And you can come and visit with her tomorrow after school. I don't want to fight you over this, Riccardo.'

'Very generous,' he had muttered with heavy sarcasm, but the arrangement had been made and now here he was, as nervous as a kid waiting to be seen by the headmaster. He swept his trench coat from the counter, drank the contents of his wine glass in one long gulp and headed out of the door.

He had a driver on permanent call, but this time he would be taking a black cab. George was as perfect a driver as he could hope to find, which meant that he never asked questions and could be counted on for his discretion, but a secret child? That might have been taking temptation too far, and Riccardo needed to come to terms with the situation himself before opening the door to the inevitable furore of gossip.

On the way, staring out at the dark, bleak and cluttered city streets, he marshalled his wayward thoughts into coherent points. Point one would be elimination of the fiancé. He wasn't going to share his child with another man and that was just something she would have to accept.

Since when, he wondered, had she become so damned *mouthy*?

He frowned and thought of her glowering in his office, *laughing* at his proposal and then refusing to budge! Indeed, walking out!

Well, the fiancé would be a thing of the past if he had to set up camp in her house and supervise her movements like a babysitter!

The taxi drew up outside the house and nerves ripped through him like a knife. He had bought a stuffed toy. A very large one. What else did one buy for a child with whom you were intimately connected and yet didn't know you from Adam?

He felt utterly foolish and stupidly terrified as he pressed the doorbell and heard it reverberate inside the house.

Charlotte opened the door, and behind her was Gina.

'What on earth is that?' Charlotte smiled reluctantly at the sight of Riccardo clutching an oversized brown-and-white stuffed dog. It was a very floppy stuffed animal and its limbs drooped over his hands as though it had decided to fall into a deep sleep, leaving its owner slightly bewildered as to what he was doing with the thing in the first place.

'It's a dog.'

'Gina, come and meet—'

'I…I brought you this…' Riccardo heard himself stumble over his words and he looked to Charlotte for help.

'It's gorgeous, isn't it, Gina? Come in. Look at this dog! It's the biggest stuffed animal I've ever seen! It's almost as big as your room, honey. Where are you going to put it? You should thank your…your…'

'Dad,' Gina said, one eye on the dog, one eye on Riccardo. She smiled shyly and took the dog, and all at once Riccardo felt foolishly, ridiculously happy. Nothing like the sort of happy he felt when he closed a deal or staged a takeover. This was a feeling that penetrated through to parts of him he hadn't known were there.

'Why don't you go upstairs and show…show your dad where you're going to put that wonderful dog.'

It was as easy as that. The door closed behind him, he removed his coat and followed his daughter up to her room. Both threw Charlotte a look of hesitancy, but Charlotte ignored that. She had told Gina about her father, had glossed over the whys and wherefores, and had left so many threads dangling that it was a wonder she hadn't become entangled in her own story. But Gina had not asked any awkward questions. Her childish eyes had lit up, and for the first time Charlotte had realised how much of a disservice she had done her daughter, although every decision made had been made in good faith.

She closed her eyes and sagged against the banister, then after a few minutes up she went, hearing their voices before she appeared in the doorway.

Gina was showing him her handheld games console, which had been her last birthday present, and explaining how it worked while Riccardo listened in what appeared to be fascinated silence.

For a few seconds Charlotte watched the scenario, then she cleared her throat and they both looked round at her.

'I thought it might be nice if we went out for a meal,' she said.

'Fish and chips?' Gina asked hopefully. 'Do you like fish and chips, Dad?'

'I…I love it.'

'Nice try,' Charlotte said dryly. She looked at Riccardo in a moment of unthinking shared honesty at the wiles of an eight-year-old. 'We try and limit the greasy food, so we'll take you to the Italian on the corner. They do a very nice, and very healthy, *pomodoro* pasta.'

'Mum hates junk food. Do you hate junk food?'

'Junk food?' Riccardo asked.

'That's not something your dad's probably ever had in his life before.'

'You've *never* had junk food? *Ever?*' On which subject Gina maintained a steady and incredulous conversation as they gathered up their coats and headed out of the house, Riccardo on one side, Charlotte on the other and Gina between them.

'What do you eat, then?' she demanded as they perused the menu and she perused them.

'Oh, all sorts of things.' Riccardo smiled, liking her directness but alarmed by it as well. 'Mostly I eat out.'

'Isn't that very expensive?'

'Gina, please!'

'Mum says you're not married. Do you have a girlfriend?'

'Well, no.'

Gina smiled triumphantly at both of them, but before she could really and truly put her eight-year-old feet firmly in it Charlotte said hurriedly, 'And let's just leave it there.'

She looked at Riccardo and could see him processing his daughter's stray remark, putting it somewhere safe for future reference.

Later, with an overtired and overexcited Gina finally in bed, Charlotte made her way downstairs to find Riccardo in the kitchen, scrutinising all the childish bits of schoolwork that had been stuck to the noticeboard on the wall behind the kitchen table.

'I thought that went okay,' she said cautiously.

'I think we need to talk.'

'What about?' Charlotte had seen hundreds of sides of Riccardo in the past, all the bits and pieces that went to make up this complex man, but she now realised that she had only ever seen a fraction of what he was all about—because tonight had been a revelation. She had watched him listen with humour and consideration, and ask questions to which he patently knew the answers. It had been a bizarre situation, a brush with true domesticity that she had never had. There had been times during the course of the evening when she had had to remind herself that they weren't a happy little family unit straight out of *The Waltons*, but two people united in a false situation for the sake of their child.

'Where to begin?'

'Not with accusations.'

'Then let's start with this fiancé of yours, shall we?'

'Okay, but—'

'No, no *buts*, Charlie.' Riccardo thought of the way his daughter laughed, the way she grinned, the way she pulled herself up straight when she thought she was on the verge of making an important point to adults. When he thought of another man sharing those moments, he felt physically ill.

'You kept my daughter from me for eight years. You tell me you won't marry me, allow me to legitimise my own daughter, and I can't force you to walk up an aisle with me.'

She thought he looked as though he'd like to have given it a good try, however.

'I explained that.'

'Keep quiet!' He banged his fist on the kitchen table and Charlotte jumped. 'I… Tonight has been one of the hardest nights of my entire life. I've had to watch my daughter and wonder at all the missed years.' He looked at her and raked his fingers through his hair. 'I won't have another man bring my child up.'

'There's no question of that,' Charlotte said quickly.

'You get rid of him, do you understand me?'

I already have. 'Or else what?' She folded her arms and stuck her chin up.

'Or else,' Riccardo growled, 'I'll move into this house, lock stock and barrel, and set up camp! Would you like that? My computer taking over the kitchen table? My shoes at the bottom of the stairs? I know Gina wouldn't mind. Did you see her eyes light up when I told her that her daddy didn't have a girlfriend? How do you think she'd react if I asked her whether she wanted me and her mother to live together?' Okay, he knew it was below the belt, but that stubbornness was driving him crazy and even worse was the suspicion that the touchy-feely boyfriend was to blame. Eight years ago one touch and she'd been his. Now he was the dinosaur, deposed by someone who could cook a mean quiche.

'That's not fair!' Charlotte said hotly.

'Then lose the boyfriend.' Riccardo stood up, but there was precious little room in the kitchen. He felt hemmed in and suddenly in need of a drink. He had dutifully stuck to water during the meal. Now he opened her fridge and extracted a half-full bottle of supermarket white wine.

'Make yourself at home,' Charlotte said sarcastically.

'Oh, believe me, I intend to. Where do you keep your glasses?'

'Sit down. I'll get them.' She reached up and her jumper rose, exposing a slither of skin. Riccardo found himself savouring the tantalising glimpse. 'You think it's all right for me to disrupt my life, chuck a guy I happen to like a great deal?'

'*Like?* That says it all, Charlie.'

'Stop calling me that!'

'Why? Because it reminds you too much of when we were young and couldn't get enough of one another?'

Suddenly it was as if the oxygen had been sucked out of the tiny kitchen. A sense of erotic, forbidden intimacy shoved its way through the tense atmosphere, and her hand was shaking as she put his glass of wine in front of him and took a hearty swig of hers.

'You're going to *marry* a guy because you *like* him?' Riccardo gave a snort of derisive laughter that made her hackles rise.

'Affection happens to be a very important part of a relationship!'

'So is passion, and I didn't witness much of that when I saw the two of you together!'

'Well, we weren't all over each other like a *rash*, if that's what you mean! And, on the subject of other halves, now that you're laying down laws, what about *your* other half? The Amazonian bimbo with the tight outfit—is she really out of the picture or was that just a fairy story for Gina's benefit?'

'What makes you think that she's a bimbo?' Riccardo asked with interest.

'Oh, sorry. Was I mistaken? Is she a nuclear physicist?'

'No, not quite,' he admitted. 'Actually, I would be surprised if she could even spell it.'

Charlotte looked at him over the rim of her wine glass and grinned reluctantly. 'Well?'

'No fairy story. I've already got rid of her.'

'You're kidding.'

'No, I'm not. And it was a hell of a lot harder than it should have been, considering you laid it on thick about love and marriage and a non-existent future.'

'Sorry. I couldn't resist.' Charlotte knew that this pause in hostilities was a dangerous no-man's-land. It was too easy to see the man she had fallen head over heels in love with and she didn't want to go there again. Any arrangements they now had would be strictly along business lines. 'You shouldn't have descended on us.'

'Oh, but I had to. I had to size up the competition.'

'There's no competition.'

Riccardo felt a flare of rage. He couldn't understand what the hell she saw in the man, and he noticed that she had yet to confirm that she would be ditching him. 'We don't have to get married. Yet. But I want us to live together. That way we can give Gina the family unit she's missed for the past eight years.'

'No!'

'Why not? Does the man live with you?'

'No, of course not!'

'Then what's the problem?'

'Don't you get it, Riccardo?' She finished the glass of wine. Now she fancied another. 'Yes, it's important for Gina to have both of us, and now that she's met you

I recognise that you're here to stay when it comes to her. But you just have to look at it from the point of view of a divorced person involved in an amicable joint-custody type situation.' Charlotte took a deep breath and looked him directly in the eyes, which made her feel a bit giddy.

'I don't want to marry you or live with you because… because…we just don't have that kind of relationship. Marriage and co-habitation should be about commitment and sharing, and *wanting* to be together. It shouldn't be a duty undertaken because of force of circumstance, if you know what I mean.' She pushed her hand through her hair and leaned on the table. 'When I say "I do" to a marriage or even to a guy moving in with me, I want to feel excited about it.'

Riccardo flushed darkly. 'Most marriages end in divorce. People start out with stars in their eyes, and then reality sets in and they find they can't deal with it. What's wrong with a business arrangement? It makes sense.'

'Not to me. And we're just going round in circles here, Riccardo.' She gave in to temptation and poured herself another glass of wine. 'I don't want to marry you and I don't want to live with you.'

'There was a time when you would have jumped at the prospect.'

'That was a long time ago.' She rested the glass on the table and ran her finger lightly around the rim. 'I was a different person then and so were you. We've both changed.'

'You mean you became a responsible adult who decided that a passion-free relationship with a man who doesn't challenge you is the safe, logical way to go.'

'Ben is *very* challenging!'

'Don't get me wrong, Charlie. I'm not saying that he isn't a thoroughly *nice* guy…'

Charlotte gritted her teeth. He managed in those few words to paint a picture of someone mind-numbingly dull, and she momentarily regretted her elaborate and fictitious description of a man who was sensitive and in touch with his feminine side.

'I *like* nice, Riccardo.'

'Because it's safe?'

'Yes, it's safe, and what's wrong with that?'

'Nothing. But right now…' Riccardo leaned towards her, every muscle in his body taut with menacing intent. 'Life's a little *unconventional*, wouldn't you agree? And unconventional situations call for unconventional solutions. Besides…' Riccardo relaxed back into the chair and twirled his wine glass lazily in his hand. 'What we had was pretty strong, if I recall; who knows if it's all still there, lying just beneath the surface? One touch and *pow*!' He made a little explosive gesture with his hand and then deliberately looked at her very slowly, a leisurely, sexual exploration that made her skin burn.

'Don't be ridiculous,' Charlotte said, clearing her throat. This was just another ploy to try and get what he wanted, whatever the cost! She pushed herself up and looked at her watch. 'When would you like to next visit Gina?'

'You still haven't told me what you intend to do about the boyfriend.'

'I'll obviously think about what you've asked, Riccardo, but I won't be turning my life upside down just to suit you. You might sneer at Ben because he's not like you, but you might also want to stop and think that he's exactly what I need. And want!' she added belatedly. She folded her arms and backed towards the kitchen door, bumping into the doorframe as Riccardo took a step towards her. She dearly hoped that the madness swirling around inside her wasn't reflected on her face.

'Hmm. Interesting,' Riccardo drawled. One step closer. 'Because you don't look all that convinced of what you're saying.'

'I mean…' now he was standing right in front of her, trapping her with her back pressed hard against the wall '…your colour's all up.'

'What can you expect?' Charlotte said wildly. 'I mean, you sit there asking all sorts of impossible things!'

'Making all sorts of impossible allusions,' Riccardo agreed on a husky note. 'Daring to suggest that we can still *do* things to each other…' He reached out and feathered a finger along her cheek. To Charlotte, it was like being brushed by a flame. She twisted her head away but her heart was pounding and her body… Her body was on fire, alive with a whirlwind of responses that she hadn't felt for anyone since *him*!

She breathed in deeply, nostrils flaring, made herself remember the crucial footnote to his behaviour which was that he was using her to get what he desperately wanted. He wasn't attracted to *her*!

'I'll call you, Riccardo.'

'Not good enough, I'm afraid. You're trembling. Why? Does the boyfriend make you tremble like this? Do you know that I can breathe you in? I remember the smell—of Italy and summer and your skin.'

'Don't!' It had meant to sound like a forceful command.

Instead it sounded like a plea. She placed one hand squarely on his chest, which was a bit of a tactical error, because instantly she was flooded with memories of how he looked bare-backed, his muscles tightly packed.

'Why not? Scared?'

'You can't just come in here and do whatever you want.'

'No, but I am happy to do whatever *you* want.' And she wanted him. Riccardo could feel it. He was also achingly aware of how much he wanted *her*. Quite honestly, he had felt the pull the minute he had clapped eyes on her. He wondered now if he had ever really stopped wanting her. Yes he had turned away, because at the time he'd been convinced that a serious relationship was not what he wanted, least of all with a kid who had lied to him about his age, but he had never sought to replace her, had he? He should have forgotten about her, moved on to have a stable relationship with someone; Lord knew it was what his mother had spent years clamouring for. But he hadn't. Instead, he had littered his life with a series of pointless bimbos. Now, here, breathing this woman in, he felt at ease with himself.

He leaned down, brushed her lips with his, and she tried to wriggle free but not with any conviction.

This was madness! She wanted to pull him to her and sink herself into his kiss. Instead, she pushed him away and found that she was panting as he straightened up and looked down at her.

'Tomorrow,' Riccardo said.

'Tomorrow?'

'I'll be in touch.'

Well, he thought as he stepped out into the bleak

blackness to hail a cab, she hadn't left him very much choice, had she?

Yes, she had given him a long speech about Mr Right, but he knew this much: Mr Right was not Mr Fiancé. She might think that safety and predictability were qualities she was after, but she was wrong. He had felt it just then in her trembling struggle to tear herself away from him.

And she hadn't told him what he had wanted to hear, that her relationship with Ben would be off. She had skilfully danced around the subject, and he had left none the wiser as to what her intentions were. But when he thought back to their conversation, he was sickly aware that running towards him, arms outstretched, for the sake of their daughter was just not enough for her.

Riccardo, accustomed as he was to life conforming to exactly what he wanted, was afflicted by an unexpected attack of mortal fear.

So what if she'd felt a little edge of nostalgic attraction to him? What did it mean? Nothing. Because she had emerged from her disastrous, disillusioning relationship with him into something she had convinced herself she wanted to be, and the fact that *he* was convinced otherwise meant nothing.

He would end up being a part-time father, taking Gina out to fast-food restaurants and trying to bond with her in two-hour sessions once a week. And eventually Ben—stolid, reliable, 'let me cook for you honey' Ben—would get his foot in through the front door until he became the full-time dad doing homework with Gina, watching her grow up, sorting out her problems.

It wouldn't happen at once. She would do her utmost

to accommodate him, because he knew that she felt guilty, but gradually the guilt would begin to fade and then the relationship that she might have put on hold would resurface. Riccardo knew human nature, knew that good intentions had a very short life span and guilt an even shorter one.

So then he came right back to his original question—what choice had she left him?

The brilliant thing about money was the way it could buy things you couldn't see or touch. Speed, for instance. A couple of calls and he had made all the necessary arrangements to have the paraphernalia of the home office ready to be installed the following afternoon.

He could have just made do with his laptop computer, but that would have felt like a temporary option, so he had gone the whole hog, including an extra telephone line and broadband internet access.

He telephoned her office promptly the following afternoon and told her to meet him at her house in an hour.

On the other end of the line, Charlotte overcame the jolt to her nervous system on hearing his voice and prepared to bristle, but he had already hung up, leaving her no option but to rearrange the meeting she had scheduled with two mortgage specialists and leave the office in the capable but slightly dippy hands of her second in command.

She was unprepared for what met her eyes: vans. Men in overalls. Items of equipment. And, of course, Riccardo in the midst of it all.

Charlotte dropped her briefcase and stared, open

mouthed, barely aware of Riccardo walking in her direction.

'I know,' he said, sticking his hands into his trouser pockets. 'Utter chaos. But once everyone's inside we can leave them to get on with things, and by the time we get back, hey presto, you'll never know they've been!' Riccardo looked at her warily. Yes, of course he had everything under control, but the woman, as he was finding out, was feisty, unpredictable and not of a disposition to take things lying down.

'Riccardo, *what's going on*?'

'But we can't get in without a key.'

Charlotte reached into her bag without thinking. Anything to sort out the Piccadilly Circus situation on her doorstep.

From her own front door, she watched in dazed silence as Riccardo took charge. Events seemed to be moving at the speed of sound, men expertly checking things, stooping and peering under bits of furniture, then after what seemed like a lifetime Riccardo joined her by the front door wearing a sympathetic expression, which should have warned her of underhand dealings, but she was still too flummoxed to pay attention to that.

'Now, here's my idea,' Riccardo said. 'We go and get Gina from school and go somewhere…fun. And warm.' He was liking what he saw. Charlotte in her work clothes, and not spitting fire at him, was incredibly appealing. She looked so damn *young* to be carrying a briefcase and wearing a stern grey suit. Her eyes looked enormous.

'Fun? Warm? What are you talking about? And

what's going on in my house? Who were all those men?' He was already ushering her into the back seat of a black cab, which seemed to have appeared from nowhere, and asking her for the name of Gina's school. It was literally a short walking distance from the house, something for which Riccardo was deeply thankful, as he could sense Charlotte's shock beginning to wear off.

It was peculiar, but he had always been intolerant of women who were demanding or argumentative. As far as he was concerned, his working life was high octane and stressful enough without his brief windows of relaxation being spent listening to a nagging harpy. The role of a woman was to soothe. In Charlotte's case, however, he found himself oddly invigorated by her outspoken and frankly unwelcome disregard for his personal boundaries. Maddened, but invigorated. Right now he could see her edging towards a major outburst, but fortunately the black cab was pulling up outside the primary school.

Charlotte looked at him in exasperation, fully aware that the taxi driver was ready and willing to sit in on a long-winded rant with his meter running.

'I'll be ten minutes,' she warned him. 'And when I get back you'd better have a few answers for me!'

'Yes, ma'am!'

Charlotte made an inarticulate sound of pure annoyance as she saw Riccardo and the cab driver exchange one of those infuriating eyes-to-the-heavens 'who knows women?' looks.

Yes, her life had been a bit boring, a bit lacking in something vital, but essentially peaceful. And *peaceful* had been good. Hadn't it?

CHAPTER SEVEN

GINA was, predictably, on cloud nine at the unexpected turn of events that allowed her to skip her final class, which was maths. She was also, even more predictably, on whatever cloud was higher than cloud nine at the prospect of an afternoon with Riccardo.

Charlotte looked down at the bobbing black head and smiled. It was surprising how readily Gina had welcomed Riccardo into her life. She had been told that he had not been around because of circumstances, but that now he was, and so happy to have her in his life. And with absolute childish trust she had accepted the story. If she had been a couple of years older, Charlotte was sure that the situation would have been very different.

When she started thinking like that, when she witnessed her daughter's excitement and realised how important a figure Riccardo was for her, she couldn't suppress the surge of guilt that overwhelmed her. Who could blame Riccardo for his fury?

He was waiting for them in the taxi, and as soon as they were inside he turned to Gina and asked, smiling, where she would like to go as there was 'some work' being done at the house so they couldn't go back there just yet.

'Work?' Charlotte asked, ears pricking up. 'I hope this doesn't involve any over-the-top presents for Gina…' She had visions of gigantic games consoles and home cinemas crowding the bedroom. Sometimes fathers with limitless supplies of money could be impractical when it came to giving presents to their offspring, and Riccardo, seeing himself as the wounded party who had been denied his child for eight years, might just find himself strolling down that inappropriate route. She would have to nip it in the bud.

'We know, don't we, Gina, that pressies are for special occasions *only*. Birthdays…Christmas…maybe a reward for something out of the ordinary.'

Gina failed to give support to this theory, and Charlotte frowned at her until she said, glumly, 'Yes, Mum.'

'Thoroughly commendable!' Riccardo agreed, and Charlotte looked at him suspiciously. 'It's crazy to buy things for kids just because you can *afford* to! Takes away their motivation to succeed and doesn't teach them how to value money.'

Gina sighed in resignation.

'So if none of that in the house is anything to do with Gina…'

'Oh, but I never said that it had nothing to do with Gina. Look, we're here.' He leant towards his daughter and pointed out of the window as the taxi slowed in front of a very exclusive-looking sports centre. 'Nice swimming pool. How do you fancy a swim?'

'But I didn't bring a swimsuit.'

'With a little luck you can get one inside. It's a small shop but well stocked. Caters for eight-year-old kids who forget to bring their swimsuits.'

'Riccardo…'

'We'll talk in a minute.'

'Okay…' They walked inside the very small, very intimate sports centre where it became immediately apparent that Riccardo was the owner. 'The minute's up. Now, tell me what the heck's happening inside my house while we…while we relax in your private little health spa!' She stood still and folded her arms, refusing to go a step further.

'It's not *my* private little health spa, although I do admit membership is by invitation only.'

'Well…?'

'Well, I would have preferred it to be a surprise, but…guess what?' He looked down at Gina whose ears had pricked up at the word 'surprise'. Then he stooped down to her level, forcing Charlotte to bend down so that she could hear what he had to say, although she was beginning to have an inkling of an idea. 'Your mum's had you all to herself for eight years, and it wasn't her fault, but…' and he took his daughter's hand and covered it with both of his '…now that I'm here, I would very much like to move in so that I can share every day with you.'

Gina beamed and flung her arms around him. Above, he heard a strangulated sound and decided to ignore it. The feeling of his daughter's head pressed into the curve of his neck was answer enough that he had done the right thing.

'Whoa!' Charlotte managed to croak out. 'Stop right there!'

'Mum! I'm going to have my very own dad at home!'

'Gina…' Since Riccardo was showing no signs of standing up, Charlotte reluctantly knelt alongside him, but at an awkward angle because of the narrowness of her skirt. 'I think you'll find that perhaps your *very own dad* hasn't quite thought the matter through.'

'What do you mean, Mum?'

'Maybe we should sit down and discuss this, honey.' The dark brown eyes were beginning to look a little anxious, but Gina nodded and Charlotte led the way, walking briskly over to one of the little circular tables by the bar area. It was comfortable and agreeably empty, just a few businessmen relaxing in the corner, and an elegant foursome of wealthy mummies decked out in very tight designer keep-fit gear. With well-bred good manners, none of them glanced in their direction although they must have been curious.

'I know it would be *super* if Ricc… *Dad* moved in. It's just not possible, as I'm sure he'll agree once he hears me out.'

'Oh.' Gina slumped. 'All my friends have dads.'

'And so do you, honey!'

'Their dads live with them.'

'And, well…' Charlotte cast her mind around wildly for the least aggressive way of saying what she had to say. 'I'm sure your dad would too but he's a *very* important man who has *lots and lots* of big companies, and he just can't run them from a small, tiny house like ours.' She shook her head ruefully and shot Riccardo a look that should have turned him to stone.

Riccardo met her look steadily and mouthed, above

Gina's head, 'Forget it'. Then he smiled down at his daughter. 'Your mum's right about one thing, Gina. I *do* have lots of companies to look after, but that's why we couldn't go back to the house straightaway.'

'Why?'

'Because lots of men are there right now making sure that I have everything I need to work as much as I can from home.'

'What?' The polite groups of people glanced across, and Charlotte modulated her voice to a venomous hiss. 'What?'

'Computer, fax, internet access, the lot,' Riccardo told her coolly.

Between them, Gina could barely contain herself, while Charlotte gritted her teeth and tried not to scream. *How could he?* How could he just think that he could walk through her door and take up residence? But she knew, of course. One reason was Ben, the non-existent fiancé whom Riccardo regarded as a threat, but far weightier than that was his determination to be a full-time father to his child. Lord knew he had no feelings towards *her*, but that, Charlotte realised, would just be a minor sticking point for him. He was Italian, and family was all.

'You can't, Riccardo,' she told him in a sibilant undertone.

'I can and I will and don't even think of stopping me.' He beamed at Gina and pointed to the small, exclusive sportswear shop. 'You run and pick yourself a swimsuit.'

'I'll call the police!'

'And say what—that Gina's father wants to share the

same house as his daughter? That he would even be willing to buy his family as big a house as they want to accommodate his simple wish?'

'Oh *please*! Since when have you *ever* done *anything* that could be classified as *simple*?'

I once loved you. The thought flashed into Riccardo's head and disappeared as quickly as it had come, leaving him momentarily shaken. Then he remembered that those times were gone and, standing in front of him now, she was simply the mother of his child, and moreover the woman who wanted to come between them.

'Don't argue with me, Charlie.'

'You're the most high handed, arrogant, *pig headed* man I have *ever* met in my entire life!'

'I'll take that as a compliment.' He allowed himself a triumphant smile at the notion that Ben the cook would no longer be able to come and go in his daughter's life as he pleased.

'And where do you imagine you're going to sleep?'

'Guest room. To start with.'

'To start with?' Charlotte felt faint.

'I might decide to build an extension, although I have to admit it would be easier all round if we just moved into a bigger house. And you're in the perfect position to find the ideal place. Why don't you consider it a priority? That way I won't get under your feet too much.'

'You...you *can't*.'

Riccardo sighed. 'We're just going over old ground here, Charlie. Why fight the inevitable?' He glanced to where Gina was dangling a swimsuit and gesticulating madly. She wanted them both to swim, and had picked out an especially charming swimsuit for Charlotte in horrible hues of blues and reds which was clearly designed for maximum exposure. Charlotte declined, preferring to watch them both from the sidelines of the pool where she could stew in frustrated silence. Riccardo, she noted sourly, was doing extraordinary things on the bonding front—teaching Gina how to swim breast stroke, tossing her into the air, balancing her on his shoulders so that she could stumble off with squeals of laughter. He didn't look at Charlotte once. But then why should he? she thought. He had got his own way after all.

The whole afternoon, drifting into early evening, was a nightmare. They ate in the restaurant, with Riccardo playing the good dad and compelling her into the role of either *good* mum or utterly miserable sour-faced mum.

By the time they were on their way back to the house, Charlotte's face ached from the strain of having to pretend.

But as promised the work was done, everything tidied up, by his personal assistant, she'd been told while they'd been at the club 'having fun'. And Gina was exhausted. Too tired for anything more than her nightie and half a story.

Which just left them and a quiet house.

'You'll need a towel,' she said wearily, sinking into a chair in the sitting room, all the better to contemplate the unravelling of her life. 'Lord, Riccardo, I can't believe you've done this.' She rubbed her eyes with her thumbs and then closed them.

'So, why don't you try making the most of it?'

Charlotte opened her eyes to him sitting on the arm

of her chair, but she was just too tired to respond to the invasion of privacy. 'How? We don't like each other, and yet I'm supposed to be happy sharing my space with you.'

For some reason, that hurt him. He stood up and walked towards the door, pausing to glance at her over his shoulder. 'Well, if it's any consolation, my routine at my office will continue as usual, and yes, I'll be around in the evenings, but if this arrangement really doesn't work out then we'll reconsider the whole thing.'

'Meaning what?'

Riccardo shrugged. 'Meaning we'll do the amicable joint-custody thing and I'll just have to reconcile myself to not being around in a full-time capacity.'

'You should have thought of that before you embarked on this crazy moving in idea!'

'I'm going to have a shower. If you need me I'll be working at the desk in my bedroom.'

He shut the door quietly behind him, leaving Charlotte a little disappointed that the argument she was fired up to conduct had fizzled out like a damp squib. But at least he had agreed to clear off if things didn't work out. Which, naturally, they wouldn't. Any fool would have predicted *that*. He didn't like her and she didn't like him. There was just too much water under the bridge, whether he wanted to admit it or not.

Except…except…

There had been moments at that wretched spa when she had forgotten her anger and experienced a little taste of family life, ordinary family life with laughter and teasing and *fun*, and someone else there sharing the little things. The frightening thing was that it could get to be a habit, but…

She stood up and headed up the stairs. It was a small house. Just the three bedrooms and a shared bathroom—and he wasn't in it. There was no sound of running water and there was a crack of light under his bedroom door. At least for the time being she would have to get used to this inconvenience. She grabbed her clothes from her room and, head still full of ridiculous but tantalising thoughts, she gave a brief knock on the bathroom door and opened it.

Riccardo, naked and shaving in front of the bathroom-cabinet mirror, saw her enter and freeze. He rinsed his face and turned around.

'What's the problem? You've seen this body naked before.'

Charlotte, clutching her bundle of clothes for dear life, glued her eyes to his face. That was safe. And right now she needed that safe haven because her legs had turned to lead.

'Argh…'

'Did you want to use the bathroom?' He strolled towards her. Eight years on and she still blushed like a virgin. He had been out with women who were willing to do the most explicit things and had never turned a hair, never mind looked as though they wanted the ground to open up and swallow them.

'Ah…umm…'

'What is it about me that you don't like?' That passing remark had been niggling away at him like a thorn in his side. Resentment and even hatred he could deal with, because he could tie them up to a reaction to how they had parted company, and whether or not he agreed with it he could now understand it. But just *not liking* him was a bit more difficult to get his head around. He knew that physically he could still affect her. Experience with the opposite sex had made him a master in reading their responses. But just not liking him implied something that bordered on emotional indifference, and for the first time in his life the physical was just not good enough. He wanted more from her, and he told himself that that was because their situation was so complicated.

Charlotte made an inarticulate sound and began feeling for the door behind her.

'No, no. Not so fast.' Physically, he had to admit, *she* certainly still affected *him*, evidence of which was all too visible should she allow her eyes to travel due south. He snatched his towel from where he had draped it over the shower rail and slung it around his waist. 'There. Better?'

'I'm not having a conversation with you in here!'

'Why not? It's as good a place as any.'

'It's a bathroom!'

'Since when did you become so conventional, Charlie? If I recall, you never allowed inappropriate locations to get in the way of what you wanted to do.' He leaned against the door, effectively locking her in.

'I don't *want* to talk to you, though, Riccardo. I *want* to have a bath.'

'Feel free.'

'This is *my* house.' She tilted her head up mutinously and swallowed down the unsettling feeling in her stomach as she stared into his eyes, feeling a bit like plummeting sharply and unexpectedly down on a rollercoaster ride. 'You may have taken it upon yourself to move in *temporarily*, because you just can't *bear* not to get your own way, but you're still under *my* roof, and just so long as you are I won't have you disrupting my life and what I want to do!'

'This isn't a question about me!'

'Yes, it is!' His bare torso was only inches away from her and she could feel her body prickling with awareness. It was unbearable, especially as she knew he was aroused. How could she not? She might have kept her eyes plastered on his face, but she still hadn't been able to miss his very obvious erection. She told herself that that meant nothing. She had fallen in love with a man who was capable of conducting a relationship based solely on sex. She just wasn't going there again.

Nevertheless, her breasts ached; every part of her ached.

'It's about us trying to make something work for the sake of someone else. Gina didn't ask to be born into a single-parent family, and I'm giving us both the chance to try and do something about it.'

'Okay. But can we discuss this somewhere else? Because…'

'Because you're really desperate for a bath? Because you call yourself *Charlotte* now and have an overdeveloped puritan streak? Or maybe it's because you're terrified I might do *this*…'

He leaned down into her and kissed her. No gentle, explorative kiss, but a kiss that was fiercely, urgently hungry, pinning her back against the door.

Charlotte could feel his hardness pressed against her, and with a stifled moan of desperation she went under.

Of their own volition, her hands reached up and her fingers curled into his still-damp hair, and when he flattened his hand in the small of her back and pulled her into him she didn't resist. She just couldn't. It was as if she had been waiting eight years for this moment to happen and now that it had she was powerless to do anything about it.

His tongue was in her mouth, probing and demanding, and when he stopped kissing her it was so that he could do more, reach for the buttons on the snappy no-nonsense blouse she was still wearing, and begin unfastening them one by one. And not nearly fast enough. She helped him, shakily undoing the last, and drowning in a sea of pleasure as he pulled open the blouse, exposing her lacy white bra. Without pausing, he slipped his finger into her cleavage and stroked the sensitive skin between her breasts.

For Charlotte, nothing had ever felt so good. But then, no one had touched her since him. Those familiar hands were like heaven. He pushed down the lacy cups and her breasts spilled out, succulent, plump fruit waiting to be tasted.

Riccardo, always in control of his body, had to steady himself to avoid the unthinkable happening. He had no idea how they had moved so swiftly to this point, but at this very moment eight years had never elapsed. She was all his as she'd been back then. Her nipples were big and defined and rosy with arousal. He teased their erect peaks with his fingers, enjoying those little noises of pleasure she made, and then he sank to his knees so that he could take them into his mouth, licking, sucking, nipping them with his teeth, until he could feel her wanting to cry out but restraining herself.

When he tugged the bra off her breasts bounced free, and he cupped them in his hands and massaged them, while he continued his exploration of her body, first trailing his mouth against her flat stomach, then squatting so that he could ease off the remainder of her clothes, and she helped, stepping out of them, eager to have no barriers between their naked bodies. He blew gently on the soft curls that guarded her most intimate place.

Her fingers were resting lightly on his head, but at that they curled into his hair. When he raised his eyes, he saw that she was arched back, her eyes shut, her breathing quick and shallow.

He dipped into her moist femininity and tasted her, a slow and lingering taste that made her quiver and wriggle against his mouth. With remembered enjoyment, she began to move rhythmically against him, a soft up-and-down slide as he took her higher and higher. His tongue flicked and slid and teased the throbbing bud, but it was only when he stood up, ready to hoist her onto him, that Charlotte opened her eyes and the full reality of her situation sank in.

'We...we can't, Riccardo.'

'Don't even think of stopping this now.' Riccardo growled his answer.

'This is what got us into the situation we're in now...unprotected sex.'

And so what if it happens again? The thought

slammed into Riccardo like a closed fist, almost making him reel backwards from the silent admission. He put that disturbing thought on hold and snatched the discarded towel back up. 'Then we'll make sure we use protection.'

'I haven't got any!'

Which raised another question, but that too he put on hold. His body was on fire and he *had* to have her.

'Leave it to me.'

Charlotte struggled to feel some healthy disgust at a man who travelled with a portable supply of contraception, but she was burning up. In those few seconds, as she tried to snap out of her crazy trance, Riccardo manoeuvred her aside and opened the door, while she flung back on her clothes in a haphazard fashion, not bothering to button or zip anything up. Then to his room, the little guest room at the far end of the landing.

'Gina…'

'Will be fine.' He locked the bedroom door, and at the sound of the key turning she felt a thrill of heady, forbidden excitement. She was also in the grip of a 'what the heck' reckless urge. She was violently attracted to this man and it had never stopped, not even when he'd no longer been around and her only bed companions had been bitterness and disillusionment. It was as if her body obeyed a different set of rules to her head.

He didn't switch the light on nor did he close the curtains, and in the silvery darkness she was mesmerised by the sight of his naked, muscular body.

She automatically stripped off her top. The bra she had left discarded on the bathroom floor. Then she stepped out of the rest of her clothes so that they were both standing only feet apart, eyes locked. Riccardo was the first to break their mutual appraisal by holding out his hand to lead her to the bed. It was a single bed, and hardly ideal, but to Charlotte it might well have been the most romantic venue in the world.

'Well, now,' Riccardo murmured. 'Shall we take up where we left off?'

'This is absolute madness.' But there was a smile in her voice that made his heart sing.

'What's the point of life if we don't succumb to a little healthy madness once in a while? Now, where were we?'

'You were…'

'Yes?'

'I see you're still the tease in bed you always were…' Charlotte murmured, guiding his hand to where she still ached for his touch.

'Only with you,' Riccardo said huskily. He was relieved that she didn't ask him to explain that, because he had no idea what he had meant or even how he had managed to utter the words, but he had meant them. *Crazy.*

He made love to her slowly and sweetly, touching every inch of her body, and the more he touched, the more he remembered, almost as if the image of her had been lying somewhere just below the surface. He even remembered the way she moved and sighed, and all the little noises she made to express her pleasure.

'So,' he said afterwards, when they were lying interlocked on the single bed. 'Tell me you can't make a go of this, Charlie.'

'I give up trying to get you to call me *Charlotte*.'

Riccardo stroked some blonde hair back and kissed her nose. 'Somehow *Charlotte* seems too proper. We're good together.'

'We're good *in bed* together,' Charlotte said on a sigh. 'And I still have a bath to run.'

'It can wait.'

'For what? Nothing's changed, Riccardo.'

'We just made love!' He pulled her against him, because he could feel her shifting to get out of the bed. 'Did you?'

'Did I what?'

'Touch him. Make love to him.' He had to know, and this went far beyond simple curiosity.

'Don't bring Ben into this.'

'Did you? Forget it. Forget I ever asked.' He sprawled onto his back and stared upwards at the ceiling. 'Go have your bath, Charlie. You're right. Nothing's changed.'

'Okay. No. No, I didn't. It wasn't that type of relationship.'

'What type is that?' Riccardo addressed the ceiling, but suddenly he felt on top of the world. So he had been right all along—it had been a passion-free zone! Maybe a kiss or two, a friendly peck on the cheek, he liked to think, and he could deal with that. He didn't know where this fierce possessiveness had come from, but he wasn't going to rail against it. She was the mother of his child and he was an Italian man. It was understandable.

'I told you. After what happened between us, I had a big rethink on what I wanted out of a relationship and I knew that it wasn't just sex. It didn't matter how good the sex was, in the end it just never counts for very much.'

As swiftly as he had hit the top of the world, he

plummeted back down to earth and straight back into the brick wall of her *not liking* him. He knew he should rise above this. Damn it, it was hardly as though he hadn't enjoyed women, having made sure that they knew in advance that he was only interested in relationships that came without strings. He was no saint, but he felt as if she was enclosed within four ice walls. And she didn't want to bring the paragon *Ben* into the conversation because she still needed him.

'Look.' She stepped out of the bed and began putting on her clothes, glad for the distraction of doing something rather than lying there next to the man she now, with gut-wrenching dismay, realised she still loved. 'I'm prepared to put Gina ahead of myself and let you stay here, at least for a while, until she gets to know you and feels safe enough to let you move out without thinking that you'll disappear for ever. But there's one big condition.'

And he would never know how important the condition was for her health, because sleeping with him had been a crazy mistake and she couldn't do it again. It would be bad enough having him in the house, but to start having a sexual relationship with him again would spell a honeyed trap which she couldn't fall into again.

'We don't do this again.' Clothes on, she looked at him sprawled on the bed, half covered with the tousled bed clothes that were a mocking reminder of her weakness. She took a deep breath. 'It was a mistake, and I guess it was a mistake we both had to make, but the same old same old doesn't work for me any more.'

'Same old same old?'

Charlotte shrugged. 'Same old Riccardo, the good lover with nothing more on his mind.'

'I proposed marriage!' Riccardo reminded her, enraged at his impotence, at her for her moral high-ground, and at his own confusion because the thought of her and her sensitive twenty-first-century wimp stirred hot, ugly jealousy inside him.

But where's the love? she asked herself sadly. 'You just don't understand, Riccardo. Anyway. That's not important. I'm going to have my bath, and like I said we'll both put Gina first and see how it goes for a little while.' She didn't trust herself with him. He could manoeuvre a conversation in directions she didn't know existed until she found herself going down one of them, and she couldn't let herself be persuaded into a relationship with him on his terms. So she opened the door and, before he could say anything else, she let herself quietly out of the room and straight to the bathroom.

Not important? *Not important?* Riccardo, staring in frustration at the closed door, was outraged. What, he thought venomously, did that man have that *he* didn't? And how could she just write off physical attraction as something that didn't count for *anything*? Moreover, would she still be able to have a relationship with the man after she had slept with *him*? He could have kicked himself for not asking her that vital question, and then it occurred to him that maybe, in the great scheme of things, he was emotionally so unimportant that their one-night *mistake* wouldn't even register.

But he was finding he damned well *wanted* it to register! He had been young and arrogant and had let her go, thinking that it was the best for the both of them. He was beginning to wonder whether that had been a mistake from which he had never really recovered. But fate had given him this second chance. He wasn't going to make the same mistake twice, not when there was so much at stake.

CHAPTER EIGHT

'WHAT'S going on?' Charlotte stepped through her front door at a little after seven-thirty, to find Riccardo right there and apparently waiting for her. This was disconcerting. In fact, the past two-and-a-half weeks had been disconcerting. She could accuse him of a lot of things, but not making an effort for the sake of his daughter was not one of them. How long he could keep it up was anybody's guess, but if the object of the exercise was to get close to his daughter then he was succeeding with flying colours.

He'd been getting back to the house by seven. He had taken Gina to the cinema twice to see shows which she couldn't imagine he'd enjoyed in a month of Sundays. He had endured a Saturday evening meal in a fast-food restaurant surrounded by babies, toddlers, young children running about and harassed mothers without complaint. He had played Scrabble and contrived to lose, Monopoly—which he hadn't quite been able to bring himself to lose—and endless games of cards which Charlotte could only think he'd found supremely tiresome compared to his previous adult pursuits. On a scale of one to ten, where, she wondered, did gin rummy figure compared to a Friday evening in the company of one of his leggy blondes at a posh restaurant?

Charlotte had watched from a distance, joining in when she had to, but protecting herself from seeing all this effort as anything more than Riccardo approaching a situation with the one hundred percent desire to succeed with which he approached all situations.

Aside from her. Because he'd assiduously left her alone. He'd laughed, he'd joked, but his attention had been primarily for his daughter. There had not been the slightest hint that anything physical had taken place between them. He had been, she was forced to admit, the perfect gentleman. The cynical side of her couldn't help but think that he was covering ground quickly with Gina so that he could clear out of the house, having realised that sex with her mother was no longer an option.

'Food,' Riccardo said succinctly. He began helping her out of her coat while Charlotte, bewildered, wondered what he was on about.

'You're wearing my apron.'

'Well spotted.'

'It looks ridiculous.' But she had to smile. Riccardo, decked out in old chinos, a tee-shirt and sporting an apron bought by Gina that declared the joys of motherhood, was priceless. 'I wish I had a camera,' she said. 'This is a moment worth capturing.'

'Go upstairs and have a bath.'

'Yes, but…'

'Gina's with one of her school friends. Last-minute thing. Going to the movies, so she won't be back home until about eight-thirty. I thought that would be all right as tomorrow's Saturday.'

'Well…' Charlotte felt a little twinge of alarm. Gina had been their chaperone for the past couple of weeks, always around with them both and filling in potentially awkward silences with relentless chatter. When she hadn't been around, Riccardo had disappeared to work and Charlotte had curled up in front of the television, always making sure to take a handy book to duck behind should he appear without warning.

'It's a good opportunity to discuss…domestic arrangements,' Riccardo said vaguely.

'Oh. Right.' So *that* was what he was up to! Now would come the nitty-gritty details of when he would leave the house. Charlotte felt it in her bones, and knew that she should have been over the moon because her life would get back to normal, but she felt an empty void settle in the pit of her stomach.

Why fight the truth? She had become accustomed to having him around the house. She had always thought that two was such a tidy number. Just her and Gina, both of them against the world. But three was just so much *rounder* and more fulfilling.

If he thought that cooking a meal was the adult, civilised way of breaking the news, then she would show him that she was fine with that idea and dress accordingly, in her usual casual, staying at home 'because I love my life without you in it' gear—a pair of comfy combat trousers, and a baggy olive-green sweater.

She was not expecting what she found in the kitchen.

Candlelight, for a start. Riccardo turned around as she walked in, and Charlotte smiled awkwardly at him.

'I didn't dress for the occasion.' She spread her hands along her randomly put together outfit, feeling a bit of a fool even though he was in casual clothes as well. Though somehow he looked considerably less scruffy than she was.

'No matter.'

'You've cooked a meal from *scratch*?' She spotted the recipe book propped against the bread bin and the sink full of pots and pans, which seemed to suggest an awfully ambitious meal just for two. Why did he have to get under her skin like that? Why did he have to make her *like* him?

'There's no need to sound quite so astounded,' Riccardo said. He fetched something from the fridge. It turned out to be avocado and prawns.

'I thought you hated cooking, and sneered at men who ventured anywhere near a kitchen unless in pursuit of a bottle of wine from the fridge.' She sat down and tried to squash the foolishly special feeling rushing through her. This just wasn't going to do, was it?

'Obviously I wouldn't make it my life's work.' He handed her the dish, the avocado and prawns both drowning under ample amounts of seafood sauce, which he had bought because the recipe had seemed ridiculously long considering the length of time that would be spent eating the damned thing. 'It might taste better than it looks,' he said, picking up his fork and diving into the starter. 'Not bad.' Fairly revolting. Ben the Chef probably did all manner of creative things involving herbs and spices, which immediately made Riccardo scowl.

'It's not that bad,' Charlotte told him, misinterpreting his expression.

Riccardo grunted. Most evenings she worked long hours. Way too long. Never mind that she had an excellent childminder. It had crossed his mind more than once that she'd need not necessarily been at work, that she could have been seeing her boyfriend behind his back. It had crossed his mind even more that he could have her followed and put his suspicions to rest once and for all, but he'd baulked at the idea. He didn't want to discover whether she had broken ties with Ben or not; he didn't want to have to deal with the confrontation that would result from such a discovery. Because it had become blatantly clear to him over the past couple of weeks that he wanted her in his life. He had no idea how he could have been so stupid as to think that the physical spark between them would be enough to cement the union he felt his daughter deserved. Charlotte might have caved in once, but she had made it perfectly clear as time had gone by that that had really meant as little to her as she had told him at the time.

Riccardo, always at the top of the game when it came to women, had felt for the first time in his life superfluous to requirements. His presence was tolerated because he had inflicted it upon her, leaving her no option but to concede temporary defeat. But he could sense her waiting for him to leave. It enraged and frustrated him at the same time.

'What's that?' He realised that she had been talking to him, making polite conversation the way you would with a stranger.

'I wondered when was the last time you cooked anything.'

'Is that a comment on the food?' he asked, still scowling, and standing up to clear away the dishes.

'No, of course not!' Charlotte protested, taken aback. 'I was just making polite conversation.'

As he had thought. 'Strangers make polite conversation.' He tried to keep his voice level and jovial. 'Usually people who have a child in common can be a bit more relaxed with one another.'

Charlotte refrained from pointing out that most people who had a child in common probably had a more conventional union. Instead she asked him brightly what he had cooked.

'Pasta.'

'Yummy. Italian food. My favourite.'

'I know.' *Steer away from confrontation.* 'Although…' he drained some tagliatelle and noted that it looked a bit on the tough side, hopefully convincingly *al dente* '…I can't guarantee it'll taste like anything you ever had in Italy.'

'Smells good, though.' This was bliss. Back from work, the smell of food in the kitchen, Riccardo busying himself… When she had invented Ben as her fiancé with a magical culinary touch, she had had no idea just how wonderful the 'man in kitchen' package could be. Thus far, she and Riccardo had avoided eating together. She had grabbed a sandwich and so had he, at a different time in the evening, and then there had been the occasional father and daughter bonding visits to a couple of local fast-food places. On weekends, admittedly, meals had been shared, but with Gina sitting solidly between them.

This situation now took domesticity onto a different and dangerous level.

Charlotte, waiting for the verbal knife to fall, decided that she would initiate the first cut. Attack was always going to be better than defence, she reckoned. Better to be empowered than reduced to being told that, yes, he would be on his way now, and thank heavens they hadn't done anything crazy like get married.

It was clear that he was on edge. In fact, as she tried to chat about the food—asking him all sorts of questions about ingredients and cooking times, while she frantically tried to work out how she could manoeuvre the conversation skilfully into the place she wanted—she noticed that he was all but gritting his teeth together.

'I'll have to try this one,' she said in a cheery voice.

'Will you?' He looked at her narrowly, wondering whether that meant that the boyfriend had been sidelined.

'Sure! I mean, it's not as though you're going to be around here for ever, whipping up mushrooms and tomatoes and tagliatelle for my benefit!' There. It was out in the open, and Charlotte was quietly relieved to have taken the bull by the horns. She stared at herself twirling pasta round and round her fork, and felt sickeningly oppressed by the knowledge that he was staring at her and thinking…*what*? Thanking God she'd broken the ice on a difficult subject? Hoping she hadn't started thinking it was going to be permanent? Thinking that he'd never thought she led such a boring life, watching television and reading books every evening, or that he'd never imagined she possessed so many dreary clothes?

Riccardo watched her downbent head and stilled. 'Right. I wasn't actually going to bring up this subject just at the moment…'

'I know. We should maybe wait until we finish eating, but why not just get it over with and discussed? You're on edge, I'm on edge. You're right about us not being strangers, so why should we beat about the bush when it comes to discussing something as important as this?' Charlotte was rapidly going off her food. 'I was horrified when you moved yourself into my house, but I have to admit that the experiment worked much better than I thought it was going to.'

'The experiment?'

'Yes.' She rather liked the sound of that word: *experiment*. It sort of removed her from being personally involved, turned them all into little white mice scurrying round and round in a cage. Little white mice didn't fall victim to broken hearts. 'Face it, Riccardo, you might think you know it all, but—'

'Hang on a minute!' He slammed his fist on the table. 'Why don't you climb down from your perfect pedestal for a minute and stop the categorizing?'

'I wasn't categorizing.'

'No? Then why do you imagine that I think I *know it all*? Would that be because I'm still the bastard who turned his back eight years ago? It's a damned long time to be still affected by the past, Charlie! Anyone would think that there's a reason for that.'

'A reason? What kind of reason?'

'So what sort of timescale do you have in mind here?'

Just at that moment, washing the dishes seemed a very good idea. He took her plate, impatiently ordering her to stay put when she offered to help with the tidying, at which she subsided into a series of polite utterances: 'Are you sure?' and 'Okay, if you insist.' Riccardo felt his mood drop another couple of notches from foul to downright filthy.

Now for the first time he could see that there would be no point to his staying under her roof. She had been right after all. An unnatural relationship for the sake of a child would have been all wrong, and sooner or later Gina would have been affected by it, far more so than if they did the inevitable now and went their separate ways.

He would not debate her decision. Pride slammed into place and settled over him like an ice-cold shroud.

'Well, I think we can both agree that you're doing an amazing job bonding with Gina.'

'And you thought that I wouldn't?' Riccardo asked coldly, his back to her as he ploughed into the dishes with the speed of someone vastly unconcerned about grease remnants.

'No! I just thought…' She might have spent the past two-and-a-half weeks watching far too much television and lurking behind books in an attempt to avoid him, but she would miss the way her heart fluttered whenever he was around, miss the way he interacted with Gina, making her smile and just being there to pick up the slack when Charlotte had been feeling exhausted. She would even miss the way they sometimes sided against her when she began giving one of her speeches about nutrition. Tears threatened, and she swallowed them back. 'I thought you might have found it difficult to bond at first. I mean, it's not as though you have a lot of experience with children.'

'She's an easy child. Intelligent. Outgoing. Outspoken.' He ran water over a plate and slung it on the draining board, where it balanced precariously against a frying pan.

'Yes. And I'm really pleased that things worked out… Well on that front. I suppose she's at the perfect age—curious, willing to give people and situations the benefit of the doubt.' When she closed her eyes, she could relive the sight of him naked, his broad shoulders and athletic, muscular frame glistening with perspiration as he drove deep into her. She cleared her throat to dispel the burgeoning image. 'But of course, that's only part of the big picture, which is why I accept that this living arrangement has to come to an end. As far as timescale goes, well, I guess you'd agree that sooner is better than later. I mean, I know it's going to be hard for Gina, because you've been on the scene for over two weeks now, but I think that you're well bonded enough with her that she can feel secure in the knowledge that even when you go she'll carry on seeing you.'

The last of the dishes now completed the pyramid which threatened to topple over, and Charlotte stood up and fetched a tea towel from the drawer. 'I can tell you don't do much washing up, Riccardo,' she joked, to distract herself from the hollowness of the reality opening up in front of her. She picked up a plate from the top and dried it, feeling his proximity like a knife wound.

Riccardo thought that that was typical, because despite all her chat about his great bonding talents—as though connecting with his own flesh and blood had really been some kind of mountain he had been obliged to try and climb—she still saw him as essentially the arrogant bastard who had rejected her once upon a time. She hadn't let it go in eight years and she never would.

'Well, no.' Riccardo shrugged one of those dismissive shrugs that spoke volumes of the man who ran an empire with a steel fist. Pride would not allow him to plead his case. If she'd dismissed him as a bastard, then why fight the image? 'Why should I?'

He stood back from her and folded his arms. From a detached point of view, he disapproved thoroughly of what she was wearing. Combat trousers and sloppy cotton jumpers that looked as though they had been through the wash a thousand times were not, in his opinion, the kind of sexy, feminine gear he liked to see women in. But oddly, over the past couple of weeks, he had grown accustomed to her curled up in her comfy clothes, and it now struck him that he, too, had begun to dress down. It wasn't surprising, really, considering how casual life was in her house. It wasn't a place fashioned for designer clothes. That he had changed without even noticing it jarred.

'Limitless money can buy limitless things,' he heard himself say, and winced internally at the high-handed bore he sounded. 'Including a dishwasher. Not, of course, that I usually find myself facing stacks of dirty dishes. Isn't that what good restaurants are for?'

'I find it more fun to do the washing up with Gina

by hand,' Charlotte said coolly. 'It's a nice time for us to catch up and chat. But I guess in the world you live in catching up at the end of the day at the kitchen sink just isn't *quite* the done thing. Anyway, who would you have to catch up with?'

She closed the cupboard door on the last of the dried dishes and retreated to the safety of the kitchen chair. It felt good to argue with him. Really, if she was going to say goodbye, then she couldn't face saying goodbye to a considerate, witty, sexy, 'cooking a meal and doing the dishes' Riccardo. She drew her legs up and propped her chin on her knees. When she glanced down, she could see her perfectly painted pink toenails. She had given herself a pedicure two days ago. It was something she never did, but Riccardo had been downstairs explaining fractions to Gina, and she had found herself in the wonderful and novel situation of being able to spend a little quality time on herself. So she had painted her toenails.

Afterwards, she had realised that a part of her had done it for his benefit. He liked women who had painted toenails. It was something he had told her years ago in passing. Not, she knew, that he would even spare a glance at *hers*, but she had done it anyway. Just looking at them now made her angry with herself because she had disobeyed all her own rules of self-preservation and allowed herself to fall in love with him all over again.

She looked at him standing there, tea towel slung carelessly over one shoulder, arms folded as he stared right back at her.

'Meaning *what* exactly?' Riccardo asked tightly.

'Meaning that you haven't exactly spent the past

eight years committing yourself to another human being, have you, Riccardo? No long-term partner, no family. Just a series of *babes*, and everyone knows that men don't catch up with *babes* over the kitchen sink. Men catch up with them over some Chablis and French food in a restaurant, followed by a hot night in the sack. I'll bet you've never even gone on holiday with any of them!' Okay, she was pushing it, she could tell by the grim, shuttered expression on his face, but perversely that made her feel good.

No, he hadn't. Many had hinted, but he wouldn't have dreamt of doing any such thing.

Riccardo pushed himself away from the kitchen counter against which he had been leaning and strode towards the door. 'A little childish all this, isn't it, Charlie?' He paused and looked down at her coldly. 'Hurling insults. When we should be discussing the next step forward like civilised adults. I'm going into the sitting room where we can talk in comfort. Follow me, but if you don't I feel I should warn you that I'll have no alternative but to get lawyers involved. I want firm visiting rights, and if you can't control yourself when you're with me then it's a pretty good indicator that you'll be impetuous and unreliable when it comes to any situation we agree informally.'

Charlotte flushed, stood up and followed him, feeling ashamed of her outburst. 'I'm sorry,' was the first thing she said as soon as they had sat down, facing one another. 'You're right. I shouldn't have commented on your personal life. I was out of order.'

'I can be out of here by tomorrow evening,' Riccardo

told her bluntly, ignoring the apology. 'I'll want to spend it with Gina, as you might understand.'

''Course.' Winter would roll into spring, then into summer, and on and on and on. She wondered how she would feel as time went by and she saw him every week, twice a week, how ever many times, there at her house, collecting their daughter. She wondered how she would feel when there was a woman's face looking out from the passenger seat of his car. 'But when it comes to these arrangements there are a few conditions.'

'Yes?'

'Gina can't be out too late during the week because of her homework. So on the agreed days you'll have to arrange to be here fairly early so that she can be brought back home by, let's say, eight-thirty. That would give her time to do some homework and have a bath before you come so that she can just hop into bed when you drop her off.'

'Fine. But you'll have to understand that I work, and I can't always plan meetings down to a certain hour. Sometimes I'll have to give you very short notice of when I can see her, but I guarantee it'll be no less than twice a week, and I want her every other weekend.'

'She's going to be pulled from pillar to post,' Charlotte whispered, on the verge of tears.

'I gave you the option of making our arrangement permanent. You rejected it.'

'For all the right reasons!'

'Then there's the question of holidays.'

'I can't think about that right now.'

'Try,' Riccardo rasped harshly. He watched as she curled herself into a tighter ball on the chair.

'I don't know.'

'I will want her to spend some time in Italy. She has relatives over there, people she's never met.'

'I hadn't thought… How are they going to react?'

'With great joy,' Riccardo said dryly. 'My mother's been after this result for years. 'Course, she would have preferred to have seen her grandchild through the more conventional route of marriage, but there you go.'

'Marriage to a girl with the right connections,' Charlotte said bitterly.

'She gave up on that ambition a long time ago,' Riccardo told her shortly. She had resigned herself to a son who went out with 'babes', none of whom she had ever met anyway because they weren't of the variety that he took on holiday. *Like Charlie had said, with bullseye accuracy.*

'And what about the rest of the world?'

'I'm not following you.'

'Your friends. Business colleagues.'

'What about them?'

'What will they say? What will they think of you? I mean, it's not every day that a big cheese finds himself embroiled in a scandal…'

'Now who's the dinosaur?' Riccardo commented wryly. 'For starters, it's not a scandal. And then gossip involving businessmen barely qualifies as gossip. Anyway…' he shrugged, '…I really don't give a damn about what other people think of the happenings in my personal life.'

Charlotte wished she possessed such insouciance. She might just have been able to deal with Riccardo's presence in her life a bit better. As it was, she had only just recovered from the curiosity of friends and work-mates, who all now knew about Riccardo, and she foresaw miserable times ahead trying to handle her broken life. Which brought her back to her original remark about conditions.

'I also would rather you kept your private life out of Gina's domain…' she said tentatively, and Riccardo frowned. 'I mean…' She continued hurriedly, just in case he thought that she was trying to angle the conversation back to an argument about the women he dated. 'I don't care what you get up to between the sheets, but I don't want Gina being introduced to a procession of your women.'

'And if it's just the one?'

'Well, that would be different. Of course.' *Was there one?* she wondered?

'And should I bring her round for your inspection beforehand? Just to make sure that I'm not contravening any of your moral laws?'

'There's no need to be sarcastic,' Charlotte said hotly.

She looked so *young*. Young and vulnerable, leaning forward in the chair with her feet tucked solidly underneath her as if anchoring them down just in case they decided to stand up and flee. 'No, there's no need. You have my word. The only woman I will ever introduce to Gina will be the woman I intend to commit my life to.'

Charlotte felt a sharp pang at this imaginary woman and nodded.

'I needn't ask a similar condition of you,' Riccardo said politely through gritted teeth. 'As I know there already is a man in your life.' Something felt as though it was being ripped out of him. 'You never said…does Gina get along with him?' God knew, the paragon of a boyfriend, who had been lurking in the background for the past couple of weeks, was probably a dab hand at entertaining eight-year-old children. But no longer could he lay down laws about *her* private life. She had no objection to Gina meeting a woman if he was in a committed relationship. He was obliged to return the favour. More so, considering Gina doubtless had an easy relationship with Ben.

'Oh, most people get along with Ben,' Charlotte said, skirting round the question. 'I'm glad we sorted that one out, Riccardo, although I feel badly that you wasted all that money setting up stuff to work at home.'

'We'll sort out finances another day,' Riccardo said brusquely. He looked at his watch. Gina would be getting back to the house at any minute. 'And I suggest we both sit Gina down and break this to her.'

'Of course.' She hadn't missed that quick glance at his watch. The conversation for him was now terminated. They would provide a united front when they spoke to Gina later, but as far as he was concerned he was through with playing house. He had probably been through with it long before his departure meal tonight. She just hadn't been quick enough to spot it, but then love was good at blurring the focus.

She'd thought that she would be the one reassuring Gina that her dad would still be around even if he would no longer be living under the same roof as they were but, in the end, it was Riccardo who did all the talking. This was the tender side to him she had witnessed over the past weeks in his relationship with his daughter. There was no escaping his devotion, and Gina, instinctively, must have recognised that and believed him implicitly when he told her that he was going to see her as often as he possibly could, at least twice a week.

It was so hard to think that this was the same man who could be so cold and hostile when it suited him.

Later, with Gina in bed, the cold, hostile stranger returned. He would get his lawyer to clarify financial arrangements, he informed her, and he wanted guarantees that her volatile mood swings wouldn't influence his agreed visiting rights.

She looked terrified, curled up on the chair while he towered above her, but it didn't suit Riccardo to lessen the impact of his forceful personality. If anything, he wanted her to know that he would do whatever it took to assume his parental rights, just in case she got it into her head that he might disappear into the background at some convenient point in the future.

'And just to warn you,' he said, walking towards the bay window and perching. 'Expect a little disruption in your life. Up until now, I've kept this situation to myself, but that's over.'

'Disruption?' Charlotte asked, bewildered. 'What are you talking about?'

'Reporters. For Gina's sake, I'll try and keep them off your back, but I'm high profile in the world of business. This unusual situation is bound to generate some interest. So…' He walked towards the door and she followed his leisurely progress across the room warily. 'No men. There's a thin line between reporting and scandal.'

'I thought you didn't *care* about what other people thought of you, Riccardo!' Charlotte said, stung by his implication that she couldn't wait to jump into a relationship the minute he walked out of the front door.

'*I* don't.' He paused, and in his next sentence he managed to tell her exactly what he thought of her. 'But Gina might find it very confusing. And she *is* the important one in the equation, isn't she?'

CHAPTER NINE

CHARLOTTE'S only brush with the press had been a year and a half ago in an article in the local newspaper about the estate agency's expansion into the Midlands market. It had been tucked away on one of the middle pages, where space was given to heart-warming anecdotes and readers' views, under the corny heading of: AND NOW ON A LIGHTER NOTE! The reporter in question had been a bright-eyed and bushy-tailed school leaver who had anxiously consulted her list of questions and written a flattering report about the dynamic young executive who still managed to be a super-mum. Instead of focusing on interest rates, difficult first-time buyer markets or the surge away from London to cheaper outlying districts, she had concentrated on the feminist angle of the woman who could have it all. Frankly, Charlotte had not recognised herself in the descriptions.

She supposed that this was what happened to the bright-eyed and bushy-tailed local reporters—they hit the big time, went to work on national newspapers and mutated into sharks that could scent blood from fifty paces away.

They had homed in on the lucrative theme of 'billionaire with a past', and a shady one at that. She had nothing to say on the subject whenever the phone rang, and least of all when she was confronted with any of them invading her private space. But she seemed to have emerged from the whole saga as a sex siren with an agenda, though how they had arrived at that conclusion she had no idea, considering she hadn't asked him for a penny in all the time she had been a single mother. It was a question she hadn't put to them, too concerned to protect Gina from the invasive publicity, and too harassed from fending off the sudden surge of interest everyone seemed to be taking in her, from close friends to nodding acquaintances. She had fielded enough words of advice to fill an encyclopaedia.

Now, with the minutes ticking past, she peered through the window and spotted two reporters skulking. Next to her, Gina was itching to be off to school. It was Victorian Children Day for the Year Fours. Gina had woken up especially early, thrilled to be heading to school dressed as a ragamuffin Victorian schoolboy with ripped shirt, waistcoat, tattered trousers held up by a piece of corded rope, and school shoes which had been specially scuffed for the purpose. Right now she was content to accept the fact that they would be leaving 'in a minute'. Charlotte knew her daughter well enough to realise that her acceptably impatient shifting from foot to foot would quickly degenerate into querulous whining.

'Oh, come on,' she said, making her mind up. 'We might as well head off.'

'Just tell them to go away, Mum!'

'I would if I thought they'd listen.'

'Then get Dad to do it! He knows how to do everything!'

Charlotte swallowed back a very sour rejoinder. Fact was, Riccardo was fast moving into the stellar category of Superdad. He had also, unfairly, managed to deflect all negative press reporting by flinging his hands up in the air and *coming clean*. A youthful romance, a baby he had known nothing about, a marriage proposed and turned down, responsibilities accepted, *welcomed*. He was the man willing to turn his whole life upside down for the sake of his daughter, but for reasons beyond his comprehension Charlotte had rejected his pleas to formalise their relationship. He made a lot of heart-warming references to old-fashioned values, respect for family life, and in short managed to make her seem not just ridiculously stupid, for turning down a marriage proposal from a man who could click his fingers and have any woman he wanted, but also selfish, cold and proud to the point of lunacy.

In the face of these implications, Charlotte kept resolutely silent, fearing that one slipped word would be embroidered into God only knew what.

But the past few days had been hellish, and the lurking men at the gate outside was proving to be the final straw.

She grabbed Gina and hurtled outside, wearing an expression that could curdle milk. She met the same old questions, this time more intrusive, as one of them snidely implied that she might be positioning herself for a custody battle considering she was prepared to put her welfare above that of her daughter's.

Charlotte picked up her pace but she was perspiring by the time she was safely inside her car, windows rolled up against the clatter of voices outside.

On the way to school, she heard herself chatting to Gina, asking all the usual questions about homework, and making sure she ate all of her lunch. In her head, she replayed what that damned reporter had said about the possibility of a custody fight.

Could that happen? She feverishly wondered where he had managed to pluck that random statement from. Had Riccardo said anything about a custody battle? He had said nothing to *her*, had been decent and sympathetic about the whole press-invasion business, but had he let slip some intention to the wrong ears?

Whilst driving to the school and dropping Gina off, the seeds of unease had blossomed into full-blown panic, and she called in to the office, for the first time ever, with a phoney excuse about getting in late because of a blinding headache.

The slightest mention of Riccardo and they would be buzzing with curiosity. Honestly, it wasn't as though her circumstances had changed! She was still a hard-working mum with an eight-year-old daughter. How could scandal have wrapped itself around her so completely when, *technically* speaking, things were pretty much the same, give or take the sudden appearance of a wealthy Italian? Admittedly with looks to die for and a surprising flair for the role of martyr…

She got through to Riccardo on the second ring and didn't bother with pleasantries.

'I need to see you right now.'

Riccardo had programmed her into his mobile phone. He knew, as soon as his phone buzzed, that she would be on the other end of the line. He also knew what she wanted to see him about.

'Right now. Interesting that you think you can just pop in whenever it suits you.' He swivelled his chair so that he was facing the window. Moving out had been an error of judgement. His apartment seemed too big and too empty for just one. Having spent a lifetime without the slightest flicker of paternal yearnings to disturb the calm, ordered and preordained course of his formidably disciplined life, he had discovered that he missed his daughter, missed watching her as she sat frowning in front of her homework, missed the silly questions apropos of nothing in particular, missed the board games which had become a long-distant memory from his own childhood.

He also missed *her*—Charlotte. After a stressful day at work, when before he had looked to his blonde, leggy bimbos to distract him with the game of flirtation and sex, he had found himself looking forward to the peace and relaxation of her company, to her quick sense of humour, and that reluctant smile that lit up her face when he'd said something she couldn't help but find amusing.

Never one to sit around brooding over emotional dilemmas, Riccardo had decided that he would not accept what he had increasingly found to be the unacceptable. He would not accept the visiting rights to his daughter, with the so-called benefits of being able to return to his former life of pointless women and meals out. Half a life was not better than no life at all. Half a life was, for him, just a challenge, and he had risen to the challenge with the same brutal precision that had seen him climb over the years to the top of the jungle.

'This is all your fault, Riccardo,' Charlotte said, not bothering to wrap up the accusation in any phoney packaging.

'So what's new?'

'I'm not going to get into an argument with you on the telephone,' Charlotte snapped. 'I'm on my way to the underground.'

'When are you ever going to listen to me and *take taxis* when you want to get around?'

'Oh, for goodness' sake, Riccardo!' Momentarily distracted, Charlotte clicked her tongue in annoyance and stifled the little spurt of pleasure his words generated. Belatedly, she remembered that this was what Italian men were all about. Give Riccardo an available blonde, and he was all passion and fire. Give him the mother of his child, and he became solicitous and weirdly old-fashioned. Hence that pious, moral stance that had resulted in her having all the negative press chucked at her front door. Which fired her up all over again.

'I'll be at your office in forty minutes or so. Now, are you going to see me or aren't you? Because I want to talk to you, and if you don't see me I shall just sit in front of your office until you do.'

Now *that*, Riccardo thought, would really cause a stir—the mother of his child camping out at his office door! The wagging tongues, which feared him too much to wag in front of him, would be in full force.

'I'll meet you in the boardroom suite on the top floor

in precisely forty-five minutes. Take the executive lift up. I'll make sure the people on Reception know that you're expected.'

Charlotte had very little doubt that they would have denied her entry, when her face had been splashed all over the gossip columns like a criminal in a 'wanted' ad.

She made it to Riccardo's office in record time and headed for the lift to the boardroom suite with her head down, not wanting to catch anyone's eye, and resenting that she was forced into hiding because of a situation over which she had had no control.

The boardroom was literally a suite. One vast room was dominated by a long walnut table with sufficient seating for twenty. Spanning out from that central space was a luxury bathroom, which perplexed Charlotte as she took advantage of arriving twenty minutes early to snoop around. What executive would suddenly find himself in need of a quick shower before the next high-level conference? Then there was a library stocked with shelves of books, the titles of which were sufficient to induce sudden sleepiness, and a table on which was fanned out every national newspaper. Including, she noticed wryly, the ones best known for their salacious girlie pictures. Finally, there was a big sitting area, decked out in soft sofas and chairs, and along one wall all the facilities needed to make drinks of both an alcoholic and non-alcoholic nature.

Charlotte took up position on one of the pale blue comfy chairs facing the door and leant forward, hands clasped over one crossed knee.

As always, the impact of seeing him momentarily

took her breath away as he entered the room, one hand tucked elegantly into his trouser pocket. It was still early. The tie was still on. Usually, when he'd returned to the house in the early evenings, the tie would have been off, the top two buttons of his shirt undone, as though restlessness had got the better of him during the course of the day.

She winced at the unwelcome reminder of what it had been like to share a house with him.

'How could you?' she demanded bluntly, watching as he sauntered over to a chair and book up position facing her. Charlotte stood up, walked across to the table groaning under the weight of newspapers, and picked up one of the tabloids, opening it to the centre pages and dumping it on his lap so that he could see the headlines in all their glory—TYCOON'S LOVE-CHILD IN TUG OF WAR!

Riccardo glanced down at it with disinterest. 'You should never read the gossip columns, Charlie. I never do.'

'Well, bully for you, Riccardo!' She planted herself in front of him, hands on her hips. 'I have no ivory towers to hide behind! I have to go out to work and take Gina to school, and there are *reporters swarming everywhere*!' Slight exaggeration, prompted by his cool-as-a-cucumber attitude. 'They're making life a living hell for us, Riccardo,' she continued, gratified to see that he at least seemed to be giving her words some consideration. 'They're asking questions, and even though I don't give them answers they're still jotting stuff down, so I'm in constant fear of what I'll read in the press!'

'How is Gina dealing with the attention?'

Seems fairly thrilled. 'Distraught.'

'She didn't seem too distraught when I spoke to her on the telephone last night.'

'She's hiding it well. She doesn't want to let you down.' She swept one hand through her hair and returned to flop down on the chair. 'Did you have to go and tell them all that stuff about proposing marriage and being turned down? You could have just kept a low profile and everything would have blown over by now. Instead, what do you do? Blather on about values and tradition, making me out to be selfish and heartless!'

'I did warn you that the press might get involved.'

'Yes, I know *that*! But did you have to be so…*long winded* with them?'

'I've found that it's the only way to get rid of them. The slightest hint of any cloak and dagger stuff and they immediately think that there's something to hide. Give them the barest bones and then walk away.'

'I wouldn't call your marriage proposal the "barest bones". Actually, I think that would come under the heading of some pretty meaty stuff,' Charlotte said waspishly.

'Have you had any breakfast?'

'How can I eat?' She glared at him. 'My stomach's a mess.'

'I'll get them to bring you up something. Scrambled eggs on toast all right?'

It sounded yummy to Charlotte. 'I'm not hungry. I've completely lost my appetite with all that's been going on.'

'Mmm. Yes. Believe me, I do understand.' For a woman with no appetite and nerves that were shredded, she still managed to look damned sexy in that little pinstriped number. '*I* was a little taken aback when I first found my face in the Italian nationals for something trivial.'

'I'm more than a little *taken aback*, Riccardo.'

'I'd get them off your case if I could, but…' He shrugged elegantly and rose to his feet to get them both a cup of coffee. His secretary had seen fit to brew some fresh when she'd known that he required use of the top floor. He was back within minutes, carrying two cups of steaming coffee and a plate of biscuits which Charlotte briefly considered ignoring, before giving in to hunger. The truth was she really hadn't eaten any breakfast. The reporters by the gate had unnerved her, and besides Gina's costume had been patched together virtually at the eleventh hour. She had still been sewing on buttons when Gina had sat down for her bowl of cereal.

'But *what*? If you wanted to, you could…could tell them to back off.'

'They're having a field day at the moment with this,' Riccardo drawled, stretching out his legs and sipping from the china cup which looked inappropriate in his big hands. 'The world's a grim place, and in a grim place there's nothing like some juicy gossip to lighten the atmosphere.'

'I don't like the atmosphere being lightened at my expense.'

'Nor do I.' Riccardo watched her flustered face over the rim of his cup. Had she really thought that he would be able to turn off the media attention the way he could turn off a tap? He felt himself puff up like a horny teenager being given a sideways glance by the hot girl in the class. 'Spare a thought for me,' he continued, and was amused to see from her expression that the last thing she felt inclined to do was spare a thought for him. 'My reputation has been put through the wringer.'

'Riccardo, you didn't *have* a reputation. Well, you did—a reputation for being successful in your field and going out with empty-headed blondes like the one I met.'

'Now if you came here to insult me…'

'I didn't,' Charlotte said hurriedly. She sighed. 'Okay. You're more used to this sort of thing. How long can I expect it to last? It's wearing me down.'

This will be someone's fish-and-chip wrapping by the end of the week, Riccardo thought. 'Who can predict the appetite of gossip mongers? And who knows how far they'll dig?'

'How far they'll dig?' Charlotte said weakly.

'Look…' Riccardo leaned forward, resting his elbows on his knees and thoughtfully rubbing his thumbs together. 'It's always ugly when the press get hold of someone's personal life. There's a reason they're called mud-rakers. Now, it really doesn't affect me, but, yes, I am concerned for Gina. She's distraught, as you have told me.'

Charlotte uneasily wondered whether that little exaggeration had been such a good idea. 'Well…perhaps "distraught" is a bit overblown.'

'Okay, then. *Distressed.*'

'Yes, well…'

'I know you might not care for this alternative…' Riccardo lowered his voice, a man giving great thought and consideration to a delicate issue. 'But I can protect Gina more if she's with me.'

'No!'

'Hear me out, Charlie!' The lazy voice was suddenly as sharp as the crack of a whip, and Charlotte sat up, momentarily lost for speech. 'The reporters that swarm around you wouldn't dare do the same with me. I have people who fend my calls, and when my line is temporarily redirected, as it is now, they simply siphon off the unwelcomed calls. If someone I know needs to talk to me, they have my mobile number. I also have bodyguards. You wouldn't have noticed them. They're very discreet, and of course will disappear if I ask them to.'

'You have *bodyguards*? What kind of world do you live in?'

'The kind of world where the wealthy are possible targets. You forget, I am Italian. My country has its own past history of kidnappings. If Gina were with me, I could ensure that at least some of the inconveniences of what she is experiencing now could be dealt with.'

'No way!' Charlotte was still recovering from the shock of knowing that Riccardo had *bodyguards*. Where had they been lurking when he had been staying with her? Behind the bushes in the back garden? Under the mat at the front door? She worried at the idea now put into her head that, with all the publicity going on like a whirlpool around them—from which she was emerging in a pretty poor light through no fault of her own—Riccardo would stand a fair chance of persuading a court of law that, decent and honourable man that he was, he might be more suitable as a full-time carer. Even though he had given no hint that he might have that trick up his sleeve. Even though logic and reason told her that judge would probably file in favour of the mother. But doubts, even unreasonable doubts, had a nasty habit of creeping under the skin like a deadly virus.

'*Why* no way?' Riccardo asked in a long-suffering voice. 'We both want what's best for her, don't we?'

'Yes, well, she's coping all right at the moment.'

'I thought you said that she wasn't.'

'It's a nuisance.'

'And you came here to put the blame firmly at my door,' Riccardo said dryly.

'No!' Charlotte flushed uncomfortably.

'You saw a couple of reporters and blew a fuse. Look, there's another solution to this problem, and maybe this time you'll give it a bit more thought. Neither of us wants to be in the glaring limelight. You have a job to do, as do I, and Gina has to go to school without her life being disrupted. We continue as we are and who knows how long we'll be a scandalous affair.'

Charlotte snorted sourly under her breath. 'None of this would have happened if you weren't such a big cheese.'

Riccardo raised his eyebrows and smiled slowly at her, and Charlotte reluctantly grinned back.

'Marry me,' he said abruptly, never imagining he would return to this place having once been rejected. He noticed that she didn't immediately recoil. 'As a couple, we would have no story. A normal life, Charlie. You could keep your job, even though it's not in my nature to see my wife work, and you wouldn't have to think that at any given time you might be pounced on by a reporter wanting an update. You've seen how the kids of wealthy people can become specimens under the tabloid press microscopes…'

'Not *all.*' So, he hadn't mentioned the 'L' word, so she still had all her arguments about marriages of convenience being empty shells—but she had lived with him...shared the same space. She had liked it, whether she was willing to admit it or not, had liked seeing her daughter with her father. In life, people made sacrifices. She would sacrifice the perfect dream and instead live out the shared one, one in which she loved but was not loved in return. She'd be liked, though, and as the mother of his child always respected. Would it really be so bad?

And no more hassle with *anyone*. The curious looks at work would come to an end, as would the nagging suspicion that she might be recognised by perfect strangers because they could place her face from somewhere. Normal had never looked so good.

'And, like you say, all this will blow over in time...' She imagined being able to rely on someone else in a way she had never been able to in her life before. Someone who could share her concerns when Gina was ill, or had difficult homework. Someone who could help with the big decisions in her daughter's life, the schools she would attend. The list of temptations grew steadily longer.

'Also,' Riccardo said silkily. 'Look at it from my point of view for a minute instead of your own: I want to be able to give Gina all the things money can buy.'

'Which is the wrong way to bring up a child!' Charlotte said robustly.

Riccardo didn't miss a beat. He could sense her coming round, and the nearer he got to his goal the more he wanted it. 'Which is why I shall rely on you to rein me in when I want to show up at the house with a ten-foot pink elephant or the latest-model quad bike.'

Charlotte shuddered, and in the intervening silence Riccardo steamrollered on, not giving her time to back-track over the old arguments against which he had no adequate responses. 'Better that than for Gina to grow up and witness the disparity in our lifestyles.'

'Meaning that you would be able to tempt her away from me just because you could lavish her with whatever she wanted?' But he had hit an open nerve, because she knew that with the best will in the world children could be swayed. The latest-model quad bike would always look better and shinier than the home-made doll's house under the Christmas tree. It wasn't fair and it wasn't right, but it was life. And, even if Gina held firm and was sensible enough to make the right judgements, how fair would it be that she should have to be put through the process of choice simply because her mother didn't want to marry Riccardo because he didn't love her the way she loved him?

'I would never, ever set out to do any such thing…'

The 'but' hung in the air between them like a sharp-ened knife ready to drop.

'Will you give me time to consider it?'

Riccardo knew that the deal was done. 'We couldn't continue to live in your house,' he said briskly, making sure that she didn't see his pleasure. 'It is too small for the three of us.'

'We managed just—'

'Which in turn might mean taking Gina out of her school, transferring her to another.'

'She's happy there, and she's not moving.'

Riccardo decided, in the interests of peace-making, not to pursue the point. 'Fine. But we move, and who better to source the right place than you?'

'I haven't yet made my mind up,' Charlotte said weakly.

'You have. Now all we need to do is sort out the details.'

Step one in growing up had been having Gina. Now, step two was the realisation that nothing really worked out the way you truly wanted. But he was right, and there was no use pretending. Her mind *was* made up bar the shouting, and, yes, the details would have to be worked out.

'We'll have to tell Gina.' She lowered her eyes because she could feel the glitter of tears brightening them.

'This evening,' Riccardo agreed. 'And, whilst you can source locations and possibilities, I would want the three of us to look at any potential houses together.'

'I don't know what kind of house you would want.' Things seemed to be moving at breakneck speed, and she tried to yank it back to a pace she could deal with.

'You know me. You know the kind of place I'd be comfortable with.'

'I *don't* know you.'

'Of course you do. You know me better than any other woman has ever done.' Riccardo shocked himself with the admission. A whisper of vulnerability threaded its way through his body and he fought it away. 'I know you probably have ideas on weddings. All women seem to. I am happy to go along with whatever you want. Big, small, fancy, simple…'

'I don't care.'

Riccardo watched her downbent face with narrowed eyes, feeling like the executioner dragging someone to the guillotine. Was this how she truly saw him? Still? Was she coming to him defeated, because he had cleverly put her in a position from which she saw no retreat? Dammit, he was trying!

'Your call. But I won't sit around waiting. If you don't care, then you won't mind getting married quietly in the Register Office at Marylebone.'

Charlotte shrugged. Gina would be over the moon, which was a cheerful thought. 'What do we do about…?'

'About what?'

'About…'

Comprehension dawned, and Riccardo gave her a slow, wolfish smile. 'Sleeping arrangements? To put it delicately.'

'You slept in the guest room before.'

'That was then and this is now,' Riccardo drawled. 'When I am your husband, then I have no intention of our marriage being in name only. And there's no need to look so primly offended at the prospect.'

He pushed himself out of the chair and strolled over to Charlotte, so that he could lean over her, hands on either side of her chair. 'We both know that when all the talk of our union being for convenience only is over, there is still left the interesting fact that we want one another. Look at you. Eyes as wide as saucers, pupils dilated.' He lifted one hand and tugged her bottom lip gently with his finger. It was all the more erotic because his eyes remained pinned to her face. 'Wouldn't you like me to touch you right here? Right now?'

'No, I would *not*!' What should have been a firm, controlled, maybe even slightly amused protest—because spinsterish outrage had just not been cutting it—emerged as a strangulated gasp for air, with a feeble denial thrown in for good measure.

'Tut, tut, Charlie. You'll really have to do a bit better than that…' He leant into her and covered her mouth with his, sliding his tongue between her lips, which were parted in surprise.

In that split second, Charlotte realised that she was no longer going to fight him. She loved him and she would take what she could, because her previous efforts at self-denial had been painful and futile. Her body melted and she arched up to return his kiss, feeding his hunger with her own. She felt his momentary surprise, and wondered whether he had been expecting her to put up her usual resistance, but then it was as if her response had fired up something in him, something savage and urgent. He pulled her to her feet, backing her slowly but inexorably towards the cool wall until she was pressed back against it.

They managed to remove her jacket without breaking apart, and she helped him as he began unbuttoning her blouse until he could reach inside and caress her aching, tender breasts through the lacy bra.

Riccardo was dimly aware of the inappropriate nature of their surroundings. He was breaking every single one of his own codes of practice by doing what he was doing in the sanctum of his working environment. Women had always been for pleasure, and pleasure had never crossed over into his working life. The two had been kept apart, physically and mentally.

But he couldn't help himself. Not when her breasts were pushing against that bra, begging to be suckled. He ground his body against her, letting her know how aroused he was, and he almost embarrassed himself by ejaculating as she rubbed him through his trousers.

His secretary would know better than to disturb him when she knew he was using the top floor. They would not be interrupted, and right now he had to have her, needed to taste every inch of her body, from her nipples all the way down to the honeyed moisture between her legs. His body was on fire and starving, and common sense would just have to wait.

CHAPTER TEN

BUMPING into Ben three days later was an accident of chance, and in the interim Charlotte had had ample time to wonder what she had got herself into. An emotional quagmire, or so it seemed, in which the main protagonists, Gina and Riccardo, were very happy, leaving her to nurse her confusion on her own. In her head.

Both she and Riccardo had spoken to Gina together. They had anticipated questions, but Gina had accepted this new, startling change of events with an ingenuous lack of curiosity. Typical eight-year-old. Precociously bright she might be, but when it had come to Mummy and Daddy getting married there had been nothing incisive about her exclaiming 'Great! Can my friends come round and meet my dad?'

And the press, alerted by invisible radar, had changed from pursuit to writing treacly praise for the importance of marriage. Within this framework, Riccardo seemed very satisfied because he had, she acknowledged, got precisely what he had wanted from the very first minute he'd realised that he had a daughter. And he even had *her* thrown in for good measure.

He had all but moved in, and when he'd been around his eyes had followed her, he'd made sure to touch her, even in passing, and when Gina hadn't been around he'd pinned her against the wall and they had stolen their heated kisses like star-crossed lovers. And that was the one thing they weren't, because 'love' was the taboo word that had been resoundingly absent in all his dealings with her. He was content with the lust, and she no longer had the strength or the conviction to resist it.

She had resigned herself to the unhappy prospect of wondering when the lust would end and when he would begin to discreetly cast his net further afield in search of more nubile pastures. She would probably never know, because he would leave no careless signs behind him, and he would continue to treat her with the respect due to her position in his life. And she would never confront him, because she knew already that ignorance would be bliss.

Ben was lucky enough to find her at midday on a sullen, overcast Thursday, sitting in her office with an untouched sandwich next to her, supposedly mulling over a report on first-time buyers and interest rates, but instead gloomily contemplating her life.

It was a few seconds before Charlotte was even aware of his presence by her door, and a few more seconds before she registered who he was, but when she did she found that she was overjoyed to see him. She had spoken to him a couple of times after the story had broken, and he was the only one she had been honest with, and the only one who had not given her a hearty little pep-talk on how lucky she was to have landed the biggest fish in the sea.

'That's not a good look for someone living out the fairy-tale dream,' was the first thing he said as he stepped into the office and shut the door behind him. 'What's wrong, Charlotte?'

'*What's wrong?* How much time have you got to spare?' She gave a manic little laugh that ended on a strangled sob.

'Okay, my girl. On your feet. I'm taking you out to lunch.'

'I can't, Ben. I've got *all this*.' She waved her hand to take in the computer and the stacks of paperwork sitting on her desk, patiently waiting for her to get her act together.

'You still have to eat. Now, up. We won't go far. I'll have you safely delivered back to the grindstone by one. I'm here for a meeting with Parry at one-thirty, anyway.'

'Honestly, Ben, don't ruin your plans for me. I know you just popped in to say hi.' She stood up. 'But I'm not getting any work done, and lunch out is just what I need. I can't tell you how miserable it is being the luckiest girl in the world.'

They went to a brasserie round the corner from the office. They could be guaranteed a certain amount of privacy there, because the food was delicious but wildly overpriced and everyone else in the office avoided the place like the plague. It was also the perfect place to have an emotional conversation without risk of being overheard. The tables were helpfully spaced apart and the atmosphere, even at midday, was curiously intimate.

Without too much prompting, Charlotte poured out her heart. Ben provided the handkerchief, and over an expensive, exquisite beefburger listened to her rambling tale of love and panic, and confusion and love, and lust and uncertainty, and more love. He remained stoic when she told him with an anguished groan that she wished to God she could have loved *him* the way she loved Riccardo. Ben, who had just started seeing another woman, hoped for the adoration Charlotte obviously still felt for her ex-boyfriend and now husband-to-be. To have that would be nice. Standing outside, he was pleased to see that Charlotte looked a lot less teary, even though he had offered no helpful pieces of advice but had just listened. When she hugged him, he freely wrapped her in his arms and gave her a brotherly kiss on her forehead.

Across the road, Riccardo was halted in his tracks. He hadn't expected this. The girl at the office had told him that Charlotte had gone to lunch at that expensive place round the corner; she couldn't remember the name but it was something French. She hadn't said anything about the man Charlotte had gone with, and Riccardo had assumed... What had he assumed? That she was tied to him in some way simply because she had finally given in to her physical attraction? Hadn't she told him often enough that lust was not the glue that held a relationship together? What the hell had he been thinking?

He watched from a distance as she stood still on the pavement for a few seconds on her own, wrapping her arms around herself. She was smiling, and from where he was standing that smile looked mighty happy indeed.

Riccardo felt the blood which had drained away from

his body rush to his head in a burst of jealous, possessive rage. He was shaking as he leant heavily against the wall and drew in one long, shuddering breath. Then he turned away and began walking. He didn't go near his office. Trying to work would have been impossible. For the first time since he had been living in London, he did the unthinkable and took a taxi to Regent's Park, which was peaceful and fairly deserted. In his head, he replayed what had confronted him outside the brasserie. His wife to be, his *woman*, wrapped up in the arms of another man. There was a heavy sensation in the pit of his stomach which felt like concrete.

He should have talked to her before, really talked. But how could he have, when he had known nothing of how he felt about her until an hour ago? When he had witnessed her in the arms of her ex-boyfriend. If indeed he *was* an 'ex'.

The prospect of living a life walking in the shadow of someone else filled him with searing rage and now he knew why. He dialled her number on his mobile phone without bothering to torture himself with self-analysis, and got through to her immediately.

'I need to see you,' he told her. 'Right now.'

'I've got a stack of work to do, Riccardo. Can it wait until later?' Having lunch with Ben had been a good idea. Charlotte felt calmer now, more resigned to her destiny. She couldn't resist Riccardo, and that being the case then she would have to stop acting as though the world had caved in. No one was more pitiful than the person who moped around feeling sorry for herself. She had made her choice and she would live with it and accept its limitations.

'No. Do you want me to meet you at your office?'

'No,' Charlotte said hurriedly, shuddering at the thought of every member of staff subjecting them to in-depth scrutiny. 'Where are you now?'

'Regent's Park.'

'You're in *Regent's Park*?'

'You can always come here, but it's a dreary day to be outside.'

'Okay. I'll meet you at the house. I can bring some of this work back with me and do it later after Gina's gone to bed. Is…is everything okay?'

'No. But I'll explain when I see you.'

It was so unlike Riccardo to say something like that that Charlotte felt a flutter of fear. She couldn't pack her things up fast enough, and on the Tube back her head was filled with sickening scenarios. Had he changed his mind about marrying her? Maybe her behaviour had finally turned him off. Maybe sleeping with a woman while suspecting she didn't like him had awakened in him the obvious desire to have more than just a body. She had lain in his arms and still kept him at a distance. She had been aware of doing that, and now she wondered whether he had finally got fed up with her sour grapes. He wasn't to know that she'd just been trying to protect herself.

Or maybe he was ill. That disturbing thought sneaked its way into her subconscious, and once there refused to go away. Why else would he have been at Regent's Park, of all places? If there was something seriously wrong with him, then what better place for peace, to think things through?

From these two scenarios, worrying offshoots wreaked havoc with her nervous system, and she was white-faced by the time she made it to the house and let herself in.

'I'm in here.'

Charlotte dropped her bag and briefcase and kicked off her shoes. She found him in the sitting room, lights off, nursing a cup of coffee. He looked at her, then back at the coffee, as if hoping to find inspiration in the mug, like a reader of tea leaves.

'What's wrong?' she demanded. 'Why were you sitting in Regent's Park at this time of day?'

'Sit down.' He watched as she scuttled across to the chair. Yes, she could melt in his arms, *had* melted in his arms, because she couldn't resist his touch, but what good was that when she still shied away from him like a scared rabbit whenever he wasn't touching her? He thought with regret of how she had wanted him all those years ago and how he had thrown it all away because his bright, glittering future had had no place for her at that time. Now, ensconced in his bright, glittering future, he could only think how much he wanted that girl back, the one who curved willingly into his arms and would never have sat watching him cautiously from the furthest possible chair, her body language stiff with tension.

'I came to your office today.' He stood up abruptly, wishing to God he had had the sense to have poured himself something a little stronger than a cup of coffee.

'You did? When? I didn't see you.'

'I was told that you had gone out for lunch.'

'Oh, right. Yes.' Charlotte thought uncomfortably about Ben and reddened.

Watching her, Riccardo now knew for sure that she still had an ongoing relationship with the other man. So maybe she wasn't sleeping with him, but she was giving him her love, and what greater gift was there, after all?

'How long has it been going on?' he asked roughly, pushing himself to his feet and pacing the room.

Charlotte wearily wondered whether she was letting herself back in for another speech about relinquishing all contact with every other man on the face of the earth, even if the contact was perfectly innocent, because that was the *Italian* way. Never mind that he wouldn't have a problem with his *Italian* way allowing him to take a mistress as and when he so desired.

She opened her mouth to speak, but he silenced her with his hand. 'No. Don't answer that. I don't have a right to know and I do not want to, anyway.'

'You mean you're not going to lay down laws about Ben? I don't believe you!' She laughed, but nervously, because this too was unlike the Riccardo she knew. Which brought her right back to the 'seriously ill' theory.

'I gave you up eight years ago, Charlie. I have no right to ask anything of you now.' He dragged a chair closer to hers and sat down heavily, raking his fingers through his hair before resting his arms loosely on his thighs.

'But I want to.'

'Want to *what*?'

'Ask a millions things of you. Ask you not to see that man ever again. Ask you never to even let him cross your *mind*. I have a problem with him. I have a problem with your friendship with him.'

'You mean you're *jealous*?' Charlotte asked incredulously, and Riccardo flushed.

'What's so weird about that?' he asked, his head snapping up. 'I am a jealous man. Of course I can't bear the thought of you enjoying the company of another man.'

'But Ben isn't *competition*.'

'No. Because you have reluctantly come round to my proposal and decided to marry me.' His eyes tangled with hers and Charlotte felt her heart do a crazy loop. She wanted to tell him to spend a little more time discussing the jealousy issue, because just the thought of that sent an illicit thrill racing through her. 'But I see now that you were right all along. Reluctant acceptance…a business arrangement, call it what you will…just is not good enough. For either of us. I thought that it would be fine, that it was in the best interests of our daughter, but now…'

'Now you've changed your mind.'

Riccardo nodded with difficulty and tried to marshal his thoughts. 'We were happy once.' *No.* Just referring to their happiness in the past tense scared him because it made him realise that it might be lost to him for ever and there would be nothing he could do about it. Money could buy him anything on the face of the earth, but if she turned him away then nothing it could buy would be of any value. 'I know what you think of me. But we could be happy again. I…was happy when we were living together, and if I didn't show it then that was my fault. Don't say anything. I just want you to think about what I am going to say to you, and if you still don't want me then so be it.'

Charlotte didn't think there was anything she *could* say, because her tongue seemed to be glued to the roof of her mouth.

'Eight years ago, I let you go. We were both too young, and there was too much living left to do to settle down with one person.'

'I know.' Her cheeks were tinged with dull colour. 'We've gone over this ground a million times before. I thought we'd made peace with the past.'

'What I am trying to say is that the best thing that ever happened in my life was the day you walked back into it.' His dark eyes met hers, and Charlotte held her breath, not wanting to shatter the moment. 'Yes, I was furious that you had had a child, *my* child, and not seen fit to tell me. But when I saw you again…' He relived the moment and briefly closed his eyes before looking at her. 'Everything that had once been there flooded back. It was as though those eight years of absence had never been.'

'What do you mean?' Charlotte was almost too afraid to ask just in case she had missed some very obvious agenda that would put paid to the soaring hope blossoming inside her.

'For eight years I did what I was programmed to do,' Riccardo said heavily. 'And I enjoyed it, or I thought I did. Women came and went, and I figured that was perfectly normal.' He glanced down at his fingers and thought how odd it felt to be at the mercy of something he couldn't rationalise. 'You came along, Charlie, and it was as though I had been living half a life. I don't want to marry you just for the sake of Gina. I want to marry you for *me*, because I can't go back to that half life. And, before you say a word, I can make you happy.'

He went over to her and sat on the arm of her chair because somehow, by being physically close, she might absorb the urgency of what he was saying. 'You think you need the safety of that other man, but you don't. All I am asking is a chance… I love you, my darling. You complete me.'

'Perhaps you could say that again?' Charlotte at last found her voice and she smiled at him, a wide, blissful smile that lit up her face.

'Come on, Charlie,' Riccardo, watching the transformation of her expression, felt deliriously happy. 'I've bared my soul. Now it's your turn.'

Neither was allowed to let the grass grow under their feet. Gina made sure of that. She wanted to be a part of everything, and no decision was to be made without her consultation. The dreaded meeting with Riccardo's mother turned out to be not quite the terrible event Charlotte had envisaged.

'She'll hate me,' she'd told Riccardo, the day before his mother was due to land for a long weekend with them. 'She'll complain about the size of my house. She'll complain about *everything*.' She could remember all too well the austere, aristocratic bearing and the disparaging, soul-destroying personality. But Riccardo had been right to reassure her that his mother had mellowed over time, and Gina had broken the ice. The two together had formed an amusing and conspirational relationship which oversaw the details of the wedding, and six months later, Charlotte and Riccardo had been married. It was a fairly small service, followed by a much bigger reception, and afterwards a fortnight in Italy, during which they'd barely seen their daughter who'd done the rounds of relatives and had been overjoyed to be the centre of attention.

Riccardo, who increasingly found it hard to understand how he could have lived his life without Charlotte, returned to their new, spacious house in Richmond every evening to the warmth of his family. And when, on their first anniversary, he was informed that he was going to be a father for the second time, he felt pride and joy swell inside his heart for the woman sitting opposite him in the restaurant, demurely sipping from her glass of mineral water.

'You'll give up work, won't you?' She had stayed on to oversee the running of the office on a part-time basis, and now she nodded, with a slow smile.

'Can't wait. Gina's settled in her new school, life is settled...' She could feel tears of happiness well up. 'And it's about time you did it the Italian way and started supporting me!' Then she grinned, because it was only what he had wanted from the minute she had looked at him and said, 'I do...'

THE RICH MAN'S LOVE-CHILD

BY
MAGGIE COX

The day **Maggie Cox** saw the film version of *Wuthering Heights*, with a beautiful Merle Oberon and a very handsome Laurence Olivier, was the day she became hooked on romance. From that day onwards she spent a lot of time dreaming up her own romances, secretly hoping that one day she might become published and get paid for doing what she loved most! Now that her dream is being realised, she wakes up every morning and counts her blessings. She is married to a gorgeous man, and is the mother of two wonderful sons. Her two other great passions in life—besides her family and reading/writing—are music and films.

Don't miss Maggie's latest novel,
***One Desert Night*, available from the**
Mills & Boon® Modern™ series in March.

To James,
a truly kindred spirit.

CHAPTER ONE

'OH, WHAT a beautiful house!'

'Yes, darling.'

'And look at the lovely horses, Mummy!'

'Yes…they're grand too.'

'Can we ride them?'

'No, sweetheart.'

'Why not?'

'Because they don't belong to us.'

Caitlin wrapped her daughter's warm palm into her own icy one and squeezed it. Outside Mick Malone's cab, which had picked them up from the airport and was taking them to her childhood home, the usually verdant but now snow-covered pastures sped past—all part of a vast country estate.

Glancing beyond the horses that were attempting to crop the frozen grass, Caitlin spied long low roofs and high hedges, and in the distance a large Georgian house, bordering on the palatial. Its long sweeping drive fanned out from a pair of massive stone pillars and black wrought-iron gates tipped with gold, and was lined with frosted conifers, sparkling in the cold January light. To a little girl raised in a cramped terraced house in a busy South London suburb Caitlin didn't doubt it must resemble something out of a fairytale, and the scene was made even more enchanting by the low orange globe setting in the west behind it.

'Who do they belong to, then?'

The child was leaning across her mother's lap to try and get a better view of the creatures that had so captivated her, her soft moss-green eyes full of hope and yet disappointment too, because she hadn't managed to procure the promise of a ride.

'They belong to a family called MacCormac.'

Her glance suddenly collided with the too-interested gaze of the florid-faced driver in front of them, and Caitlin squirmed a little in her seat as a wave of uncomfortable heat assailed her.

'I'm sure they're very nice people to have such nice horses,' the little girl chattered. 'Perhaps if we ask them ever so nicely they might let us ride them. What do you think, Mummy?'

'I think you're asking far too many questions just now, Sorcha,' Caitlin admonished her daughter, not unkindly.

Whether the MacCormac family were 'nice' people or not was hardly on her agenda right now…even if the very name was apt to deluge her stomach with wild butterflies. Not when she'd come home for the first time in four and a half years for the sole distressing purpose of attending her father's funeral.

'Kids! They drive you mad, but you wouldn't be without them,' Mick Malone cheerfully observed, determinedly catching Caitlin's eye in his mirror. 'And sure she must be a great comfort to you, now that both your parents are gone, God rest their souls.'

'Yes, she is,' Caitlin murmured, silently wishing that the man—a long-time friend of her father's—would not try and engage her in any more conversation until they pulled up in front of the small farm cottage where she'd grown up.

She was almost too weary and heartsick to talk to anyone. It simply took too much energy to respond to polite and well-meant niceties when she felt so drained and hopeless inside. *Both her parents gone...it didn't seem possible.*

Deliberately withdrawing her glance, she threaded her fingers distractedly through her daughter's fine wheaten-gold hair and prayed for the strength to deal with whatever must come in the days ahead. As well as her grief at losing her father there was another shadow looming on the horizon, and she was more than anxious at the prospect of facing it. It was one that had been weighing down on Caitlin's heart for four and a half long years, dogging her every waking moment. She was going to need all the help she could get to deal with that particular daunting spectre.

It was a throwaway remark made by one of the farmers at the local inn, while Flynn was supping his pint and wrestling with the intricacies of a legendary chieftain's battle plan for his latest book on mythological Ireland, that made him suddenly concentrate with razor-sharp acuity on the conversation being conducted at the bar.

'Tommy Burns's daughter came home for his funeral, so I hear. She was a fine-looking girl, that one…must be a grand young lady now.'

'Must have broke his heart when she took off like that. No doubt he wanted her to marry one of the local lads and stay close to home. Being as though she was his only child an all.'

'Wasn't there a rumour going round that she had a thing for that MacCormac fella? You know? The one that inherited the estate and practically half the county?'

'Aye, there was.'

Flynn froze in his seat, the blood raging so hotly inside him that he sensed sweat break out on his skin, then chill again so that he was almost shivering. He couldn't have been more shocked if he'd just heard that World War Three had been announced. Caitlin was home and her father was dead? Staring at the two thickset farmers perched on their barstools as they mutually paused in their conversation to drink their pints of Guinness—both of them clearly having no idea that he was sitting in a booth not far behind them—he grimaced and shook his head. They could not realise what a bomb they had just detonated.

Setting his own half-drunk pint down on the deeply grooved and scarred wooden table, he found that all desire to finish it had abruptly deserted him. He tugged the collar of his battered leather jacket up around his ears, then stalked from the near empty bar out into the bitter wintry afternoon. His lean face with its hollowed out cheekbones was sombrely set—as if he was preoccupied with a battle plan of his own.

As his booted feet hit the deep, impacted snow that blanketed the narrow pavement and he headed towards the corner where he'd parked the Land Rover Flynn wondered how it had not reached his ears until now that Tom Burns had died and Caitlin had returned for his funeral. Someone known to him—either family or friend—would surely have heard and told him? Nothing much went unreported in their small rural community. Was there some kind of unspoken conspiracy going on amongst the people who were close to him?

Caitlin's return had always promised to be a potential minefield after what had happened—even though he had long-ago given up hope that he might ever see her again. Certainly his family hoped he would not. The way they saw it, she came from poor farm labourers' stock and inhabited a very different world from the rich and powerful MacCormacs and their ilk… Theirs was a world that didn't willingly invite or encourage integration. They certainly hadn't been happy when Flynn had started an affair with the girl.

But Flynn had been in no mood to entertain so much as one single complaint from any of them at the time. Not from his mother, his uncles, his brother or his brother's wife…Not when he'd already buckled under familial pressure once before, when he'd been young, and had married a girl from the 'right end of the social spectrum' who'd then ended up pregnant with another man's baby while still wed to Flynn. What had sickened him the most was that he hadn't discovered that the child—a boy they'd named Danny—wasn't his until he was six months old and his wife had finally confessed to both the affair and her desire to be with her lover rather than Flynn. She'd only stayed because of the privileged lifestyle that he had been able to provide for her—apparently her lover was not quite so well off.

Devastated, Flynn had been deeply humiliated and hurt. He'd grown to care for the child. But, having no choice other than to give Isabel the freedom she'd asked for, he'd ended his travesty of a marriage and filed for divorce. But, God, how he'd missed the boy! To all intents and purposes, until he'd discovered the truth, he'd been *his son*. After that, Flynn had vowed that he would never leave himself wide open to deceit again.

It had been so refreshing to meet a girl as sweet and uncomplicated as Caitlin after that painful and bitter episode in his life. Yes, she'd been young—only eighteen at the time they'd met—but Flynn had fallen for her hard. She'd completely swept him away with her beauty and innocence…so much so that he hadn't had the slightest suspicion that she too would eventually betray him. Not with another man, but by leaving him high and dry when he'd just started to believe they might have something worth holding on to.

Flynn had never dreamed Caitlin would act so cruelly. Her feelings had always been written all over her face, and he'd had no clue that she might make such a devastating move. To be treated with such contempt by someone you were falling in love with burned worst than corrosive acid. He would have given her the sun, moon and stars if she'd stayed with him—even if he'd never got round to telling her so.

It hadn't helped his case that her father had despised him with a passion. Tom Burns had never hidden his dislike. He'd scorned Flynn at every turn, even once telling him that he wasn't good enough for his daughter and who did Flynn think he was using his position to take advantage of her? Flynn didn't doubt that Tom had encouraged Caitlin to leave. It was clear that her father's continual besmirching of Flynn's character had influenced her in the end. So she'd left, and Tom had refused point-blank to tell Flynn where she'd gone. In contrast, Flynn's family had breathed a collective sigh of relief at the news…

Reaching the snow-laden Land Rover, Flynn imagined his blood pressure rising to dangerous levels if he didn't soon have some outlet for the rage that was brewing inside him.

Caitlin was home again. The pain jack-knifing through his taut hard middle almost doubled him in two. It might have been only yesterday she'd walked out, instead of almost four and a half years ago. *Wasn't time meant to be the great healer?* What a joke that had turned out to be! Jamming his key into the lock of the driver's door, he cursed the air blue as, in his haste to turn it, his numbed fingers slipped and he almost ripped off a thumbnail.

It was two days after her father had been buried when Caitlin first set eyes on Flynn again. She'd sensed his gaze on her long before she'd turned in the street and had her intuition confirmed.

Leaving Sorcha at home with a kindly neighbour who had offered to sit with her for a while, she'd come into town for some groceries, welcoming the chance to have a few moments to herself outside all the grief and sadness that lingered back at the cottage. It felt like cloying ghostly cobwebs clinging to her very skin. Her progress from shop to shop had been unexpectedly impeded—not just because of the snow that dictated she walk more slowly, but because she'd found herself stopped every now and then by people offering condolences. It seemed that she hadn't been forgotten, even though she'd moved away.

And then there had been that intense warning prickle at the back of her neck that had alerted her to the fact she was being watched. Her heart jolted hard against her ribs as she moved her head to the side and saw Flynn MacCormac, standing there on the other side of the street. For a moment the whole world seemed to turn on its head, and then in a split second was transformed by complete and utter stillness…as if everything around her was holding its breath.

A small gasp—a sound only Caitlin heard—eased out slowly from between her lips. Straight away she detected a disconcerting change in him. Not a physical one, but one more psychologically rooted. Her intuition told her that he'd closed in on himself even more than before, and the knowledge sent her stomach plunging to her boots. It was as though an impenetrable glass wall now isolated him and his feelings firmly away from the rest of the world.

He'd ever been reclusive—keeping his deeper emotions and thoughts mostly hidden and resisting anyone getting too close—but he was so beautiful he was like a burning flame to a moth. His very presence elicited excitement and a forbidden sense of danger too. Tears burned in Caitlin's eyes, and although the fabric of them was deeply sewn with unbreakable threads of sorrow for what she had lost, they were also shot through with a fierce, almost violent joy at seeing him again.

She barely moved as he crossed the road to join her—a tall, broad-shouldered figure, dressed from head to foot in black, moving with the predatory, almost feral grace of a creature. She couldn't take her eyes off him…

'I heard you were back.' His voice sounded slightly rough—as though some unexpected emotion had partially locked his throat.

Caitlin's own mouth was so dry she could barely get a word past its arid landscape. His jade thick-lashed eyes were intense and hungry. 'My father died…I came home for the funeral.'

His hard jaw seemed to tighten, but there were no immediate condolences forthcoming. She hadn't expected there would be. He would have nothing good to say about her father, and although it grieved her she couldn't really blame him.

'So I see,' he said instead, and then, before Caitlin could reply, 'I won't ask how you've been keeping because you look well enough…but you might tell me where you've been living all this time?'

She put a shaky gloveless hand up to her straight blonde hair and the edge of her palm glanced against her cheek. Right at that moment she was convinced that there was not a scrap of difference in the temperature of her skin and the hard-packed ice covering the pavement.

'London…I've been living in London. With my aunt.'

'That's where you went when you left?'

Beneath his harsh, accusing glare, Caitlin felt like the worst criminal in the world. 'That's right.'

'So you didn't fall ill, get abducted by aliens or lose your memory?'

'What?'

'How the hell would I know what happened, seeing as though you never even thought to tell me you were going?'

She flinched as though he'd slapped her hard. It took her a few moments to recover. 'Must we discuss this in the street? If you want to talk, I'll talk…but not here.'

Glancing across Flynn's broad shoulder, Caitlin's blue eyes briefly scanned the snow-covered street that was dotted with mid-morning shoppers. She felt suddenly intensely vulnerable. She'd already discovered that there were people here who knew her, and some of them had no doubt heard about what had happened between her and Flynn. The idea that people were watching them made her skin crawl. All the odds had been stacked against their relationship from the outset. Nobody had wanted them to be together, and nearly everyone had disapproved. *But none of that would have mattered if Flynn had truly let Caitlin into his heart…and if she had allowed herself to fully trust him…*

'Tell me something. Would you have come to see me at all if I hadn't bumped into you like this?' he demanded.

'I was intending to do so…yes.'

'I wonder when that would have been, Caitlin? After all, you must have such a busy life…so busy that you couldn't even pick up the phone and ring me! Not even *once* in four and a half years!'

'I know it must have seemed heartless what I did, but—'

'Heartless?' he mocked. 'Sweetheart, that doesn't even come close!'

'What I mean is—' She faltered, her heart going wild. 'You obviously want an explanation, and you have every right to one, but this is hardly the right time or place, Flynn.' Knowing that her eyes must convey at least some of the tremendous guilt that was churning her up inside, Caitlin frowned. 'We haven't seen each other for years, and believe me—

I deeply regret that everything went so wrong in the end.'

'Do you?' Flynn's glance was unflinching in its raw intensity. 'And why did it go wrong, Caitlin? I'll tell you why! Because you ran away! You ran away without even having the damn decency to tell me why!'

Shivering, Caitlin lowered her gaze. What could she tell him? He no doubt believed that it had been her father who had influenced her decision to leave and end the relationship. God knew Tom Burns had made his dislike of Flynn and his family only too clear. His antagonism had gone deeper than mere dislike…he had actively resented the MacCormacs with a vengeance—despising their wealth and the influence they had in the community. But if Caitlin's only hurdle in being with Flynn had been her father's temper and his aversion to the match she could have got over it. She'd loved Flynn with all her heart. He had become as essential to her as her own breath. But she hadn't left him because of her father…It had been much more complicated than that.

There'd been that humiliating conversation she'd overheard between Flynn and his mother, during which Estelle MacCormac had been so unstintingly cruel in her summation of Caitlin's motives for seeing her son. *'She's only sleeping with you for what you can do for her and that dreadful father of hers! Don't kid yourself that a girl like that cares a fig about you personally! Next thing you know she'll be trying to trap you into marriage by telling you that she's pregnant!'*

Hearing herself spoken about as if she were the most awful little trickster, Caitlin had reeled away in shock and horror. After that, coupled with her father accusing her of bringing 'shame and disgrace' on him, by behaving like a little slut with Flynn MacCormac of all people,' she'd had no choice but to phone her aunt Marie in London and ask if she could go and stay there for a while. Especially as she had also just found out that she was indeed pregnant with Flynn's baby…

It would have done no good trying to talk to him and explain. He would hardly have been likely to believe anything she'd said after his mother had done her worst. And, although Flynn had passionately demonstrated that he wanted to be with her, he'd never actually said that he loved her. In fact he'd hardly ever opened up to her about his personal feelings at all. Consequently Caitlin had found herself unable to trust him with her doubts and fears. So, instead of screwing up her courage and confronting him, she had fled to London.

She hadn't meant to make it a permanent move, but time had overtaken her and, consumed by her new parental responsibilities, she had had no choice but to stay and try and make the best of it. Every day she'd been away from her homeland…away from Flynn…her heart had grown heavier. But how could she ever have gone back when her news might only have confirmed to him his mother's belief in her motives? She'd had no choice but to let him go.

As the years had passed and she'd made a life for herself and Sorcha it had grown ever harder for Caitlin to contemplate returning home. She'd always known Flynn must despise her by now, and she'd been heartbroken at the thought of facing his contempt…as she was facing it right now. And he didn't even know about the child they had made together yet…

'So, what is it you want to do now, Flynn?' Her heavy sigh made a plume of steam as it hit the near freezing air, and Caitlin at last lifted her gaze to face him again. The formidable chill in his glance had not lessened any.

'What is it I want to do?' His green eyes narrowed to icy slits. 'You know what I'd *like* to do? I'd like to cross back over the road the way I came and pretend I hadn't seen you! Why couldn't you have just stayed in London and not cursed me with the sight of you again? Why did you have to come back at all?'

She'd never heard him sound so frighteningly bitter. His tongue lashed her like a whip, almost cutting her knees from under her and making her shake. Her blue eyes watered alarmingly.

'My father died…I told you. I only came back for the funeral.'

'I want to talk to you. I want to talk to you, and it had better be soon! You're damn right you owe me an explanation, and I'm not letting you run away from me again without it!' Letting out a harsh breath, as though every word he'd uttered had caused him some considerable pain, Flynn raked her from head to foot with his burning stare, as though daring her to even *think* of defying him.

'The standing stones at the top of Maiden's Hill.' Her voice sounded as if it had been dragged through gravel. 'I'll meet you there tomorrow afternoon at three. I want to sort through some of my father's belongings in the morning and decide where they're going to go.'

'Three it is, then. And, Caitlin?'

Her heart slammed like a wrecking ball against her ribs at the look he was wearing. 'Yes?'

'Don't let me down. If you do…I'll come and find you.'

And with that he left her there on the pavement, her legs shaking so hard and her heart beating so fast that she couldn't move for several minutes, until she had calmed down sufficiently again to think what she was doing. By which time she was numb with cold and desperately in need of some warmth.

Seeing the little blue and yellow sign above Mrs

O'Callaghan's bakery swinging back and forth in the wind, Caitlin headed over there—to the prospect of a steaming mug of milky coffee to help thaw the chill and the *dread* from her bones.

CHAPTER TWO

CAITLIN arrived at the standing stones early, bundled up warmly in corduroy jeans and a chunky knitted sweater beneath her coat, to stave off the relentless slicing wind that was already making her face burn with cold. Standing on the edge of the ridge with the stone circle behind her—all six-feet-high shale stones erect, apart from one recumbent in the middle—she stared out at the stormy Irish Sea, smashing wildly onto the rocks hundreds of feet below, and sensed a small flame of pleasure light inside her. It was a breathtaking location, and one she'd often yearned to go back to when she was far away in the busy traffic-jammed streets of London.

A magical haunt, with or without the numerous legends that surrounded it, it had taken on an extra enchanting quality after many times spent there with Flynn. They had even made love there one warm midsummer's night, with the moon's shining face showering them with its silvery light…as if it approved of their being there together.

Her blood throbbed with a primitive and powerful need at the recollection. Perhaps it hadn't been such a good idea after all that this be the place they meet? There were too many memories that lingered here…stirring, soul-ringing memories of love that were only taunting shadows of a path not taken. And now Flynn wanted answers…answers that behoved Caitlin to tell him that she'd had a child, and that *he* was the father.

She knew exactly the moment he arrived, because there was a frisson of electricity running through the air that made her scalp tingle in alert. It was ever thus that she had been so psychically attuned to his presence. As if they'd had some strange other worldly bond that mysteriously linked them together.

Wrenching her hypnotised gaze from the commanding sight of the foaming white-capped sea below her, Caitlin turned and saw his masculine dark figure striding towards her over the brow of the hill. The savage wind that was swiftly gathering force was now accompanied by spots of sleet that flattened his clothing against his lean hard body and turned his gleaming black hair to wet silk. Her violent shiver wasn't just because of the icy cold that seemed to penetrate her own clothing and lay its death-like fingers on her bare flesh. A powerful swathe of want and need throbbed through her, and—too swept up in its passionate grip to move—she remained where she stood, a prisoner to its force, nervously watching him approach.

'You came.'

Flynn didn't smile as he released the words that were swiftly borne away on the soughing wind. Instead, he stared at her like a man possessed by a dream. Sleet clung to his ebony lashes and made the fascinating jade of his remarkable eyes glitter like flawless gemstones.

'It's bitter.' Her teeth chattering and her boots shifting on the slippery frost beneath her, Caitlin wrenched her gaze free from his unsettling, diverting glance and started to move past him. 'It's a day for staying by the fire…not freezing to death!'

'Let's go over by the stones,' he sombrely suggested. 'It might shelter us a bit.'

Trying to brush back the windblown hair from her face, Caitlin glanced up into his solemn visage as she stood with her back to one of the standing stones, its dark companions making up a loose enclosure around them. Closely observing the way the taut skin stretched over his hollowed-out cheekbones, she saw how it rendered the implacable bones of his jawline rigid as iron. There was no spare flesh there. None. Its stark and fascinating definition could have emerged out of granite or marble, it was so faultlessly constructed. There was a fair smattering of dark growth shadowing the mainly smooth surface, though it was likely he had probably shaved only that morning, and his face reflected an austere and sombre beauty that seemed to come from the earth herself. It was no wonder that he seemed to blend so well into this wild and rugged landscape.

While Caitlin was so earnestly examining him, Flynn wasted no time in doing the same to her. Her chest tightened as she became weakly, stunningly aware of the raw need that was reflected back at her. To be observed in such a primal, voracious way by him snatched the breath from her lungs, made her feel as if she was drowning in a sensual aquamarine sea that commanded the total surrender of all her senses.

'We'd better get this over with,' she heard herself say, and there was an emotional catch in her voice as her hand moved to restrain the dancing wheat-coloured strands of hair that the wind was buffeting around her frozen face.

She realised in that moment the devastating extent to which she had missed him. As though Flynn was the absent part of her soul that she'd always ached for—a silent, hurting emptiness that never diminished. Only Sorcha had made her life worth living again since she couldn't be with him.

'Why?' he murmured gruffly as his hands

dropped loosely to his hips. Then, before she could answer, *'Why?'* with all the primitive force of a glacier splitting open. His expression was savage.

Flynn's heart was pounding with more force than a blacksmith's hammer as he searched Caitlin's shocked white face for an answer. Did she have any idea of the wasteland of misery and pain she had consigned him to when she'd left? Did she know how it felt to have every day of your life since feel as if it were a hundred years long? Without love, without warmth. Winter, spring, summer and autumn—all had turned into one long, never-ending season of darkness and unhappiness.

Only his work gave him any solace. His writing career had really taken off after Caitlin had left—but then how could it not have when he'd made it his sole driven focus? His dedication to learning his craft, to improving and refining the books that had university professors and television producers alike clamouring for him either to lecture or make programmes about Ireland's Celtic mythological legacy, had become vitally important to his psychological survival, and took up a large proportion of his time. But other than that time hung about like stale cobwebs in an empty, long-disused room.

Flynn had good people to help him run Oak Grove—the impressive MacCormac estate—and it had not been that difficult for him to pursue his chosen career. Even though his family still believed that looking after the estate should be more than enough…

Now, as he considered the brilliant sapphire-blue eyes and the beguilingly shaped lips before him, he realised that no matter how much his heart was secretly thrilled to see Caitlin again forgiveness would be no easy matter after what she had done. There was no excuse on earth that he would accept for her deserting him like that. *None.* And that included her father persuading or bullying her into break off their relationship, people gossiping about them, and the difficulties they'd faced in trying to be together in the face of their families' hostility to the idea. Clearly, whatever feelings Caitlin had harboured for him, they hadn't been strong enough to persuade her to stay.

Flynn knew his shortcomings where relationships were concerned, and he was quite aware that he wasn't an easy man to love or to be with. Hadn't Isabel already proved that? He could be both taciturn and morose, and the tendency to both had worsened after his ex-wife had so sorely deceived him. But when he'd met Caitlin he had started to hope that the trust Isabel had violated might one day be tenderly reinstated. But it was not to be…

In search of the peace of mind that so eluded him, Flynn had renovated an ancient cottage in the mountains and turned it into a writing retreat. Pretty soon it had turned into a retreat *per se*. It was simply easier *not* to be around people sometimes, and it helped to have a place to escape to. Once upon a time Caitlin had managed to come somewhere close to penetrating the hard shell he'd built around himself, but when she'd gone he had strengthened it doubly.

Now—and not for the first time in all the years they'd been apart—Flynn mused on whether he had imagined her tenderness and affection towards him. Could her seeming attraction for him have been just a product of a young girl's fickle nature? An attraction for an experienced older man that had been there one minute and gone the next? What if she'd had a better offer of a more tantalising future somewhere else, and she'd been unable to resist and couldn't bring herself to tell him? Was *that* why she had left?

Flynn deliberately slowed his breathing in a bid to calm himself down, even though his hands had clenched into fists of bitter frustration by his sides.

'My reasons aren't—they aren't easy to explain,' she said now, reluctantly answering his question.

The wind tore at her lovely yellow hair, and Flynn longed to grab a handful of its spun silk and submerge his senses in the wild, rain-washed scent of it. He intimately knew her body's perfume, and time had not dulled it in his mind. But his fury hadn't abated, and he clung onto its force to ground him, to try and kill the almost painful desire that was surging through his bloodstream just because he was near her.

'I've got all the time in the world, darling," he mocked, his glance hard and impervious as the standing stones that encircled them. 'If it means we stand here and freeze to death until I get a satisfactory answer then…so be it.'

'Well, I don't want to stand here and freeze to death!' Caitlin retorted with some spirit. 'I want to get home. I have a lot to do to sort my father's house out before I go back to London, and there's only me to do it!'

'So you're going back to London?' he ground out through gritted teeth. 'I suppose you can't wait to leave? Once upon a time you said you wouldn't want to live anywhere else in the world but here…that you loved the landscape, the weather and the wildness…that it was in your *soul*. Clearly the temptations of London held far more allure for what I now know to be your true fickle nature, Caitlin.'

'I'm not fickle! And I still love it here! In London it's hard to breathe sometimes…too many people, wall-to-wall traffic and everyone on a treadmill they can't get off! If it's got a soul at all I never came close to finding it…not in all the time I was there. Not like this place.'

'But the fact still remains that something lured you there!' Flynn shook his head, still fighting to hold onto his temper. 'What was it? Another man?'

'No!' She looked aghast, the gusting wind turning her corn-coloured hair into a gilded fan across her face. She pushed it impatiently away. 'How could that have been possible? I spent all my spare time with you, Flynn! I only wanted to be with you!'

'You're lying. You must be! You forgot this place—this land you purport to love so much—as easily as you forgot me!'

'I didn't forget you. I never—' She stopped, her expression bleak.

Fighting a dangerously treacherous urge to hold her, Flynn deliberately took a step back—as if afraid his body would act of its own volition without his strict and guarded control.

'Nobody wanted us to be together, Flynn… Can you remember how difficult it was?' Her voice was too soft, and he almost had to strain to hear the words beneath the howling of the wind. 'My father…your family…they kept trying to keep us apart.'

'Not good enough, sweetheart. Try again.'

'I was only eighteen! What could I do? I had no power, no say in anything! And it was always perfectly obvious that your family wanted you to be with someone much more suitable, from your own class and background, not some farm labourer's daughter like me! Did you think I wanted to hang around and eventually see that happen? I know I should have told you that we should finish and that I was going away, but—but when it came down to it I just couldn't face you. You probably think I'm a terrible coward, but everything was just getting me down back then. Including the way my dad was with me.'

'You should have *told* me that! Not left me in the dark about how you felt!'

'It wasn't so easy for me to talk to you about personal things back then.'

'Why not?'

She looked as if she was struggling to answer him, and Flynn sensed the tension inside him build almost to the point of pain.

'You—I didn't think you'd understand. You always seemed so impervious to feelings. I was afraid you'd just try to brush my fears off…tell me not to be so stupid.'

'I'd never have done that!' He was genuinely shocked.

'I'm just telling you how I felt.'

'If you'd done that four and a half years ago, instead of just walking away like you did…out of the blue and without warning…we might have been able to salvage something out of the situation. Instead you left me with nothing, Caitlin! *Nothing!* And then to have your father gloat in my face that you'd finally come to your senses and realised you were better off elsewhere! A place he had no intention of giving me the location of! *That* I can neither understand or forgive!'

'I—what can I say except that I'm very sorry? Sorrier than I can ever begin to tell you.'

Touching her hand to the large standing stone at her back, it seemed as if she was lost in some melancholic memory Flynn couldn't share. He fought like a Trojan to keep the urge to shake her at bay, even as the scent of the sea filled his nostrils and more sleet settled in his hair.

'So that's it? That's all the explanation I'm going to get?'

'It's—it's freezing out here. We ought to go—'

'Didn't you hear what I just said?'

This time he completely failed to keep his frustration at bay. It didn't seem enough somehow, what she'd told him. Surely there had to be something else to complete the puzzle of her desertion? And what did she mean by him seeming so impervious to feelings? Dear God! It was his *feelings* that had damn near crippled him these past few years with her gone!

But in the end Flynn knew that whatever embellishment Caitlin might come up with none of it would make him feel one damn bit better. He should accept that something about him hadn't been enough to hold her and just forget her. Get on with his life as he had been doing until she had so unfortunately returned for her father's funeral.

Now the chill in his bones was nothing to do with the sharp-bladed cruelty of the weather. It was just too bitter to see her again and watch her walk away a second time…

Staring at Flynn, at the dismay and disappointment etched into the haunting lines of his face as though they might take up permanent residence there, Caitlin didn't have the courage to just come out and tell him about Sorcha...the beautiful child they had made together. She was frightened of how he would react, and was undone by the thought of him hating her worse than he must do already for her desertion. To learn that she'd had his baby and had kept the news from him for all these years would be far too devastating a blow for him on top of having to deal with her unexpected return.

It had stunned her to consider that he'd cared for her to such a degree that he was still furious at her leaving. The Flynn she remembered had not been a man who had readily or easily revealed much about what he was feeling. Except when he was making love to her... Then there had been no barriers to stop him from showing her exactly how he felt. Sometimes, alone in her bed at night in London, Caitlin had no difficulty in conjuring up the thrilling memories of how this man had loved her, and it had kept her warm even when she'd felt as if her heart was rent in two for ever.

There was no doubt she would have to tell him about Sorcha some time soon. But it just couldn't be right now.

'I know we have unfinished business, and there are things that I should say...things I should have told you before I left. Maybe when you've calmed down we can—'

'Calmed down?'

She could see that wouldn't be happening any time soon. She exhaled a resigned sigh into the frigid air. 'I can see you're still mad at me, but maybe that's why we should both have some time to think things through before we meet again?'

'Think things through? What the hell do you think I've been doing for these past four and a half years?'

He took a step towards her, put his face up close to hers—so close she could see every tiny grooved line and pore indenting his skin. She could see the midnight shadow that studded his well-defined jaw, and Caitlin's heart thudded in shock at the barely contained anger that rolled off him towards her.

'I thought—' She took a nervous swallow. 'I thought you might have married again or—or perhaps be living with someone by now?'

Oh, how she'd dreaded that. Even though there was no earthly or logical reason why Flynn shouldn't be with someone else by now.

'I'm no celibate priest, but I'm not in a relationship, no. Why, Caitlin? Did it make it easier for you all these years living in London to think of me being with someone else? Sorry to disappoint you. I guess betrayal leaves a nasty taste in the mouth that's not easy to relinquish. These days I have only one real use for women, and I'm sure you don't need me to go into details!'

'No, I don't.'

It was almost more than she could bear to imagine him for even one second with another woman, doing the things he had done with her. *Oh, God...would this pain ever heal? This longing for him abate?* Fixated on the beautiful sensual mouth that hovered so near, Caitlin could almost taste the kiss that her lips longed for. His kisses had been heaven and forbidden fruit all at the same time. Her knees went weak as water at the memory.

As if not trusting himself to be so close to her, Flynn moved abruptly away again—but not before his jade eyes made a blistering examination of her face.

'And what about you, Caitlin? Do you honestly mean to tell me that there's been no other man in your life since you left? That you've spent every night in your bed alone?'

'It doesn't matter what I say, does it? You'll believe whatever you want to believe!'

'Can you blame me?'

He strode right away from her then, driving his hand in mute outrage through his sleet-sodden black hair.

'Flynn!'

She ran after him, cold to the bone and shivering uncontrollably.

'Please don't just walk away!'

'Why not?' he growled, his expression bleak. 'Isn't that what *you* do?'

'Please, Flynn,' she implored again, too weary in mind, body and spirit to argue any more—knowing whatever she said would likely be a red flag to a bull while he was in this frame of mind. 'I don't want us to be enemies. I know we can't be friends, but don't you think we could try and resolve our differences and at least be civil to each other?'

'We'd better get out of here.'

Ignoring her plaintive question, Flynn pulled up his jacket collar as far as it would go, with freezing hands almost blue with cold. In spite of his animosity and anger towards her, he could see that Caitlin was in even worse straits. Her wheaten-gold hair was drenched and flattened to her head, and her lips were almost colourless…like wax. The last thing she needed after just burying her father was to come down with a bout of flu…or even…pneumonia.

'This wind is getting worse and the light is going. Did you make your way here by yourself?'

'I got a lift to the road and walked from there,' she replied, her teeth chattering.

'My Land Rover's parked down at the bottom. I'll run you home.'

For a moment she looked as if she might refuse

the offer of a lift, but a second later she briefly inclined her head.

'Thanks… Just halfway down the lane will do. I can walk the rest of the way from there.'

When Flynn pulled up in the lane that led to what had been Tom Burns' old cottage, he switched off the ignition and turned in his seat to regard his now silent passenger.

'We could meet at the house tomorrow at around ten. Do you want me to come and get you?'

'No, it's all right. I prefer to walk. Ten it is, then.'

She pushed open the door at her side and stepped down onto the snowy road without another word.

Flynn sat and watched her walk up the lane—a slender, duffle-coated figure with bright hair whipped by the wind—and he gripped the steering wheel as though he would break it, shuddering out a long, slow breath.

CHAPTER THREE

SHIVERING, Caitlin wrapped her arms around her chest to try and retain some warmth inside. Since returning from Maiden's Hill with Flynn she had hardly been able to get warm at all. It was as though some of the ice and snow that covered the beautiful, haunting Irish landscape had seeped into her very bones…drip by freezing drip. Knowing she was finally going to have to tell him about Sorcha tomorrow, she fleetingly mused on how his family would react to the news that the girl they'd so looked down their noses at had a child by Flynn. No doubt they'd instantly believe that she'd come home to try and trap him—just as his mother Estelle had once told him she might.

With her daughter tucked up safely in the old iron-framed bed she had slept in as a child, Caitlin stared out through the back door of the small farm cottage into the inky darkness of the freezing night, lifting her gaze to the sprinkling of bright stars that were like a glittering breast-plate above.

None of them burned with the same intense flame or hue as Flynn MacCormac's unforgettable eyes… And today those same eyes had regarded Caitlin with fury and loathing in their depths for what he clearly perceived as her careless and thoughtless desertion. It was so unfair! And why should all the blame fall on *her*? If only he had been more emotionally giving and less remote sometimes, she might have been able to open up to him as she'd wanted. How could she have told him she was carrying his child when she'd had no clue at all as to how he might react to such momentous news? What if Flynn had believed that Caitlin really *was* some conniving little gold-digger, out to try and trap him into a commitment he didn't want or desire? Such a destroying assumption would have made a complete mockery of her love for him…a love that she had known to be pure and true.

Her throat tightened painfully when she remembered how hard she'd cried on that plane journey across the sea to London—far from her home…far from the man she loved.

When Flynn found out about Sorcha she knew his heart would probably petrify against her completely…that it was likely he would never forgive her. How would she live with that? Especially if he wanted regular contact with Sorcha from now on?

How would she cope if he wanted his child but viewed her mother as somehow not good enough or trustworthy enough to be associated with his illustrious family? Her humiliation at the hands of the MacCormac clan would then be complete…

Returning from his early-morning ride on the stunning grey mare he had recently purchased from an elite stables in Dublin, Flynn left the horse in the capable hands of his top stable-hand, with instructions to get her dry and warm as quickly as possible and give her a feed. Then he went back to the house for a quick hot shower and a change of clothes before Caitlin arrived.

The elegant Georgian mansion he had lived in from a child contained four different wings, each with its own self-contained living quarters. But now Flynn was the only one who lived there. Although, truth to tell, he spent more time these days up in the remote cottage he'd renovated. After Isabel had done her worst, he had more or less viewed the big house as a place in which to conduct the business of the estate and little else. He took no pleasure in its timeless elegant beauty, and found himself brooding far too much when he was there. When Caitlin had run out on him he'd almost come to despise the place. It was as though all the vast rooms and corridors mocked his unhappy inability to turn it into anything close to a home…a home with a wife and children and all the comforting paraphernalia that came with having a family.

Danny's nursery was empty and cold, and Flynn had finally locked it up—unable to bear even glancing at the door that led into the room where his little boy had slept.

Now, today, after a mostly sleepless night spent thinking about Caitlin's visit, he was irritable and on edge. That was why he'd had to get out of the house early and expend some energy with a brisk ride in the hills. The glacial air had chased away most of the fogginess in his head and the tiredness in his limbs, and now his body was thrumming with renewed purpose and anticipation. He probably shouldn't be giving Caitlin the time of day after the way she'd treated him, but she'd hooked him by telling him there were things she should have told him when she'd left, and he couldn't help but be intrigued.

And somewhere in amongst his feverish thoughts was her accusation that he had been 'impervious' to feelings. It had prompted a curiously defensive reaction in him, because he intuited that her statement skirted too close to the truth. He knew he would have to maintain his usual rigid guard throughout their encounter. The force of Flynn's attraction for Caitlin hadn't diminished over the years…it had simply been lying dormant, like a silent but ever-flowing and forceful river.

Having showered and combed his hair, he wrapped a towel round his lean, hard middle and crossed the huge high-ceilinged bathroom to the marble vanity unit on the other side. Squaring his jaw, he stood in front of the gilded antique mirror, preparing to shave. Seeing the ridiculous gleam of hope and excitement flaring in his green eyes, he turned impatiently away to mutter a harshly voiced oath…

Caitlin had visited Flynn's private quarters at Oak Grove before, of course, but it intimidated her no less to visit the grand, imposing house again. Standing in his elegant sitting room, with a good fire blazing in the exquisite fireplace, surrounded by gracious, comfortable furniture and with fine paintings adorning the walls—each no doubt valuable beyond belief—she felt a little like Alice in Wonderland after she'd drunk the potion that had rendered her so impossibly small.

The contrast between his wealthy background and the impoverished one of her personal humble beginnings had never stared back at her with such clarity. Thinking of her father's damp, rundown cottage all but brought tears to her eyes. Then, quickly remembering that she had nothing to be ashamed of—she'd come from staunch, hard-working stock—Caitlin lifted her chin a little and declined Flynn's less than warm invitation to sit down.

'I won't stay long,' she asserted, her blue eyes

nervously arresting on his sombre face. 'I'm busy sorting out some of my dad's things to give to the church for their next jumble sale. Not that there's a lot to give. He wasn't one for acquiring material things. There was only himself after I went, and as long as he could listen to the racing on the radio and buy himself a pint now and again he was happy.'

Was that true? Caitlin's stomach seemed to plunge to her boots at the realisation that she hardly knew if her father had been happy or not. He had had too much anger and resentment in him to be happy. After her mother had died, she had rarely seen him even smile.

'Come and stand near the fire.' Moving towards her, Flynn intensified his gaze. 'You're shivering.'

'I'm all right.' Her lips trembled on a little half-smile, but the gesture was quickly gone again as Flynn drew level with her. Now she experienced a different kind of intimidation. Her awareness of his daunting masculinity and strength almost robbed her of the power to speak…especially knowing what she had yet to reveal to him.

'You're not coming down with a chill after yesterday?' he demanded, his expression surprisingly concerned.

'No…no, I'm not. Flynn, I—'

'You cut your hair.' His voice had lowered to the hypnotic nap of luxurious velvet, and Caitlin sensed her whole body tighten in exquisite response.

'It's more practical for work to wear it short. Easier to manage,' she murmured. 'I see you've grown yours.'

He was staring at her and didn't look away. 'I'm viewed as quite the bohemian these days.'

'You always went your own way, as far as I could tell.'

'You didn't seem to mind.'

'I liked it that you were...different.'

'So, tell me...do you still have a penchant for older men, or have your tastes changed since you've been in London?'

'That was unnecessary!'

To Caitlin's consternation Flynn reached out and touched her hair, completely immune to her discomfort at his definitely barbed comment. Her heart went wild as he drew his palm over its softness.

'What do you do in London, by the way?'

'Do? I—I work in a bookstore.'

She saw an interested gleam in his aquamarine gaze. Yes, she knew about his books—and she had thrilled to see them, to see his photograph on the inside jacket sleeve. For a while it had given Caitlin the confirmation she'd yearned for. He still inhabited the world safely. He was now a much-admired author and clearly doing well.

Her breathing became shallow. His hand still brushed against her hair, and was sending little flashes of disconcerting electricity up and down her spine. *He should stop it. He should stop it now, before she had no will left to summon for her protection.*

'You're a writer now yourself, I see? They sell your books in the store. I got—I got quite a shock. I knew you wrote a bit, but you never told me you intended to write books. Your family must be very proud.'

'Proud that I haven't made Oak Grove and all its doings my one and only passion?' He wryly moved his head. 'I don't think so. Besides…I don't see them much these days.'

Lifting his hand from her hair, he positioned his fingers beneath her chin instead. His warm breath skimmed over her, and although his skin smelled mainly of soap and aftershave, she detected the arresting scent of snow-covered hills and valleys and sweet fresh air too. Flynn was a true Celt, both in heritage and in spirit. He simply worshipped nature in all its myriad forms, and loved nothing better than to be outside, breathing it all in—whether that meant strolling, hiking or riding through the countryside, or simply being at one with the beauty of it when watching a sunrise or a sunset. There wasn't a house in all creation that could contain that restless spirit of his. No wonder he'd chosen Celtic mythology as the subject for his books.

'What are you doing?' Caitlin asked—aware that

everything in her had tightened in exhilarating anticipation as he lowered his dark head to hers.

He didn't reply to her question, simply breathed out on an impatient sigh and then boldly took what he was so anxious to savour, touching his lips avidly to hers.

At the first pulse-racing contact her spine seemed to turn to mush, and protesting against his embrace was not even in her mind. Instead, her hands reached out to rest on his waist, in a bid to balance herself as he impelled her hard against his chest. His objective was to angle his kiss even more intimately, and as his tongue thrust hotly into her mouth his fingers pressed hard into her back, to try and obliterate any sense of separation between their two bodies at all…to make them as one.

Four and a half years ago a kiss like this would have had only one destination, and both of them would have moved heaven and earth to get there. But now, as the memory of her daughter waiting at home with a neighbour for her return stole suddenly into Caitlin's brain, reminding her of the real reason she was here—not to make love with Flynn, but to tell him that he'd fathered a child—she started to pull urgently out of his ardent embrace.

His frustration was immediately evident in the harsh-sounding breath he expelled, and the slightly dazed look in his darkened jade eyes. His lips twisted wryly.

'I would apologise,' he asserted mockingly, 'but I'm only human—and you do seem to have this inconvenient ability to raise my temperature at the drop of a hat. Given what's happened between us, I should learn to resist it better.'

'We should talk about the reason I'm here,' Caitlin announced abruptly, striving to sound confident when all her senses were still under siege from his sexy, knee-trembling kiss.

Hugging her arms over her chest in the soft dove-grey sweater that she wore with her jeans, she found herself moving nervously across the room towards the fire. As the flames spat and crackled and hissed round the logs she stared at the fiery dance, silently searching for the right approach…the best way to break the news. News that would stop his world and change its pattern for ever… *Or maybe it wouldn't?* In the end she knew that there was no correct protocol or any sensitive couching of words to soften the blow—she simply had to state what it was and leave it with him to do with the information as he may.

'I have a child—' she began—and, intimately attuned to every nuance and gesture he made, she easily sensed his immediate confusion and shock.

'A child?' he echoed.

'Yes. A little girl… Her name is Sorcha.'

'Well, now…' Nodding his head, Flynn more than adequately reflected the derisive bitterness of that one telling phrase in his tone. 'So you didn't lack for male company in London after all? Of course you didn't! What normal red-blooded male could resist a girl who radiates innocence and sex in the same seductive package as you do?'

'I've never slept with any other man but you, Flynn.' Her expression was in earnest. '*You're* Sorcha's father…no other.'

'Good God, woman! You must think me the biggest fool that ever lived!'

His words were like the score of a sharpened blade across her heart. She sensed the wound gape open even before he'd finished speaking.

'Of course I don't think that! And I'm not trying to treat you like one either! I'd never deceive you about such an important thing. *Never!* I'm not interested in playing those kind of cruel, manipulative games. I know you may think that I've left it a little late, but I only want to try and put things right…to set the record straight. I realised when I was coming back for the funeral that it was time you found out the truth about what happened after I left. Sorcha is nearly four. I've got her birth certificate with me if you want to see it and the date is self-evident.'

At first he couldn't believe it was happening to him again. That another woman was declaring him the father of her child and expecting him to unquestioningly accept it as fact—as though he lacked even the most basic capacity to discern truth from falsehood.

It was several seconds before Flynn could see past the red mist that seemed to rise up and blur his vision. It had been bad enough when Isabel had lied to him about the child she'd carried being his. Especially when he'd found himself growing to love little Danny and making the discovery that he actually *welcomed* becoming a father. He'd known that the marriage itself probably wasn't destined to last—but then how could it have been when he'd been all but 'coerced' into the relationship by his parents? Yet he would have worked hard to make the union work if the child had truly been his and not some other man's. What cut deep was that somehow Flynn had always expected better and more from Caitlin. He'd honestly believed she was incapable of acting wilfully in anything. *Until she'd left him, that was…*

'If she's my child, as you say she is, why didn't you contact me before now?' he demanded furiously, hardly knowing how he contained his rage. 'And what if your father hadn't died? Would you have even bothered to let me know about her at all?'

'I—I didn't contact you before because I didn't know how you'd take the news. You were always such an enigma to me, Flynn…I never knew what you were thinking from one moment to the next! You rarely shared your private thoughts with me. How could I know that you'd even *want* a child? When we were together you never expressed whether you thought our relationship would lead anywhere or not. I just thought—I just thought you believed it was an affair we were having…something that would sooner or later come to an end. And I didn't want you to be with me just because I fell pregnant with your baby.'

'So instead of even giving me an opportunity to say what I wanted, you ran away?'

She hung her head and stared at the floor. 'You make it sound as though the decision was easy for me.'

'Well, clearly you overcame any scruples you might have had and left anyway!'

'Don't, Flynn!'

'You're seriously telling me I have a child, and that she's nearly four years old?'

'Yes.'

Her lip quivered, but Flynn ignored the tears that he saw glistening in her eyes. If this latest experience with women's deceiving ways didn't scar him for life, he didn't know what would!

'And you've raised her by yourself during all these years? There's been no other man involved?'

'No!' Her expression was wounded. 'My aunt Marie helped me to raise her. She looked after Sorcha for me and I had to find a job to support us.'

'I must be in the middle of some kind of nightmare!'

'Please don't say that! Is it so terrible to learn that you're a father?'

Danny's cherubic face hoved into view in Flynn's anguished mind, and the pain that accompanied the picture was indescribable. Swallowing hard, he strove to recover his bearings.

'And where is she now? The child, I mean?'

'Back at the cottage. A neighbour is sitting with her while I've come here…Mary Hogan.'

'Mother of God!'

He turned away then, allowing a reluctant acknowledgement that she might—just might—possibly be telling him the truth. He might be the father of a little girl he had never seen—a child who was nearly four years old.

He definitely hadn't always been as scrupulous about contraception as he might have been, he guiltily recalled. There had been times when his passion for the woman who now stood before him had broken all its bounds and pure wild feeling had had its untrammelled way instead. He had started to let down his guard a little with Caitlin…had started to trust her. He had never guessed that she would desert him as she had.

There were hardly words to describe what he felt right now. Shock, disbelief, soul shattering astonishment… Nothing could come close to conveying the fierce tumult of emotion that rocked through him.

'I'm sorry.'

Her words were so soft Flynn barely heard them.

But they made him turn back to face her just the same. The heat from the fire that blazed behind her had tinted her smooth pale cheeks to a healthy rosy glow, and her gold hair gleamed with the sheen of a polished blade—as though she stood beneath direct sunlight. Even now—even when his life had been thrown into profound chaos by what Caitlin had told him—his body blazed with an unholy fire for her. Yet he had to fight the attraction. Because there was a hell of a lot at stake here…not least a child's future, as well as Flynn's sanity.

'Sorry, is it?' he mouthed harshly, shaking his head. 'Such a small word to convey what must be no less than your complete and utter *contempt* for me! All I can say is that you'd better not be lying to me! If you are then by God you'll be the one who's sorry, believe me!'

'You don't need to threaten me. Why don't you come back with me now and meet Sorcha for yourself? She has a look of you about her, even though her colouring is fair like mine.'

'You've told her about me?'

Flynn hardly knew what to think about that. The pain of losing Danny had made him fear loving another child ever again. Was he even capable of such a thing when it felt as if his very heart was wrapped inside a steel cage these days? Yet he couldn't deny there was a strong sense of anticipation and excitement flowing through his veins too—

even though he was bitterly angry that Caitlin had deliberately kept this momentous revelation from him.

'I haven't told her. No. I didn't know what you'd want to do, so I thought it best not to say anything until you'd reached a decision. I can tell her you're a friend, if you like? Perhaps that would be best for now.'

'Best for whom?'

'There's no point in telling her you're her father if you decide you don't want anything to do with her…that's all I meant. It would be too upsetting for her and she wouldn't understand. She's only a baby.'

'If I *am* her father—' a muscle ticked clearly in the side of Flynn's smooth-shaven jaw '—then I want her to *know* that I'm her father. There's to be no more pretence or lies. God knows, I've had my fill of lies to last me a lifetime!'

'I hear you.'

Her small chin went up then, as if to show him she was not intimidated either by his threats or his temper, and a part of him secretly admired her courage. Even though he was in no mood to be conciliatory after what she had just revealed.

'I'll get my jacket, then we'll go.'

He walked to the door, leaving her to quickly collect her duffle coat from the chair he'd laid it over and hurry after him.

When Caitlin and Flynn arrived back at the cottage Sorcha was sitting at the small table in the parlour with Mary Hogan, poring over the thick, generous-sized pieces of a puzzle they were doing together.

Immediately self-conscious about the poor decorative condition of the tiny cramped dwelling—its only bright point the blazing fire that burned in the grate—Caitlin couldn't help but see what had once been her home with Flynn's no doubt highly critical gaze. After the opulence of Oak Grove, this cottage must seem like very mean fare indeed. The chairs around the table were roughly hewn and old as the hills, and the rest of the sparse furniture looked about ready for chopping up into firewood. The stone floor had but one faded rug to adorn it, and was hardly conducive to making the room warm and welcoming.

Swallowing down her embarrassment, and sure that all Flynn's attention would naturally be on the little girl who was his daughter anyway, Caitlin smiled at the diminutive Mary Hogan, thinking that the woman must be in shock at seeing one of the illustrious MacCormacs walk into the room.

Although he was wearing just a plain dark sweater and jeans beneath his three-quarter-length black leather jacket, the sheer quality of his clothing and his handsome looks easily set him apart from most of the folk who lived in that small rural community. And that was *without* the knowledge that his family practically owned everything and anything worth having in the area. There was even a mountain named after them, for goodness' sake!

'Hi, Mary. I've brought home a visitor, as you can see. This is Flynn MacCormac. Flynn, this is my father's neighbour—Mary Hogan.'

'Mary.'

Flynn courteously shook the elderly woman's hand, but his gaze moved from her almost immediately to alight on the small elfin-faced child who was presently assessing him with a stare that was openly curious.

'And this must be Sorcha?'

She knew she hadn't imagined the slight break in his deeply resonant voice. Caitlin wondered if Mary had heard it too, and what on earth the woman must make of it all. Luckily for her, her dad's gentle neighbour wasn't an inveterate gossip, like some. She took a deep breath to steady herself.

'Sorcha, darling…say hello to Flynn.'

'Hello.'

The little girl's thumb was immediately inserted into her mouth after her shyly voiced response, and her small hand slipped swiftly into her mother's, seeking reassurance. Caitlin tenderly ruffled the silky blonde hair.

'It's all right, sweetheart. He might look fearsome, but he won't bite you!'

Desperately seeking humour to decrease the

tension, she glanced nervously up at the man standing by her side, and saw to her relief that there was a definite flicker of a smile touching his otherwise stern mouth.

'I only bite when I'm very, very hungry,' he teased. 'And, luckily for you, I had a big breakfast before I came out this morning!'

'Now, who would like a nice cup of tea? Mary?'

'No, thanks, Caitlin dear. I'll be getting along home now, if you don't need me for anything else. Now you've got company. I'll pop round in the morning before I go to the shops…see if you want anything then. And don't forget the casserole I've left in the oven for you and the little one. You can have it for your tea.'

Stooping to collect the large dyed cloth bag in which she kept her knitting and two sets of spectacles, Mary moved towards the parlour door.

'Thanks a million, Mary…you're a godsend! And thanks for taking care of Sorcha for me this morning too.'

'My pleasure. She's a grand little girl, so she is! Your father often used to show me her picture…he was so proud!'

Catching Flynn's eye as she turned towards him, Caitlin sensed a shiver of unease go through her. He was no doubt furious that Tom Burns had kept the news from him that he was the father of his daughter's child. She just prayed he wouldn't give rein to his temper while Sorcha was there. It wouldn't be a good beginning for the child to see them arguing.

'Nice meeting you, Mr MacCormac! I'll see myself out, Caitlin. You go on inside and be with your visitor.'

'Mind you go careful back down the lane. That ice is treacherous!'

'Don't worry about me. I'll take my time, so I will.'

When Caitlin stepped back into the parlour, Flynn was sitting in the chair Mary had vacated, talking softly to Sorcha. At the sight of her daughter's bright hair and her father's midnight-dark locks leaning towards each other over the slowly forming picture puzzle, her heart almost lost its rhythm. They looked so right, sitting together like that, and Caitlin couldn't help but feel profoundly guilty that it was she who had kept them apart all these years.

'I'll have that cup of tea now—if you're still offering?' His implacable jade glance briefly touched hers before swiftly returning to Sorcha and the jigsaw. 'Now…I'll bet you any money that this little fellow slots in here… See! What did I tell you?'

'You're right!' Sorcha exclaimed in delight, clapping her hands together.

As emotion swelled inside her throat, Caitlin turned hurriedly away into the kitchen to make the tea…

CHAPTER FOUR

CAITLIN couldn't ignore the fact that after Flynn's initial good humour around Sorcha a definite awkwardness and reticence had seemed to steal into his manner. It was as though he were deliberately holding himself emotionally apart from his child—as if he didn't trust that she was *indeed* his daughter.

It had been a fraught couple of hours, with Caitlin doing her level best to cover the tension-filled gaps in conversation and Sorcha regarding her mother's visitor extra-warily…as if she too sensed his discomfort with her. At first Caitlin had thought Flynn would stay just a short while and then quickly leave. He'd clearly need time to take in the news that he was now a father. But, in spite of his withdrawn manner, he'd surprised her by seeming in no hurry to go at all.

After making them lunch, and then settling Sorcha down on the threadbare couch with a blanket tucked round her for her afternoon nap,

Caitlin felt she could finally talk to Flynn more freely.

'We're leaving in a few days, and I wondered if you'd decided what you want to do about seeing Sorcha again?'

Her voice had a tremor in it, and she really wished it didn't.

Taking up the too-small old-fashioned armchair with his impressive physique, his long legs stuck out towards the now simmering fire, Flynn studied her for several long seconds before replying.

'You were right about her looks,' he said. 'There's definitely a family resemblance. The MacCormac genes are strong.'

Caitlin found herself holding her breath. She folded her hands in her lap and waited.

'I can't believe your father knew all this time that you'd had my child and deliberately kept it from me! I used to see him from time to time in the town, and he always walked past me without saying a word, or looked right through me as if I didn't exist. And people think the MacCormacs are arrogant!'

'He was only acting out of concern for me. You were—you were who you are, and an older man. He believed you were taking advantage of me. He was only protecting me, that's all.'

'But to keep your whereabouts from me, and the fact that you were carrying my baby a secret! If he were still alive I'd— Never mind! It's just unbelievable he did what he did. Surely it must have crossed his mind that I'd want to see the child, have some part in her upbringing, for God's sake? No doubt he concluded that I didn't *deserve* to know.'

He'd raised his voice, and Caitlin glanced anxiously towards Sorcha on the couch. But the little girl went on sleeping peacefully, her plump round cheeks flushed from the heat of the fire.

'I don't know what he thought—except that he was furious with me when I told him I was pregnant. He accused me of bringing great shame on him. He was very old-fashioned about things like sex before marriage...his strict Catholic upbringing, I suppose. Anyway...we rarely made contact after I left to go to England. I sent him letters, photos of Sorcha, but he didn't often reply. I was totally shocked when Mary said he'd often shown her Sorcha's picture and indicated how proud he was of her! She might just have said that to be kind, though.'

Pulling her troubled gaze away from his too-intense examination of her, Caitlin linked her hands awkwardly together in her lap.

'I'll want to have access now that I've seen her, of course.'

'Are you sure, Flynn? You seem—you seem hesitant. It must be a great shock to you to learn that you're a father. I understand it might take time for the reality to sink in.'

'You have no idea *what* I'm feeling!' he came back, jaw clenched tight.

'Then tell me!' Caitlin implored, blue eyes glistening. 'At least then we might get somewhere! You must know that I would never try and force you into doing anything you didn't want to do. Even acknowledging that Sorcha is yours!'

He seemed to mentally regroup, as though he regretted his telling outburst. 'I want you both to come to my place in the mountains tomorrow. We can continue this conversation there. Right now I have to go and prepare some work to take with me.'

He pushed to his feet, his imposing height and broad shoulders relegating the already small room to doll's house proportions.

'You bought that old cottage in the mountains?' In spite of her sorrow that Flynn obviously couldn't trust her with the truth about his feelings, Caitlin felt his comment pique her interest.

She stood up beside him, all of a sudden remembering that he'd taken her there once, to show her the dilapidated dwelling that the estate agent had drolly referred to in its advertising blurb as 'a pile of stones with a resident goat'.

Flynn allowed himself a smile. She'd been utterly charmed by the place, seeing all kinds of whimsical possibilities in the rundown building *and* the goat.

'I not only bought it, but I had it completely renovated too.'

'Really? How wonderful! And that's where you write your books?'

'It is.'

'You can't lack for inspiration, then. You'd have to go far to find a more spectacular location!'

For a moment Flynn forgot to be mad at her—forgot that she'd walked out and kept her pregnancy from him—and in place of his anger a rogue arrow of warmth and affection helplessly pierced his heart. Perversely, once upon a time the only peace he'd ever really known had been with Caitlin. Her innocence and joy in the simple things of life had accorded him great pleasure. But that had been a long time ago, and a lot of turbulent water had flowed under the bridge since then…

'That's true enough.'

'And what about the goat? What happened to him?' she asked.

'I donated him to a local farmer.'

'You should have kept him. He was a real character.'

Feeling oddly chastised, Flynn firmed his mouth.

'I'll come and pick you up around one. Make sure you're ready and wrapped up warmly, the both of you. It'll be a bit of an arduous journey in this arctic weather, so it's just as well to be prepared. I'll see myself out. Until tomorrow, then.'

He went out through the front door before he

caved into the powerful urge to pull her into his arms. It wouldn't be the wisest of moves, under the circumstances. He surely needed to keep a clear head to think through all that had happened.

Braving the wind and sleet with his head down, Flynn negotiated the icy pathway to his vehicle with his mind focused astonishingly on the fact that he was a father now, and would once again have to learn how to be around a child…to maybe care for her, when to do so would make him risk his heart in a way he'd never thought to do ever again.

The following day, when the time came, Caitlin honestly couldn't attest to how her legs carried her towards the waiting Land Rover at the end of the lane. She'd crossed the first major hurdle, in telling Flynn he was a father, but she didn't doubt there'd be many more challenging obstacles to come. She was entering into the realm of the unknown and she couldn't help but fear it.

A thought had crossed her mind last night that, when he'd mentioned access with regard to Sorcha, had Flynn possibly been referring to a joint custody scenario? It was a prospect that filled her with trepidation for several reasons—not least that they lived in two different countries. It might mean longer separations from her daughter than Caitlin could tolerate…

Beside her now, her daughter's normally cheerful chatter had stilled to an apprehensive silence that tugged at her heart, and the little girl gripped her mother's hand with uncommon tightness.

'You know the man you just met?' Caitlin had told her yesterday, when she'd woken from her nap. 'I have to tell you, darling, that he's your daddy.'

Sorcha's soft green gaze had mirrored her innocent confusion straight away. 'Really?' she'd asked, her voice falling to a captivated whisper. 'I didn't know I had a real daddy!'

'Well, you do, sweetheart. It's just that when Mummy had you, we weren't together.'

'So Flynn—the man that helped me with my puzzle—is my daddy?'

'Flynn MacCormac…yes.'

'The same name of the people who own the lovely horses?' Sorcha had excitedly exclaimed.

'That's right,' Caitlin had answered, the inside of her throat feeling scratchy as sandpaper.

'But, Mummy…what if he doesn't want a little girl like me?' the child had responded, her smooth brow puckering. 'He waited such a long time to come and see me! Why did he, Mummy? Why did he wait so long?'

Caitlin had had to glance quickly away then, to hide her tears…

The snow covered the hedgerows in a glittering white shawl as they made their way up the lane, their booted feet gingerly negotiating the hard icy surface beneath them.

Flynn's practical Land Rover was one of the only all-terrain vehicles that had a chance in this seriously inclement weather which closed roads and made frustrated motorists abandon their cars. It would be the only possible means—apart from hiking or helicopter—with which to reach the secluded mountain cottage he'd purchased.

Caitlin had loved its remote location as soon as she'd set eyes on it. It was a wild, mystical place, surrounded by areas of concentrated woodland full of ancient oaks that made a patchwork of the sky and held a silence where you could hear every beat of your own heart as well as the sound of your thoughts. And not far away was a clear path to the top of a mountain peak from which there was the grandest view of the majestic sea, in all its myriad hues: aquamarine, duck-egg blue, misty grey and mossy green. That view would ease the sorest of hearts…

Yes…Caitlin knew intimately why Flynn had been unable to resist the chance of having a refuge in such a place. If a man sought any kind of peace or solace away from the world then he would surely find it there.

Up ahead, he'd stepped out of the driver's seat and stood watching them as they approached—a dark imposing figure that even from a distance seemed to convey command. Caitlin felt the power of his searching gaze—first on herself, then on their child. What was he thinking? Would he be examining that sweet elfin face with those soft innocent eyes that held traces of both her blue and his jade colour in their fair-lashed depths, to ascertain that she was really his? Would he still hold the possibility in his mind that Sorcha might be another man's child after all? Her heart lurched as they drew level.

'Hello,' she greeted him, her lips moving in an uncertain smile. He didn't answer her. Nor did he smile. Instead he stooped down low, so that he was level with the little girl standing quietly at Caitlin's side, her hand still holding on tightly to her mother's.

'Hello, Sorcha,' he said gently, gravely. 'It's nice to see you again.'

'Hello,' the child replied quietly, stealing a glance upwards at her mother before returning her gaze solemnly to Flynn. 'Did you know that I'll be four years old on my next birthday?'

'I did know that. Sure, that's a great age, isn't it?'

His smile was clearly in evidence now, and the dark beauty of it was purely breathtaking in its effects.

'Are we going to your house now? The one with the horses?' Sorcha asked, her voice sounding undeniably hopeful.

'Horses?' Flynn glanced up at Caitlin and frowned.

'She saw the big house on the way here from the airport,' she explained, sensing hot colour rush into her face. 'She asked me who owned the horses in the paddock and I told her it was your family.'

'I see.'

He rose to his full height again, and his hand glanced gently against the top of Sorcha's woolly indigo-coloured hat. 'I'll take you there to see the horses very soon,' he promised, 'but right now I'm going to take you to see my house up in the mountains. It's quite a long way to go, so I think we'll get in the car, shall we? It's not good to stand around for too long in this perishing cold.'

'Take off your coats,' Flynn instructed, serious-faced, as they entered the rustic-styled porch of his secluded mountain home. 'I'll put the under-floor heating on but we can have a real fire too—if you'd like?'

'That would be nice,' Caitlin agreed, surprised he'd consulted her on her opinion.

He'd hardly spoken a word on the treacherous journey to get there, no doubt sensibly preferring to concentrate his well-honed driving skills on getting up the narrow mountain passes safely. Behind him, Caitlin had sat quietly, with Sorcha snuggled deep into her side, her wary sapphire-blue gaze often resting on the back of Flynn's dark head, as well as on the sheer drops they skirted so breathtakingly close to.

The tension produced by the dangerous conditions of their journey, coupled with the unspoken strain that lay between them, had felt as heavy as a dragoon's thick dark cloak, enveloping them all, and Caitlin had longed for something light-hearted or diverting to ease things a bit. But now at last they'd arrived, and the scene that greeted them was like a winter wonderland illustration from a child's book of fairytales—low roofs at the centre of mountainous white peaks and frosted treetops. Her heart lifted at being back—in spite of the tensions of the journey.

Although the renovations Flynn had made to the ancient stone cottage and its various outbuildings had been by necessity quite major—to make it habitable and also to bring it up to modern-day standards—Caitlin knew he had a preference for the natural heat that came from glowing turf fires and, in the less inclement weather, sunlight. Consequently she'd intuited that the interiors would also be sympathetic to the cottage's stunning surroundings, and reflect as much as possible a natural environment.

As she and Sorcha followed Flynn's tall figure into the comfortable living room, with its wood-panelled flooring, attractive muted-toned rugs and huge open-plan windows at the back of the far wall, which seemed to invite the snow-covered landscape inside, Caitlin found she wasn't disappointed. And as he stalked over to the wide stone hearth, with its carved wooden mantelpiece, crouching low to light the already made-up fire in the grate, her senses were swamped by memories.

He had done this for her before…lit a fire so that they could talk, eat and make love with the dancing flames warming them on a cold day just like today…Her heart skipped a beat when she saw the poignant selection of seashells positioned on a little walnut table next to the window. She was certain they'd collected them together on one of their long walks on the beach. And there on the wall were the four simple prints of the mountain view in spring, summer, autumn and winter, which Caitlin had bought Flynn for his birthday. They would have looked entirely out of place in his grand apartment at Oak Grove, with its valuable antiques and paintings, but here they were just perfect. She was inexplicably touched that he'd put them here, in the place where he retreated from the rest of the world to write…a place he had brought Caitlin to see before anyone else, because she had instinctively known what it would mean to him.

She frowned as she stooped to undo the buttons on Sorcha's light-coloured sheepskin jacket and remove her gloves.

'There you go, angel!' Snapping out of her reverie, she grinned lovingly at her child, her hand ruffling the waving golden hair that fell about the small shoulders as she lifted off her woolly hat and stood up straight again.

Immediately she sensed Flynn's watchful eyes on them both. 'I expect the pair of you could do with a drink?'

Rising from the hearth, where the fire had started to crackle nicely, he dusted down his black cord jeans with his hands. There was so much they needed to discuss—but how to accomplish it with Sorcha so close by?

Caitlin's nerves bit with frustration and tension. 'Why don't you let me put the kettle on?' she suggested, inserting a falsely cheerful note into her voice that was a feat in itself, given the strained circumstances. 'You could talk to Sorcha on your own for a bit, if you like?'

She was trying to make peace, of sorts. Hard in view of the threats he had issued yesterday, and what he might yet demand regarding parental access, but she had to try for her daughter's sake.

'Sure. The kitchen is just to your right there. You should easily find everything you need, but shout out if there's something you can't.'

'I will.'

Her automatic smile had all the effect of water glancing off a duck's back. His sombre expression didn't change one iota. He seemed to be brewing a lot of resentment towards her today. No doubt time to think had only increased it.

Caitlin willed herself to try and relax. 'I'll go and make some tea, then.'

'There's some fresh juice for Sorcha.'

'Great.'

In the large bright kitchen—traditionally the hub of Irish family life in these old cottages—Caitlin had no trouble in locating the makings of a pot of tea. Everything was in beautiful order, and was indeed easy to find.

As she watched the kettle start to steam on one of the iron plates of the beautifully restored old-fashioned range she heard muted conversation coming from the living room with bated breath—Flynn's velvet rich tones and Sorcha's answering softly childish one. She knew she couldn't hold back the tide now that her secret was out, but she feared for the backlash she might come under from Flynn's family when they heard the news. That was, if they hadn't heard it already.

'You found everything?'

Suddenly Flynn came through the doorway, his tall, broad-shouldered presence in his dark clothing seeming to dominate the room—for it was impossible to look anywhere else when he was near.

'Yes, thanks… What you've had done with this place is amazing! It's beautiful, Flynn,' she added warmly, pouring boiling water onto the leaves in the ceramic teapot.

He ran his gaze over her curves in the light blue

sweater she wore with her jeans, and for a long moment silence stretched ominously between them. Caitlin tried in vain to keep her hand steady as she continued to pour the water.

'It was definitely a labour of love,' he finally admitted, again surprising her with the admission.

'I can see that.'

'She's so bright… Her vocabulary for a child so young is quite extraordinary.'

The unexpected comment elicited a burst of warmth inside her, and Caitlin looked straight at him. It was a shock to see the depth of emotion written there in the compelling planes and angles of his darkly riveting features.

'Yes. She picks things up very quickly. She's also got a will of iron, and can be a right little madam when the mood is on her, so don't be fooled altogether by that "butter wouldn't melt" expression!'

'Like her mother, then?'

The softly spoken remark sent goosebumps chasing over the smooth surface of Caitlin's skin.

'You said you had some juice?' she mumbled.

'In the fridge. There are some biscuits in the cupboard too.'

'We can't leave it too late to get home. Those roads were treacherous, and you shouldn't be driving them in the dark.'

'Anxious to leave already, Caitlin?' A muscle

visibly throbbed under the skin of one shadowed cheekbone.

'Not at all!' She coloured as she put the tea things on a nearby tray, to carry them back into the living room. 'I know there's a lot we still have to discuss.'

'An understatement, if ever there was one.'

Throwing her a glance that drove away the previous warmth she'd felt, he turned and went back to rejoin his daughter.

While Sorcha was stretched out on the rug in front of the fire, drawing in one of his unused sketchpads with some crayons Flynn had found for her, he moved his gaze to her mother, sitting on the far side of him. She was sipping her tea and staring into the flickering blue and yellow flames as though transfixed. The reflection of the fire's warmth turned her hair into a rippling stream of gold and he couldn't help but secretly admire it.

It was hard to believe she was back. If he closed his eyes and opened them again would she disappear altogether? If she did it would be proof that she was just a figment of his fevered imagination—because this place had lost some of its meaning for him since the day she'd left, no matter how much a labour of love it had been, or how beautifully it had been transformed. He sighed, and Caitlin immediately transferred her gaze from the fire to him.

Studying the serene face, with its smooth untroubled brow and shimmering china-blue glance, Flynn sensed a bolt of despair pulse through him. Why had she treated him with such contempt by keeping Sorcha's existence a secret? He still couldn't understand it, no matter how hard he tried.

'Where is the bookshop you work at in London?' he asked, grasping a neutral subject out of the sky and willing the fire in the pit of his stomach to abate—because he wouldn't lose his temper in front of the child and risk frightening her.

'Just off Tottenham Court Road…it's quite a well-known one. You can get practically any book you want there.'

'And does this aunt of yours know that you were intending telling me about Sorcha at last? What's her opinion of the whole debacle?'

He knew he was glaring, and he saw Caitlin pull her glance awkwardly away for a moment at his swift change of subject, as if to garner her defences.

'We did discuss my telling you…and she was, of course, anxious.'

'I'll bet she was,' he replied, low-voiced and grim, and saw her flinch. 'Seeing as she must have colluded with your father all these years to keep your whereabouts and the fact that you'd had my baby a secret.'

'She advised me to try and heal the past the best I could by telling you the truth.' Leaning forward with her hands in her lap, Caitlin implored him with her eyes. 'Aunt Marie didn't condone my father's behaviour *or* mine. But she helped me because we're family, and she loves me.'

'And did either one of you spare *me* so much as a thought, while you kept me from my child as you did?'

Inevitably his voice—underscored by emotion—had grown louder, and Sorcha glanced up at him gravely from the picture she'd been so busy with.

'I want to build a snowman!' she declared, and in the next moment was scrambling to her feet and planting herself in front of Flynn, small arms akimbo. She didn't look dissimilar to some seriously ticked-off schoolteacher, confronting her wayward class. 'You *have* to help me!'

Surprise and pleasure swiftly acted as a salve to the anger that had seized him, and Flynn stood up and held out his hand to the little girl. 'It's been years since I've built a snowman, darlin'. You'll have to show me how.'

'Don't worry,' Sorcha replied confidently, smiling as she slipped her small pale hand into his. 'I will!'

'Don't forget your coat and hat and gloves, Sorcha Burns!' Caitlin called, and twisted round on the couch to watch them as father and daughter headed off towards the front porch.

Stopping for a moment to glance back at her,

Flynn let her know with the hardening of his gaze in no uncertain terms what he felt about his daughter not having *his* name. When Caitlin's cheeks coloured softly, he knew a certain grim satisfaction that his unspoken disapproval had hit its target.

CHAPTER FIVE

THE snowman was a resounding success—even if Flynn said so himself. His daughter seemed delighted with the results, at any rate. She was a robust little thing, he thought with unexpected pride, watching her clap her hands together with glee as she stared up at their handiwork beside him, even though her gloves were soaked through and she must be frozen to the bone.

She'd worked hard and without complaint, piling handfuls of snow upon snow as Flynn had strived valiantly to fashion some sort of recognisable snowman shape out of the powdery ice. He was out of practice with this sort of thing…*years* out of practice. That was the trouble. There hadn't been many children in his life at all since his own childhood. And because that had been a somewhat solitary one, in spite of his brother Daire—who'd had his own set of friends and scorned his big brother's company whenever he could—Flynn had not found a lot of pleasure in childish pursuits. Apart from reading and going off into the woods on expeditions of the imagination.

All the same, he'd derived a fierce enjoyment from meeting his daughter's passionately voiced request. They'd finished the large rotund figure off by inserting a pair of coals for eyes, a withered carrot for a nose, and wrapping a striped woollen scarf round the solid wide neck. After adding a smiley face with his finger, at Sorcha's eager instigation, the job was done. And now Caitlin stood in the doorway of the porch to assess the results of their labours, her arms folded against the raw wind that swirled fresh flakes of snow everywhere and her face wreathed in an admiring smile.

'He's fantastic, isn't he? A real character! Well done, both of you!'

In a totally unguarded moment Flynn got swept up in the radiance and warmth of that smile, and to his alarm found himself reciprocating. Then, in the next instant, he remembered the suffering she'd caused him and the gesture was withdrawn as swiftly and emphatically as though it had never been.

'Better get her inside and warm her up,' he murmured, putting his hand between Sorcha's small shoulders and guiding her towards the porch.

'I'm going to call my snowman Tom, after my grandad!' the child announced proudly as she climbed up the steps towards her mother.

'That's a grand idea,' Caitlin agreed, wrenching her wary gaze away from what Flynn knew was the less than animated expression on his face.

Personally, he neither wanted nor needed any reminders of the man who had played a part in driving Caitlin away from him, and thereby depriving Flynn of his child. As Caitlin turned away towards the living room, and the fire he guessed she would have kept blazing to warm them on their return, Flynn moved past her to go into the kitchen.

'I'll make her some hot chocolate while you get her warm again. There's a blanket in the box at the side of the couch—you should wrap her up in it.'

'Thanks…I will.'

Her expression even more guarded now, and her smile banished, Caitlin continued on into the living room.

With growing anxiety she had watched the cold day's short span of light rapidly fade outside the windows, as the fire she'd tended continued to throw off its glowing welcome heat into the room. On the comfortably upholstered sofa beside her Sorcha had fallen into a deeply tired doze, her little body worn out by the afternoon's strenuous snowman-building and by the relaxation encouraged by the big mug of milky hot chocolate Flynn had made her. She was wrapped in the luxuriously soft tartan blanket that he had urged Caitlin to use, and only the child's small pink-cheeked face and spun-gold hair showed above the blue, red and green checked wool as she sank ever deeper into a more contented rest.

They would have to leave soon if they were going to get home at all tonight, Caitlin thought worriedly, her glance flicking once again to the windows and the dusk that was descending outside, along with more snow. It would be madness to attempt the drive back down the mountain in near darkness.

Flynn had left them alone for quite a while now, but she knew he was in the kitchen preparing food by the delicious scents that were wafting through the cottage, making her tummy rumble with hunger. But, hungry or not, she would have to insist they left directly.

Just as Caitlin decided she would have to go and tell Flynn so, he came back into the room, his gaze falling at once upon the sleeping child, her feet stretched out on her mother's lap and her golden head resting on a multicoloured cushion.

'I thought that might happen,' he commented, moving towards the fire and tending it with the poker that lay on the hearth in front of it. Little orange sparks flew up at the disturbance, and settled again to make the flames dance higher and brighter.

'She couldn't fight it any longer.'

Pursing her lips before continuing, Caitlin felt her heart flutter wildly at the sight of that strong, resolute profile of his, and the way his well-defined thigh muscles had stretched the fabric of his jeans as he crouched before the fire. The flickering light from the blaze made his handsome visage an almost intimidating bronze mask, and at that moment she wondered if she'd imagined all the times she'd been able to coax him out of a black mood and make him smile. *Never again...* Never again would the power to do that for him lie with her. It was like waking up one morning and learning that there would be no more spring, only winter for ever.

'Flynn, I think we'd better get—'

'Remember what the Celts called this time of the year?' he asked, turning his dark green glance towards her.

How am I expected to remember anything when you look at me like that? Caitlin thought frantically, as her body was suddenly stormed by hot licking waves of intimate heat.

'No...no, I don't.'

'*Anagantios*...stay-home time.'

'I suppose it makes sense. What else would you really want to do in this weather if you had the choice?'

He'd always shared his love of the Celtic way of life with her. In fact it had been her own interest in the folklore and wisdom of her ancestors that had led her to the library in town to hear Flynn talk about the major Celtic feasts and festivals one soft rainy night just five years ago. Enthralled beyond words by both the man and the talk, she'd shyly sought him out afterwards, amid a queue of others waiting to ask questions. The fact that he was a MacCormac, and an educated, cultured man with a sharp intelligence that could be intimidating, should have given her pause—but she'd managed to put aside her apprehension and speak to him anyway.

One thing had led to another when their gazes had locked for that very first time, and neither of them had been able to readily look away from the other. Before she'd returned home that night Flynn had invited her to join him the next evening for a drink. Caitlin had known her father would likely want to kill her when he found out—but what she'd experienced when she'd set eyes on Flynn that very first time no threat or lock and key devised could have prevented. She could still recall the passionate, intense excitement of it all, and the astounding revelation that love really could happen at first sight.

'You and Sorcha are going to have to stay the night. Obviously I shouldn't attempt the drive back down the mountain in these conditions tonight. Besides…it's been snowing heavily again.'

Getting to his feet, Flynn laid the poker carefully back down on the hearth. Now Caitlin's heart really did pound in alarm.

'We can't stay the night! You know we can't!'

'Why?' His lips twisted with derision. 'Do you think I might try to get you into my bed again? Do you think I have no pride left after what you did to me? Don't worry, Caitlin…as irresistible as you are, I do have some scruples left, even if you don't!'

Admonishment blazed in his eyes, enough to ignite her where she sat, and Caitlin was submerged by a cloak of the utmost desolation. She'd killed what little trust he'd begun to extend to her when they were together completely with her actions…even though they'd been committed under duress, as well as in the inexperience of her youth.

'I'm sorry. I'm sorry I hurt you so badly that you can never forgive me.' She swallowed across the lump that seemed to swell and burn inside her throat. 'But you hurt me too, Flynn. I know you can't see that, but you did. You shut me out emotionally and made it hard for me to get close to you. I don't understand why, when I made it pretty obvious that I was mad about you! But there… What's done is done, and we can't turn back the clock. I know we had something special, and that I smashed it all to dust when I left without telling you. I've had to live with that knowledge every day! Every time I look at Sorcha and see your likeness in her eyes, in her smile… Every time she reaches another milestone in her childhood and you're not there to witness it… Don't you think I think of what I've done and regret it? Regret it with every breath in my body?'

'Yet you clearly didn't regret it enough to come back and face me with the truth!'

There was not a flicker of compassion or forgiveness in Flynn's chilling glance, and Caitlin saw to her frightening cost that her initial summation when she'd seen him in town the other day had been right. He'd closed himself up so tight against any future possibility of hurt or slight that there was no getting through the iron wall of his defence. Not even a battering ram could make a dent in that impenetrable armour of his.

'You and Sorcha can sleep down here.' He shuddered out a long breath. 'It's the warmest room in the house. That other sofa opens up into a bed. I'll bring down some bedding later. In the meantime I've made some soup, and there's new bread too. We'll eat in the kitchen, if you like, while she sleeps. She can have some when she wakes.'

He saw that Caitlin had barely touched her food. Flynn's own appetite faded similarly as he broodingly observed her from across the kitchen table.

The snow that blanketed the house and its surroundings muffled every sound, leaving an eerie silence in its wake—a silence that was akin to a still, frozen lake after all the birds had flown. But beneath the deceptive appearance of calm surely it was only a matter of time before something had to crack?

Her face was alabaster pale, and there were soft purplish and green smudges of fatigue beneath her vibrant blue eyes. She probably hadn't slept much since hearing of her father's death and coming home for the funeral. And she'd accused him of hurting her too, by making it hard for her to get close to him, and Flynn's conscience was pricked because he knew she was right.

Fighting hard against compassion, steeling himself against the treacherous attraction that flared just as fiercely as it had always done—despite his recent affirmation to Caitlin to the contrary—he suddenly pushed away from the table, his chair scraping loudly and discordantly against the stone-flagged floor, so that the silence was shattered as shockingly as breaking glass.

'If neither of us is going to eat then I may as well put on the kettle for some tea,' he ground out.

'We haven't talked about how often you'll want to see Sorcha after I go back to London.' Pushing aside the steaming bowl of aromatic soup she'd been unable to enjoy, Caitlin's voice was low. 'We ought to come to some arrangement since we're both stranded here for the night...don't you think?'

The sky-blue glance she settled on him was piercing in its pristine hue. For a moment Flynn was dazzled, and heat swirled into his belly with a deeply primeval force...the kind of heat that could enslave a man's desire for her for ever... Filling the kettle and placing it on the range, he fought through the debilitating fog of lust that had entrapped him, trying to centre himself.

'I've been giving that some thought,' he announced, turning back to face her.

'Well...would you like to share your views with me?'

'It's clearly nonsense to imagine we can make something work with you living in London and me here. Now that I've met Sorcha I know seeing her once or twice a month wouldn't be enough. Which is more than likely how it would go if we continue to live in separate countries. Our only real solution to the problem is for you and my daughter to move back here.'

'Back to Ireland?'

'Clearly the prospect doesn't appeal to you.'

Flynn could not curtail his profound dismay. But he was not about to let a second child slip out of his life so easily—even if the prospect of fatherhood daunted him more than ever because of what had happened between him and Isabel.

'It's not coming back to Ireland *per se* that doesn't appeal,' Caitlin answered softly, her brow furrowing. 'It's just that I've made a life for Sorcha and me in London, and she'd miss my aunt too much if we left. She's all the family she's known. I can't just uproot our whole lives without thinking about that.'

'Even if it's best for Sorcha?'

'How do you know it's best for her? How do *I*, for that matter? Parenthood is fraught with so many impossible choices.'

Flynn kept silent.

'I'll think it over… But I can't make any promises now,' she told him.

'Have you forgotten who I am, Caitlin? What I can give her? Her situation here would be much more secure… Would you deny her a better start in life than she's got now?'

'I wouldn't deny my child anything that was ultimately going to help her, but I have to consider my own position too, Flynn!'

'And what's that? You're a single mother, living in a big, careless city, trying to make ends meet by working in a bookstore!'

Even as Flynn spoke the words he felt a jolt of something painful tug at his heart. For the first time it crept into his consciousness just how tough that situation surely must be for Caitlin. It made him all the more determined to alleviate some of the struggle—even if he was still disinclined to forgive her for what she'd done.

'Since I've now acknowledged that Sorcha is mine, it stands to reason that I should support her—and *you* as her mother.'

'*Help* support her, don't you mean?' Pushing her fingers agitatedly through her hair, Caitlin stared at him with growing anxiety in her eyes. 'I'm willing to accept that our child should be a shared responsibility…and I wouldn't deny Sorcha your support…not if you're willing to give it. But I need a measure of independence too. I'm used to working…to taking care of things. And last time I looked jobs were few and far between in this part of the world. I can't just come back here and let you take over everything, start making all the decisions where the both of us are concerned!'

'I'm not taking over everything! And *I* am Sorcha's family now, as well as you and your aunt! Do you think I could stand back and watch her go, knowing that if you both lived here she wouldn't have to struggle at all? There'll be opportunities here with me that won't be open to her is she stays in your current situation in London. You talk about impossible choices. Is it really so hard to make the decision between penury and wealth?'

Taking a deep breath, Flynn moved restlessly from one end of the room to the other.

'Moving into Oak Grove with me is your only

sensible choice. You certainly can't stay in your father's old place. Seeing it the other day, I was appalled by its unkempt and rundown condition! I certainly wouldn't want any child of *mine* living in such squalor!'

Caitlin shot to her feet. 'It's not unkempt! How dare you? My dad may have neglected the general upkeep of the cottage a bit—he was a one-man band, trying to work and take care of things on his own when I left, and there was very little money for luxuries—but there's no need to look down your nose at what was our home! We may have been poor but my parents were honest and hardworking! After I lost my mum it wasn't easy for my dad…but he did the best he could with the resources he had and I've nothing to be ashamed of. So don't you *dare* act so superior just because you've come from money and I haven't!'

Her breasts were heaving in her soft blue sweater, and her face was flushed with temper, and for a moment it was hard for Flynn to hang on to any desire to argue. Not when a quite *different* desire was storming through his veins.

'You sound just like your father. He had a real chip on his shoulder about wealth too! Stop being so damned defensive and see some sense, will you? Whatever way you look at it, who in their right mind could argue that Sorcha wouldn't be better off living here in comfort in Ireland than in a situation in London where you're struggling to put food on the table?'

'It's not as bad as all that! I don't earn a fortune, but I've made it work with my aunt's help for the past four years!'

'With your aunt's help?' His tone was disparaging. 'So you and Sorcha are living in *her* house, on her say-so? What kind of security is that for a child?'

'She's loved and cared for! That's the kind of security she has in abundance! Something that you and your own family clearly don't set a lot of store by!'

'And whose fault is it that I haven't been able to love my own daughter? I didn't even know of her existence until a couple of days ago! Answer me that while you're busy being so damn self-righteous!'

A stricken look came over Caitlin's face. 'I'm sorry,' she whispered brokenly.

As she started to turn away, Flynn was by her side in two long-legged strides, gripping her arms, his expression caught somewhere between intense frustration and despair.

'That word again!'

Would he ever forgive her? Staring up into that carved, long-boned, troubled face, Caitlin found it hard to see a way out of the fog of misery that had descended.

'You have to give me some time to think over what you've suggested. I—'

'Mummy!'

The rest of her words were cut off by the sound of her daughter's frightened cry.

His expression alarmed, Flynn had left the kitchen even before Caitlin. Reaching the living room, they found Sorcha sitting bolt upright on the couch, her hair a golden tangle from lying on the cushion, her pretty face damp with tears.

'Mummy's here, darling! What's the matter? Did you have a bad dream?'

Pulling her into her arms, Caitlin cradled the child against her, feeling the slight body tremble. Her own heart was beating much too fast.

'I dreamt that you went away and never came back! Just like my daddy did!'

Flynn's gaze locked with Caitlin's, something close to devastation reflected in his haunting jade eyes. For a moment Caitlin didn't think she breathed…

'I haven't gone anywhere, angel! I've been here all the time, with—' Her mouth went dry as sand. 'With your daddy.'

Lifting his hand, Flynn pushed away some of the hair from his daughter's tear-damp face. His lips were trying to curve into a smile, but seemed to be having some difficulty in completing the manoeuvre.

'Hey, beautiful. You know what? I'm not going anywhere soon without you. That's a promise.'

Stopping her quiet sniffling, Sorcha struggled to sit up in her mother's enfolding arms. Her gaze upon Flynn as he crouched down by her side was unwavering and direct.

'You mean you really will be my daddy—for ever?'

CHAPTER SIX

WHEN he stirred in the early hours, his duvet a crumpled mound over his body where he'd apparently wrestled with it during the night, Flynn knew that he'd hardly closed his eyes. All night long his racing thoughts had driven him near crazy, and his memory had played back time and time again the look on Sorcha's face and her sweet infant voice when she had asked him if he would always be her daddy.

An exceptionally perceptive child for her age, she had obviously thought about the fact that there had been no father figure in her life since she'd been born. Damn Caitlin! How could she have done that to him? Walked away like that when she knew she was carrying his baby? And yet allowing his affection for the little girl to deepen and grow would be no easy feat after the trauma of losing Danny. What if Caitlin decided one day that she didn't want him to be in Sorcha's life after all? What then? Dear God, he'd likely end up going mad if that happened! When Isabel had taken Danny away for a long time afterwards he had felt like a broken man.

Cursing the dread that loomed up inside him at the prospect of a similar scenario occurring, Flynn groaned out loud and dropped his head into his hands. It didn't help. It just seemed to stimulate more unwanted and troubling thoughts, and it was his thoughts that he was so desperately trying to get away from. Easing himself up into a sitting position, he rearranged the rumpled duvet and tugged it up to his shoulders. The temperature in the room was icy and his body shivered with cold. It was six in the morning, and as black as pitch outside, his head was pounding and his eyes felt as though someone had thrown a handful of sand in them. Usually he welcomed any opportunity for solitude… Right now he wanted anything *but*.

His fears were almost too much to bear by himself, and he decided he might as well get up as sit there plagued by demons. But, not wanting to disturb the two females sleeping downstairs, he hesitated. The knowledge that Caitlin was not far away had hardly assisted his aching, restless body during the night either. His libido was as entranced and taunted by her presence as it had always been—even though she had so badly let him down and he couldn't trust her.

Determined not to venture into even more unhelpful areas of his mind, Flynn strove to insert a little clarity into his thoughts. *First things first...* To help himself come to, and banish the effects of a night with no sleep, he badly needed some strong black coffee. Perhaps he would risk going down into the kitchen after all, to make some? After that, when Caitlin had risen and got dressed—he tried not to think of her wearing the white linen shirt he had lent her to sleep in—he would have an earnest conversation with her about his plans for their daughter's future welfare. For, in spite of his thoughts giving him no peace, what he wanted had suddenly become very clear to him...even though he couldn't fully acknowledge the reasons why.

'I've thought about what you suggested yesterday. About me and Sorcha moving back to Ireland and coming to live with you.'

Staring at Caitlin across the breakfast table as she spoke, Flynn knew his mercurial gaze was immediately alert.

'And?'

Outside, the relentless fall of snow had at last abated, and everything as far as the eye could see was thickly shrouded in an extra-generous coating of frosted white. Even Sorcha's snowman had doubled its girth.

'And...I've decided that we'll do it.'

The small but painful nugget of tension between

Flynn's shoulderblades eased. Suddenly he could breathe again without impediment. He'd thought he'd have a fight on his hands about the matter. He was stunned that she had conceded so easily in the end.

'What made you decide?' he asked, his voice a little gravelly because he hadn't slept.

She shrugged and put down the mug of tea she nursed. 'Everything you said last night made sense, I suppose. I think it's only fair that you should have a proper chance to get to know Sorcha, and she you...but only if you're certain that's what you really want?'

'I'm certain.'

Everything outside was still frozen, but inside Flynn's beleaguered heart something had thawed.

'So there's nothing to stop you both moving in with me today?'

'Today?'

'Why not? The sooner the better, as far as I'm concerned.'

'It can't be today, Flynn.'

Apprehension sounded in Caitlin's voice, and Flynn wondered briefly if she was already regretting her decision. But in the next instant he was thankfully reassured.

'I've still got my dad's things to sort out and get rid of, and the cottage to tidy before I give the keys back to the landlord. Plus, I—'

'Your father didn't *own* the cottage?'

'Of course he didn't!' Touching her fingers briefly to her lips, Caitlin sighed. 'My parents could never afford a mortgage. Unskilled work doesn't pay a lot, and my father worked the land all his life. They rented the cottage from Ted MacNamara. He said I could stay there as long as I wanted to after dad's funeral, but obviously he knew I had to go back to London at some point.'

If her father *had* owned the place then she and Sorcha might have had a bit of a nest egg for the future, Caitlin mused, but no such luck. Still, she was a pragmatist if nothing else, and there was no use crying over spilled milk. Having spent most of the night tossing and turning—mulling over and over the fact that Sorcha seemed to be forming a definite attachment to Flynn, and the idea of him being a permanent fixture in her life—she had concluded that the prospect of crucifying herself with even more guilt for depriving her daughter of a daddy and Flynn of his child was too much of a burden to be going on with. That was why she had decided in the end to comply with his suggestion about their moving back to Ireland.

'Then you've definitely made the right decision.' Flynn was on his feet in a trice. 'And, while we're on the subject, I've also thought about you going back to London. After Sorcha getting so upset last night, I've decided the only way you're going to go back and get your things and draw a line under your life there is if I go back with you. I'm not risking you either changing your mind or…more importantly…Sorcha believing that I've deserted her.'

Her heart tripping at the look of steel on his face, Caitlin absorbed his announcement with genuine shock. It took her aback that Flynn was sounding so possessive about the child he had only just met. It stunned her that he should care enough about Sorcha being upset that he would postpone his no doubt busy and demanding life to travel back to London with them and stay there until Caitlin had tied up the loose ends of her life there. Perhaps some of those hidden depths she'd long suspected him of harbouring were beginning to show…

'I'm not going to change my mind now that I've made my decision, and I'd never let Sorcha think you had deserted her! I'd reassure her that we'd be coming back to you. But, while we're on the subject, I have to tell you that the prospect of staying at Oak Grove doesn't exactly fill me with confidence. What will your family think of the arrangement? And, more to the point, what are they going to think about me turning up with your child?'

'Their opinion hardly signifies. The fact is, Oak Grove belongs to *me*—I live there and they don't! It's entirely up to me who I move in.'

Lifting his second mug of strong black coffee to his lips, Flynn took a long draught to finish the treacle-coloured brew and all but slammed the mug back down on the table. Wiping the back of his hand across his mouth, he threw Caitlin an impatient look, as if the subject was now definitely closed.

'I'll go and bring Sorcha in from the garden, and then we must get ready to leave. I don't want to risk another heavy fall of snow while we're travelling back down the mountain.'

Turning on his heel, he left Caitlin standing there.

She brought up the subject again on their journey home, and finally persuaded Flynn to agree to her and Sorcha going to stay at Oak Grove the following day instead. There were practical things to do to facilitate their move, and these would take time. Their suitcases had to be packed, and she needed to finish parcelling up the items her father had left which she was going to donate to the church for a future jumble sale. Plus, the cottage needed a thorough and final clean before she handed the keys back to the landlord.

But, most of all, Caitlin needed time to assimilate the events that were racing towards her with all the subtlety of a runaway juggernaut. She didn't doubt that Flynn was insisting on their move to his ancestral family home for Sorcha's sake and Sorcha's sake only. He was the type of man who would always meet his moral obligations, whether he welcomed them or not. She sighed. At least there was honour in him… But, although he might be dismissive of what his family would think of her and Sorcha turning up and moving in with him, Caitlin was nursing a real dread of being confronted by Estelle MacCormac again. The memory of her telling Flynn that Caitlin was more or less only using him for some kind of financial and material gain, and would probably try and trap him with a pregnancy, still had the power to revolt her.

The next day the temperature rose a couple of degrees, and the snow that had blanketed the countryside for days finally started to melt. The sound of ice dripping steadily off the cottage eaves provided a rhythmic backdrop to Caitlin and Sorcha's hearty breakfast of porridge, toast and marmalade.

There was a damp patch in a corner of the parlour ceiling that was leaking water. Discovering an old plastic bucket under the kitchen sink, Caitlin resignedly positioned it beneath the drip. It seemed to be a clear sign that the cottage definitely *wasn't* the place for her and Sorcha to see out the rest of their stay. Already it felt as if the damp and cold that the rundown dwelling reeked had taken up permanent residence inside her marrow.

Glancing at her watch, she saw that she had but half an hour before Flynn's promised arrival. In that time Caitlin had to clear the breakfast things, do a final check round, and leave the bags of jumble she'd sorted out on the back stoop, from where Father O'Brien from the church had promised to send someone to collect it.

Pausing for a moment between tasks, she had the strangest feeling that by agreeing to stay with Flynn she was casting her fate and Sorcha's into the great unknown, and the wild butterflies that seemed a given whenever she thought about him were suddenly back inside her stomach. At least in London—as difficult as life could be—she was resourceful and strong, and had faith in her ability to cope with most things. Becoming a single mother had definitely shaped her that way. But here in Ireland, around this enigmatic man who had turned her life upside down from the moment she'd set eyes on him, she felt anything *but*…

Her two frayed green suitcases looked starkly unprepossessing in the centre of Flynn's elegant sitting room floor. Like a shop-bought Christmas tree next to a sumptuous Norwegian Spruce. It was a dead certainty that they'd never been put down anywhere near as elegant before.

As Sorcha inquisitively skipped from room to room of their opulent new surroundings, Flynn indulgently having told her to explore wherever she wanted and make herself at home, Caitlin remained standing there in her duffle coat, jeans and sweatshirt, feeling as out of place as her unimpressive luggage.

'Aren't you going to take off your coat?' Shutting the door that led to the hall behind them, Flynn regarded her expectantly.

He wore casual clothing that was clearly not off the peg and was obviously expensive—and his unquestionably fit physique had all the bearing of a seasoned warrior from old Celtic tales of valour and honour. And with his black hair gleaming and newly washed, and his chiselled jaw freshly shaved, he was definitely possessed of all the beguiling attributes that could so easily ensnare a young girl's heart. Just as he had ensnared Caitlin's, at the tender age of just eighteen… Contemplating the prospect of living with him over the next few days, she couldn't deny she was feeling a little like an embattled fortress, under siege yet again.

'I'll take it off in a minute.' She smiled uncertainly. 'I'm still feeling the cold a bit, if I'm honest.'

Moving nearer to the warmth of the fire—presumably lit by his housekeeper—which beckoned welcomingly in the graceful surround of the fireplace, Caitlin stretched out her hands towards it.

'It's a wonder the pair of you didn't end up with pneumonia, staying in that draughty old cottage!'

Flynn remarked in exasperation. 'You should have come here yesterday, like I suggested.'

'I told you—I had things to do. As it is, there are bits and pieces of my dad's belongings that I just had to leave there. They wouldn't be of any use or interest to anyone…not even for a jumble sale.'

'If you want to keep some of them, I can find somewhere to store them for you, if you like?'

Her blue eyes mirrored her surprise. 'It's okay. It's not that important. I'm not sentimental about material things…just—'

'Just what?'

'It doesn't matter.'

To Flynn's examining gaze, Caitlin appeared extra pale and tired today. No doubt her recent bereavement was taking its toll, as well as the situation concerning him and Sorcha. He fought against feeling too much sympathy for her, yet something in him—some treacherously tender impulse—yearned to bring the light back to those pretty blue eyes.

Telling himself such a dangerous urge would likely be his downfall where she was concerned, Flynn yet again steeled his heart. Women couldn't be trusted. If he hadn't found that out by now, he really *was* in trouble. Celtic mythology was full of examples of the myriad ways the feminine sex practised to deceive. If he wanted to protect himself from future betrayal he should definitely not let his guard down for even a minute while he was around Caitlin.

'I'll take your cases into the spare bedroom. You and Sorcha should be quite comfortable in there.'

'Flynn?'

Her soft voice stopped him in his tracks.

'Do you know—can you guess how hard this is for me? Not just staying here in your house, but being here with you, knowing that you must hate me for what I did? How are we going to make things good for Sorcha if you won't even allow an opportunity for us to be friends?'

He shut his eyes for a moment, then opened them again. 'I'm not your enemy, Caitlin,' he said, with the suggestion of weariness in his voice, 'and I don't want you to feel unwelcome in my home. But right now we have to put Sorcha's needs and feelings before our own, to help her settle in. After that… Well…I've no powers to tell the future.'

Lifting the suitcases, he disappeared into an adjoining vestibule, then opened the door into what Caitlin knew from old was a sumptuous spare bedroom. In spite of her promise to herself to stay strong, emotion overtook her and her eyes welled up with tears. He seemed determined to maintain the distance between them by being aloof and detached, and he was not relenting towards her in any way. The hurt was immense.

By the time Flynn returned to the living room she'd scrubbed away all evidence of distress, taken off her coat, and silently vowed to make the best of a situation that was likely going to tax every sensibility she possessed. She owed that much to her daughter at least.

'At least the snow's started to melt.' Her glance towards the large Georgian windows was only brief, and she hardly registered the impressive view at all in her attempt at some light conversation to ease the tension.

'Hmm.' Clearly not predisposed to talk about the weather, Flynn narrowed his jade eyes. 'I've been meaning to tell you—'

There was a distinct rap on the door. In just a few long-legged strides he had crossed the large expanse of parquet floor to open it.

'Bridie,' he greeted the generously figured middle-aged woman who stood there, a patterned overall covering her clothes. 'Come in. I want you to meet Caitlin…and running round somewhere is Sorcha. I'm sure she'll find her way back to us in a minute or two. Caitlin, this is Oak Grove's housekeeper—Bridie Molloy.'

'Pleased to meet you, Bridie.'

Finding her hand clasped warmly in the older woman's, and faced with a pair of merry brown eyes that radiated both kindness and acceptance, Caitlin somehow sensed she'd found an ally. The previous housekeeper, Peg Donovan, had been *much* more formidable, and Caitlin had given her a wide berth whenever she'd seen her coming down one of the house's endless corridors towards her. Flynn had often used to tease her about her dread fear of the woman, then made it worse by telling her that as boys he and his brother had called her the 'ould witch'.

'I heard about your dad…I'm sorry for your trouble, my love. It's a hard thing to come home to, so it is.'

'Yes, it is.'

'Mummy! It's so big here it's like a palace! It's just like a king or a queen must live here!'

Bursting into the room, her golden hair a soft halo around her eager flushed face, Sorcha stopped shyly in her tracks when she set eyes on Bridie.

'Now, who can this beautiful young lady be?' The housekeeper smiled. 'If this is a palace, then I think she must be a princess…don't you Mr MacCormac?'

'Aye…she's definitely a princess.' Flynn's smile was like a sunburst as he turned his gaze upon his daughter. Watching him, Caitlin sensed her heart soar. 'Sorcha…come and say hello to Bridie.'

'Hello, Bridie.' She solemnly held out her small hand to the older woman.

Bridie crouched low, so that she was on the same level as the child, and her face was wreathed in delight as she gently shook it. 'Well, now. A princess, is it? I'm honoured, so I am!' Glancing up at Flynn and Caitlin she gave them a conspiratorial grin, 'What do you say I give Her Highness the royal tour of the house? And when we get to the kitchen there just might be some fairy cakes about ready to come out of the oven. Would you like a cake and a glass of lemonade, Your Highness?'

'Yes, please!'

Hopping from one foot to the other, Sorcha clearly had no qualms about going with the housekeeper for a while.

'Be a good girl, then, and mind your manners.' Dropping a kiss on top of the bright blonde head, Caitlin nevertheless reluctantly watched the child leave with the other woman, apprehensive at finding herself alone with Flynn when she wasn't at all prepared for such an event.

'She seems lovely,' she commented, as the housekeeper closed the door behind her.

'After the dour Peg Donovan, she's like a breath of fresh air!' Flynn agreed.

'What happened to Mrs Donovan? Did she—she didn't die?'

'Die?' His glance flared briefly with amusement. 'No...she didn't die. Would you believe she fell for a visiting gravedigger holidaying here for a while with his sister? She married him and went off to live in Dublin! We were all gob-smacked when it happened. It would have to be a strong fella with nerves of steel to take on our Mrs Donovan, that's for sure! But no doubt he was used to seeing a lot of frightening apparitions in his line of work!'

Caitlin couldn't help but laugh. Flynn's obvious enjoyment in telling her the unlikely story of his stern housekeeper's unexpected bid for romance contributed to the bubble of joy that suddenly burst inside her.

They both stopped smiling and laughing at the same time, and now the air crackled with something as different from humour as dark from light.

Feeling as though her skin had suddenly brushed up against electricity, Caitlin nervously tucked some stray blonde strands of hair behind her ear. 'You said you'd been meaning to tell me something before Bridie knocked at the door?'

Breaking out of the trance he seemed to have fallen into, looking at her, Flynn rubbed his hand round his jaw.

'I've been thinking about what you said about your independence…and you're right about jobs round here being thin on the ground. I wondered if you'd consider helping me out with some administrative stuff now and again? I'd pay you, and it might help alleviate some of your concern that I'm somehow taking control of your life. What do you think?'

Now it was Caitlin's turn to be gob-smacked. She definitely hadn't expected such an olive branch.

'Seriously?'

'I'm perfectly serious.' He allowed a rueful smile, and Caitlin's heart gave a little skip. 'You only have to take a look at the pile of unanswered correspondence on my desk to know that I'm definitely in need of some help!'

'When would you like me to start—and what about Sorcha?'

'Take a couple of days to settle in first, and I'll talk to Bridie. I'm sure she'll be only too happy to watch out for Sorcha while you work.'

'All right. Then I accept your offer. Thank you.'

CHAPTER SEVEN

IT WAS late in the evening and Flynn was in his study working. His concentration was hardly what it should have been, considering he had a book to deliver to his publisher by the end of the month, but right now ancient Celtic chieftains' plans for reinforcing their fortresses and their strategies to protect their *tuath*s against invaders from across the sea did not rivet his attention as emphatically as they usually did.

For one thing, he wasn't alone in the huge apartment, as he normally would have been. Every now and then during the day his attention would be diverted by the sound of his daughter's laughter, or her mother's calmly voiced reply. Sounds that even the thick oak doors that guarded the various rooms could not completely dim because Flynn was so intimately attuned to them. He had even found himself deliberately listening out for them. They'd been living with him for almost two whole days now, and already the pattern of his quiet, fairly ordered existence had been altered irrevocably.

At some point during each day Caitlin would take herself and Sorcha off on a longish ramble around the estate, and if Flynn hadn't already known she had a passionate penchant for fresh air whatever the weather—he would have been seriously impressed by her dedication to being in the great outdoors. That was one of the things he'd found so irresistible about her when they'd first met…her appreciation of the elements and her love and respect for nature, which he shared.

Both Caitlin and Sorcha spent a lot of time with Bridie while Flynn worked on his book, and he'd arranged with the housekeeper for their dinner to be brought up to his own private dining room in the evenings, so that Caitlin wouldn't feel things were uncomfortably formal. He'd seen the strain on her face, and he didn't want any tension she felt affecting her relationship with their daughter. Instead he wanted to help her realise that this was their home now.

After dinner he chose to spend time with Sorcha, playing or reading her a story before bedtime. He tried not to think too much about the hopes he'd had when Danny was born of doing the same with his son, but already Flynn had grown to anticipate the precious moments with his daughter with increasing pleasure. It was *after* Sorcha had gone to bed that was proving the most testing time for him. Even if he decided to go back to his study and continue working into the early hours of the morning, as he was doing now, he still had to deal with the fact that Caitlin would have settled herself in an armchair by the crackling fire, her head in a book, her feet bare and her soft blonde hair a golden and too touchable cloud around her head.

His body inconveniently tightened and he shifted in his chair. Why couldn't he trust himself to be alone in the same room with her? That wasn't difficult to answer. His body's lustful craving for her hadn't diminished any, despite the tension between them. He sighed and stared unseeingly at the screen on his desk. Whatever came about he was going to do everything in his power to get Caitlin to realise that she was better off here in Ireland with him. There was no way he was going to risk losing Sorcha like he'd lost Danny. The allure of her old life in London would surely soon diminish…and as he'd said to her, who would choose penury and struggle over wealth?

Flynn would just have to live with the fact that he himself would never be the main attraction, and it didn't matter that Caitlin still had misgivings about staying with him at Oak Grove—somehow she would have to learn to live with her reticence and weather the changes, just as Flynn had to.

Shutting down his computer, he stood up and

stretched with a yawn. Glancing down at his watch, he saw how late it was. As he walked across the room towards the door he told himself he was just going to have to somehow learn to stem the irrefutable urge to touch Caitlin whenever she was around. He hoped that she had yet again decided to have an early night. *Liar!* he silently mocked himself as his hand curved expectantly round the door handle. He was praying that she would still be sitting in the armchair, reading her book…

'Good book? It must be if you're still up reading at this hour.'

Tearing herself away from the compelling Celtic tales of heroic journeys, heartfelt challenges and lost loves she'd been reading, Caitlin stared up at Flynn's tall dark figure in his black sweater and jeans like someone in a trance.

Her father had often accused her of having one foot in this world and the other in a realm unseen, and he'd probably been right. As a child she had avidly scoured the surrounding woodland for sprites and fairies, and she had talked to imaginary friends whenever she was lonely or afraid. She'd also stared up at the sky and made castles, birds and animals out of the cotton-wool clouds that softly scudded by.

So many times she'd longed for something magical to happen, to take her far beyond the predictable pattern of her days. She'd feared even then that her future might hold a similar soul-destroying design as her parents, lives with nothing but struggle, and working hard, and no joy to lighten the load and look forward to. Caitlin had yearned for a world that promised enchantment and a love that would last for ever. When she had met Flynn her heart had beat so fast because she'd truly believed she'd found it.

Now, as he walked towards her, his aquamarine gaze reflecting spellbinding lights of blue-green fire as he rested it on her, she knew she couldn't hide her heartfelt need for him quickly enough. Laying down the book, she attempted to divert him.

'It's one of yours…I hope you don't mind? I helped myself from the bookshelf.'

'Let me see.'

To Caitlin's intense alarm, Flynn crouched down beside her and plucked the book from her lap. After examining the cover for a moment, he flicked idly through the pages. All the while she couldn't tear her eyes from his face, from the blue-black lights that glinted fiercely in his hair and his hard chiselled jaw, and neither could she ignore the warm, sensually musky scent that drifted up to her from his body.

'Which story are you reading? The tale about Deirdre and Naoise?' His mouth softened a little as he said this, but only someone who'd been on intimate terms with his moods and expressions would have detected such an infinitesimal change. 'So you like tales about wicked women who put spells on innocent young men and get them to elope with them?'

'Naoise was a warrior…a champion. Hardly an innocent.'

'Maybe. Clearly you still enjoy them? The old tales?'

'They're magical, and they have a purpose too. There's deep wisdom in the telling of them, and they can teach us so much about life. I've always loved them…you know that.'

She couldn't help but think of Flynn when she thought of the handsome warrior that the maiden Deirdre had indeed eloped with. He'd had hair as black as a raven's wing and had been heartbreakingly handsome, so the tale went…

Her voice had unwittingly lowered, and Flynn put the book aside. But instead of moving away, as Caitlin had expected, he stayed exactly where he was. The fire that danced with orange and blue flames in the fireplace next to them made the haunting lights in his eyes like the effect of sunlight on a still blue-green lake. Caitlin was caught in the spell of them, her whole body holding itself in abeyance. Almost in slow motion he slid his hand behind her neck and brought her head down to his.

The first touch of his lips was like cool satin

overlaid with velvet. Overwhelmed, relieved—*hungry* to assuage an ache she hadn't even realised she was nursing—Caitlin gasped her need into his mouth. Behind her neck Flynn's warm hand grew firmer, to hold her still so that he could drink from the fountain of her lips as thirstily as he desired.

If she'd forgotten what the taste of heaven was like, she remembered now. A wild tremor shivered through her body at the pleasure he was igniting—a profound, shuddering, soul-deep pleasure that melted her as easily as the winter sun had melted the icicles hanging from the cottage eaves the other morning. Then he moved his hand from her nape to follow the path of her spine, and soon after he was urging her down onto the rug beside him, touching her breasts through her shirt and dragging her hips towards his so that she felt his growing desire hard against her.

Their lips were magnets for one another, clinging and tasting, stoking a fire that felt as if it had been kindling all these years, just waiting to burst into flame again. Drawing back with a ragged breath, Caitlin glanced up into Flynn's passion-darkened eyes with a question in her own dazed blue.

'What?' he murmured, gravel-voiced, impatient to draw her back into another hungry and sensual embrace.

'What are we doing, Flynn?'

'You mean you don't know?' He raised a dark brow with grim mockery. Feeling a cold shiver slither down her spine, Caitlin sensed her desire start to cool. This wasn't about *love*...she knew that. And, whilst the knowledge was apt to shatter her still unmended heart into a thousand tiny fragments yet again, she also knew it had very little to do with affection or regard either. None of those attributes had she sensed in Flynn's ardent demand. Nor would she, when all he seemed bent on was a kind of revenge for what he saw as Caitlin's deliberate rejection of what they'd once had. This was purely and simply about sex...about answering a primeval white heat that would scorch them both but leave Caitlin ultimately feeling like a used and empty well.

She would sacrifice much for her child, but she would not give her body to a man who neither loved nor respected her. No matter how powerfully she desired him. Extricating herself from his hold, she eased up onto her feet.

'I don't—I don't know what I was thinking. This can't happen between us. You know it can't. We need to implement some strict rules about this sort of thing while I'm here.'

'Rules, is it now?'

A sardonic smirk touched the lips that only a few moments ago had been devouring hers. He stood up beside her and his frustration was easy to sense. His hard, lean body radiated it.

'You wanted it as much as I did!'

His harsh accusation spared her nothing, and made Caitlin's face burn.

'Desire means nothing without love,' she commented sadly, hugging her arms over her chest.

'You stand there and talk about love when you walked out on me as if my regard meant less to you than some "blow-in" you'd only known for five minutes? Love!' He spat out the word, as though he scorned the very sound of it.

'You've become so bitter, Flynn. Did I do that?'

'What do *you* think?'

The look he gave her practically froze the blood in her veins, and Caitlin nervously touched her hair before turning her face away in a bid to hide the grief and despondency that welled up inside her.

'I know I said I left because of all the family opposition we had to us being together, and because the rows with my dad about us were getting me down…I didn't lie.' Choosing her words carefully, she swallowed hard before continuing. 'But there was so much more to it than that, Flynn.'

'Go on.'

His stern visage hardly invited her confidence, but then Caitlin was used to that. Somewhere along the line she had to find a way through her reticence and doubt and risk telling him the truth. How could there be any chance of an improvement in their relations if she didn't?

Sighing, she made herself continue. 'Would I have left a man I trusted with all my being as well as loved? My father hardened his heart and didn't let me anywhere near after my mother died. He probably did it unconsciously, to protect himself, but it still hurt. Then I met you—and you did the same! You were kind to me, yes, and you wanted to be with me. You made that clear…with your body, with your eyes. But you rarely gave me any insight into the real man. There was a distance between us even then, Flynn, and I defy you to deny it! How could I tell you what was in my heart—let alone that I was pregnant with your child—when you never revealed anything to me about what might be in your own? I still don't know what ails you…why you hold back so. Maybe you can tell me something…*anything*…that would give me a clue?'

Something flared deep in his eyes, but his lips remained sealed. Caitlin knew instinctively that sometimes secrets were not revealed in actual words, yet silence could touch upon so much. She sensed the power of silence now, and made herself wait. And if she added a prayer or two to help things along, then only she was privy to that.

'This isn't the first time I've believed myself to be a father.'

Now Caitlin was stricken silent, but the thud of her heartbeat sounded like cannonfire in her ears.

Flynn's hand tunnelled restlessly through his thick dark hair, but his gaze remained steady as he continued to focus it on her.

'I told you I was married before, and that I ended up divorcing the woman in question? Well…she had a baby. A little boy named Danny. For six months I believed him to be mine…that I was his father. Then she told me she'd been having an affair, and the child was this other man's. She'd had a paternity test done to prove it. Her lover had insisted on it, and because she was in love with him and not me she agreed. For six months she let me think I was the boy's father—until finally her lover gave her an ultimatum and told her to choose between the two of us. Well, she chose her lover. And, taking Danny with her, she moved out and went to live with him. That's it. End of story.'

Turning away, Flynn laid his hand on the marble mantelpiece over the fire.

Remaining where she stood—partly out of shock and partly because she sensed he needed some space right now—Caitlin's deeply affected gaze never left his haunting, absorbed profile.

'But that's *not* the end of the story…is it, Flynn?' she questioned him softly. 'You're still hurting over what happened. You miss your son. Oh, God! If only you'd told me this when we were first together!'

'So you'd have stayed with me out of sympathy?' His glance was brutal. 'I don't think so!'

'It's not about sympathy, Flynn! Though I wouldn't be human if I didn't feel for you in such a cruel situation. It's about allowing *intimacy*…trust. It's about knowing that your secrets are safe with me and mine with you.'

'That's as maybe. But what happened isn't something a person gets over in five minutes! And then to have *you* walk away…' He clenched his jaw, as if contemplating so much perceived betrayal was too much to bear, then turned and crossed the room to the door. 'I'll leave you to enjoy your book in peace. Goodnight, Caitlin. I'll see you in the morning.'

She knew there was no point in going after him. Not now, when all he really wanted was to be alone and tend to his wounds in private. But what he'd told her was a revelation that gave her more than just a small clue to his aloof, detached persona, and somewhere deep inside her Caitlin knew it was a breakthrough.

Almost too restless to contemplate sleep, she chose to stay up long into the night reading instead—but her thoughts were not on the pages of print in front of her. They were on Flynn, and the little boy that his ex-wife had cruelly taken away, whom he had clearly loved deeply…

After that, was there room in his broken heart for her and his daughter?

CHAPTER EIGHT

'THERE'S something I've been thinking about,' Flynn announced the next morning, as they breakfasted together in his private dining room.

'Can I get down now, Mummy?' Sorcha interrupted, eager to get back to the toys that Bridie had brought yesterday, which had once belonged to her own now grown-up daughter.

Leaning forward to wipe some strawberry jam off the child's rosebud mouth with a linen napkin, Caitlin nodded. 'Go on, then. But you'd better get Bridie to take you to the bathroom and brush those teeth before you do anything else! I'll be checking to see if you've done them, mind!'

'All right.'

The soft green eyes demonstrated immediate reluctance for carrying out this mundane but necessary task, and Flynn couldn't help grinning. 'You'd better do as your mother says,' he advised, ruffling his daughter's bright hair. 'You don't want to end up like that "toothless old hag" in the fairy story I read you last night!'

Sliding off her chair, Sorcha placed her hands indignantly on her hips and affected a look of great mortal offence. 'I'm *not* going to be an old hag! I'm a princess, and a princess stays young and beautiful for ever! Silly Daddy!' And off she flounced, completely unaware that she'd left Flynn sitting there with astonishment written all over his face.

'I swear she's a sixty-three-year-old in the body of a child!'

Shaking her head in amusement, Caitlin smiled. Having naturally noted her daughter's poignant reference to Flynn as 'Daddy', and thinking about the secret from his past that he had so reluctantly revealed last night, she hoped her smile hid the sudden wave of emotion that deluged her.

'You said there's something you've been thinking about?' Taking a careful sip of her hot cup of tea, she settled her wide blue eyes expectantly on Flynn.

But he was still busy absorbing the incredible fact that his child had just casually addressed him for the first time ever as her daddy. He felt as if his heart had just burst wide open.

'What was I saying?' He scraped his hand distractedly through his midnight hair, thinking hard. 'Ah, yes… Two things occurred to me after we'd spoken last night.' His eyes sought hers.

For a long moment their gazes clung, surprised, enthralled, as if they couldn't bear to look away from each other, then Caitlin blushed deeply, and carefully returned her cup to its matching porcelain saucer.

Flynn had always loved that 'shy' aspect to her personality, and he discovered that that hadn't changed.

She was looking exceptionally pretty this morning—a factor that seemed to provoke a deep carnal heat in him that uninhibitedly travelled to his groin as he gazed at her. Reflecting on the events of last night, he wryly recalled that they'd done a bit more than speak. He was riveted by the way the soft pink sweater she wore clung to the sweet perfection of her lovely breasts, unknowingly inviting his ardent examination and increasing his rather inconvenient desire. Endowed with the kind of lovely, unforgettable face that any man would thrill to find on the pillow next to him in the morning on waking, Caitlin also had the body of a siren. The combination was intoxicating. And motherhood had clearly enhanced those stunning attributes.

Although she had sworn to him that there had been no intimate relationships for her during the past four years, Flynn wondered if she'd ever got lonely for the feel of someone's arms around her. She wouldn't be human if she hadn't—but it damn near killed him to think of her with anyone else but him. After his unexpected confession last night, he had to own to feeling particularly vulnerable where she was concerned.

'First of all we need to talk about when you're planning on going back to London.'

'We're due to leave this Saturday…I told you. Are you still intending to come with us?'

'Of course. But we can't return this Saturday—that's what I wanted to talk to you about. I need you to postpone the trip for another couple of weeks at least.'

'Another couple of weeks? Why?'

'Because my workload is such that I just can't leave it.'

'Then why can't Sorcha and I travel back on our own and you can join us?'

'No.'

'What do you mean, *no*?'

Flynn immediately detected that his seemingly inflexible attitude had upset her. But he had his reasons for not wanting her to leave without him, and in his opinion they were sound ones.

'You're not taking my daughter anywhere without me.'

'Be reasonable, Flynn! We *have* to go home on Saturday! My plane tickets aren't transferable for one, and secondly I need to let them know at work what I'm doing. I might have to work a week or two's notice before they'll let me leave.'

'You don't need anyone's permission to quit your job, and you won't be working *any* notice.' His tone disapproving, Flynn coolly conveyed his intransigence on this point. 'There's no need. You're simply going to tell them you're resigning for personal family reasons, and that your resignation has to take effect straight away. In fact, the more I think of it, you could probably deal with the whole thing on the telephone and follow it up with a letter.'

'And what about my aunt?'

'What about her?'

'She's expecting us home! What am I going to tell her?'

'Tell her that *I'm* going to take care of you and Sorcha now.'

'I don't need taking care of! I'm not a child.'

Caitlin's darkly golden brows had creased in protest. Determinedly Flynn tried to deflect her unhappiness.

'Think about it… You could probably do with a break after what's happened with your father. Surely your aunt understands that? What's the urgent need to go back to London? You're basically resigning from your job and packing a few things for you and Sorcha. Apart from that…you're free.'

'Free?' Her blue eyes visibly darkened. 'That's a strange way to put it! As if there's no emotional attachment to the place I've lived for the past four and a half years at all! I'm not saying I'll exactly miss London, but I will miss my aunt. She's my closest friend, as well as my relative. We've been through a lot together.'

Her comment instigated a train of thought that instantly perturbed him. Reflecting on the momentous event of her having had a child alone, without him as the father to support her emotionally as well as materially, Flynn all but winced. He should have been there with Caitlin to help her when she had Sorcha. If he could have been—he would have been.

'We were friends too, once upon a time,' he replied thoughtfully, his huskily voiced words making her glance up at him with surprise. 'Remember, Caitlin?'

He barely heard her reply, it was so quiet. 'I remember.'

'So that's settled, then? The London trip is postponed until I finish my work?'

'If there isn't any other way round it, I suppose it is. Look…if you're feeling overwhelmed you should let me help you, like you suggested. We could start today, if you like?'

Again she had surprised him. He'd thought he'd have a royal battle on his hands about delaying her trip back to London, but instead it seemed she'd chosen to acquiesce with his wishes rather than argue. Was that because of what he had revealed last night? Flynn abhorred the idea that Caitlin was, after all, feeling sorry for him.

'Why not?' he agreed, shrugging. 'I'll talk to Bridie about looking after Sorcha for a while. There's something else too...'

Automatically starting to clear away the breakfast things, Caitlin paused.

'I've been thinking about our living arrangements.' Folding his arms across his chest, he exhaled a resigned-sounding sigh. 'It came to me that you might be happier and more comfortable if you and Sorcha occupied the apartment in the east wing rather than stay here with me. You would have your own private space and yet still be under my roof. What do you think?'

She noted he'd asked what she *thought*, not how she *felt*. Somewhere hurt and dismay surfaced, because she wondered if he wasn't subtly trying to keep her at a distance. Determinedly, she pushed away her doubt.

'I think it sounds like a good idea,' she heard herself say, though she was not at all convinced.

'The other thing I've been meaning to ask is, can you drive?' Flynn continued. 'I know you hadn't had any lessons when we were first together...'

'I still haven't.' Pursing her lips for a moment, Caitlin was genuinely rueful. 'I wish I could drive, but there was no need to learn living in London. I simply used public transport. I know it's a very different kettle of fish getting around here.'

'Then I'm going to arrange lessons for you as

soon as possible. I'll get you your own car, and you can have all the freedom you want. Perhaps living with me might not be so difficult for you then? How does that sound?'

It sounded as if he was being both generous and thoughtful, despite his reference to living with him being difficult, and Caitlin knew it would be churlish to complain. Having her own apartment in the house and her own space was probably wise at this point in time, when things between them were still under somewhat of a strain. Even though there had been that breakthrough of his story about the boy he'd believed to be his son—a first in terms of personal confessions from the heart…

Going back to the issue of their living arrangements, it crossed her mind that perhaps she and Sorcha disturbed Flynn during the day when he was working. Even though his apartment was huge by anybody's standards. Yet she couldn't help returning to the thought that he'd leapt at any opportunity to install a little more distance between them. The barriers were still there, and he wasn't going to relinquish them easily. He was prepared to give Sorcha all the time in the world, but when it came to his ex-lover he still had no intention of letting his guard down.

'It's a kind offer on both counts, and I don't think I'll refuse. Thank you.'

Before Flynn could say anything else, she turned away to go in search of their daughter.

* * *

The spare apartment in the east wing was delightful. With its varnished wooden floors, high ceilings and light and airy aspect, there was enough space contained within it to house one large family or two smaller ones. Either way, Caitlin was unused to inhabiting the realms of such unmitigated luxury.

Once she'd unpacked her own and Sorcha's suitcase, hung their meagre selection of clothing in the cavernous wardrobes and then deposited their equally minimal toiletries in the vast luxurious bathroom, she found herself longing for some of her personal things from home to arrange around the place. She didn't have much, but she would have liked her photographs, her books and her CD collection at least. Never mind. At least the apartment was fully furnished with everything even the most discerning occupant might need or desire.

Suddenly restless, Caitlin walked over to the huge Georgian sash window in her bedroom, which overlooked the parkland where Flynn had taken an excited Sorcha to look at the horses. There was a hollow feeling in her stomach now, that seemed to have replaced her previous optimism that at last he might be more prepared to talk about his past and open up a little.

Perhaps she should have resisted his offer of living in a separate apartment from his? What if her acceptance had merely confirmed to him that she wanted to have as little to do with him as possible other than their dealings concerning Sorcha? That would be no good to them at all! It was clear that he was still grieving for the little boy he'd lost, and Caitlin turning up after all these years with Sorcha had surely dredged up aspects of his past that were clearly still blisteringly raw in their intensity. How could she get him to see that she wanted to *help* him heal by being with him…not make things worse?

But at least father and daughter seemed happy together. She should be relieved that Flynn hadn't rejected Sorcha altogether after what had happened to him before. Again she sensed the heavy cloak of guilt deaden her shoulders. Perhaps she didn't *deserve* happiness? What if her impetuous and frightened actions of four and a half years ago had robbed her of the possibility of being happy for ever?

The thought wasn't at all helpful—bruising her soul as it did—and, feeling impatience at indulging in such destroying self-pity, she elected to ring her aunt. Apart from seeking the comfort of someone who really cared about her, she needed to explain why she and Sorcha wouldn't be returning to London on Saturday after all. After that, she would get on with the task of resigning from her job.

There was a knock at the door. Having fallen into an exhausted doze on the sumptuous living room couch whilst reading her book, Caitlin guiltily jolted upright and hastily tried to fix her tousled hair as she hurried out into the vestibule.

'Flynn!'

'I just came to see if you were settling in okay. Bridie offered to take Sorcha into town to do some shopping. I let her go. Was that all right?'

'Yes, but—'

'Can I come in?' His expression inscrutable, he swept past her without waiting for a reply.

Caitlin stared after him, slightly muzzy-headed after being woken so abruptly. 'What's up? You look as if you've got something on your mind,' she commented, wondering what this visit was really about.

'Since you ask…there *is* something.'

Heading into the living room, with its air of calm and its gracious antique furniture and elegant rugs, Flynn waited for Caitlin to join him.

Her heartbeat slowed inside her chest as she saw the definite strain between his brows—as though the tension inside him was rendering any equilibrium or even a pretence at it impossible.

'I want you to tell me about Sorcha's birth,' he said, his jade eyes flaring with so many shades of feeling that Caitlin was momentarily struck dumb.

Of all the reasons for his unexpected visit, she hadn't expected this.

'What?'

'I need to know. I've been with her for the past couple of hours and I've been wondering…'

'Why don't you sit down and be comfortable? I'll willingly tell you anything you want to know.'

They sat on opposite sides of the couch she'd been dozing on, and Caitlin felt like a novice climber at the foot of her first significant mountain. Did she have the necessary courage to negotiate this particular daunting ascent?

'Where do you want me to start?' she asked.

'What was your pregnancy like?'

He sat with his elbows resting on taut long-boned thighs beneath dark denim jeans. A lock of sable hair slipped forward onto Flynn's brow, and Caitlin longed to sweep it tenderly back for him. But taking a deep breath, she started to recall what carrying her baby for nine months had been like.

'The first three months were the hardest, I think. I was awfully sick, and couldn't keep anything down. But after that…I just felt this incredible sense of well-being and rightness somehow. As if—as if Mother Nature herself was minding me in some way.'

She felt heat surge into her face, suddenly self-conscious, but Flynn was looking at her as though every word she uttered was somehow vital and important. It spurred her on.

'The last six weeks were a bit of a challenge… moving around, I mean. I was used to nipping about like a two-year-old, and I felt slow and ponderous. I got very tired too. But Aunt Marie was wonderful, and encouraged me to rest whenever things got too much.'

'And what about the birth? What happened on that day?'

'I woke up at one in the morning with pains. I knew it was the real thing because I was about a week overdue. My aunt called an ambulance, and they came and took me into hospital. I was in labour for a night and a day.' She grimaced. 'There was a complication, and at one time the baby got a bit distressed inside the womb. They talked about giving me a Caesarean, but I so wanted to have my baby naturally! Somehow I knew it would be all right—blind faith, you might call it—and in the end it was. She had a fine pair of lungs on her right from the first moment she drew breath, I can tell you! I should have known from then on she'd come into the world with plenty to say for herself!'

Flynn sensed the tension inside him lock tight as he thought about Caitlin being in labour for so long. A night and a day, she'd said. When she'd first returned to Ireland and he had seen her, he had wanted retribution for what she'd done to him. Now, hearing about his daughter's birth, it made something that had previously been an abstract idea entirely personal—and very close to home. Now he found he couldn't even tolerate the thought of either Caitlin or Sorcha being in distress.

'And then, when you took her home…what was her sleeping like? Danny used to—' He abruptly cut off the thought that had crept up on him unawares, and the jolt it caused in the pit of his stomach was sickening.

'Danny used to what, Flynn?' Caitlin urged, gently leaning towards him, her blue eyes concerned. 'Was he a poor sleeper? Did you have to get up to him during the night?'

Slowly he let out the breath he was holding, that was near cutting him in two. His fingers found the wayward hair that flopped onto his brow and pushed it back to no avail. 'Several times sometimes. Isabel complained about being disturbed, so I saw to him. I never minded. It was an opportunity for the two of us to spend time alone together in the still of the night, with no one else around.' Hardly believing he was telling her all this, Flynn ruefully moved his head and swallowed hard over the intolerable ache in his throat.

'He must have meant so much to you.'

'Let's just concentrate on Sorcha, shall we? Tell me some more about her as a baby.'

He knew that she would have encouraged him to talk some more about the other child who had been in his life, but Flynn already felt he'd said too much about that. It was their daughter, the little girl who was quickly making dangerous inroads into his heart right now, that he needed to discuss.

Leaning back against the luxurious upholstery, Caitlin let a smile steal onto her lips like the sun peeping from behind a cloud. 'She was just adorable! She was surprisingly contented, in spite of everything, and she could sleep for England *and* Ireland, so thankfully there were no problems there! I'd never have entertained the thought of going back to work when she was eighteen months old if she'd had trouble sleeping. I don't think I could have coped with the lack of my own sleep and taking care of everything else.'

'But you *did* cope. And from what I can tell looking at Sorcha you did a grand job, Caitlin. Motherhood clearly comes naturally to you.'

'I don't know about that! I'm quite capable of making a hash of things sometimes. I'm not perfect, but I do my best. And I love her very much.'

'I can see that too.'

'Was there anything else you wanted to know?'

His answering smile seemed to come naturally...with hardly any reticence at all. 'I think that's fine for now...'

CHAPTER NINE

For a while Caitlin simply basked in the feeling of calm that swept over her after Flynn had spoken. It was a rare thing since she'd been back, and she wanted to savour it. His smile too had caught her unawares. Unguarded, like honey to a bee, it had made everything inside her feel as if it was indeed drowning in sweet enticing nectar.

But, finding him in this more conciliatory mood, she wanted some answers of her own. Replies to more personal enquiries that he might not have contemplated giving even just a day ago…

'Your ex-wife…Isabel…?'

Gazing directly up into a hypnotic glance that led her thoughts down a very provocative road indeed, Caitlin struggled to concentrate.

'What about her?' he asked.

'You never told me much when we were together…except—except that things didn't work out between you.'

'Nobody likes talking about being made a fool of by someone. Though the blame doesn't all lie with Isabel. I was the prize fool who kidded myself that I could somehow transform a travesty of a relationship into a real marriage…even though I quickly realised I'd mistaken physical attraction and lust for something more meaningful.'

'Why did you marry her, then?'

The question was out before she had fully realised her intention to verbalise it. When someone had been hurt, or carried a deep emotional wound, it wasn't necessarily the right thing to try and force a revelation, in Caitlin's opinion. One had to tread carefully. But, nonetheless, Flynn didn't hesitate in answering.

'A temporary lack of judgement capitalised on by family pressure.' He shrugged. 'They were all for it, and convinced me that everything would work out given time. She came from the right social strata, she was pretty, educated, and both sets of parents approved.'

'And the affair she had? That started *after* you got married?'

'Before, as a matter of fact.'

'And you had no idea that she was seeing someone else?'

He shifted in his seat and glanced momentarily away. 'I was glad she chose not to spend a lot of time at home. She had a tight-knit circle of friends, and she was always doing something with them…travelling, shopping, indulging herself on a regular basis. Until she told me she was pregnant I was more than happy for her to go her own way.'

'But you welcomed the news that you were going to be a father?'

There was a flash of the intense light in his eyes that Caitlin had seen reflected before, when he'd spoken about the little boy he'd lost, and her heart turned over.

'I did.'

'Oh, Flynn… It must have been terrible for you when you found out that—'

'Danny wasn't mine? *Terrible* is perhaps too mild a word. Anyway, I'm weary of talking about it. Do you mind?'

'So you never—you never see him?' Caitlin ventured one last question to complete the puzzle.

'Isabel and her lover moved to Italy after she left me. Apparently he had family there who offered him a home and a job. We both agreed that it was probably best I didn't keep in contact… She wanted Danny to have the chance to get close to his real father.'

'What a dreadful situation! You must have— It must have broken your heart into a million pieces!'

He neither moved nor spoke. Everything about that indomitable visage of his denoted great strength of mind, uncommon passion and purpose, but Caitlin was beginning to see that she had misjudged Flynn. She'd worried that he was incapable of great love towards anyone, but now she knew that the reverse was true. Underlying the words that had come so reluctantly and with such obvious difficulty when talking about the loss of the child who had clearly meant the world to him were emotions that ran fathoms deep.

He would never forget the little boy he had loved…not until his dying day. He'd carried the wound around with him for years, and the scarring must be indelible. Caitlin could hardly breathe for the hurt she felt on his behalf.

'You were Danny's father for a while, Flynn!' Leaning towards him, she reached out her hand and tenderly, so *carefully*, touched the side of his jaw. With the pad of her thumb she stroked across the shadowed stubbled surface. 'A part of that little boy's spirit will always know that—no matter where he is. Some part of him will know that there was this incredible man who loved him so much, and that can only enhance his own ability to love deeply when he grows to a man. That's your legacy to Danny. Love never dies, Flynn. It's a power…a force for good in the world like nothing else!'

'Sweet heaven!' Capturing her hand, Flynn turned it palm up and pressed his lips against the centre. His mouth was warm, intoxicating, a poem of tenderness and passion, and Caitlin sensed her need for him break all its bounds and make her very insides ache.

'No one but you could say such a thing…could even understand,' he told her, keeping hold of her hand and avidly examining her face.

'I meant it, Flynn. I so want to—'

'What?'

'I so want to show you—to tell you—'

Closing the gap between them even more, Flynn momentarily touched her lips with his fingers, then beguilingly brushed back a strand of her hair. 'Do you think I'd try and stop you?'

The room fell quiet, and a sensual undercurrent filled the air between them with an exquisite expectancy that was as taut as a harpstring.

'Do you not know that I'd die a thousand deaths if I couldn't touch you right now the way I yearn to touch you, Caitlin?'

Her blue eyes grew very wide…as though a sublime ocean of feeling resided in each.

The ancient Celts believed that in the act of gazing deeply into a lover's eyes, making love with them, your spirit inhabited theirs for a little while, and vice versa. It was a momentous thing. It reinforced an ancient and sacred circle of belonging that was there when your twin souls first recognised each other.

Staring into Caitlin's bewitching gaze now, Flynn remembered the quiet, yet explosive excitement that had erupted inside him that very first occasion when their glances had met. Whole futures spun and wove far-reaching webs on such moments. He'd known then that his own path would irrevocably be tangled up with hers.

Moving her into this vacant apartment, his desire had been to give her some space, so that she could grieve for her father in peace and by degrees come to see that living with Flynn at Oak Grove would have benefits—material ones, at least—that she might come to welcome as time went by. But the truth of it was he was having the devil's own job trying to resist her, and no distance was great enough to keep his desire for her totally under lock and key. Not when his whole body was consumed by the frustrating need to touch her on a daily basis.

'I feel the same.'

'Good.' His lips formed a smile that would stop the tides. 'Then let me take you to bed.'

Finding herself in that neat and orderly bedroom, where not so much as a loose thread on the dulled gold counterpane disrupted its perfect symmetry, Caitlin knew her wild emotions were the exact opposite. Now, with her limbs entwined with Flynn's, she knew she was exactly where she yearned to be. Where she was meant to be.

It was a joy unparallelled to have the freedom to slide her hands down that strong, lean back with its taut, well-developed muscles and silky skin, to feel that amazing well-defined mouth of his tasting her lips as though he was a man near desperate for air. And when that same voracious mouth turned its attention to her tingling, aching breasts, her passion-filled moans permeated the surrounding silence like something wild, suddenly released after long imprisonment.

How had she survived without this utterly necessary intimacy with this man for over four long years? Apart from Sorcha's presence to lighten them, the days had indeed been like prison walls—because her spirit had been here with him all this time…

'I feel like we're doing this for the very first time,' she admitted softly, her voice a broken whisper as she at last allowed herself the freedom to push back that rogue lock of coal-black hair from his lightly grooved forehead. 'I've missed you so, Flynn. I've longed for your touch.'

His mercurial glance blazed down at her.

'And do you know how long I've needed *your* touch?' he responded, his rich voice threaded with unconstrained passion.

'I never meant to hurt you.'

For a long, unsettling moment she sensed him grow still, and his gaze seemed to excavate deep inside Caitlin's soul. Her chest grew tight with trepidation. Fearing he might leave her, she started to withdraw her hand from where it lay across his tightly bunched bicep, her heart almost torn in two with despair at the idea that he'd changed his mind about making love to her. But then he emitted a harsh-voiced groan and kissed her hard—so hard that his teeth and lips connected bruisingly with hers.

'I need this. I need this like I will die if I don't have you! But I need to protect you too,' he told her, when he could finally bear to tear his lips from hers.

'It's all right, Flynn…I'm on the pill,' Caitlin answered quickly.

Anxious that he shouldn't think that it was because she'd been sleeping with anyone else, she started to explain that she took the oral contraceptive purely to ease her period cramps, but to her relief there was no doubt in his eyes, and with the sound of her own heartbeat drowning out further thought Caitlin sensed Flynn's hands slide firmly beneath her bottom, urging her hips towards him.

There was no gentling her for his possession. His uncontained hunger reached out to her and filled the wild, empty spaces in her own longing, so that when he took her with one long, penetrating deep thrust everything inside her softened willingly in answer. It had always been like this. The first heated touches when they'd been together had always elicited this raw, elemental explosion of need—and then, when that had been assuaged, would come the tender, quieter, yet equally fulfilling counterpoint of their loving.

The profound, soul-searching glare from Flynn's disturbing black-fringed jade eyes possessed Caitlin with as much hunger and need as his body did, and she couldn't hold back the ocean-tide of feeling that seemed to gather strength inside her until there was nowhere else for it to go. Instead it got caught up in a passionate eddy that made her release a cry of wonder and indescribable pleasure as it reached its zenith.

Her moans of satisfaction swiftly turned to tears of joy touching on regret. Why had she let him go when she should have held on to what she'd had with her life if need be? Why hadn't she been stronger and braver and somehow *made* him open up to her?

'Hush, now…hush…It's all right.'

Kissing her tears away, Flynn drove hard into her body and finally fell against her, his breathing harsh and his forehead lightly sheened with sweat. As the erotic scents from their skin mingled and the fragile winter light of the day started to edge its way towards afternoon Caitlin wrapped her arms around her lover and willed her tears of regret away. Instead of dwelling on the past, she would hold these precious moments to her like an unexpected matchless gift. And nobody could take that away from her.

Moving to her side, Flynn urged her against him, fitting her body into his as though she was the missing part of him he'd long been searching for.

Thinking back over their conversation earlier, when she had asked him about his ex-wife and his son, he knew a great longing to have trusted Caitlin more when they'd first met—to have shared the truth with her about what he'd been through. Maybe if he had she wouldn't have left as she had, and he wouldn't have spent all this time resenting her as well as blaming her father for her leaving. He was beginning to see that he had played a not 'insignificant' part in driving her away. He had been too quick to blame others, instead of looking at himself, and now Flynn saw that he'd allowed his ex-wife's cruel actions to make him bitter, closed-off, suspicious of anyone wanting to get close to him.

No wonder Caitlin had felt she couldn't trust him with the news that she was pregnant!

Storing away the information until he could properly consider it, Flynn tenderly stroked Caitlin's hair, then gently kissed the top of her silky head. 'Why don't you try and get some sleep?' he suggested. 'I'll get up and see to Sorcha when she returns.'

'I promised to help you with your work, remember?' she said, stifling a yawn.

'Work can wait.'

'Are you sure?'

'Absolutely.'

'Then in that case I might just take a nap—if you

promise me you'll stay a while?' As she murmured her reply, her eyelids clearly were struggling to stay open, and her warm breath feathered softly over Flynn's bare chest.

A few moments later he heard her sigh and knew she was sound asleep. Staring up at the high vaulted ceiling, he exhaled—perhaps the longest, most relaxed breath he'd experienced in ages. If it hadn't been for the fact that it was his daughter whose return he was awaiting nothing barring an act of God could have induced him to move from that bed. His spirit soared at having this beguiling woman back in his arms again. Being inside her, feeling her scalding velvet heat enfold him, as well as the erotic sensation of her long legs clasping his waist in passionate surrender, had been the culmination of a long-held dream. He'd missed her more than he could ever say.

And as Caitlin's hand splayed out against his back in sleep, the brush of her satin skin once again instigating his passionate arousal, Flynn battled hard to contain his longing for her. Sliding his hand down over the smooth, undulating contour of her hip, he found himself willing her to wake in time for him to have her again at least *once* more, before he absolutely had to get up and go and collect Sorcha from Bridie's care…

Later that afternoon, having left Flynn in his office taking a phone call, Caitlin followed her daughter down the grand curving staircase, watching closely to make sure she didn't fall and hurt herself as she skipped happily ahead. They were heading for the huge country-style kitchen, where Bridie had promised to spend some time making iced buns with Sorcha so that Caitlin could help Flynn with his work.

Outside, the dull weather had been lifted by a welcome display of fierce sunshine, and nearly all of the snow that had covered the countryside for days was gone, leaving a shimmering verdant landscape in its wake. Caitlin was sensing a sea change of hope arise inside her since making love with Flynn, and her mood was buoyant. As they reached the bottom step a figure appeared through the opened front door at the end of the hallway—a familiar figure that took her aback.

It was Estelle MacCormac—Flynn's mother. Despite the shock that ebbed through her like icy ocean waves, Caitlin determinedly tried to cling onto her upbeat mood. Why hadn't Flynn mentioned she was coming today? She would at least have been better prepared for the confrontation.

The older woman was the epitome of elegance, dressed in a black coat over an emerald-green tailored suit and cream blouse, a rope of antique pearls at her neck. Immediately conscious of her own less elegant attire, of serviceable black sweater and jeans, Caitlin sensed her heartbeat drum hard.

Estelle's critical gaze seemed to freeze on mother and daughter as she considered them. Instantly protective of her child, Caitlin settled her hands over Sorcha's small shoulders and drew her in close to her legs.

'Hello, Mrs MacCormac.' She forced the words out through reluctant lips, despite her vow to err on the side of optimism. 'It's been a long time.'

'It certainly has, Miss Burns.'

The other woman moved down the stone-flagged floor towards them, her hands busy removing her elegant black gloves as she did so. 'Is Flynn around? I told Bridie to let him know I was coming. I gather he was occupied when I rang earlier.'

Her implication seemed to be that Caitlin had clearly had something to do with that, and the younger woman found herself helplessly colouring. 'I'll go and tell him you're here, if you like,' she offered.

'No—wait. I think I'll take this opportunity to have a word with you first, if I may?'

'All right.' Caitlin shrugged, unable to think of an excuse to refuse, and thinking too that it was time to stop running away and instead face her fears. Perhaps lay a few ghosts too.

'And this is your child?'

'Her name is Sorcha.'

It seemed to Caitlin's sensitive hearing that Estelle was suggesting it was doubtful she could be Flynn's child too.

'Pretty little thing…lovely eyes. Hello, my dear!' She leaned forward to address the child.

Pressing closer to her mother, Sorcha stayed silent.

'I expect she's shy. Why don't we go into the drawing room? I'm sure Bridie must have a nice fire going in there.'

Wary of the unexpectedly warm manner Estelle was affecting, Caitlin tried to mentally prepare herself for the conversation that lay ahead.

'I want Bridie!'

Before Caitlin could stop her, Sorcha broke free from her mother's restraining hands and dashed down the hallway in the direction of the kitchen. In a way relieved that she had done just that—because she wouldn't want her daughter to witness any ill feeling that Estelle might extend towards her—Caitlin pushed her fingers a little anxiously through her newly washed and dried hair.

'Bridie's promised to make some buns with her,' she explained, shrugging again.

Without inviting her to follow, but somehow conveying that was precisely what she expected, Estelle turned and swept into the vestibule, then beyond into the drawing room. There was indeed a welcome fire burning in the beautiful marble fireplace, and the bright winter sun that streamed in through the Georgian windows settled on the floral and striped fabrics of the elegant furniture and soft furnishings, highlighting the faded grandeur that was so stylishly evident here and there. Flynn's housekeeper clearly took meticulous care of this grand old house, and lavished much loving attention on it.

But Caitlin very quickly turned her attention from the appearance of the room to the woman who had gone across to sit quite regally in a graceful striped armchair with a winged back.

'I don't know if you're aware, but relations between myself and my son have been under a bit of a cloud since you left these shores Miss Burns. This is the first time I've visited Flynn for at least a year, perhaps more, and the last time we met the situation was unhappily as difficult as ever. He's borne a lot of anger towards me about the way he thought I'd treated you. He partly blamed me for your leaving. That's been made clear to me on more than one occasion.'

For a moment Caitlin's heart lifted at the idea that Flynn had defended her to his mother and not entirely heaped all the blame on her.

'It must have been very difficult for Flynn all round,' she said.

Her regret was genuine. It had to have hurt him to be estranged from his family. It could only have added to his sense of isolation after what had happened with his ex-wife *and* Caitlin. However, anxious about what Estelle might say next, Caitlin elected to remain standing rather than sit down.

'I miss my son, Miss Burns. You have a child yourself…as a mother you must only want what you believe to be the best for her. Is my son the father of your daughter? Tell me the truth.'

In shock, the younger woman stared, stunned that Estelle would even consider that not to be the case after all this time. 'Yes, he is.'

'So clearly you were pregnant with her when you left?'

'That's right.'

'I thought she looked about the right age to be Flynn's child. But despite being pregnant you decided not to tell him?'

'I—I couldn't.'

'And why was that?'

Was she imagining it, or had she seen the glimmering of regret in Estelle's shrewd gaze as she regarded her? Caitlin inhaled a steadying breath.

'I heard what you said to Flynn that day, Mrs MacCormac…the day you were arguing with him about seeing me. I'd come to Oak Grove to find him, the drawing room windows were open and your voice carried clearly. I'd just been listening to my father berate me for being with him, and I was already upset and distraught. But then to hear you tell Flynn that I was only using him and would probably try to trap him with a pregnancy! How do you think that made me feel? You made a terrible judgement about me when you didn't even know me! Wasn't it enough that your son chose to be with me?'

'I interfered where I shouldn't have…I see that now. If I'm big enough to admit to making a mistake, Caitlin, are you generous enough to accept my apology?'

Surprised, Caitlin needed a moment to absorb this unexpected turn in the conversation.

'I don't believe in holding grudges. But I want you to know why I left that day. I truly feared Flynn might believe what you'd said about me. Coupled with my own doubts about how he would react at the news he was going to be a father…the only thing I could think of to do was to leave. In a million years I would never have wanted to trap him into staying with me. I loved him! It broke my heart to leave him even though I was carrying his baby at the time.'

By the time she had finished speaking Caitlin's heart was beating like thunder inside her chest.

Sighing deeply, Estelle put her hand up to her head, as if needing a moment to get her own emotions under control.

'What have you been saying to Caitlin? I hope you haven't been stirring up trouble while my back's been turned!'

Both women glanced up in shock at the tall, furious-looking figure outlined in the drawing room doorway.

CHAPTER TEN

'YOUR mother was only talking to me, Flynn.'

'That's what worries me!'

Striding into the room, Flynn glanced from what he considered to be the too-pale pallor of Caitlin's face to his mother's tightly controlled, perfectly made-up features. Frustration eddied through him. If only Bridie had told him sooner that Estelle was paying him a visit then he could have discussed it with Caitlin.

'I didn't come here to cause trouble, Flynn.' Rising to her feet, with the tight mask of her self-control slipping and distress stealing over her features instead, Estelle looked highly nervous. 'I've missed you, son, and I want to put things right between us.'

'I'll go,' Caitlin said quietly next to him, but Flynn glanced at her in alarm.

'No! Stay. This is *my* home, and if anyone's going anywhere it won't be you.'

'I'll go for a walk…give you two some time together. I'll be back, I promise.'

As her wide blue eyes met and held his, Flynn tried to quiet the small storm going on inside him. Fear of losing what he had only so recently gained was almost overwhelming.

'Don't be long,' he told her, reluctantly agreeing.

Caitlin left the house and walked into a wind that almost cut her in two. The sunlight was deceptive. The temperature could surely not be much above freezing. But right then she couldn't have cared how cold it was, because she had other, more pressing things on her mind.

It seemed as though her life had come full circle after her meeting just now with Estelle. The other woman's apology had come as a total surprise. Caitlin found herself hoping and praying that this time the outcome would be different—that she would at least have a chance to make things right with Flynn. Could she trust this new feeling of optimism that was slowly coming into being, starting to bud like a spring flower that had been lying dormant all winter, waiting for the time to blossom at last?

If she had to leave him again she didn't think she could stand it. She had been pierced to the core by the longed-for sight of him in town that day, and even then Caitlin had known that some how, some way, she had to help create another more hopeful ending to this story. And now…seeing the way he was with Sorcha—how he delighted in his little daughter as much as any doting, loving father—how could she possibly believe it right to go back to England, taking his child with her?

And yet…could Flynn love Caitlin as she longed for him to love her after all the bitterness and pain? Did he even have the ability to do that after the hurt he had suffered at the hands of his ex-wife?

Crossing her arms over her black sweater, to try and protect herself from the worst of the wind, she followed a winding gravelled path to the secluded garden at the back of the house. There was a charming old summerhouse there, she remembered, and she could take shelter inside if it wasn't locked.

Finding no barrier to her entry, Caitlin let herself inside and shut the door. With the wind howling around her—the stand of slim fir trees at the bottom of the garden was almost bent double by the force of it—she sat down in a simple chair fashioned from local rush work with a cross-stitched cushion at her back and dropped her head in her hands…

'Caitlin?'

Lost in her thoughts, it took a couple of seconds for her to raise her head at the sound of that masculine voice. Flynn stood framed in the narrow doorway, the top of his head almost reaching the lintel.

'You should come back into the house now. It's cold out here.'

'Has Estelle gone?'

'She's getting acquainted with her granddaughter. Is that all right with you?'

'So you've made it up, then?'

Entering the light-flooded space, Flynn carefully shut the door behind him. 'She told me you heard us arguing that day…that you heard what she said about you trying to—'

'Trap you by getting pregnant.'

Caitlin couldn't help wincing at the memory.

'No wonder you left.' As he moved to stand in front of her, Flynn's expression was painfully rueful. 'I made it hard for you to trust me, to tell me that you were carrying my baby, and then you heard that! Maybe I would have done the same in your shoes, if I'd been eighteen and hurt like you must have been. We all let you down, Catie…me, my family, your father…I see that now. But if I had been more willing to open up to you, to confide in and support you, it wouldn't have mattered what anyone else thought or did.'

'I never wanted to trap you into staying with me, Flynn. I only ever wanted you to be with me if you wanted that too. But I was so confused about what I thought you felt. How could I have known at the time what you'd been through? What made it so hard for you to trust?'

'I think I—'

'Mr MacCormac!'

The summerhouse door flew open and Bridie stood there, puffed and out of breath, looking as though she'd run all the way from the house.

'It's Sorcha! She took a tumble down the stairs and knocked herself out!'

'What?'

'Oh, my God!'

The three of them ran out together, Flynn grabbing Caitlin by the hand and sprinting past the housekeeper to get to the house as quickly as he could.

When they arrived in the generous-sized entrance hall, Estelle was sitting at the end of the carpeted staircase, cradling a tearful Sorcha in her arms. The child was awake and gazing around her, and Caitlin sent up a quick heartfelt prayer of thanks that she wasn't still unconscious. But she knew they weren't out of the woods yet.

'She was showing me how she could skip, and before I realised what her intention was she'd run up the steps and turned round to skip back down them. It happened in an instant. Oh God, son, I'm so sorry!'

Estelle's distress was genuine and heartfelt, her features the colour of whey.

As Bridie came back into the hall behind the little group, Flynn turned immediately to the housekeeper. 'Bridie, go and phone the doctor, will you? Tell him what's happened and ask him to come right away!'

'Yes, Mr MacCormac.'

She bustled off to do as she was bid.

'Oh, sweetheart—did you hurt yourself?' Tenderly stroking back some silky fair hair that had fallen into her daughter's eyes, Caitlin saw the egg-sized lump that was forming on her forehead as she did so. 'Mummy told you to be careful on the stairs, didn't she?' Her stomach somersaulted with the strain of the fright that had seized her.

Behind her, Flynn leant forward to carefully examine the contusion himself. 'How long was she unconscious for?' he questioned his mother.

'It can't have been much more than twenty seconds,' Estelle replied anxiously. 'She started to open her eyes just after I got to her.'

'Do you hurt anywhere else, *mo cridhe*?' His voice infinitely gentle, Flynn lifted one of Sorcha's small pale hands and held it.

She shook her head, her bottom lip quivering, trying not to cry any more. 'I hurt my head!' she told him plaintively.

'I know, angel, but you're going to be all right. The doctor is coming to take a look at you to make sure. Do you feel a little bit sick or dizzy?'

Sorcha nodded. 'A little bit sick.'

'You won't feel like that for long, I promise. We'll soon have you feeling well and comfortable again.'

Bridie appeared from the direction of the drawing room. 'Dr Ryan's on his way. He said he'll be here in about twenty minutes. You're to stay with her and make sure she doesn't try to get up until he arrives.'

'Let me take her, Mother. We'll take her into the drawing room and lay her down on the couch. Bridie…can you go upstairs and fetch a blanket?'

They all had an anxious time until the doctor arrived. Flynn sat holding Sorcha's hand, telling her stories to help distract her, while Caitlin sat at the other end of the couch, closely watching for any signs that might give further cause for concern.

After doing a fair amount of pacing and watching herself, to Caitlin's surprise Estelle went into the kitchen with Bridie, to help make them all tea, and returned with it all set out on a tray to serve it.

Dr Ryan turned out to be a very gentle, affable man—just the sort of caring professional a parent would want to tend to their hurt child—and after thoroughly examining Sorcha he took great pains to assure Caitlin and Flynn that the little girl was going to be just fine. For the next twenty-four hours they should keep an especially close eye on her, he advised, but other than that the following day she should be back to her old self.

Estelle and Bridie left them alone with their

daughter after the doctor had departed. Caitlin sat with knots in her stomach for a different reason. Flynn sat there, not saying a word, and she couldn't help but be anxious about what was going through his mind.

Sorcha's accident had shaken them all up, and there was a sense of something changing in the rhythm and shape of things that she couldn't deny. As for herself, she felt emptied and drained—as wrung out as a dishcloth. But in a strange, inexplicable way she felt cleansed too. A light had been shone into all the protected and dark corners where secrets had been hidden for too long, and the truth was at last exposed. But what Flynn intended to do about that truth, she hardly dared guess.

One thing was clear—Sorcha wouldn't be going anywhere very far without her father. Even now, her little face gazed up at him from the plumped-up pillow behind her head, as though he hung the moon and stars combined.

'Hey, there…you okay?'

His warm, vibrant tone interrupted her preoccupied thoughts, and Caitlin stared back at him for a moment, not comprehending. Every time he turned that too-striking gaze on her she experienced an answering anticipatory tug deep inside her womb. It wasn't just for Sorcha's sake she wanted to be close by.

'Better now,' she admitted, her slender shoulders drooping a little beneath her black sweater.

'Our resident ghost has more colour than you!'

'You have a *ghost*?'

'A very benign one…a lady who watches over the broken-hearted, so legend has it. Her lover was a reckless young MacCormac she'd recently married, whose sense of adventure drove him to spend a large part of his life at sea. His ship sank in a storm in the Atlantic one night long ago. She set a lantern in her bedroom window and kept watch every night, waiting for him to come home.'

'How sad! What was her name?'

'Lizzie. But enough of sad tales and family ghosts…I'm more concerned with how *you're* doing.'

'I got the fright of my life when Bridie said Sorcha had knocked herself out! I told her not to play on those stairs, but she's a mind of her own, that one.'

'How can she not, with you and I as parents?' Flynn commented wryly.

He was smiling at her just as he'd done in the old days, when they'd first been together—a smile that was a sensual threshold to the man's true beguiling nature. Feeling heat rise inside her, Caitlin knew her own smile was tinged with sudden shyness.

'Talking of ghosts…your mother didn't look too good there for a while either.'

'Yes, well…' A flash of his old resentment tightened Flynn's mouth. 'Perhaps she's finally realised it's her grandchild that almost ended up in hospital today!'

'She was as shocked as we were. You could see that. Don't be mad at her.'

'You've got a heart as wide as the ocean, Caitlin Burns!'

'What are we going to do, Flynn?' Tracing the fine intricate lacework on the cushion she held in her lap, Caitlin glanced back at him with anxiety in her eyes. 'About *us*, I mean?'

'We have to talk,' he said straight away, his expression becoming almost stern. 'But not now… Let's just see to Sorcha's needs for today, and tonight, when she's asleep in bed, we'll have every opportunity to discuss things.'

'Everything all right?'

Flynn glanced towards the door as Caitlin returned from the bedroom, where she'd gone yet again to take a peek at the sleeping child. 'She hasn't stirred since the last time we looked.'

'Good. Come and sit down before you fall down. You look barely able to stand up!'

To say he was on edge was an understatement. Concern for both his daughter *and* her mother cut deep. Sorcha had put the fear of God in him when she'd fallen down those stairs. It had hit him then how great was the responsibility of fatherhood…how strong the bonds of love that tied him to his child for ever. There would always be a place in his heart for the little boy he had lost, and he would never forget those early days when he had been a father to him, but now he knew it was his daughter who needed his love.

Now that Flynn was reassured she was all right, and was sleeping a perfectly natural sleep—not succumbing to any dangerous drowsiness that suggested her accident was the cause—he could give all his attention to Caitlin. Something he'd been craving all day. There was so much to say—but where to start?

CHAPTER ELEVEN

How did you heal a fracture that had been left untended for much too long and was so bent out of shape that perhaps there was no restoring it to its former health?

Watching Caitlin, her flawless skin far too pale against the funereal black of her sweater, Flynn determinedly fielded the deep sense of rejection that overwhelmed him when she sat on the couch at the opposite end to him. Assuming distance between each other—*any* kind of distance—should not be happening after the sensual delight of earlier today. Not after Flynn had experienced the fiercely sweet excitement of her body again, and she had matched him kiss for passionate kiss, their racing hearts beating as one.

But perhaps she wanted to put distance between them after the way he'd treated her—shutting her out as he had done. He could hardly blame her when he must have caused her untold grief with his aloof behaviour.

'I thought you might like to look at these.' She was handing him a small red photo album the size of a wallet. 'I keep these in my bag…I remembered I had them just now. There are some baby pictures in there, as well as a couple of Sorcha at one and two.'

With a tight feeling inside his chest as he took the proffered album, Flynn briefly met the serious blue eyes that tentatively locked with his. Here in the flickering firelight the colour took on the bewitching hue of a sky caught betwixt twilight and dusk. He knew only too well what looking into them did to his body…

'Thanks.'

Silently he studied the photographs, taking his time, his thoughtful sculpted profile seeming to drink in the details as though to consign them to memory for however long he lived.

As Caitlin glanced from Flynn towards the fire and back again, she reflected on the long, painful journey of 'growing up' that had culminated in her return to her homeland. Remembering her folly of once believing that falling in love should be so simple—that love could and *would* surmount any obstacle with ease—she felt as though she'd aged a hundred years since then, with all that had happened. Now, studying Flynn again, she silently conceded that the web of passion and hurt that had enmeshed them both was probably going to tighten when they started to discuss their future…a future Caitlin was by no means certain would turn out the way she longed for.

'I like this one.'

'Which one's that?'

Before she realised she'd done it, Caitlin had scooted up the couch to sit right next to Flynn, and peered over his shoulder at the particular photograph he had referred to. It was one that her aunt Marie had taken a couple of hours after Caitlin had given birth to Sorcha. She was sitting up in the hospital bed, a pink knitted shawl courtesy of her aunt draped round her shoulders, holding the baby in her arms. Her smile looked wan and tired, but somehow happy too.

Oh, how she had longed for Flynn to be there that day to see their child born! Thinking of the strange mix of elation and sadness she had experienced at that momentous time, she tried to stem the torrent of emotion that inevitably throbbed through her.

'I'm not exactly looking my best in that picture.' She made a face.

As he turned to study her, a deep furrow creased Flynn's handsome brow. 'You both look incredible. It's the most beautiful picture I ever saw,' he told her, a distinctly husky catch in his mesmerising voice.

'I wanted you to be there that day,' Caitlin confessed, her own voice barely under control. 'I couldn't sleep that night for thinking of you…even though I was exhausted.'

'I don't like to think of you in so much pain, giving birth alone,' he admitted, the palpable tension in him giving powerful weight to his heartfelt words.

'Aunt Marie waited outside, and the midwife and doctors were very kind. And it's true what they say—you forget the pain you've been in as soon as they put that baby into your arms. I remember looking down at Sorcha for that very first time, and I thought, So this is what they mean by a miracle. But actually…' She paused as she gazed into his eyes, knowing that her own were like crystalline windows, giving him access into the deepest part of her soul. It was too late to stop him from seeing inside, and much too late to hold anything back now that the floodgates were opened. 'Actually it was missing you that caused me the most pain, Flynn. It was like a part of my heart was cut out, not having you there.'

The tightly clenched jaw and self-deprecating twist of his mouth took her aback.

'I'm surprised you can still say that after all I've done!'

'What do you mean?'

'I thought I could never forgive you for walking out on me…but I've learned that it's *you* that needs to forgive *me*. All this time I wore my resentment towards you like a shield. A form of protection, I suppose…to guard against ever being so enraptured again. Instead of realising that I'd given you very little access to my true self, not enough for you to trust me, I chose to blame you for leaving.' As he closed the little wallet, his sigh was deeply regretful. 'I let what happened with Isabel make me bitter, Caitlin. So bitter that I didn't really realise how fortunate I was when you came into my life. It wasn't until after you'd left that it came to me what a gift I'd had within my grasp. The truth is I should have made a better effort to find out where you'd gone—but I let my pride stop me. Instead of licking my wounds and feeling sorry for myself I should have gone to your father and pleaded with him if need be for him to tell me where you were!'

'Ah, sure…you're not the pleading type, Flynn!' Caitlin's smile was both tender and forgiving.

Flynn caught her hand and, capturing her fingers, raised them to his lips and kissed them.

'Isabel's actions taught me to be very wary of relationships. When I met you I was terrified at how easily you could unravel me, with just the simplest of smiles. You had a way with you that could reach places inside me nobody had ever reached before. I knew you were dangerous from the very first time I saw you.'

'Dangerous?'

For a moment there was doubt on Caitlin's face.

'I know you don't have a calculating bone in your entire body, Caitlin! I don't doubt my mother knows it too now. That's not what I meant.'

His hand moved to cup her small delicate jaw. 'I meant that you were dangerous to my very heart…you couldn't help but crack it wide open.'

'And now?'

'Now we have to start to mend what was broken. I must have put you through hell! You were a young girl, alone and pregnant in a strange country, and I should have been there to help you! I want you to know that I'll always regret that. But we need to take this one step at a time, sweetheart…and I'm not saying it's going to be easy.'

Sensing the reservation in his voice, Caitlin tensed and pulled away from his tenderly stroking fingers.

'If you think it won't work…If you think we can't—'

'There's been hurt on both sides. All I'm saying is that some healing needs to take place first, before we can make a more permanent commitment to each other.'

His words made sense. There was no rushing this. They both had to be certain this was what they really wanted. There was Sorcha to think of too. They couldn't afford to make any more mistakes.

Sighing, Caitlin rested her head against the top

of Flynn's muscular arm. Carefully he moved her so that her head lay against his chest instead, his arm protectively around her shoulders.

'Tell me one of your stories, Flynn,' she entreated him softly, her eyelids fighting to stay open after the tensions and drama of the day. 'Tell me a story where everything seemed to be lost but in the end hope won the day.'

Staring into the fire, Flynn allowed himself a small, satisfied smile. Luckily for her, he knew lots of stories like that.

Their moving forms cast shadows on the wall in the dark gold lamplight of Caitlin's bedroom. Flynn's hands enclosed her hips, and she received him into her with a small breathless sigh, shutting her eyes to absorb the sensation of their two bodies now moving as one. A sense of rightness and completeness washed over her—almost a sense of being 'home' at last. That was what being there, with all the barriers down—mental, physical and spiritual—meant to Caitlin.

'Open your eyes,' he ordered softly, and she did, her gaze touching all the planes, shadows and sculpted angles of his strong long-boned face with unashamed love.

'Did you miss this?' she whispered, smiling as she adjusted her body to take him even deeper.

His eyes darkened in the lamplight, and he

released a sensuous groan that made her shiver with pleasure. It wasn't just his touch that held her spellbound—his voice, with its rich velvet timbre, had always had the power to affect Caitlin deeply. Now his hands moved to stroke and cup her breasts, his fingers squeezing and releasing the tight aching buds of her dusky-rose nipples with increasing pressure.

Caitlin barely heard his answer to the provocative question she'd phrased because she was so swept up in the tide of soul-drenching pleasure that drowned out every other thought.

'Aye…I missed it badly. Now you're just going to have to make up to me for lost time.'

He guided her head possessively down to his, and his kiss was hot, hungry and rough with need. The tension inside Caitlin magnified and almost took her over the brink.

'I promise,' she gasped. 'If you just let me—if I could only—'

'This?' Flynn said throatily against her mouth, and thrust upwards strongly into her core, holding himself there deliberately until he sensed her tight, quivering muscles convulse around him.

Then and only then, with her soft-voiced cry echoing in his ears, did he let go of the barely leashed control he'd been holding onto with an iron will ever since Caitlin had opened herself to take him. With his body's longed-for release he spilled his hot, urgent seed inside her and kissed her again—the longer his mouth stayed in contact with hers, the more tender the kisses he wrought.

His feelings seemed to consume him and fill up every previously fiercely guarded corner of his heart. There was no other woman on God's green earth that Flynn wanted to be with but *her*. What had he been thinking about earlier when he'd suggested some healing had to take place before they could make a more permanent commitment to each other? Just being here with Caitlin and Sorcha was more than enough healing, wasn't it? It was certainly more than Flynn could ever have dreamed of having during all those long, lonely years he'd spent without her…

Caitlin had told Flynn that she was on the pill. But now—without the worry of falling pregnant, and able to make love freely without fear—she found herself idly wondering if she might ever have any more children with Flynn. Sorcha was nearly four years old, and part of Caitlin had never really wanted her to be an only child. But whatever happened she wouldn't bring another child into the world as a single parent. The years she'd raised Sorcha alone had been the toughest, most challenging years of her life. It just wouldn't be fair to visit that struggle on another child. In her opinion, if at all possible children needed both parents in their lives. Look how Sorcha had blossomed and seemed to grow more confident since she had been reunited with her father!

'What are you thinking about?' Flynn demanded gently, as he helped ease Caitlin down next to him on the bed.

'You mean you expect me to be able to *think* after that?' she laughed huskily.

To his amazement, Flynn felt himself grow achy with desire all over again. 'Tell me,' he urged, his jade eyes intense as they roved across her flushed and lovely face.

'I was wondering if we might ever have any more children together,' she admitted softly. 'I know we still have things to work out between us, but I—'

'I'd like a son.'

'What did you say?'

'I'd like a son—a brother for Sorcha.'

'You would?'

'Are you going to doubt everything I say from now until we grow old?' he asked, feigning vexation.

'Until we grow old?' Comprehension dawned, and her eyes went very bright. 'To be honest, I much prefer harmony to arguments. I grew up with enough of those between my father and me to be frankly weary of them!'

'I'm sorry that he hurt you and then you lost him.'

'He's in a better place now.' Her arm went confidently across Flynn's chest and she snuggled her body up close to his. 'With my mam.'

'Aye.' He pressed his lips against her honey-scented hair. 'And you, Caitlin? Are *you* in a better place? A place you might consider staying for some time?'

Her heart almost missing a beat, Caitlin sucked in a steadying breath. 'Oh, yes, Flynn! This is where I want to be...with you and Sorcha. Most definitely.'

'Good.'

Smiling to himself, Flynn moved his hard, muscular body carefully atop hers, sensing a thrill ripple through him at the surprise and then pleasure that registered on her face.

'Because I swear to God, I don't ever want to be without you again!'

Bridie breezed into the family dining room downstairs, where they were eating breakfast, and placed a small, somewhat tattered envelope on the table in front of Caitlin. There was no name or address on the front.

'Mary Hogan dropped by with this a few minutes ago. She wouldn't come in when I asked her. Just said to make sure that I gave this to you and to tell you that Ted McNamara found it down the side of the couch in your father's parlour.'

As Bridie caught Caitlin's eye the older woman's smile was full of her characteristic kindness, as if she'd intuited that the letter would be both a surprise and a shock to the young woman.

His handsome face wearing a frown, Flynn studied Caitlin closely as she picked up the envelope and stared at it.

Her stomach tightening with anxiety, she turned hot and cold all over. To calm her nerves, she put down the envelope and spread some marmalade on her toast, then turned briefly to smile at Sorcha. Thankfully she seemed none the worse for wear after the drama of yesterday, and even the lump on her head had gone down considerably.

'Aren't you going to open it?' Flynn asked her in surprise.

'Of course I am!'

Gathering her courage in both hands, Caitlin picked up the letter again. Sliding her finger under the barely sealed yellowed flap, she opened it and drew out the single sheet of paper that was inside. Instantly recognising her father's large spidery handwriting, she started to read the sparse contents.

Dear Caitlin
I've tried many times over the years to tell you how much I've missed you, but after your mam went it wasn't easy for me to be with you. You are so like her in so many ways that it almost hurt to look at you.

I'm sorry that you went away and that I never asked to see the child. At first I wouldn't look at the pictures you sent, but after a while

I made myself look at them. Sure, she's a grand little thing, isn't she, your Sorcha? I wish you would come home so that I could see her for myself, but if the truth be known I don't suppose I will even have the courage to send this letter. I've been very foolish, and not a good father to you, and I know your mam would wipe the floor with me if she were around!

I see that MacCormac fella around from time to time, and I'd like to tell him where you are but I don't have the heart for it. Would he have made you happy? I don't know, but I am sorry I stood in your way when you wanted to be with him.

Look after yourself, Catie—and give the little one a kiss from her grandfather.

Dad X

Hardly trusting herself to speak right then, Caitlin kept hold of the letter as the tears welled up hotly in her eyes.

'What's wrong, Mummy?' Sorcha asked, a spoonful of cereal poised in mid-air. 'You're crying!'

'Bad news?' Flynn too was staring at her, his handsome face grave with concern.

'Dad must have written this some time ago.' She wiped at a tear and made a feeble attempt at a smile. 'But he never got round to posting it.'

'Can I see?' Holding out his hand expectantly, Flynn took the scrawled page and avidly scanned it.

All this time Caitlin had believed that her father had never forgiven her for 'disappointing' him and winding up as a single mother. He'd been so hard on her, and she'd never understood why. Now, astonishingly, she'd learnt that he *had* loved her after all—but she had reminded him too much of her mother, the woman he had loved and lost too soon. And she had also discovered that he had indeed thought about his grandchild, and would have been happy to meet her. However, on the downside, it had pierced her heart to read the part about Flynn.

'What a foolish old man!' His voice gruff, Flynn leant towards Caitlin and gently touched her damp cheek with the back of his hand. 'If only he had made himself post it! Look at what he lost out on because he didn't!'

'He was afraid. After he lost my mam he was afraid of everything. His whole life was ruled by fear. I can see that now. I can see it and forgive him.'

'Like I said…' His arresting glance wry, Flynn shook his head. 'You've a heart as wide as an ocean, and I for one wouldn't have it any different!'

'It's all in the past,' she said with a determined smile. 'It's the present and the future that's the important thing…don't you think?'

'Daddy, I want to go and see the horses! Will you take me?' Sorcha glanced expectantly up at her father, milk from her cereal glistening on her small chin.

'Later, darling…I promise. But first I have to go somewhere with your mother this morning.'

His commanding glance towards Caitlin clearly denoted that he expected complete agreement with this previously undisclosed plan, and apprehension mingled with surprise inside her.

'Bridie thought you might like to go and play in the garden for a while, if you wrap up warmly,' Flynn continued. 'She might even let you plant some bulbs in your own little patch for the spring.'

'Yes, but I have to have my own shovel!' the little girl replied with relish.

The two adults laughed aloud in unison.

'What have I raised?' Shaking her head, Caitlin wiped at her mirth-filled eyes.

'In a few years she'll be running for Taoiseach, that's for sure!' Flynn grinned in agreement.

Emerging from an alley of hornbeams that in the spring would create a magical canopy of lush green growth, Flynn pulled the car up in front of an elegant Georgian country house with a graceful white-pillared portico. It was a beautiful dwelling that anyone would be proud to live in, surrounded as it was by dense woodland and verdant lawns. And because of its secluded position it was naturally very private.

'Are we visiting someone?' Twisting round in

the passenger seat to rest her gaze on her companion's implacable features, Caitlin frowned. 'I wish you'd told me! I would have dressed up a little.'

Not that she had much of a wardrobe to choose from since most of her clothes were still at home with her aunt Marie. But Caitlin would have preferred something a bit better than the habitual jeans and sweater combination she'd been wearing since she'd arrived in Ireland if she were going to be introduced to some of Flynn's friends.

'There's no need for you to dress up when there's only you and me here, *mo cridhe*.' He smiled, using a Gaelic endearment, his compelling eyes crinkling at the corners.

'I don't understand…' Shrugging with frustration, even though her heart squeezed tight at his affectionate address, Caitlin drew her dark blonde brows together in puzzlement.

'I own this house,' he explained.

'You do? It's lovely!'

'It needs a bit of a work done on it, seeing as though it's been standing empty for a while. The tenants left just before Christmas. But I won't be letting it again.'

'No?'

'No.'

Suddenly his expression was very serious.

'I'm giving it to you, Caitlin.'

'Giving it to me? How do you mean?'

'The deeds will all be in your name. It's a wedding present…so you'll never be without a place to call home again.'

It was hard to believe the evidence of her own ears. To be given a house—and a house such as this! That was amazing enough…but to be given it as a *wedding present*?

Tears swam helplessly into her eyes. 'A wedding present, you say?'

She sat quietly, her hands scrubbing at her increasingly damp cheeks, and it was Flynn who—driven past all endurance—pulled her fiercely into his arms and kissed her. When he lifted his head after doing the job more than thoroughly, he grinned at Caitlin like the cat that had got the cream.

'Can I take that as an acceptance? I should have asked you four and a half years ago, if I'd had any sense at all, but I was too damned cautious for my own good back then!'

'It's what I've always wanted…from the moment I saw you…to marry you. I *knew*…I knew even then you were the one for me.'

'It was the same for me.'

For just a moment Caitlin saw such unfettered emotion in Flynn's glance that it seemed to suggest he was on the verge of tears, and then he brushed back her hair with slightly trembling fingers and gazed at her as if it was *she* who hung the moon.

'I love you, Caitlin. I've waited a long time to tell you that.'

'I love you too, Flynn...and it's a love that will endure for ever. I have no doubt about that.'

'Well, then...this will be a new beginning for both of us. You have complete *carte blanche* as to how you do the place up, by the way. When it's been decorated to your satisfaction we'll move in here—you, me and Sorcha.'

'But what about Oak Grove?' she asked concernedly.

'I still have to help oversee the place, but my brother Daire can help with that like he's always done. He's away travelling at the moment, but when he gets back I'll put him in the picture. We'll keep my apartment there for visits—and I've got my writing retreat up in the mountains too, don't forget. But once we're married this will be our home—if you're in agreement?'

'If I'm in agreement? I'm in seventh heaven! But, as wonderful as this gift of yours is, I have to tell you that I don't mind where I live as long as I can be with you. The ancient circle of belonging can't be broken, Flynn...you of all people know that. Wherever you and me and our children are together...*that's* home.'

Laying her head against the warm, protective wall of his chest, Caitlin sighed softly as she realised with joy that this was exactly the sort of homecoming her heart had always dreamed of.

MILLS
BOON
TM

0311/05a

We're thrilled to bring you four bestselling collections that we know you'll love...

featuring

THE KOUVARIS MARRIAGE by
Diana Hamilton

THE GREEK TYCOON'S
INNOCENT MISTRESS
by Kathryn Ross

THE GREEK'S
CONVENIENT MISTRESS
by Annie West

featuring

WEDDING AT
WANGAREE VALLEY

BRIDE AT BRIAR'S RIDGE

CATTLE RANCHER,
SECRET SON

by Margaret Way

On sale from
18th March 2011

By Reques

The Man She Loves to Hate

by Kelly Hunter

Three reasons to keep away from Cole Rees...

Our families are enemies.
His arrogance drives me mad.
Every time he touches me I go up in flames...and it's infuriating!

The End of Faking It

by Natalie Anderson

Perfect Penny Fairburn has long learnt that faking it is the only way—until she meets Carter Dodds... But can Carter get her to drop the act outside the bedroom as well?

The Road Not Taken

by Jackie Braun

Rescued from a blizzard by ex-cop Jake McCabe, Caro finds the hero she's been looking for—but to claim him she risks losing her son to her jerk of an ex...

Shipwrecked With Mr Wrong

by Nikki Logan

Being marooned with a playboy is NOT Honor Brier's idea of fun! Yet Rob Dalton is hard to resist. Slowly she discovers that pleasure-seekers have their good points...

On sale from 1st April 2011
Don't miss out!

Available at WHSmith, Tesco, ASDA, Eason and all good bookshops
www.millsandboon.co.uk